Voyage
to a
Phantom
City

Voyage

to a
Phantom
City

Christopher Bernard

A *Caveat Lector* Book

REGENT PRESS
Berkeley, California

PAPERBACK
ISBN 13: 978-1-58790-342-7
ISBN 10: 1-58790-342-3

E-BOOK
ISBN 13: 978-1-58790-343-4
ISBN 10: 1-58790-343-1

Library of Congress Control Number: 2015956048

First Edition

1 2 3 4 5 6 7 8 9 10

Printed and Produced in the U.S.A.
REGENT PRESS
Berkeley, California
www.regentpress.net
regentpress@mindspring.com

We were led, not knowing where.
Like mirages before us there receded
Cities built by miracle;
Wild mint laid itself beneath our feet,
Birds travelled the same route that we did,
And in the river fishes swam upstream;
And the sky unrolled itself before our eyes.

— Arseniy Tarkovsky

Contents

The Sun Above Ur

It skims the southern clouds.
Bowed, glowing, white.
Majestically vague, as old as light
on earth. It sees nothing. Like a god.

At the table where you sit, you look up from the book you have
just opened, past the broken lamp, toward the broad view of the
sea. You were almost afraid to open it again, a little notebook
lying at the bottom of a cardboard box you hadn't looked at it
in years—and there it was, a volume of pages, once blank, later
covered with a maze of barely legible writing.

The broken lamp stares at you admonishingly in the early
winter light. You will fix the lamp later. When the night comes.
And the notebook calls you back to it.

You scan the obscure little poem. And hear in imagination,
once again, the voice of the young man you once were, trailing
away into silence.

Kitt's Rock

The moan of the ferry dies away and a breath of air passes in from the sea.

You hear a creak, an animal-like squeal, and feel the breeze and hear the sound of surf against the rocks. The kitchen back-door pauses and swings, in a little dance, awkward as a child; you must have forgotten to latch it. It finally makes up its mind and stops, stuck on the threshold like a half-open book, and you turn back to the broken hurricane lamp and the unopened letter near it.

The taciturn ferryman, with a glower and shrug, had handed the dirty envelope to you, and you had tucked it into your pocket before walking up the path with the week's supplies, past the rusting piles of old cars and pickup trucks, vans, the ancient SUV, that gagged the driveways of the vacated island compound.

The address is, unusually, handwritten, in a penmanship you don't recognize. The letter leans, half-crushed, against the old notebook you had been reading earlier, as you work on a chore you have been putting off for a week.

The wick bunches in your fingers. Again you hear the creak, and a chilly breeze creeps up your arm. The wall calendar shifts on its hook, on its face a photograph of a pale young woman, a dark red rose perched above her ear, who reminds you of someone you knew many years ago . . . Then something gives way, and the wick slips up through the brass slit.

The letter, lifted by the breeze, slips to the scuffed floor.

Not now. You've had too much bad news in recent years. You can't face any more right now.

The grand houses, handsome and abandoned, stand off to the side along the cliffs; staring out over the restless sea, their computerized safety features ludicrous and useless despite the aging solar panels and the elegant wind turbines. Dead television dishes point toward the sky like wistful faces.

You move up the dirt road, avoiding the mud from the early snow melt.

You haven't seen a plane pass in months. Even freighters on their way to Bangor, or south toward Boston, are becoming rare. Maybe the threats of the climatologists are coming true after all.

A raven lands on a gable and watches you suspiciously as it flexes its wings. Then a sudden blow of wind unbalances it into the air.

Then, as you move past the last house before the dunes begin, you too are met by a blast. Over a dull ocean choppy with whitecaps you see an advancing cloudbank, and you pull tight your macintosh and plough through the wind on the way to your errands at the weather station and lighthouse.

Squinting past the lighthouse array, half crystalline, half insectoid, of blazing lights, half-blinding you, you can just make out, in the far distance beyond the rock piles white with surge, a black cloud closing over a last hole of blue. You blink as a rain drop spits you in the eye.

Quickly retreating, you scuttle past the wind cups whirring like a top and see the wind flag go wild, shifting in one direction after another, like a scared fish. When you face into them, the gusts stuff your mouth so you can barely breathe. Then the storm slams into the island.

A veil of sand, lifting from the ground, nearly blinds you.

You curl your body in and fight your way against the wind.

Your path takes you along a cliff edge, and, at one point, leaning into the rock face, you stop and peer over the cliff.

Eighty feet below, down veils of rain, the surf boils and churns white and black among columns of granite. The sea sweeps to the horizon where a layer of clouds closes over it like a shell.

Your foot slips as a hard blast strikes you, and you take a wild grab at a rock cocked from the wall like an axe head, and hold onto it with both arms. You can feel your legs flailing. *This is it,* you think, strangely calm. *I'm going over. . . .*

A wet blast of wind sweeps up the cliff.

You slip again, your arms almost giving way, then the wind strikes again, pushing you, like a rough hand, against a sand bank, and you roll toward another rock, grasp it, and stare, your heart racing, over the flying wind and water.

Not this time, you think, the water pouring down your face. *Not yet . . .*

The wind, spiked with rain as with tiny, needle-sharp stones, flails at you as you stagger back toward the house.

The compound is dark when you get back, groping for the unlocked door and almost knocked down by the water flooding the rain gutter.

The hurricane lamp is finally lit under your fingers, and the light, when it burns, shows the reflection of a shaken, wet old man with small startled eyes, his hair nearly all white, staring back at you from the storm-beaten window.

The letter lies open on the sofa.

So they managed to find you. Even in this hidden place.

You trail your eyes again over the words: "Dear Mr. Ariel Hunter . . . We are very sorry to have to inform you that Frankie Palmer, who, we understand, was a friend of yours from many years ago . . . We have been asked by his family to get in touch with all of his old friends in case . . . Please accept our deepest sympathy and sincere condolences . . . A memorial service will be held at . . . Yours very truly . . . "

You see Frankie's little puckered face, smiling at you as you walked through the door one day.

Rain against the window.

You have no tears. Almost no sorrow. Only vacancy and numbness.

Suddenly the wind smites the house with fury, as though this time it will, at last, knock it down.

The fire wakes up, writhing and spitting in a cavern of shifting spectres of landscapes, cities, faces ....

An icy draft seeps in, and you take the hand bellows and blow the fire bigger.

The fire flashes an image of familiar mountains that instantly vanishes.

Frankie's face appears in the flames.

A view of distant desert. A twister whirls across the sand, vanishing in smoke.

A boy in a cowboy hat riding a bull, his arm waving. The arena is silent, empty.

The profile of a little girl in a hijab as she picks through a garbage can. An explosion behind her—she doesn't seem to notice. Then she suddenly looks at you.

The two towers against the Manhattan night.

You shake yourself, striving to make your mind blank.

The wind again strikes the house.

"You didn't get me that time!" you shout. "Not then, and not now! . . ."

A spit of rain hisses down the chimney, and you remember a young woman's ice-blue eyes . . .

You stare into the fire until the last ember dies in a little plume of smoke.

On the way upstairs you stop and listen to the rain. It's lightened, the wind has died down.

Thunderstroke and thrashing rain.

You start up from the first sleep.

Flash.

. . . 6, 7, 8, 9 . . .

A crack and split across the sky. *O deep and mighty roar. Tongue of God.*

Clash of cloud and earth, swarming ions minus and plus, then they can't take it anymore, like randy teens in an empty house, and flash, bang! Unless I'm sleeping. Still sleeping. Even if I am. Am I sleeping if I think I'm sleeping? Am I dreaming if I think I'm dreaming?

I am the One.

For those of you who have found God, as a Unitarian minister once put it to his Easter audience. There are no atheists or Unitarians in foxholes. Tongue of God to render you speechless.

Darkness around meets darkness within. Through darkness, from darkness, to . . .

A long cry . . .

You wake up. The room is freezing, you pull the blanket tighter around you.

You listen to the wind, the downpour.

Another cry, almost a moan, and the sound of a weeping child.

You start, suddenly alert, and listen more closely. The sound seems to change: from the sound of a child crying to that of a wounded animal, a whimpering dog, and back again. The sound of the rain confuses it.

I should get up and go find it.

But where is it? In somebody's yard? But there are a dozen, abandoned, nobody's left on the island. There's nothing but lightning to look for it with . . .

I should get up and go find it.

Whatever it is cries again, whimpers.

Leave me alone, I want to sleep, I'm an old man, it's cold, I should get up and go find it. Miserable thing . . .

A sound like sobbing.

Get up get up. Get up.

You pull yourself groggily from the bed, grope across the freezing floor to the window. An occasional flash shows the warren of backyard fences, back walls of houses beneath a driving icy rain. . . no sign of anything alive.

You stumble back to bed.

Maybe I dreamt it after all . . .

Again the wind shakes the house.

A longer cry, going on and on, animal, human . . .

You stare into the darkness.

I'll find you . . . I'll find you in the morning . . .

You listen, half asleep.

More whimpering, quieter now . . .

. . . please . . . please be a dream . . .

Quieter, fading . . .

I couldn't have found you tonight . . . anyway . . .

Your thoughts become confused, going back and forth between the sound of whimpering, rain, wind . . .

Flash. Then long thunder.

In the Mountains

Somebody laughs. There's a murmuring of voices, mostly male, though a woman's chimes in at one point, then a girl's. You can't make out what they're saying.

A shadow twitches above your head; then a penetrating cheep, for a moment unrecognizable, soars away.

You shake your eyes open and stare straight up, trying to remember where you are, and pull the sleeping bag closer against the early chill.

It was a strange dream. You've already forgotten most of it: something whipping in a hard wind, the taste on your lip of a splash of rain . . . you were much older: an old man, gone all white . . . then something else, just at the edge of your aware-ness . . . Then the memory, like that of all dreams, vanishes.

A hand switches back the tent opening and a familiar grin greets you.

"Ready for your tea in the desert, sir?"

"Go to hell."

"You're a little late for that, mate." Peter cocks his head at the desolate landscape dimming through the flap. The air is already hot. "I think we're there already."

You kick yourself out of the bag. A palm frond falls a few feet outside the tent, hits a floor of dry fronds, dead scorpions, sand.

The "bear" comes up to you, an unfolded map in hand. You call him that to yourself because that's what he looks like: big, bearded, melancholy.

"The Trans-Saharan Highway is marked here clearly, Mr. Hunter. I knew there was something we needed to talk about."

You're already tired of your clients on this trip. Let the desert-guide guide them through the desert—that's what they pay you for. Professors were the worst.

"Right." You pretend to peer at the paper. "It's been on the map for a generation at least, but we aren't likely to find it." You smile painfully up at him. "It's been gone the last decade and a half. Along with the taxis and the bus service."

The bear smiles wanly.

"It was never much good even before it disappeared. Plows can't even protect a town when the sand decides to swallow it, let alone a road. When you've lost a mile of highway in this country, you may as well have lost all of it."

A few yards away, Peter gestures questioningly toward the lead car.

"But it looks like it's time we were going," you say, and head toward the back Hummer. You are, after all, the guide for these people, if they'll let you.

Husayn and Umar finish packing the tents; tall, dark, bony Husayn, and Umar with his funny face shaped like a flattened egg. The professors and the trio of grad assistants check the cameras and maps. The old man takes another look at the satellite photos where he thinks he sees signs of an ancient city, its walls marked in a depression between the southern ranges and the sand sea stretching a thousand miles south.

You had seen the photo that so excited him, and them: it showed, against a light gray background, a loose polygon-like box inside of which appeared ambiguous, stainlike spots and a maze of broken lines, like the remains of a labyrinth; the whole seen from straight above and crossed by a small cloud.

The sun is already entirely—a golden ball of blinding fire, a cloud of knives of light—above the horizon.

A plain sweeps from the camp south to a distant range of mountains, deceptively clear in the morning light: you can almost count the canyons between them. They seem not ten miles off.

You look around at the edge of Ouadane, the scrabbly last oasis you'll enjoy for the next couple of days, if the chart is right and Amri, your old friend who regularly provides you with updated maps of the ever-changing Sahara—a smiling middle-aged Berber with a fat belly and spindly legs and arms, who you call "the spider" to yourself—hasn't lied to you.

"Time to ride, folks. The desert waits for no man—and no girls either!" Peter, the Aussie driver, calls out. "And that, children, is why it never got a date."

Groans from the other drivers—Cees, the melancholy, tow-headed "little Dutchboy," and Jack, the Okie.

Umar and Husayn get into the corroding Hummer a sand-storm once ate the paint off in a couple of hours and you never bothered to have repainted. Whenever you see it, it reminds you of the Humvee driven by your old boss in Baghdad, a head man in BlackRock Security: stripped to its metal and as ugly as he was. . . . The year that left you battered and obsessed by the desert . . .

You lower himself into the driver's seat as Umar and Husayn chatter in Arabic in the back seat. They seem to be already calculating their pay. You glance at them in the rearview mirror—Husayn's long, handsome face, Umar with his odd-shaped head and perennially puzzled expression; they catch your eye and stare solemnly back. They always look hungry. You give them a handful of figs from the front-seat bag.

The expedition had come through one of your friends in Oran, who had known someone who'd trekked with the nominal lead, Charles Duden, thirty years back, during the '90s, on a journey from Morocco to Libya. The details had been vague, firmed up on the ground a week ago after the band of profs and their staff gathered in an Oran suburb, and they worked their way to this small oasis a few days later. The press for secrecy was puzzling. At first you had wondered if it might be government work: the CIA was still cleaning up from the great jihadist wars of fifteen years back—ambushing aging Al-Qaeda and ISIL targets, mopping up from the ghastly mistake of a war you tried to keep *as far behind you as possible*. . . . But no: it seemed less dramatic than that: more a professional desire to prevent some rogue archaeologist from the University of Pennsylvania or the British Museum from beating them to the mysterious city they had discovered on a satellite flyover from a sampling of digital photographs.

Over breakfast that very morning, the professors had debated, with a weary sense of going over much-traveled territory. Had the city been a Roman town, "flourishing" when the northern half of the Sahara was fertile? A camp for the legions protecting the North African trade route between Egypt's Thebes and Hippo, Augustine's city? Far outpost of the ancient Carthaginians? "Or," an ironist among them suggests, "Prester John!" That fabled city often sought, never found, last Christian redoubt in North Africa to survive the Muslim onslaught. A favorite destination for generations of amateur explorers, most of them never seen again.

They seemed a sufficiently professional bunch, led by the old man, the lean, tough-looking, snowy-haired Duden—a nervous, intently smiling, no-nonsense type who seems to enjoy lording it over his little cell of spies into the past. There are two middle-aged men—the bear, born Brian Lexington, and Ralph Smuts, a rangy man with a clipped mustache, who seems always on the verge of making some unpleasant revelation he is magnanimously holding back. And a woman, more reserved than other female pottery nerds you have trekked with before, who tend toward the floridly eccentric: a certain wounded look in her eyes never quite disappears no matter the hilarity of the moment. And moments have come when everyone briefly succumbed to not taking the whole thing completely seriously. Though, unfortunately, never for long. Something about her reminds you of someone, but you never have the leisure to work it out.

Completing the motley group are the grad assistants: a young girl-woman and two academic boy-men—Cecilia, Sean, Chad—almost caricatures of their elders in their mannerisms.

By late morning the "reg"—a bleak plain of gravel and sand littered with larger broken and splintered rocks—is a blaze of heat expanding around the little four-car caravan. Ouadane has shrunk to a tiny tuft of palm trees trembling above a silver sea-mirage in the rearview mirror.

The plain spreads around the little caravan like a shimmering ocean; spilling on each side of the invisible path they've taken, flickering like tin foil lying lightly on the ground under a breeze.

"Like shining from shook foil." Hopkins. God's grandeur . . . The much-anthologized poem you first read in high school. The poet who first made you fall in love with poetry, or what you thought at the time was poetry: overheated verbiage, a dictionary forever on fire. That Jesuit had much on his conscience. Also Shelley and Keats, and a handful of Frenchmen, superbly damned. The delicate exterminating angel of Amherst, dark opposite of the logorrheic fool of Camden. To say nothing of Crane's bleak dribbles of ineradicable ink. You too, like half your generation, had wanted to be a "poet" once, though Ginsberg and Kerouac had never been your personal toxic temptation. No, you preferred the overwrought idealism and nightmarish disillusions of the century before: their more frank hopes and desperations and despairs. They were less well defended than the callused, titivating moderns and their bastard

25

children, the "posts." So out of touch you were . . . ! But you preferred it that way. The howlers, hipsters, rockers, the cool, the punks, disgusted you. Let them scream and snark. Let them burn.

You irritably shake off the memory, and focus harder on the mountains, which, despite hours of traveling, seem no closer.

They look flat against the horizon. "You can never tell real distances in this place," you had told the old man when asked how far away the mountains were, "even with a map."

The mountains have turned into a graying bluish wall locked on the horizon, they resist and flee, like a bedouin band drawing you into the wilderness.

One of the many illusions the desert provides to keep us entertained. And I can't help being taken in by it no matter how much I try reasoning against it.

You remember, in childhood once, sticking your finger into a little water spring and watching the end of your finger suddenly seem to swell and break under the surface.

White silence.

A buzzing loops around your head where you lie for the mid-day siesta on the towel across the front seat. The buzz moves away, then returns, circling you face. Off again. Back.

Dozing: broken images of the professors blend with memories of your flat in Oran, the schoolyard of your middle school near Columbus, a road in New England, a silent bar in the East Village during the summer before the attacks on September 11, a rowdy Cairo dance club, a train stopped in the middle of a pasture in Spain, a foaming vanilla shake sliding toward your mouth, then the blocky face of your long-dead father turns toward you from a game of Monopoly (a game you had never seen him play) with a tragic look and the words "I'll take Broadway" coming out of his lips strangely, as in a badly synchronized film, then a white, silent explosion by the side of a dirt road near the ruins of Babylon, the startled look in the eyes of a young woman in a scarf; then you are suddenly in an ancient fighter hurtling toward the earth, and your eyes start open.

Umar and Husayn are folded up in the back seat in kufi caps and T-shirts. Then the quiet sound of "rai," Egyptian pop music, trickles from Husayn's small radio. He likes to nap with it next to his ear.

The heat of the day is at its height.

The buzzing that turned into a fighter screaming out of the sky is a thirsty mosquito: they must have collected it at Ouadane. It lands on your ear, you flick it off and abruptly sit up.

The reg surrounds the sleeping caravan in monotonous, oppressive flatness. The palms of the oasis have vanished to the north.

You see a mirage on the horizon: it looks like the reflection of a Hummer caravan much like your own, also of four vehicles, as it moves across a glassy lake of heat water – but you only see the reflection of it, *upside down*, as it drives southward.

Jack's arm suddenly hangs down outside his window in the van just ahead of yours, and the vehicles roll to a halt.

The hot breeze through the open window on your side (the vehicle's air-conditioning died long ago) stops, and a solid wall of heat leans against your face.

Hatted, booted, with sunglasses of various shapes, the caravan members climb out, stretch, take drafts of water still cool from the oasis spring. The air is baking.

You walk toward the front. Umar and Husayn sit inside the Hummer with the back door open, their bare, brown legs visible against the ground in the van's shadow.

"Is this spider country?"

It's the woman. You turn to her, slightly surprised. The tacit code of the uneasy class system of the caravan usually prevents clients from addressing other than practical questions and brittle cordialities to the "help," at least for the opening days of the trek. You peer at her and try a smile, though it feels stiff.

"Only if you're a fly."

The smile she gives back is big, awkward, tense. As though she's almost forgotten how to smile easily. Or as though she is no longer sure how her smiles will be returned. She had approached you, when you first met in Oran, with the implausibly broad smile that some of your compatriots—usually from California—had a habit of using when first meeting strangers. One could never tell what it meant: you've forgotten long ago.

"Seriously!"

"I *am* serious."

"I was just wondering if I should watch out for scorpions. Back home, that's the one thing they were really afraid of for me...."

Vivian Callan. One-time beauty, still lithe and limber, sharp-eyed, hair like an auburn casque, mole near her left nostril. A hungry look.

"It's a concern, especially for sleepwalkers. You should check your shoes before putting them on, that sort of thing. The horned viper is another one. The snake that walks sideways. Like a crab."

"We have one like that, in Arizona. A sidewinder."

"There's nothing more should scare you then."

"I'll know where to turn if I should."

"Always happy to serve."

The Okie bobs up from the open hood.

"Water's out, I filled the sucker this morning. I'll have to tap the drinking water."

As you turn away, you notice the third man in the party of archaeologists glaring at you. Smuts, the mustache.

Right. All we need is a brawl over the woman.

"Peter, you hear what Jack said?"

The Aussie grins under his broad hat: he always seems to grin, even when he's not. Not as irritating as the American smile since it's never meant to be believed. The way his mouth and eyebrows work together, or just an Aussie tic . . .?

The other professors and their assistants stand about, looking like a band of spirits or ghosts in their whites, their pale hats and kerchiefs, their black sunglasses: the lean, tough-looking older man; the wry, nervous moustache; the young aliens with their bizarre slang. The bear gazes moodily at the far mountains.

They're from a small university in Massachusetts—one of the lesser-known prestige schools they are very proud of and a little defensive about when you said you'd never heard of it (you were lying, of course, to see their reaction). There was some nameless tension (professional? personal? bit of both?) between the mustache and the bear: they avoid talking to each other and when they do, avoid eye contact.

The woman completed the leads. She was friendlier with the big man than the moustache, and was trusted most, it seemed, by the old man. The teenagers were sweetly defensive, idealistic, cringingly sexy, opaque.

They were personable enough, at least superficially: broadly cheerful among themselves, though it masked professional rivalries between the two middle-aged profs, and sometimes between them and the old man (who sometimes played them off each other), though the woman seemed to stay out of the discussions if they brewed too hot; and when they did and she couldn't very well keep silent, she usually sided with the old man. They seemed to make an effort to keep the professional lingo to a minimum, but it would break out despite, and then the discussion became as interminable as it was an impenetrable labyrinth of debitage, provenience, seriation, biface, cache pit, petroglyphs, varves . . .

The woman slept alone. The eyes above the mustache sometimes lingered on her.

You hear something like running water from a spring behind you and turn expecting to see the Okie pouring water into the engine radiator. But he isn't there.

Again you can hear the sound of running water behind you. You turn again, and see only broken stones, split volcanic rock, small polished boulders, dangerous if driven straight over, and beyond these, the plain, with its shallow depressions and remains of ancient lakes and wadis able to toss a truck if driven across too fast. A vibrating layer of heated air blurs the horizon.

You shake your head. You're about to ask if anyone else hears the spring when the clear glug-glug of the Okie pouring water into the vehicle sounds close to your back. This time you don't turn to look.

The old man is scowling at the tire.

"We just rotated them last week," the Okie says, defensively, "not a worn tread on them. We buy them new every November."

The old man scratches his bald patch, then motions toward the mountains. "And is it common for them not to seem any closer even when you've driven most of the day?"

"Then suddenly they're on top of you," you say. "You can't always trust what you see out here."

The woman gives you her uneasy, tight smile again.

"Devious, like a genie."

"The jinns are active today. Maybe they got bored at the oasis and stowed away with us."

Umar catches the word "jinn" and, startled, makes a sign against the Evil One and spits.

As the new tire is being screwed onto the axle, a little gravel gets kicked from underneath, and the woman stoops for a closer look, smoothing away the gravel.

Polished, laid out as if by a craftsman, the surface stretches out in all directions around them like a carpet of smooth stone under the sand and rock.

"It's like the floor of a Byzantine palace, or a cathedral. Beautiful! Brian, look at this."

The big, melancholy specialist in the interior tribes of North Africa, with a minor in the Eastern Empire, stoops beside her.

"Reminds me of the mosaics in Ravenna." The bear looks almost shyly at Vivian. "How did you know?"

She smiles.

"I didn't!"

"Theodora's robes in San Vitale have the same colors. She looked just like photographs of my mother. I kept a reproduction from the Internet tacked on my wall all through high school. She died on me before I was two. Mentally speaking, I wasn't even born at the time. Those mosaics have a lot to answer for," he says, looking up with a pained expression. "They got me into this business. Looking for a past I may never find."

"Pretty defeatist for an archaeologist," Vivian says.

He responds with a dry smile.

There's something comic about getting a blown tire in the middle of the desert, you think. *Maybe someone put a tack on the "road" just to be a nuisance. The jinns are active today.* You spit on the ground. The saliva evaporates almost immediately on the overheated surface.

The bear pulls at something, then yanks it out like a weed and waves it at Vivian.

"Think I found it!"

The long, corroded nail is bent in an L-shape. Curious, with square head and shaft, like a nail from a sailing ship of centuries ago, a hundred miles from the nearest ocean. Or from a time when this desert was just another arm of the sea.

That evening the Aussie comes up to the campfire, a book in hand.

"Here's a little something, children, in a book I found under the back seat, about those precious efreets we're always talking about."

"What does it say?" the girl pipes up.

"Let's see." Peter clears his throat. " 'The *djinn* . . .' "

At the word "efreets" Umar and Husayn, sitting whispering nearby, stop and listen. At the word "*djinn,*" they laugh.

31

"'. . . are *not*—italicized and in capital letters—fallen angels.'"

Pause.

"Well, *that* is certainly a relief," says the mustache.

"'They were created from a smokeless flame of fire.' In the Koran it says something about man being made from mud and jinns from smokeless fire. I remember that one at least!"

"Why 'smokeless,' I wonder," says the woman.

"Maybe it suggests purity, even in their malevolence. Or maybe they were created instead of the smoke, maybe they're a kind of spiritual smoke, a noxious waste product," you speculate out loud.

"'The first recorded *djinn* to be disobedient is *Iblis*.'"

"Rings no bells."

"Isn't there some classical figure named Iblis? Ibis?"

"There should be but there isn't," speaks up the specialist in classical antiquity. The mustache puts on his professorial voice and bristles slightly. "The Egyptians worshiped the sacred ibis along with Thoth, their god of wisdom, a bit like the Greek Hermes. It's associated with big tempests like hurricanes—last to hide, first to poke out after the storm. And Ibis is a poem by Callimachus inveighing against the ingratitude of the poet Apollonius, his student. It's quite negative."

"Timon," says the woman.

"What?" Smuts asks petulantly.

"Of Athens. The Shakespeare play. Well—according to some. There's some controversy. About ingratitude. There's Lear, of course. 'Sharper than the serpent's tooth.' Or the ibis' beak?"

"A favorite of yours? Timon, I mean. Whether the Bard's or not."

"Hardly!" She smiles briefly at you—a strained smile. "I'm more a 'Troilus and Cressida' type."

"'Disbelieving, disobedient *djinn* and *humans*'—and is that, or is that not us, o infidels? – 'are known as *shayateen*.' Satans!"

"Shayateen!" Umar and Husayn repeat, together, with their purer accents, though it's uncertain whether they are correcting the Aussie's pronunciation, practicing a spell, or just repeating the word for its own sake.

"So maybe *we* are the *djinn*. Is that what you're telling us?" From the woman.

"They come in grades too, our *djinn*," says the Aussie, clipping the last word hard and laughing at Husayn and Umar beside him, as they again repeat: "Djinn."

"Listen to this, from—" Peter's voice goes low and slow with authority. "*The World of the Djinn and Devils*, by Ibn Abdul Barr."

"Sounds like a British convert," says the mustache.

"Not with this sort of prose style, mate. 'If one is mentioning the *djinn* purely of themselves, they are called *djinni*.'" The Aussie over-pronounces the Arabic word, and you can hear him mischievously cast the word at the two young Arabs beside him as they giggle uncomfortably.

"'If one is mentioning the *djinn* that live among mankind, they are called *aamar*, whose plural is *amaar*.'"

"Amaar!" says Husayn, drawing out the last syllable.

"'If one is mentioning the ones that antagonize the *young*, they are called *arwaah*.'"

The Aussie almost shouts the last word as he turns, laughing, on Umar and Husayn. They laugh back.

"Arwaah!" cries out Umar irritably.

"Arwaah," Husayn says quietly.

"'If one is mentioning the evil ones that antagonize humans, they are called *shaitan* for the singular. *Shayateen* has already been given for the plural.' Ever the careful grammarian, even when covering devils."

"Wasn't the devil the first pedant?" the woman asks.

"Shayateen!" says Umar, boldly, as if challenging one of them.

"'If they cause even more harm and become strong, they are called *efreet*.'"

"Efreet!" says Umar, sharply.

"Efreet," says Husayn, in a more subdued voice. Then again, "Efreet," almost in a whisper.

"Haven't seen stars this clear since I was a girl in Indiana."

You can't see her face but you can feel her smile.

"Wait till the moon rises. It'll feel just like home."

"I can't wait, then."

"You'll just have to wait then," you reply, teasing. "But it won't be long, I promise. They tell me you only see the stars this clear at sea. And this used to be ocean before it was desert."

You both stand at the edge of the camp beneath the black curtain of the night scattered with stars like enormous handfuls of salt or vast processions of candle bearers winding over your heads. Corridors seem to branch off behind the curtain, into rooms, chambers, more hallways, corners, attics, closets, spare rooms, in a mansion that feels at the same time infinite and strangely self-contained: vast darkness held together by thousands upon thousands of tiny points of light. The Milky Way stretches across the sky like the bed of an enormous creek.

How small I feel under it. And how grand! Like a child in a dark house.

"What did you say?"

"Nothing. Was I muttering again? Just thinking out loud. The night sky brings out the kid in me."

She laughs lightly.

"Used to bring out the bacchante in *me*! Shades of wicca and the pagan rites of midsummer."

"In Indiana of all places."

"And why not Indiana? Corn circles, witches' covens, corn wizards—corn was the basis of Mayan blood rituals. That's what got me into archaeology, when I discovered *that*. Midwestern corn no longer seemed like such an embarrassment. We had a secret, we were wild and weird, dancing bare-chested beneath the slowly fattening cobs. All summer long. The thought still brings out the crazy kid in *me*!"

She suddenly spins in a shadowy dance move in front of him, a crazy glance in her eyes. Then stops, abruptly, as though afraid of something.

"So," you say, with a laugh, "why did you change?"

"Why did I change what?" she asks, suspiciously.

"From Maya to the Maghreb, for one thing."

"Oh! *I* didn't, *it* changed. Funding dried up for the Maya, but it kept up for the Middle East."

"But this is North Africa!"

Her mood suddenly slumps.

"It's the Middle East as far as the oil companies are concerned: they fund these things. They're so desperate to find new sources they're even co-opting strange little creatures like us."

"So that's what you folks are looking for."

"Not quite. But we aren't discouraged from keeping our eyes open. I'm hoping to find an old, forgotten outpost of Carthage. Duden's an Egypt man. Brian is for the Tuareg or Chaamba, but when did they ever build a city? Ralph is for Rome. Ralph is probably right, but it would be very boring."

"Nobody's mentioned Arabs."

"No." Dismissive? Or responding reflexively to some other arcane competition in the field? "Afterwards, we'll write up a report and send it to a journal for publication a decade from now when there's a slow news quarter."

"No tweeting?"

"No tweeting. Too many ears."

"And if you find a little oil seepage along the way . . ."

"We message the company – encrypted – that is, if we can find a local node somewhere." She gestures ironically toward the wilderness. "It's not in our contract but it's understood. If we want to be funded next year."

"You don't sound so upset about it."

"I hate it, I loathe it, I despise them and myself for it. But it's a minor jinn in a world of efreets. It's reality, now that government funding has dried up and foundations are leery of 'soft science.' So we've got to deal. It's where the money is, so we play."

"Right."

"What brought you out here?"

You give her a weighing glance before answering.

"Drifting. I left school after 9/11, wandered about for a while . . . maybe Iraq did it . . ."

"You were *there*?" She sounds surprised.

"I was a kid. I dropped out of school after the attacks, everything just seemed too pointless. I was hurt and angry about a lot of things. And vengeful. Like everybody else in the country, I guess. Of course I was against the invasion, but once it happened I wanted to do something. I'd been drifting too long by then . . ."

"So you joined the army?"

"No. I was practically an anarchist at the time. I joined BlackRock. The security company that practically ran Iraq till the country's third or fourth elections. Maybe they still are, for all I know. The pay, the promise of adventure, were too tempting for a footloose kid in his mid-twenties with a bad conscience to turn down. I thought I'd avoid having to kill anyone. Do my bit. Maybe even do some good. . . ."

You snort, then you both fall silent.

The moon rises, huge and watchful, its rays slowly erasing the stars in the eastern part of the sky.

Vivian speaks, very softly.

"If I were twenty years younger, I'd be dancing right now."

You say nothing.

"If I told you something, do you promise you'll tell no one else?"

You can just make out her face in the darkness.

"I won't tell yours if you won't tell mine."

"No one else knows this and no one suspects. Duden has only told me."

"What's the mystery?"

36

She looks at you keenly in the moonlit darkness—maybe already regretting what she's about to say.

"Duden thinks the city in the photograph might be Zerzura. The city that Bagnold and Almasy spent years in the desert looking for in the '30s. The city that people have sought for centuries; coming back empty-handed or not at all. He thinks he has a chance to make the greatest discovery of his career, now he's just retiring. If he's right, it'll be worldwide news, even if only for a day. It will make him very happy. It would finally make his name. He hasn't had many triumphs. But you mustn't tell anyone else—no one else suspects what he's hoping. He's almost ashamed of it."

Rather than mocking her and her deluded mentor, you look solemn in the dark moonlight.

The eastern half of the sky is as black as silver and glows above the abandoned sea, now desert. The stars have been erased. The reg shines as if oiled.

"All right then. Let's do what we can to get him to his city. Whether it's lost or not."

You can't see but you can feel her smile—for once, entirely spontaneous.

Like the smile of someone you once knew. Your mind gropes at the memory, later, as you fight your way to sleep.

———

You pick up the thin blank book with the classic moleskine cover, of the type you sported in your early twenties but never used again, from the bottom of the box, and it opens, almost by itself, to a page where the following poem is written, in roller-ball ink, in the seething, hit-or-miss calligraphy of your youth. You had almost forgotten about it, though the moleskine book was not something you would ever forget. The words "Contra Mundum" are scrawled at the head of a trail of words that move uncertainly down the page.

37

A thin, high whine cuts the silence,
circling it like a wire —
a scream far off, at the end of the sky of your mind,
filling the skull with a cat's cradle
of gossamer shimmering in no wind
in the alert stillness.

An animal waits just beyond the perimeter of the camp,
its eyes invisible to the soldier's night-scope,
his laser-eyed armory, his spider web
of connectivity to the circling bombers
and shrieking satellites in silent space:
it does not move, it only breathes and waits.

It turns its eye. You cannot see its eye,
and yet it turns it. The retina shifts its arc
reversed, withdrawn, its world a dish of
mercury and unimpressed unknowns,
shallow and bright and unimaginable.

The ink that drew it dries. The idea lies
in the folds of gray softness. The idea dies
in its expression — is born, flies up, and dies.

———————

A roaring floods your ears as an electronic voice, crackling,
shakes you awake.

"Hey Arik!" a youthful voice shouts. "This is better than
Judas Priest! It's Wagnerian . . ."

There's a lurch and a sweeping turn, and then a stom-
ach-hollowing descent.

A silvery wing is suspended in a cloudless sky. A river
appears, far below, like a huge winding snake.

Through a gray whirling zero of propellers, you see a row
of great jagged shapes looming along a careening horizon.

They are the exact replica, white and charcoal gray, of a photograph in a children's encyclopedia you saw years ago: like the front of a cathedral, a cluster of spires and towers smeared with snow and clouds . . .

Beside you is your old high-school buddy. Alive again. Steve.

A fan of rain falls beneath the cloud-cover that rides just behind the peaks of the Grand Tetons. Lightning flashes in the shadows.

The plane banks—Steve pulls back into his seat, and the view cuts to a foaming caldron of cumulus starkly white in the afternoon sun—and then circles down in a long plunging arc.

It happens as you're waiting to check in at the hotel. A middle-aged couple in Polo attire blinks blankly around them near a potted plant. A young family stands glumly at the counter.

"She was hot?" says Steve, with a leer.

"She was hot," you assent.

"So why didn't you make your move!"

You shake your head.

"Why not? She smiled at you, man. She was giving you the eye."

"She had a ring, she's married . . ."

"So what? These flight attendants have a guy in every airport. Show some initiative, man. You should have at least asked for her phone number."

"Right."

"Hey, I thought one of our goals on this trip was to get laid."

A porter, rolling up a truck covered in baggage, glares at the two boys standing in his way. A security guard lounges with a bored, irritable look near the entrance. In the doorway to the dining room, an almost theatrical cowgirl outfit flashes past, a cowboy hat hanging and bouncing down her back: a tall, big-boned girl with reddish hair and an ivory-pale face, in profile, smiling at someone past the door—a bright, almost delirious smile. You have one of your instant affairs—flirtation, seduction, romance—you often have these days with half-glimpsed girls. Then she vanishes with a long roll of laughter.

The view from their room is over the parking lot.

"We came all this way for a view of a back alley," Steve sneers.

"I could eat a buffalo," you say.

"You came to the right place, dude. Gnarly!"

You and Steve try the bar but are stopped at the door.

"Get *out* of here!" the guard laughs.

Guests in formal attire—couples of various ages, young men alone, young women in groups, even a few children dressed in diminutive formal dresses, miniature tuxedos—wander in and out of a ballroom down the hall, carrying paper plates and plastic flutes of champagne, chatting and giggling; they poke each other, with quick jokes, wink slyly, with knowing looks. A murmuring fills the wide hallway, an occasional big laugh bursting through a thin layer of piped-in music. A woman, casually twirling a corsage, chatters to a plain-faced friend. A young man looking uncomfortable in his tux, and scowling, stands with his legs spread apart near the entrance at the far end of the hall, his arms crossed assertively across his waistcoat.

A flash of the bride in a blindingly white gown—she is smiling brilliantly at someone you can't see (not the groom, you're sure, somehow)—disappears through the entrance into a crowd of tuxedos and formal dresses of silk and satin and flowers and table cloths of white damask.

The hotel's dining room, nearer the lobby than the ballroom, is empty except for two families in a corner, celebrating a birthday—a quartet of fleshy middle-aged adults, a gaggle of kids, several teenagers sitting together watching the vacuities of the adults and sillinesses of the youngsters with superior detachment.

Sitting among the teens is the girl in the cowgirl outfit, her hat hung over the back of her chair, and sitting next to another girl in similar garb; they whisper together when the adults aren't looking. The first girl—pale, her hair a strange, orangey

40

red—rocks a little in her seat, restless. She had given the boys a darting glance when they walked in.

A burst of music comes from the reception down the hall: the band has just started. You flash on a memory of the bride dancing with her unseen partner, and the smile you saw on her face—complicit, sly . . .

You find as you sit down that, by chance, your seat gives you a perfect view of the cowgirl across the room. You grab the menu and stare over the top of it at her flickering, restless form.

Not long afterward (as you will remember often again in the future), you're standing alone in a tiny corridor in front of a door marked "Cowboys." Couples in formal splendor cross the hall. You try not to stare, but sometimes someone catches you, and you glance bashfully away.

Suddenly, the two girls at the birthday party appear from around the corner of the corridor, and stop near you, in front of a door marked "Cowgirls." The redhead remains outside as her friend enters.

Her eyes are startling. Pale, ice-blue, like the eyes of an Alaskan husky, with a little fold over the lids, which gives the upper half of her face an almost Indian look—strange, since her milky skin and reddish hair make her look Irish. She has childlike cheeks, funny, humorous lips. Taller than you had thought—almost exactly your own height. Her eyes are level with yours. . . . A buzzing wave of thrill, a swell of electricity, sweeps over you. . . . You keep yourself from looking directly at her; nevertheless, you can feel her moving restlessly, even while standing still, in a constant flow of tiny, nervous motions as she watches the wedding guests come and go through the ballroom door. A red rose above her ear flashes in and out of view as her eyes follow them.

"A w-wedding reception," you say, with obtuse obviousness and the stutter that betrays you whenever you're nervous.

She turns to you with a bright, ironic little smile.

41

"Yes," she says. "From what we can see of it from here."

You freeze, then, after what feels like about half an hour, but can't have been more than a few seconds, you hear your voice, as if coming from very far away.

"Want to, want to . . . check it out?"

She cocks her brow and glances at the door marked "Cowgirls."

"Sure," she says tranquilly.

And the two of you walk through the stream of wedding guests to the ballroom entrance.

A jungle of streamers, balloons, great fabric swags, enormous bouquets of flowers seem to burst and blossom across a room vaster than seemed likely, even possible, from the view of the entrance down the hallway.

Two walls of the ballroom are covered with gigantic mirrors; between them, they create the vision of an infinite ballroom filled with an infinite number of brides and grooms, brides-maids, ushers, family, friends, trickling lines of kids dressed like tiny replicas of the formally attired adults, waiters and bartenders and band members and dancers, a vast array of white tables expanding in diamond-shaped patterns down enormous illusory halls, scores of guests turned into hundreds, into thousands, into tens of thousands, crowds, hordes, dancing, gesturing, joking, sitting over remains of catered savories, bottles of champagne, piles of party favors and the crushed remains of wedding cake, standing about talking, ribbing each other, making sly comments, listening, comparing, laughing, shrugging, dancing, staring, watching. The bride, with her infinite reflections, sits, with her veil falling down her back, laughing with several young men in waistcoats in infinite reflections, with their infinite number of doffed jackets and open collars in the hot room. The groom is dancing with the bridesmaid you saw before with the corsage—and an infinite number of grooms dance with an infinite number of bridesmaids with an infinite number of corsages. The bride's mother, in an infinite number of reflections, is pretending to talk to the groom's mother, also in an infinite number of reflections, but sends an acid, disapproving look at the groom, who seems extremely happy to be dancing with the bridesmaid. The bride suddenly slaps one of her listeners on the shoulder, but the deep grin under her frowning eyes suggests that she is not really as angry as she pretends—or is far angrier. The band strikes up an old-fashioned polka and everyone—the entire infinite cloud of them—rises and swirls away in an infinite dance.

The girl says, with wistful detachment, "It's the happiest happiest happiest day of her life."

You smile. The repetitions are strange, sweet, charming.

"That's not very politically correct."

"Still, it's probably true." She gives a little sigh as she watches the mob of happy dancers and their reflections swell, fragment, combine, and swirl to the music, like a pond filled with water lilies. "It's never going to happen to me."

"You don't want to get married?"

She gazes with a calm, desolate look across the room and the dancers, some of whom have forgotten the steps and are laughing, some of whom laugh giddily as they show off their dancing; some faking the steps, some making them up.

"Never never never." Then she thinks for a second. "Unless I can invent my very own!" She turns to you. "How about you?"

You've never really considered it before.

You don't answer but watch the crowd, partly real, partly reflected, as it "dances dances dances" across the ballroom. Both of you watch, detached for the moment, breathing in the scent of the flowers near the door. An old man in a tuxedo, with a squashed face, and standing in a corner, drinking from a bizarrely huge glass of champagne, stares at the girl at your side. For some reason—perhaps the angle is wrong—he isn't reflected in the mirrors. Like a ghost.

The girl stares back at the man for a long moment, then drops her eyes.

43

"Knock, knock!"

The dark-haired friend is giving you an almost ludicrously murderous glare when you turn to look. You blush, confusedly, as though you'd been caught in a crime. Though you have no idea what the crime could be.

"I must go now," the red-headed girl says quietly and walks away down the hall, with her dark-haired friend in tow.

You stare after the girl till a burst of applause and cheers after the final chord of the polka makes you turn back to the ballroom.

You wake to a windless gray fog of airborne dust filling the air so thickly, you have to cover your lower face with a wet scarf to be able to breathe.

You avoid talking, and constantly wipe the dust from your eyes. The dust has no effect on the heat later in the day; if anything, making it worse. It turns your skin gray.

You drive slowly, headlights penetrating only inches before diffusing in a nebulous glow; hoping for the dust to dissipate or blow off. But there's no wind, and the fog of dust hugs the ground.

Twice the lead van lurches into a depression and has to be pulled by the other vans out again. Later you edge gingerly around a prehistoric pool bed. The vans constantly stumble over boulders big enough to crack an axle. By day's end the caravan has gone less than ten miles.

At one point you deliberately slow down your vehicle. Jack's tail lights gradually merge with the dust, then disappear.

You feel suspended, alone in a kind of void the color of pewter.

You hardly seem to be moving as the van inches ahead; then the occasional clunk of a stone against the running board or a lurch over an obstacle reminds you. The grayness is like a vast, soft, comforting silence under the rumbling of the engine.

After a while you gun the van a touch. Nothing emerges in

front but more gray. You gun it again. Nothing. Again; again nothing.

You stop the vehicle and listen.

Husayn pokes his head between the front seats and stares into the dust.

Scrufty, Brillo-haired, keen-eyed, greedy little creature you picked up in a souk in Oran: the eldest of a large family you had negotiated with for several days before getting a good price for the boy's services. Then Umar showed up—a year or two younger, Husayn's natural follower, with his funny head, he came even cheaper: maybe his family wanted to get rid of him for a few weeks, though he seemed docile enough. Umar's father had been the usual unreadable mixture of pride, obeisance, and cunning. The two boys were inseparable, never bickered without breaking off with a giggle; they often simply sat at the edge of whatever was happening, watching thoughtfully the ridiculous actions of the nazreens.

You are about to push the klaxon when a small break in the dust shows Jack's tail lights just ahead, like the eyes of a sea monster in a polluted sea, glaring at you scornfully.

That night you hear whispering in the next tent.

"So you think he's crazy."

"As a loon."

"Well . . ."

"He actually expects to find this mythical city that nobody has ever seen? Isn't that the definition of delusional?"

"Maybe this time he's right."

"Fat chance."

"Look, there are signs of some city on the sat photo. So we'll find something, even if it isn't that."

"Personally, I think they're all nuts. I think I may change to museology after this. Nothing personal, but I've never been so bored, hot, and uncomfortable in my life."

"You just don't have what it takes."

"Fuck you!"

"Keep your voice down! Duden will be on our ass."

The three assistants, whispering in the boys' tent: one of the boys, Chad, awkward, vulpine-faced, jumpy, assertively smart, the other more reserved, brooding, stubborn, red-haired and pink-skinned, Sean, afraid to look like a nerd, but sharp, and the girl, Cecilia, anorectically skinny, tomboyish, chop-haired, smile-scared.

"It's Roman." The wolf's voice, with the exasperating certainty of youth.

"Not so fast, it's too far south. It's probably Tuareg." The redhead. "At least that would be right geographically."

Silence.

"Carthaginian," says the girl primly. "It's almost certainly an outpost, it's on the exact route from Carthage to the Sahel."

"You just say that because Callan thinks so," says the redhead.

As if the judgments of the boys did not reflect those of bear or the mustache.

"Pro*fess*or Callan. And I certainly do not!" responds the girl.

"Your *lovah*."

There is a sound of rough-housing and tittering and rustling of tent and bags.

"Leave me alone!"

More tittering and rustling.

Horseplay. Flirtations between professional rivals, you think, with a smile.

A long silence follows.

"I have to go back now," says the girl in a quiet voice.

But you don't hear her leave before finally falling asleep.

The Tetons stand, jagged, craggy, massive, above you as you rise in the aerial tram: like huge, peaked hats streaked with white and separated by chasms as by gigantic ax blows.

46

The landscape drops below the tram—an enormous floor arrayed with topographical forms for the contemplation of hawks, clouds, aviators, and other sky gods: Teton Village, where their hotel looks like a toy box, shrinks far below them as you ascend; to the north awkwardly splays a blot of a town, with an expanse of lake beyond that and long lines of road cutting across the valley floor; to the east lies the local airport, where a plane descends like a long white bird across your line of vision; the city of Jackson is a blur toward the south; behind the valley, rolling green hills stretch far away into the early summer haze.

Your mind soars across the landscape, new as you are to flight, its anxieties, its thrills (the fear of crashing, the awe of the views of sky and earth)—the lift itself is like a little flight—you feel half-tipsy at the sight of the earth sweeping beneath you. *Life,* you think, remembering a poem, *is beckoning, no matter the reckoning of wind and water and tide . . .*

A flock of birds flickers far below toward the distant river.

You flash on a memory of the girl you just met, turning to you her laughing face at the discovery of his name. Her face briefly eclipses the landscape.

Steve and you, still half asleep, had been entering the hotel breakfast room when you came nervously awake.

The girlfriend—a tough-looking brunette who had the look of a suspicious canine, a boxer—gave you a death-glare as you approached.

"Hello!" said the girl with the pale blue eyes, turning with her enigmatic little smile.

The two girls are standing at the end of the breakfast line, right ahead of you. Almost as though waiting for you. Romantic serendipity, or one of fate's cruel little jokes.

Show some initiative, man! you distinctly hear Steve shouting in your mind's ear.

"This is my buddy, Steve," you say, too loud.

47

"And this is my friend, Elizabeth," she returns, with a wave of her hand.

Elizabeth glowers in silence.

The girl gazes expectantly at you.

"I'm Arik. For Ariel. Hunter."

"Really?!" the girl says with gleeful wonder. "Really truly?! Your name is Ariel? Like in the play?"

"People never let me forget it."

Mischief gloats in her grin.

"Bet you can't guess mine!"

Your mind does an iron frozen, and you stare at her *like a complete idiot*, you can feel your eyes turning into great spinning plates.

"Not . . . Miranda?"

She gives a little yip. "From *The Tempest*, my favorite play! And my favorite movie, *Prospero's Books*!"

"Don't believe her," interjects Elizabeth. "Well, her *middle* name . . ."

"Don't listen to *her*. Elizabeth has these quaint delusions that my name is Sally, as in 'Sally in Our Alley.' But it is not. It is not not not. It is Miranda—as in 'Miranda Decision.'"

"Your name is Miranda Decision?" you ask bewilderedly.

"She wants to be a lawyer when she grows up," says Elizabeth, grimacing. "*If* she ever grows up. Which I doubt."

"And *your* name is Caliban!" the girl twits Elizabeth gaily.

"Sal-ly, who's Caliban?" pipes up a little girl standing in front of them.

The girl emits a playful groan.

"Caliban," she says patiently, "is a pathetic fellow who is horrified when he looks at himself in the mirror."

"Her name is Salina Miranda Wild," Elizabeth continues, with a smirk. "And mine is Elizabeth Tudor."

"Impostor!"

"And she's crazy. As you may have noticed!"

The girl flicks Elizabeth's arm in punishment.

"Liar!"

"Liar!"

"She's just jealous," Sally, or Salina, or Miranda, or whatever her name is, says, to you, who feel a wave of nervous joy —like the touch of a passing wing—as all four of you sidle up to the breakfast board. Her eyes are shining with laughter.

You detect a surge of panic in Elizabeth's face as she turns, wordlessly, to Sally.

"Oh?" Sally says, bumping into the table with its over-bearing display of breakfast items, and herself turning abruptly to face it.

You take a napkin and, as the rest are choosing breakfast, rapidly scribble something on it: something you read just last night in a book of poetry by Percy Bysshe Shelley, a poet you'd discovered recently, after falling hard for Gerard Manley Hopkins. The lines are so apt, so perfect, it feels like fate is knocking quietly at your door. You either respond, or you do not. But only a fool . . .

But maybe you have to be a fool. You can't *not* do it. You fold the napkin quickly. As Sally "Miranda" turns to her friend, you slip the folded napkin onto her tray.

The pair of families trundles, like a small herd of blended but distinct species, to a couple of tables joined near the windows.

The girl turns to the two young men.

"You're coming . . . ?" she asks with a sudden, alert shyness.

Elizabeth glares at her and them.

"There's no room at the inn!"

Elizabeth nudges her forward with her tray. Then "Miranda" half turns.

"Maybe not . . . Maybe we'll see you at the rodeo."

The look on her face flickers and vanishes, like a flame. She gives a little wave and an apologetic shrug.

"I've never *seen* such an obvious *pair*!" Steve giggles uncontrollably as they sit. "What are their parents thinking? It's so blatant, it's hysterical. They aren't even trying to hide it."

"Be quiet, they can see you," you growl, your mind singing and soaring with joy, calculation, fear, hope. "What is it that's so 'obvious,' anyway?"

Steve stares at you and again nearly collapses with giggles.

"What is it?"

"You can't see it?"

"Can't see what?" Steve stares back, clearly enjoying your torment.

"Can't see *what*? . . ." And you are seized by a fear that drains the blood from your face.

Your friend looks at you pityingly.

"Forget it." And digs into his eggs.

"No way—tell me what you know . . . !"

"I don't *know* anything about it," Steve says with mock judiciousness. "But my guess is . . ."

"Spit it out!"

Steve looks at him with sly candor.

"Watch how they act with each other. It's almost constant mirroring—and when they don't, it's fireworks!" He pauses. "They're *dykes*, all right? They're a couple."

"No way," you practically sputter. "No *way!*"

"*Lipstick lesbians*," Steve goes on. "At least 'Miranda Decision' is—so like real girls they're, like, unreal. It's all an act. They're so close it's scary."

"Shut up!"

"Elizabeth realizes you like her friend so she *hates* you. They were playing us on a string."

What an idiot . . . ! Inside, you curdle into rancid milk at the thought of what you just *wrote on that goddam napkin:* a quotation from that goddam book of poetry you've been soaking up all goddam spring. You cringe, your spirits sinking into a pit of shame, not only because you wasted half a day daydreaming about this gorgeous girl with the red hair and pale eyes and enigmatic smile and the rose over her ear, whispering to you in the corridor, but because you had been so stupid, so thick-headed, so inexperienced that you can't even see what everybody else sees, you can't see the obvious; you have made a complete, total, radical fool of yourself *in your own eyes* . . . which is the worst humiliation of all because there is no defense against it.

"Still," says Steve, "not to despair, old man. She could be bi."

"Thanks a lot!"

You stare across at the two girls, already bickering over breakfast (you can imagine Elizabeth already accusing the false Sally: "You were *flirting with him outrageously!*" Well, she *was* . . . damn it!). The folded napkin is still lying on her tray. She'll never open it. It will end up in a garbage can and later a landfill somewhere outside Jackson, smeared with egg yolk, coffee grounds, and grape jelly as a hungry crow impatiently tears it to pieces.

The Tetons disappear behind a curtain of pines and the landscape diminishes to a strip of green toy railroad pasteboard and plywood as the gondola smoothes to a halt.

The air is keener and drier up here. Below them, Teton Village is no more than a set of carefully lined-up cubes, the hotel shrunken to a matchbox: the day before has shrunken to a nearly forgotten defeat in a silly romantic game.

"Almost makes you feel religious," Steve says as he gazes across the valley at their feet.

Steve the atheist—you both despise the Bible thumpers at school, of whom there is a steadily growing contingent, though Steve, the more mercilessly skeptical, is also the more brutally tactless.

You reply with a sly little stab of insincerity.

"We'll overlook that, considering the altitude."

"Watch out who you're calling light-headed. I wasn't the guy trying to get a date with a dyke."

"Fuck you." You grin.

You ascend the trail and, through a clearing in the trees, enter a rough plain of unfamiliar brush and rock. It's like

51

nothing you have ever seen in Ohio, where the hills have been weathered down to loam and clay for a hundred million years. The air has a thinner, a cooler edge under the quickening heat of the sun and shifts in little dry scurries across the path.

You pass through sagebrush and mountain ash and berry bushes with little bright green fruit (you pluck and nip at a few with your teeth, then spit them out; they are sour, blood red, hard). Clustered on a rock bank a wall of honeysuckle hosts a haze of bees, then the overpowering smell of sweetness is swept away on a breeze.

You poke at the broken, shaly ground at your feet, keeping an eye out for fossils: your eleventh-grade history teacher, a youngish man with a wizened smile, who spent a summer in Jackson as a teenager and waxed lyrical about the Wyoming sky—"But the only history in Wyoming since the glaciers was the Bloody Year on the Plains and the Chinese Massacre"—had been encouraging.

"It's a young range," Parry had told you. "Less than a hundred million years old. Barely out of diapers for mountains. But a hotbed for trilobites."

You pick up a promising chip of rock, then hear a click and look up.

Steve lowers the camera.

"Fossil hound staring at stone for signs of life," he says.

You kick a ground pebble at him.

"Give over."

Steve hands him the camera and strikes a pose.

"Wait . . ."

He hefts up his backpack and plants himself with the peaks in the background.

"Mountaineer at rest before conquest."

They then dig out sandwiches and take drafts of bottled water, crouching near a rock, roll out the trash bags they'd brought for the damp and lie back.

The Tetons look naked, intimate, towering silent in a

landscape lacking any human sound. Like immense witches' hats. Or like signs pointing toward an inaccessible height, beyond airplanes and satellites, beyond moons, suns, stars.

"I had no idea it'd be so quiet," you say.

"And to think that it's all just for us."

A swirl of cloud snags on the highest of the peaks, hiding it in a white blur.

You first saw the Grand Tetons in a tiny black-and-white photograph in a children's encyclopedia when you were little. The snowy, raked-back range, the clearly spaced-out peaks standing in a row like sentinels on a distant horizon, first intrigued, then fascinated you. They were peculiarly glamorous things. They seemed almost conscious, alert, alive: gigantic and beautiful, powerful and serene.

Maybe one day you would see them, even climb them and view the world from one of the peaks.

But the hope they came to signify was bigger, vaguer, than just a chance to gape at them, like catching sight of a movie star in her natural habitat: they seemed in some way to symbolize a hope that life held in store for you: marvels, wonders, miracles standing under a bright sun for all to see and to admire. No illusory dream, but the real thing. An embodiment of hope. A promise of happiness.

If you could see them, visit them, if you could know them face to face (you daydreamed), you would be able to do anything else you hoped to do. They seemed to be a guarantee of something. . . . You couldn't put it into words, and whenever you did, it sounded silly, childish. You avoided thinking it out; you only felt it, confusedly. You told no one about it, suspecting the condescending laughter that would greet you; you would have denied it scornfully if anybody had accused you of harboring, let alone cultivating, such ideas. But your mind echoed with them often when you just seemed to be sitting, quiet, with your thoughts.

Steve and you are descending a low slope in the late

afternoon when, circling a boulder, a small lake holding in it a piece of the sky, like a compact mirror, appears.

You're soon on the lake bank covered with little mountain flowers, purple, blue, white. Something underneath pokes the surface—or, too quick for the eye to see, dips and flies off—sending ripples toward the bank across reflected clouds.

You are about to turn, looking for a campsite, when you both see it: it flaps up from the trees across the water in a long, low curve toward the sky, its great wings gradually gaining altitude as its head twitches to left and right—maybe catching the two of you in its gaze—then facing forward as it climbs into the dusk, finally staring down, looking for its dinner—its white head and tail clear as it soars into the lingering sunlight.

"Holy shit!" Steve exclaims. "He was watching us. Did you see that? He was *watching* us. Man! . . . A bald eagle."

The fire crackles in the stillness. Sparks fly up. A crescent moon glows, like the white of a huge finger nail of a hand (you think) holding the sky.

The two of you, wrapped in your sleeping bags, stare up in silence.

"You know, I never knew . . ."

"Yeah. . . ."

". . . I never knew it really does look like a river . . ."

". . . yeah . . ."

". . . of stars . . ."

Looking up into the starry sky as the fire clicks nearby, you remember something one of your teachers once quoted, from some German philosopher—the two grandest things he had ever known: ". . . the starry night above me, and . . ." What was the other? It didn't really matter. Now you knew what he meant about the stars.

At last the fire dies down. You stare into the red glow flexing in the paper-like hive of ashes.

"Did you ever think that . . . ?" you ask.

"What?" in a muffled voice from Steve.

"That the whole thing seems *alive* somehow. You know? And aware. Somehow."

"The whole what thing?"

"Well . . ." you hesitate. It seems silly to say it so baldly. "The whole world. The whole frickin' universe."

You can hear Steve snort and shift in his bag.

"It's just the altitude, dude!"

You wake briefly, turn over in the sleeping bag.

Huge black wedges cut across stars. Must be *them*. The Big Dipper has moved from where it was when you turned in. What time is it? Must be hours since.

You remember Shelley's poem, "Mont Blanc"—confusing the lines, mixing them up—that you had read again before turning in, that you'd been reading and rereading on the plane from Denver when you fell asleep—just about the perfect poem for the time and place: "Mont Blanc yet gleams on high:—the power is there, the still and solemn power . . . that dwells apart in its tranquility . . . remote, serene, and inaccessible . . . the secret strength of things . . ."

And you drift off to sleep, with the thought of the night sky slowly turning, like a kaleidoscope. And your mind begins to turn with it, the night sky's stars turn and turn around you, in a great sweep between the poles and a long, flat horizon, as though you were on a sea or in a desert: a turning wheel of dark and light above your head, that turns faster and faster, the stars streaking in white arcs against the blackness, as long as comets, sweeping, swirling, faster, faster, until you feel yourself, as it were, shooting up in a fountain, a geyser, of stars, thrust into the sky, and you're flying, the earth shrinks below you to the size of a toy train table, of a doll house, of a map, as you soar into the night, the earth's shine surrounding the horizon like a corona, and you hear a voice saying, "This is you," and it says again, "This is you . . . this is you . . ."

You suddenly wake up, exhilarated by the dream.

"And the moral law within me," another voice says. That was what you'd been trying to remember, that was what the old German philosopher had said was the other one of the two greatest things he knew.

You feel sobered as you stare up into the mass of stars cut off by the mountains.

And what is the "moral law within me"? Love thy neighbor? do unto others, before they do unto you, no that isn't it, survival of the fittest, the race goes to the swift, no, the race goes not to the swift nor the battle to the strong, compassion before all things or enlightened self-interest maximize returns and increase efficiencies, the war of all against all or turn the other cheek, life liberty and the pursuit of or from each according to his ability to each according to his or an eye for an eye or thou shalt not this thou shalt not that thou shalt not suffer a witch to live or . . . or . . . ?

The questions fade in a stream riding up into the air, like flying sparks, and then go out.

You go up to the bear, who is sitting on a rock in a white hat, taking his morning coffee and staring up at the black, forbidding mountains towering enormously in the first light, sharp, immense, and clear.

Wispy mists touch the mountaintops here and there—one of them is a peculiarly shaped, toffee-beige dome; thin and gauzy as decomposing lace, the mist vanishes as they watch. Across the mountainsides slices of black are smeared like dramatic shadows: recent slides. The sun is as pink as a new baby.

"What's the next oasis again?" the bear asks in a flat voice, without looking at you.

"Ceruza," you reply. "On the other side of that dome, according to the map. An old desert stop, Amri told me," you go on, remembering "the spider's" eyes popping out as he described the oasis beyond the mountains. "He called it a city.

But anything with a mosque, a fort, and a waterhole is called that by the locals."

"A white city?"

"We'll find out."

"We've got a white enough welcome mat," the bear says, gesturing to a broad depression, a dried-up lake bed, blanched with salt, stretching between them and the mountains like a huge rug. He looks at the lake bed with strange intensity.

The old man stands near the Hummers, quizzing the three assistants, it seems, from their awkward expressions.

Wonder if they told him they think he's crazy.

"Good a place as any," the big prof suddenly says with a sigh, and stands up.

"Sorry?"

"Did I say something? I was just thinking good a time as any to get a move on." He walks with his coffee cup, his head bent, to his tent.

Half an hour later you're heading toward the first row of peaks, your Hummer in the lead.

You pass a few words in Arabic with Husayn and Umar.

"Is it hot yet?"

"It is not hot yet."

"Will you tell me when it is hot?"

"I will tell you when it is hot."

"*I* will tell you when it is hot!"

"Do not fight! I will tell both of you when it is hot!" And you laugh.

The dust stirred up from the gravel drifts away as you cross onto the salt. The lakebed is a tease: after the once-a-year rain, its water is salty enough to kill anything desperate enough to drink it.

Past the lakebed, you cross an incline of rock slide more treacherous than anything on the reg, and find your vehicles' springs tested as you bounce up the slope.

The Hummer sways and tosses, and Husayn and Umar laugh as they bounce in their seats. You join them.

"Yee ha!" you shout out the window, making them laugh even harder as the Hummer lurches over a ridge.

On the other side, a petrified wash of rock layers shines, dips, and then seems to flow up to the base of a tall butte, like gigantic frosting on a cake: the petrified remains of an enormous dune.

You point it out, with a big grin, for Umar and Husayn's benefit.

"Look!" you say in Arabic. "Is it not a wonder!"

It looks alive, by God, you think: *an anaesthetized mountain put to sleep by some old god before your very eyes. Like some crazy conceptual sculptor's environmental binge. My God, the beauty of it. . . .*

The two boys gape at the stone dunes, but you can't tell whether they are impressed or just humoring you, or are dumbfounded at your wonder. They babble the all-pervasive "Allahu-akbar" that signs, for them, all wonder, grief, enchantment, puzzlement, fear. God is great! Or are they just laughing at you? Dumb nazreen enthusing over a rock.

You move across the ridge lying just below, and the other vehicles follow.

It's already mid-morning, and the sun is pressing on you like a foot.

"Is it hot yet?"

"It is not hot yet."

"Will you tell me when it is hot?"

"I will tell you when it is hot."

"*I* will tell you when it is hot!"

The way before them is a flat incline to the base of the toffee-colored dome, so you lurch suddenly ahead, kicking up gravel and leaving Jack the Okie behind. The two boys cry out with ringing laughter as the van guns forward. "Come on, cowboys!" Jack guns his motor, and the van jerks forward to give chase. It's then you hear the long klaxon blare coming from behind Jack.

You stop, stick your head into the heat. Jack has stopped too and is getting out, looking behind him.

As you walk back the smell hits you. The Okie is staring down at the ground: a dribbling track of gasoline disappears under the Dutchboy's front fender. The Dutchboy, pushing his blond bangs out of his eyes, stands staring silently nearby. You drop to your knees: a broken line pouring gas into the sand.

"Shit."

How long has *this* been going on.

"Did you check the meter?" you ask the Okie from where you kneel half under the van.

"The meter's stuck, it isn't measuring anything."

"Check the tank."

"It's almost empty."

"Shit. Shit shit."

"What's wrong," the old man asks, "what's the matter?"

"Looks like a rock cut the gas line. We're leaking gas . . ."

You almost gag on the fumes. The dribbling line of gas leaves a mark like a welt.

You kneel for several minutes, holding the broken line.

"We can get by on a temporary fix," you say as you get up. "We can get a new line at Ceruza, it's not far past the dome. . . ."

"Ceruza?" says a skeptical voice behind him. The mustache. "Sounds sufficiently mythic."

Vivian hovers near you, her hair swept back.

"Could this help?"

A hairpin. The mustache watches them. A few yards away, the old man is poking at the base of the dome.

"No, not . . ." you say, then gaze at it a moment and flip it like a spring. "Wait a minute . . . Umar!"

You motion the boy down beside you and, taking his hand in your own, press your fingers around the slippery rubber tube. Umar grunts and lies flat in the gravel, and you scramble out.

You take the hairpin into the shadow cast by Umar's body, and start to wind and unwind it.

"Got any more of these?"

Vivian takes several from the back of her head.

"Didn't think women used these anymore. . . . "

"As long as women have hair."

You coil and uncoil the pin, check its springiness, then clip three other pins to the ends of your fingers.

"Do you have any sewing thread?"

"Now that *is* politically incorrect." She smirks genially at him.

You remove the hairpins from your fingers, take off your boot, and unravel a portion of sock. It stinks. You take several long hunks of yarn from the sock and wrap them around your wrist, then replace the hairpins on your fingers. Then you kneel back beside Umar, who blinks at you and grins at the decorations pinched on his fingertips.

"No guarantee how long *that* will hold . . . ," you comment after re-emerging from the vehicle's undershadow.

The old man grins at Vivian, half avuncular, half faunish. "You've saved the day, you weren't my favorite student for nothing. Nothing personal, Ralph, Brian," he says, turning to the mustache as it bristles; the bear gives a pinched smile. "By the way," he gestures toward the dome, "that's a coral reef, you can still see the fossils of its parasites. May have boiled away during the last warming. I knew we should have brought along an oceanographer."

"We should have brought an experienced guide," the mustache sneers.

You glare at him.

"And maybe a mechanic, and a spare gas tank or a camel or two. That would have been convenient."

Stiffly, they re-enter their vehicles and slowly cross the ancient seabed.

You suppress the sense of insult from Smuts. *There are no experienced guides to this world.*

There should be signs of the next oasis as soon as you cross the scree flanking the old coral reef. What you get is a valley of volcanic pillars scattered like the remains of a set of innumerable chess pieces: a hamada of torn rock in a vast gallery of grotesque shapes spread out to the horizon.

Like standing before an enchanted forest in a fairy tale that has appeared overnight just as you were about to reach home.

Amri's map lies flat over the lead van's hood. The old man squints at it, glancing between it and the view.

The bear gazes intently over the vista, his hand above his eyes. The mustache gives the south a long, slow sweep with the binoculars.

"How's the water supply?" he asks.

"Enough to last an extra day or so," you say. "We'll ration it to be safe."

The Okie gives you an odd look.

You scowl back at him. *The radiator, I know. Don't scare them. We just need to get to water in a day or two.*

The old man's mouth twists funny, then goes slack. His neck looks curiously vulnerable under the whitened back edge of his hair.

The sun removes the last shadow from the hills and the dome of petrified coral behind them, and presses, hot, down on them.

"Hey Hunter, it was your idea to climb this thing!"

Steve is grinning at you.

"I'm just saying."

"We can always turn back."

"And tell everybody I only climbed half way when I could have made it to the top?"

You're climbing the long switchback trail to the crag jutting over your head. The city of Jackson Hole spreads beneath under the relentless sun, a shining blob turning the valley into a huge vanity table covered with abandoned jewelry.

"They've got to be kidding. A *bicycle*?"

It lies abandoned not far from the trail's end—the first thing you see, even before the panorama across the mountainscape and the dramatically reduced gully of Jackson Hole, for which the city was named—a slip of a valley among dozens at your feet streaming up and down the wrinkled fastness of mountain country surrounding them like a vast rumpled cloak.

"Somebody *biked* up here?" Steve marvels, pulling the rusted dirt-bike up and straddling it.

The sky is empty except for a blinding sun.

You take deep, painful heaves of breath in the thin, keenly blowing air.

You feel half amazed, half obscurely disappointed. . . .

"That must be Montana," you say, gesturing toward the north. "And Idaho."

"There's desert thataway . . ." Steve looks southward.

Slowly you scan the landscape. You suddenly feels light-headed, and both of you squat.

You hear voices, thin and far away. Peering down the mountain side, you see several tiny distant specks.

Little high-pitched sounds, bickering, a harsh laugh, more sounds.

Then, suddenly, singing.

The wind comes back with a blow and you can't hear it any-more, though you can still see them, moving among the rocks.

A noise startles you. The wind has knocked the bike over, and you stare blankly at the fallen bike, looking like a wounded skeleton with a horizon of mountains in the distance behind it.

A peculiar-looking stone lies beside the front tire.

You pick it up: a broken bit of rock impressed with a form, like a light embossing; you look closely, smooth it lightly.

"What is it?"

"I'll have to ask Parry. Maybe a trilobite." You look at your friend. "It means we're walking on an ancient seafloor."

"Ever seen the ocean?"

"Nothing bigger than Lake Erie. Which doesn't count."

You bring the fossil close to your eyes. "First time I get to a mountain top I find something from the bottom of an ocean. How cool is that?"

You slip it into your shirt pocket and gaze over the landscape.

"I can see why they call it God's country."

"No shit," Steve replies sharply. "That's why Wyoming is full of hicks, Republicans, and fundamentalists." He frowns across the landscape, pushing the hair from his eyes, but the wind won't quite let him. "All it takes is a bunch of big rocks and a sky bigger than they are to make them fall to their knees and shout hallelujah. It's a big beautiful accident, like a giant ink spill. Just chance, buddy, and the laws of physics. And one hella lot of time."

Early evening.

"That must be the creek."

You can hear light gurgling of water to the right but see nothing. It seems almost to be speaking, and, fatigued from the day-long hike, you think you hear voices, a gurgle and rumble of a party or a crowd, individual voices whispering just to you, as you used to pretend as a boy. You've been following the sound for the last half hour, but you can see no sign of the creek.

Then you pass a screen of brush and an expanse of open ground surrounded by shattered granite spreads before you. The sky shows tufts of fiery gold straight above; it looks like the wing of an enormous butterfly about to take off into the twilight.

A single campfire burns in the distance, and you hear angry voices. The fire blinks as figures pass before it in rhythm to the sounds.

A creek winds near the campfire and crookedly toward you.

"Hi."

A young woman with a blond streak down a mass of coal-black hair and a thickset man with a shaved head, crouching near the fire, turn to look. The woman's face is expressionless. The man's face is bloated, jowly, saturnine, his eyes squint as if he were savoring a private joke. Another young woman, a butch-cropped brunette, sits at the creek edge, staring into the gathering shadows. The three look like they have been caught in the middle of a quarrel.

"How's the camping?" Steve asks in his squeaky, I'm-innocent voice.

"Perfect." The man shrugs. "Clean water, a clear night, a warm fire, loving company."

"Are there any other good sites?" you ask, trying to ignore the sarcasm. "We need to set up."

"No," says the man. "We took the only good one." He pauses. "Why not camp here?" he continues, with a lazy sweep of his hand. "I'm caught between two nutcrackers and I could use some reinforcements." He grins brightly. "And these two maneaters could use some fresh meat."

"Max!" cries the brunette near the creek.

You look at Steve, who shrugs.

"Sure," you say. "Great."

There's no place else to go, and the light is quickly fading, so you unpack, unroll your sleeping bag, open your dry food, set up.

"I win!" the man cries out as you're finishing.

You and Steve trade a look.

The half-blond glowers back and forth between you and the man, who gloats, swelling like a frog as the campfire makes his face go pink. Just beyond the glow of the fire, the night surrounds them like a black wall.

"We made a bet when we saw you coming. I bet I could get you to stay with us, they bet you would camp anywhere *but* with us." He grins.

Later you learn that these were the people you'd heard earlier in the day talking and singing down the mountainside.

Next morning, the falls, the source of the stream, are roaring above you.

You shout to the woman with the blond streak: Maven, "It's called Hidden Falls!"

"What?" she shouts back with a stern look.

You shout into her ear: "Hidden Falls!"

She looks at you blankly, almost hostilely, then leans over and shouts back.

"What?" you shout.

She shouts again. It sounds like a question.

"I can't hear you!"

She just stares at you, like a cold, beautiful face painted on a wall.

Suddenly you realize what she had just asked: *Hidden from what?*

The thundering white wall of water scatters away in a thousand plumes of spray and rainbows.

Near you runs a narrow stream that runs into the creek bordering the previous night's campsite—the creek that teased you with its invisible muttering the evening before. Here is the white, raging giant that is the creek's source. No more hidden than the mountains themselves. Unless the falls themselves, with their enormous curtain of white, are doing the hiding. But there seems to be no way to penetrate their secret.

Oblivious to this mystery, or maybe just impatient or indifferent, Max motions toward a trail twisting upward, and the group set off behind his hairless head with its watch cap that make him look homeless.

You and Maven take up the rear.

"So," you begin. "Where in Illinois are you from?"

"It depends on my mood. If it's good, I say Bloomington. When it's bad I say Normal." Her face is strangely expressionless. Almost dead.

You laugh awkwardly.

"They're evil twin cities. They made a mistake surveying our property when they built it in the '70s. The city line dividing Normal from Blooming Crazy, as the Normalites like to call it, goes right down our backyard. Right through my swing set, actually. When I'm swinging forward I'm in Bloomington, when I'm swinging backward I'm in Normal. Which seemed about right."

"And what do the Bloomingtonians call Normal?"

"'Ab-Normal,' what else? Like we always tell the Bloomies, 'You can call us lots of things, but one thing we'll *never* be is Normal.'"

"I grew up in Ohio. Near Columbus."

She makes no response, and you both walk without speaking a few paces before the silence gets too much for you.

"What do they do in Bloomington?"

"Lots of things," she says serenely. "There's the Midwest Fish and Feather, and the Illinois Deer and Turkey Classic, there's the Hands All Around the Quilt Show and the American Passion Play, to say nothing of the Kickapoo PowWow and Keep the Bloom in Bloomington. I ran away after high school and never looked back. Chicago, New York, Boston, San Francisco, Bolinas. Then Max stole me from the bar he managed and he bore me away to the Far North. Long as they keep the Ill in Illinois, I'll be happy."

You laugh again, less awkwardly.

"Sorry! I didn't mean to laugh at your home state."

"That's okay. We all do. If you're not in Chicago, you might as well be in Indiana." She sighs. "So. You always wanted to see the Tetons. Have they met your expectations?"

"Well . . . so far. How 'bout you?"

"I didn't have any. I'd never heard of them till a month ago. But then, Americans aren't supposed to know geography. I had never heard of Vancouver till Max moved me up with him. Then one day he decided he couldn't live without a visit to Grand Teton, so here we are and here I am." Her face remains expressionless. Even when she looks you in the eye. Her eyes are opaque. Like coffee-colored marbles.

"Ever feel homesick?"

"I hated Abnormal Bloomriddington. Well, I liked it when I was a kid. It can be quite charming walking by the Veterans Parkway under the sunset. You stare in disbelief? Or getting lost on the Wesleyan campus with half the students doing their nails on the lawn—and those were the guys. Most of it—most of *them*, since like every twin cities the place is schizophrenic when it isn't bipolar, full of self-loathing masked as hatred of the Other, or something like that—most of it is not charming at all. Get a few blocks away from a campus and it's your usual sterile suburb with tree-lined streets and suffocating competitiveness and well-manicured despair. Unless you belong to the universities—and we have three of the little beauties—your life can seem perfectly meaningless. It's like living in Las Vegas and not working for a casino." You stare hard at her black hair with its streak of peroxide blond as a breeze blows a few strands and she brushes them from her face. You register, for the first time, that her face is asymmetrical: the two halves don't quite match. It's very sexy.

She looks at you as the two of you brush between two bushes budding white and pink.

"So what are you staring at?" She looks at him with a face that is both blank and defiant.

You quickly pick a flower from one of the bushes and hand it to her.

"For the bloom in Bloomington."

Without changing her expression—or rather lack of one—she takes the flower and and sticks it in her hair.

"There's no going back. And there's no staying in Vancouver. Max wants to make more money."

"What do you want?" you ask.

"That is the question! What does Maven want? The Canucks are starting to get on my nerves. They're so awfully nice but they don't know how to pronounce English. And why are the winters there so friggin' cold!"

She pauses.

"I want to move back to America, but far, far from Abnormal Dead Bloom."

You look up to catch her staring coolly into your eyes.

"Thank you for the flower."

A rap against your window wakes you. You had been dreaming again, during the mid-day siesta . . . and you drift back to sleep.

You are in the desert again, though one you haven't seen before. You are surrounded by flowing swells of sand, swirled as if with an immense pastry knife: a frozen ocean of sand, on which you are embarked as on a voyage across a petrified sea. On the horizon ahead of you, like a tiny filament of black against whitish gray and an immensity of pale azure above, you see a figure, at first motionless, yet as though looking back at you; one arm (is it a man?) rises over its head, then lowers to its side, rises, lowers, then rises and waves, in a stately rhythm, the figure's body dark against the horizon. The figure seems at the same time tiny and far away, and yet also huge and near, at the edge of a sea of glass, or water, shimmering at its feet, for a moment reflecting the figure's shape, a vast reflection shimmering and wavering in the windless light, then breaking into an earthy yellow, no, the figure is at the top of an enormous hill of sand formed like a huge bread roll, scooped at one side in a crescent. Is the figure enormous and a hundred miles off, or merely of average size and standing no farther away than the edge of the next plain or above the next wadi? The figure seems to beckon you on, to a camp, to other men, to an oasis, just over the high edge of the star dune or the barchan, to the edge of the desert perhaps, out of the desert, maybe even to the goal of your wandering here. For you are wandering, you have been wandering for a long time. Whatever: it is a direction, you need a direction, one to stick to no matter what, and you need to hurry if you are to get there, wherever "there" is; to survive, to live, alone as you are, without shelter, without provisions, though

68

how did you get here, you seem to have been born here, maybe you were born here and are now just waking up, yet there is no sign of life elsewhere on the horizon: the desert stretches around you, a frothing, billowing, solidified sea of sand, to the south toward dim lumps of mountains and tablelands and outcroppings and pillars of eaten granite and sandstone, in the north and west to a deceptive, a falsely hopeful brightening of the sky. In the east stand the figure and the shimmering mirage and the slope up to the cresting lip of the dune. The figure raises its arm and then lowers it again. Is it beckoning you on? Is it possibly warning you away? Something about the figure you distrust, you don't know why. Something seems wrong. You hold your hand across your eyes, hiding them from the light. Then the figure suddenly turns its back to you.

You see the face of a girl you knew over two decades ago—it flickers a smile at you and immediately turns away.

A loud thumping seems to come from the figure in the distance. You try to move faster, to run away from the figure; but the harder you try the more you are held back, the sand grabs at your legs, the air becomes suffocating, you wake to see the bed in flames, then you really wake, with a gasp . . .

It's Vivian rapping at the window, her head wrapped in a long scarf like a hijab. She hurriedly gets in. A trickle of Egyptian rai can be heard from the radio next to Husayn's ear. Remembering the two Arab boys in the back, napping, you raise a finger to your lips.

"Thanks," she whispers, dropping the scarf from her face. "I've been thinking about the . . . situation. I have a bad feeling about this. I'm not saying we should turn back . . ."

You stare at her a moment . . . then shake yourself.

"I'm not exactly ecstatic myself."

"I know we have less water than you claim we do."

"So I'm a worse liar than I . . ."

"I checked it."

"Not all of it, you didn't check mine."

"I factored that in. My doctorate is not in knitting. Jack's radiator took all of his, and his group has been drinking from . . ."

"Slow down, there's more water than you've counted. We can stretch it out for a couple of days, even longer if we ration it."

"Will that be enough?"

"Maybe."

"Then there's the broken gas line . . . "

"You're alert."

She sits back. "I think you were right."

"About our stowaway jinn?"

"Exactly."

"Not a scientific hypothesis, but more comforting than sheer chance."

"I hate chance."

"Maybe we should pray to our jinn and ask him to be merciful."

She's silent, as though considering it.

"We have a Hobson's choice, doctor," you say. "We could try going back, but that probably means dropping the expedition. Have you talked to Duden?"

"He wouldn't like that. He's retiring, and emerituses don't get grants the way they used to. He needs this. His career hasn't had many successes."

"Like you said."

"He's insanely proud, behind all that Yankee . . ." She grins. ". . . pride! I know him, I was his student."

"As he made sure we all heard. On Maya blood rituals?"

She ignores this.

"So I want your opinion before I bring it up with him."

"I'm the worst person to ask."

"Why?"

"I hate going backward almost as much as I hate chance."

"So you think we should push on."

"I don't know what we *should* do. My impulse is to push on

70

if there's anything to push on *to*. And to find Zerzura, skeptical as I am . . . or not find it! Let's just say you've got me interested, so you only have yourself to blame. But I'm just a serf."

Vivian gazes through the windshield at the valley of rock forms grotesquely arrayed before them like a huge sculpture garden by a megalomaniac artist of the last century.

An hour later, just past the worst heat of the day, the caravan lumbers cautiously into the valley.

The rocky defile opens out to a canyon descending at their feet in a tableau of cascades and whitewater streams.

Maven stops and stares at the view with a hard, serene look. She cocks an eye at you.

The air tingles. A stand of aspens glitters in the motionless air.

As they scramble over a boulder, Maven grabs your hand and your blood lurches to attention. She doesn't let your hand go, pulling you closer to her as you both walk, with increasing slowness, behind the others.

Your mind draws a blank. You can feel her eyes glancing coolly back and forth between your face and the trail at your feet, are almost afraid to look her in the eye; you can barely control the idiotic smile on your face, the blush, a sudden urge to chatter.

Her lips rise to meet yours.

"Look!" you say, panicking, and point.

Across a stream thirty yards off, an elk stands in profile against the flank of Mount Moran. It's an older male, a gnarled set of antlers crowning his blunt head.

He seems to have just lifted his head, perhaps from drinking. It notices you and stops, watchful.

You both stare at the animal.

Its tail switches from side to side.

"He's watching us," Maven says with a quietly appraising look at you.

71

The others disappear behind a turn in the trail, and you and Maven are suddenly alone.

She turns to you, glances over at the elk, and then up at you again.

"Are you afraid?" she asks after a moment. She almost seems to be testing you. There is a light in her eye that gleams and goes out.

You stare down into that strange, unexpressive, unbalanced face.

The water sings and roars around you.

The elk has vanished: an empty frame of aspens against the mountain flutters where it stood.

You stare at each other for a long minute.

She leans up and whispers into your ear, "Let's catch up with the others."

Then she walks swiftly ahead, abandoning your hand.

As you both turn the trail, you see the others, who seem to be wondering what had happened to you. Max's expression is ominously flat.

Maven speaks up, in an innocent tone: "Did you see the elk?"

Steve smirks at Maven, then gives you a strangely threatening look. You stare back at him. *Why are you looking at me like that? Nothing happened.*

Yet you aren't sure nothing has.

They turn back to the trail and continue on. Maven moves to the head, near Max, and walks silently beside him. The brunette—a Canadian named Charlotte—gives you a sharp glance over her shoulder.

Steve leans in close.

"You're working fast, old man."

You whisper furiously in reply: "What do you mean? Nothing happened! We just stopped to look at an elk . . ."

"Not to worry. He can only kill you."

The grin your friend gives you is flat, shining.

Their progress is slow. Peter's van gets stuck in a sand pocket they have to rock the vehicle out of. By nightfall they've only gone a few miles, with no sign of the end of the valley.

A slightly unreal heartiness has set in as they sit around the campfire at dinner.

Umar and Husayn squat to the side, carefully watching the infidels.

". . . so you think that . . . 'oil civilization' is finished?" says the redhead, with grad-student hesitation, to the bear.

The prof wipes his forehead.

"It's finished all right. In a few years only a millionaire will be able to afford a trek like this one." He gives you one of his strained smiles. "Better work up your prices."

"Not a moment too soon!" says the wolf. "Or we'll cook in our own heat."

"It's only a hypothesis so don't drink the Kool-Aid yet." Smuts glares at the wolf and pretends to ignore the bear. "There are probably another trillion barrels of oil, on the continental shelves, in Central Asia, the Andes...."

"Antarctica. . . . With no ice, it'll be that much easier to drill."

The mustache bristles.

"I won't hold my breath waiting," says the old man. He squats forward, his lumpy pate shining in the firelight. "Not that *I*'ll see the results. The last time the temperature rose this fast was at the end of the Permian. I *know*. I was there!" He smiles ruefully. "The following die-off was 90%. Roughly."

"I'd just as soon retire the internal combustion engine while we're still ahead," says the bear.

"And go back to horse buggies and clipper ships!" the mustache sneers.

The animosity between the two of them perceptibly warms the cool night air.

"It may be time to retire the human species," the bear says quietly, still staring Smuts in the eye.

"No more archaeological expeditions in the Sahara," says the wolf, "at any rate."

"I beg your pardon," the old man smiles. "Camels will do fine for me. But we're ingenious monkeys, we'll think of something clever."

"We'd better," says the redhead, the intense, quiet one, under his breath.

"The next trek in the desert will be the one looking for *us*," says Vivian, her face blank as she stares into the camp fire.

Smuts sits just across from her. He glances at her, which she makes a point of not returning. Sometimes he glances coldly at you.

Just beyond the circle of the fire light, you suddenly see them: two bright points of light, a diminutive fox's eyes, its huge ears outlined in the darkness where it sits watching them. Man and fox stare at each other for a few moments before the two eyes disappear, and you hear the sound of its paws scampering away.

Vivian looks over her shoulder, startled.

"Nothing to worry about," you say quietly. "Just a little visitor, meaning no harm."

"I wouldn't be so sure," Smuts says sharply.

"Varmints will inherit the earth." Peter grins. The fire is starting to flicker out. He suddenly lifts his boot and smashes it to the ground.

"What is it?"

"Nothing, just an itch, I must have fleas…."

You go over when Peter gets up to go to bed. In the ground near his flank is the smashed body of a scorpion.

"Looks like a storm's coming." Maven has drifted back beside you and is now looking into your face with her strange, blank, expressionless look.

A lip of black cloud has drawn up behind Mount Moran, sinking the tip of the peak into a black-bellied white shading into gray.

"I don't know," you reply evasively.

"Let's move it!" Max calls out, looking back. He hustles forward, double time, and the rest scramble after him. Maven walks quietly beside you; you glance at her in some confusion.

"Maybe," she says coolly, not looking at him, "we won't make the ridge."

Then a wall of wind rocks the trees, and the sky goes black. They all start running. A single charge of hail followed by a brisk, cold wind sweeps down the mountainside. Lightning forks one peak, then another, and another, and thunder cracks in a violent fugue cross the sky.

They scatter to find shelter—beneath rocks, in stands of bushes. More hail rattles over them. Then something soft and white flurries and swirls down from the June sky. You stick out your hand: snow.

The others quickly unpack tarps and sleeping bags, and you yank out a garbage bag and pull it and your sleeping bag to a little spruce-grove close by, where you quickly unroll the bag and slip in.

Maven is immediately beside you. She removes her orange backpack and pulls into the bedroll, then zips the flap over their heads.

The hail sings in hard clicks as it strikes against the bag. A flash of light penetrates the bag, then more thunder. And you find yourself clasping Maven loosely, almost gingerly, in the musty brown darkness.

You can see her, a shadow with a feminine smell, staring back at you.

"Hold me," she says. You don't realize it then, but only later, that she says it coldly; like a command.

As you feel another charge of hail followed by the soft pattering of snow, Maven pulls your hand beneath her soft flannel shirt to her small, soft-skinned breasts. Thunder rolls more distantly. Your hand seems to burn at the touch of her skin, the soft loose flesh, the rough ends of her nipples.

She notices you have stopped, as if hypnotized, and she pulls your hand down her jeans to the brush of hair and the purse of moisture between her thighs. Your mind goes white—the hail, the snow, the storm, the other hikers, are suddenly very far away—as you pull her jeans down and open your own over your hardened penis, then cautiously seek an entrance into her body . . .

"You're in me," Maven whispers into your ear, guiding you. "You're in me. . . . in me . . . more . . . now . . . now . . . slowly . . . slow-ly . . . "

But you unleash in a gallop of half-terror, half-joy, as the snow softly buries the two of you. You thrust your nose into her ear, rub your face across her dark hair, rub your nose along her eyebrows, kiss her face in long spirals, follow the edge of her chin with your lips and tongue, blindly following instinct, blindly following the rolling of her face and head and hair beneath your greedy mouth.

The sounds of the storm have vanished, all you can hear are little groans, little sighs— . . .

"Maven," you whisper in her ear. "Ma-ven . . . Maa-ven . . ."

There is no other sound in the world.

Then, abruptly, there is a sharp spasm, and there is no you, no Maven, no world—just an ecstatic nothingness. . . .

The snow has stopped.

You are somewhere outside space and time, light and darkness, still and quiet in the half-light, in the warmth of a flesh sweet, slightly salty, of grassy hair, a sweet tangle of arms and legs, a slippery mass of vines, a soft slow explosion, a kind of jelly-like blowing of skin and moisture, at one and the same time crystallized and liquid, in which you lingeringly sink, pulled into a current, a tide, you have no desire to be rescued from.

You lie listening to the humming of your blood, of her blood, of the blood of both of you, unable to distinguish your blood from hers, your body, your breath, your sensations, from hers, what hers must be (you think): swimming in luminous darkness, sailing over a fluctuating ocean, shoreless, formless, where you are vanishing into a dream of, for a moment unburdened of . . . of what?

Suddenly you feel yourself coalesce out of a kind of viscous mist into numbness, vagueness, sleepiness; you feel a breathing against your neck, feel a layer of snow lying lightly over folds of darkness covering you; you hardly feel you are there at all—or as though what's left of you is being held in a cocoon, in a hand, in a bed warm and dim, and something has broken off, melted, split off and sailed away in the darkness; you are no longer who you were just a few minutes ago, whoever that was, before, before what; you no longer have, are, what you had, were, before, whatever that was, you have, are, something else now, after . . . after what? . . .

You caress your sudden lover, softly moving your fingers across her face, her thin cheeks and lips, her chin, the line of her hair, her eyebrows, smoothing her, cuddling her. You feel sleepy.

"Ar-ik!" you hear Steve calling in the distance. "Ar-ik!"

Maven's breathing calms, and she turns her face back to you.

"That'll do," she says quietly.

You open your mouth but can think of nothing to say.

You pull up each other's jeans, and Maven unzips the bag. Her head pops out into a powder of snow shaking from the pine branches.

Outside, a thinly powdered world of white covers the trees and grasses and rocks, already melting in the sun despite the cold of the air.

Winter at your feet, your head in summer.

The storm clouds have already moved on, breaking past the Tetons to the south.

A dozen feet away, Max and Charlotte, rolling up a sleeping bag, catch sight of the two of you.

"Too bad we didn't bring our skis!" you say, with a volatile mixture of light-hearted cockiness and guilty panic.

The two stare at you, Max with an ominous grin, his bald head shining in the sun.

Maven looks off into the trees, ignoring you.

"So you haven't frozen yet," says Steve.

At first you don't catch the flat note in Steve's voice. Your feeling of cockiness returns, and you give Steve a soft punch.

"Hey!" Steve apes a massive counterpunch, pulling back at the last moment to a patronizing finger flip, brushing your shoulder with contempt.

Steve turns away abruptly and walks off. You ace him with a snowball, and the two of you erupt into a snowball fight in the melting mush, your giddy, oxygen-starved laughter nipping the chill from the air. But Steve is not laughing. Off to the side, Max and Charlotte watch.

Steve throws one last snowball, his eyes glittering with something you have never before seen in them.

You're struck in the chest, and a rock drops to the ground.

"Hey!" you shout, and Steve stares at you grimly.

Maven grabs Steve's arm, and you watch them uneasily as they tramp up the snow-covered trail.

A bizarre thought hits you, a thought you refuse to believe but still can't shake. *She slept with Steve last night.*

"Excuse me, was Dr. Lexington here anytime last night?"

The question from Smuts has an edge of irritation. His face hovers in the opening of the pup tent near his feet. Groggy from sleep, you have to think a moment.

"No, why . . . "

You climb out of your sleeping bag and stand in the chilly dawn beside the old man, Smuts, Vivian. The rest are still asleep. Streaks of wild green fade into indigo over their heads, and sunlight just touches the top of the dome to the north.

"Who saw Brian last?"

"I must have," says the old man, who shares the bear's tent. "I remember thinking he must be getting up to take a leak. If I thought at all. I woke up in the middle of the night, I heard a

78

terrific report, like a gunshot. His bag was empty."

"I heard it too," says Vivian. "A whole series. Weird booms, then crashing rocks."

"Hot rocks," you say. "Too hot during the day, exploding at night when it gets too cold too fast."

"Remember the time?" Smuts asks the old man.

"No. Two, three?"

"Can I look at your tent?" you ask.

"Of course."

Brian's sleeping bag is flipped open neatly as if he'd just crawled out of it. Next to a knapsack bunched into a pillow is a pack of freshly opened cigarettes—American Spirit—and a book, a murder mystery. Brian's boots lie inside the entrance, next to his white hat.

"I saw a pack of cigarettes but no matches," you say, once outside again.

"He uses a lighter," says the old man.

"No lighter then. He may have gone out for a smoke. Or gone looking for the source of the booms. They can sound almost human."

"I never knew he smoked." From Smuts.

The old man looks at him wryly.

"That's something you would only know if you *lived* with him. I think he's ashamed of it."

Vivian smiles nervously.

"I suspected as much. No booze, no meat, no sex, no drugs. He had to have *some* vice."

"The one sure to kill him," says Smuts.

"Maybe he passed out, or fell into a wadi, or was bitten by a snake …?" Cecilia sputters.

You walk toward where Brian's footprints point across the sand. Beyond in the slowly lightening air, you see more rock pillars, outcrops, shapeless masses of gravel.

Someone calls out Brian's name. Someone else picks it up. The calling voices begin to disperse.

"Bri-an! Bri-an!" Male voices from your right and behind you, then from your left, two female: "Bri-an!"

The sense of being in a huge sculpture garden strikes you again—or as if surrounded by forms that had been suddenly frozen, petrified from long ago—or just yesterday. You can almost see animals, plants, water twisters, the shapes of birds, snakes, giants, men, faces in profile just turning away, or just turning toward him, staring.

The voices fan out. "Bri-an! Bri-an!"

A little desert rat with a long tail leaps from under your feet. Near a lava plug sticking out like a big thumb lies a butt end—a filter-tipped American Spirit, smoked almost to the tip. There was a moon last night, he could have seen his way to get here, he probably crouched near the boulder. You touch the rock, which is split in three large sections, with raw-looking dust at the bottom. *Last night? Could it have happened while he was standing there? Scaring him? So he runs off . . . gets disoriented . . . lost . . .*

Foolish not to have worn his boots.

"Bri-an!"

No signs past the boulder. Must have walked on. Walked, *not run in a panic.*

But if he could see to get here, why couldn't he see to get back?

Suddenly you stare at the sand at your feet.

Could he have deliberately . . .?

Later they stand in a rough circle, looking blankly at each other. The grad assistants look frightened, the girl teary-eyed, the two boys fit to burst with advice nobody asks them for.

"We can't leave till we find him."

"Of course."

Silence.

"We might have to go back and bring a search party."

"It might be wiser to push on to Ceruza, it has to be closer than Ouadane, we can bring back a search party," says Jack.

Smuts gives him a keen look.

"But we don't know how far away it is," you say. "We do know the distance back."

"What about gas?"

"We can double up, we can leave a van with supplies here."

Silence again.

"If we have to go back to Ouadane, he could die of exposure," Peter says. "If thirst doesn't get him first."

"Could he have taken any water with him?"

"His thermos is still in his pack."

"But somebody else's . . . "

"No one else's is missing. Anyway, why would he take water to go for a smoke."

"Could he be a sleepwalker?" the Dutchboy asks. "I used to be, when I was a kid. I once woke up in a field of tulips."

The Dutchboy is usually so quiet, everyone looks at him in puzzlement.

"Possibly," says Smuts, breaking the silence. "He never told any of us about it." He turns to Vivian. "Would you know?"

"I wouldn't know," she says, looking daggers at him.

"Maybe we ought to stay one more night," says Cecilia in the little-girl voice she uses with the adults. "Maybe he'll come back."

"Nice thought," you say, "but it's too dangerous to stay here."

The old man suddenly speaks up.

"Is night driving possible?"

"Part-way, but you saw how it was on the reg . . . "

"But it's still possible."

"Possible though not recommended."

"Then we have to go back." Though the old man's voice is firm, his large, fluttering eyes are watery. You glance at Vivian: she winces. "We have to go back and get a search party, we can't do this by ourselves. We can leave him a supply of food and water and shelter for him if he shows up."

"We can leave behind one of the Hummers," you say. "He can catch up with us if he finds it."

"I'll stay and keep looking for him." From Smuts, *somewhat surprisingly*, you thinks. *Triumph? Guilt? A professional rival suddenly removed . . .*

"There aren't enough supplies . . ."

They continue standing and staring, as if nothing had been agreed to.

Then they disband and begin to pack up, moving reluctantly, slowly, as if on the moon or the sea bottom.

"We need to hurry."

Yet their motions remain slow, packing up, topping off gas from the van they're leaving behind. It takes almost an hour before they are ready to leave, and the heat is rising.

"We'll have to drive straight through to Ouadane."

You tell Umar and Husayn they're going back; they look, puzzled, at you, then each other. They look wistfully in the direction they're no longer taking. They also will miss discovering Zerzura. Chattering to each other, they climb into the back with Vivian, who smiles at them.

You look at the old man before getting into the Hummer. "He might make it, you know."

The old man looks back at you, then his eyes skim away. His mouth sets before speaking.

"Of course he can. It will take more than a couple of warm days to kill Brian. He's from New Mexico."

The caravan lurches reluctantly north.

After a time the old man speaks up: "Brian was my best student in the class of '09. He's always been a little too independent for his own good, that boy."

"That's true enough," says Vivian quietly, from the back. "I worked with him at Northwestern for a couple of years. He always managed to get his own way."

"Stubborn as they come!"

"A gentle giant," says Vivian.

"And sometimes he's even right!" the old man tries to grin at his joke, but it comes out strained.

There is a silence. Then you ask, "Do either of you think he might have done it . . ."

"No!" the old man almost barks in response; the idea has been on everyone's mind. "Absolutely not. Brian wouldn't do such a thing. He's still a young man, he has his whole life ahead of him, so what if it's getting harder to attract funding for our sort of thing? He's tough enough to know these fashions change. There's nothing I know of in his private life. Absolutely not!"

After a short silence, Vivian speaks: "Brian is more fragile than he . . ."

The old man interrupts: "It's not possible. Some people you just know could not do such a thing. For Brian, it's absolutely out of the question."

They say no more as they move ahead.

Maybe the desert just swallowed him. As it has been known to do.

A few hours later they're back at the base of the coral dome, then move back across the petrified dune and over the scree, toward the sebcha and the barren plain north.

The campers soon reach Paintbrush Divide, a high ridge scattered with namesake flowers, and they pause to drink in the view of snow-patched mountains and pine-shaggy valleys—with distant dots of people working down a trail or edging around the rim of a lake—in great sheets of distance, like enormous scrims, toward a vague horizon.

Something odd is happening in the valleys just below them: a stirring as of a rug under the trees. Then they see them: masses of elk, moose, bison, a few bears, ground animals, moving down the slopes into the valleys—a vast horde moving silently, as if to escape the winter they think (after the brief summer snow flurry) has returned.

The five campers stand silent, watching the mass of

retreating animals. Maven, ignoring both Steve and you, stands between them, gazing over the landscape. The two friends trade looks across Maven's withdrawn face as she gazes: for the first time, neither friend can read the other's expression—and neither tries to clarify it for the other—not a shrug, not a smile, not a raised eyebrow. Between the two, like a curtain, hangs an enigmatic, watchful stare.

Suddenly Max cups his hands and lets out a rebel yell. It echoes across the mountains.

"I love America!" Maven, startling the two boys, sings out across the magnificent scenery, the valley alive with fleeing herds. And the echo rings back from the mountain walls, "America . . . America . . . America . . ."

The five stand hesitantly near the shuttle bus to Teton Village. Every so often the driver turns a newspaper page where he sits in the back.

No sign of hail or snow. The bus gleams dustily in the early evening shadows, a smell of diesel and burnt rubber surrounding it like a mist, a sickly smell after the high mountain air.

Dull and dependable as civilization, you think.

The sun disappeared an hour ago as they descended Paintbrush Canyon. The shadows of the great peaks, gathered like a coven of witches, seem to lean against the sky.

Maven had hiked the long trail down from the divide between you and Steve, not trading a word with her friends, a brittle silence between all of them.

Steve and you haven't traded a word in hours.

The five now stand awkwardly outside the bus, pretending to look at it, at a nearby campsite with three small fires and a handful of campers, up at the sky.

"Well . . ."

"Well . . ."

Steve suddenly gouges you with a resentful look and heads for the open door.

84

"I have a rodeo to go to. So I guess I'll be seeing you folks," he says before getting in. "Nice to meet you." He nods decisively to Max and Charlotte and somewhat warily to Maven, who gazes evenly back at him. "Hope you all have a nice trip."

"Right," you say suddenly. You turn to Maven.

"Do you . . . ?" you ask.

She shakes his hand firmly.

"Maybe we'll see you. Later."

"At the hotel?"

"Maybe," she says, strangely unsmiling. "Maybe at the rodeo. Anything can happen."

And she turns and joins Max and Charlotte.

Max gives you a weirdly triumphant smile. He waves. A walk-light goes on. Max's bald head shines in the electric brightness.

The two of you wave as the bus pulls onto the park road, and the three wave back—Max abruptly turns before the bus leaves and walks firmly off. You look back and see Charlotte turn to Maven, put her arm, eerily you think, around her waist, and lean over as if to kiss her on the neck. Maven leans over and seems to whisper something into Charlotte's ear, then Charlotte starts to hoot with laughter and looks back at the bus. You think you can see a sneer in that look. But then a screen of pines scrapes across the window glass, and you can see no more.

What was that *all about?* you think bewilderedly, partly about the scene you have just witnessed, partly about the episode that has just, it seems, ended.

"Ancient history," Steve suddenly growls. He pauses, then turns to his friend with the first friendly, if sarcastic, words he has offered in hours. "Still got your fossil?"

You had almost forgotten; you check your pockets.

It's still there: the backend of a trilobite (maybe) from a seabed at the top of a mountain.

You gaze at it moodily, smoothing your finger across its surface.

It suddenly seems irrelevant.

Just as the bus turns into the hotel parking lot under the darkening twilight, you remember your first sight of Maven by the campfire the night before.

I know "hidden from what," you think with bewildered bitterness, remembering the falls and Maven's teasing question. Hidden from me.

You toss the fossil out the bus window.

Horse and rider launch into the arena. The rider's legs flail above the animal's flanks, his free hand waves high, like a broken doll's, his number (46) flapping against his back like a broken sign in a gale, his hat flying off as the horse churns under him, its eyes filled with panic as it leaps across the arena, kicking its back legs skyward.

A mob of locals and tourists cheer and whistle in the stands. A few assistants in muddy chaps stand in a half-crouch, ready to spring to the rider's aid. A smell of horses—leather, hay, manure, urine—blows from the holding pens. One rider, especially young—almost your age—perches on a gate, a bright white hat raked back on his head, his expression fluctuating between frowning self-consciousness and open-faced excitement. He rocks excitedly on the gate.

It takes the horse less than the statutory eight seconds to throw the rider, and the crowd erupts in a good-humored cheer, whether for the rider for a game attempt or for the horse for so quickly freeing itself, you can't tell, but you pretend to join the cheering anyway, your shouts almost angry, as the horse is settled down and coaxed from the arena, snorting and reluctant, and the rider pulls himself from the dirt, shrugs and grabs his hat, and limps off in the opposite direction, not acknowledging the crowd.

I know just how you feel, you think.

You've been watching with a curious, detached apathy, unable to quite feel the excitement of the rodeo—preoccupied, feeling a cramp of anger and confusion, and yet also anticipation and nervousness, of seeing Maven again, possibly here, as she'd said he might. There had been no sign of her or her companions at the hotel that morning. You scan the packed crowd, uneasily searching for an orange backpack. . . .

Had it meant something? Anything? <u>Nothing</u>?

The judges' verdict blares through the loudspeakers, honking and incomprehensible. The sea-sound of the crowd barely registers a response.

The crowd is made up for the most part of fleshy Midwesterners, half-dressed and lathered with sunscreen, wearing silly hats and Bermuda shorts and shouting things like "Yippee-ay-yo!" and "Giddap!" and "Sookie, sookie, sookie!" The locals are less giddy, less theatrically dressed; more focused on the event. Vendors selling cokes and hot dogs work the crowd. The Tetons loom, aloof, in the distance, tufted with fog-like cloud.

Down several rows to his left, you see the two families you saw at the hotel almost a week ago: the two pairs of parents comparing notes, and the gaggle of youngsters lined up beside them like a long tail.

A lifetime ago.

The two girls Steve said were lesbians sit side by side in the same cowgirl outfits; "Miranda" wearing her hat and chatting volubly to Elizabeth.

You watch them with a detached, almost irritated curiosity: you feel a certain disillusioned superiority to the self you were just a week ago, and to the dreamy, half-brained ideas you had then.

That *child* . . . , you think almost contemptuously, with the sarcasm you've been using with yourself for the past day or so.

A lucky miss . . .

Another horse and rider launch from a pen nearby, and you suddenly stand with the rest of the crowd and angrily shout, "*Yes!*"

You must have shouted louder than you realized, for

Miranda suddenly looks around and up, shading her hat brim with her hand and looking directly into the sun. You wonder if she recognizes you in the glare, and stare back at her. She opens her mouth as if to call out, but stops and looks a little to your right, still staring.

You have an odd feeling, a sort of pang, or a regret that is also a kind of impulse. And prohibition.

Suddenly Elizabeth looks around too, following her friend's gaze.

You look back at the bucking bronco and rider. But the ride is already over, and the crowd gives another subdued cheer, for number 7 as he picks his hat up from the dirt and hobbles from the arena.

You look down at Miranda's hat, which is turned toward Elizabeth in an intense tête-à-tête. The odd feeling comes back, now with a certain queasiness.

You turn to the next rider, your blood suddenly tingling.

Number 18 lurches from the chute on a big pinto and holds, holds, holds—even after a whirlwind of manic corkscrews by the cunning stallion kicking up sprays of dust and gravel, then—after the buzzer sounds, just holding on for the sake of it—horse and man swoop along the edge of the arena in a round of perfectly executed high-kicking leaps, coming within stroking distance of the first row of spectators. Suddenly Miranda reaches her arm out as the horse and rider pass, the horse kicking at the air near her hand, and she turns back with a startled laugh to Elizabeth, and the rider bucks past like a controlled dummy, his limbs smooth and loose, his free hand, which never loses its grip on his hat, waving it, free, high over his head, his head nodding with the horse's bucking, regular and controlled as a piston, the crowd's ovations rising and falling in waves, and the crowd cheers when he is finally bucked off and lands in a dust cloud, then pulls himself up and turns, saluting the crowd with the hat he never dropped, and the crowd goes crazy, standing and cheering—the young cowboy perched on the gate whoops and whistles, waving his hat, wild with joy—and the rider walks, refusing assistance, with an overly controlled tread to the center of the arena and waves to the crowd, and then walks out with a little swagger, though it may just be a limp. It takes the pinto a while to realize it has lost its rider, before it settles down, wild-eyed and furious, and the crowd rises to a second ovation as the horse is trotted around the arena.

The judges seem to take forever to give their verdict—and then the crowd cheers wildly again when the rider gets the highest points for the day, real justice done for once. Then a Willie Nelson song comes on over the sound system, and they take a break before the bull rides start.

The two families head for the refreshment stands, Elizabeth and Miranda bickering about something: Elizabeth seems teary-eyed and pleading, Miranda shaking her head vigorously.

You soon lose them in the swarm of spectators leaving the bleachers. After a pit stop in the crowded men's room, you wander aimlessly around the refreshment stalls, wending through the holiday crowd, with the smell of hot dogs, sauerkraut, mustard, burgers, peanuts, Dr. Pepper, sawdust and horse manure thick in the air. You sulk near a pillar.

Then you see something dull orange, just behind a coke machine near the viewing stand entrance, and walk determinedly toward it, your heart pounding.

There's nothing, no one. You catch sight of a young woman with a papoose for her baby across her back: a dirty orange Gortex. She stands patient and bored in line for the ladies' room. Her baby is fast asleep in the orange papoose.

"Where's your friend?"

You turn to see Miranda's eyes looking directly into your own. She wears that same enigmatic smile as before.

"Steve had something to do. . . .," you mumble, startled by her unexpected appearance. "He said he'd come later. . . . He'd better hurry up or he'll miss . . . Where's—" You break contact with her eyes. "—your friend?"

"Oh, Elizabeth," Miranda replies with cheerful dismissiveness, "is having a nervous breakdown back in the car."

You stare.

"It's all right. She has one every so often, usually over a political issue. She's a bit late for one, so we've all been wondering when it was going to happen. She thinks rodeos are cruel to animals, and she refuses to see the bulls! But that's the reason we came to Jackson. If she's so sensitive about it, why did she come? If you're an animal liberationist, you shouldn't go to the zoo."

"Are you an animal liberationist?" you ask irrelevantly.

Stupid question! But then, you find yourself saying stupid things whenever you're around her.

"No!" she says gaily. "I'm a carnivore. Are you?"

"What?"

"A carnivore."

"It's very un-PC, but . . . "

"Arrgh!" She gives a playful roar. "That's the one problem between us—between Elizabeth and me, I mean. She's so PC I can't stand it sometimes. Now she is having a crying jag over that poor horse we just saw—the pinto. Now, that horse probably just had the most glorious moment of its life. Everybody loved it, admired it, applauded it—all just for ten seconds of leaping around an arena with a man on its back." She gives you a look. "It even got to throw its rider, and nobody punished it!" She grins. "Triumph on all sides. What's to feel sorry for?"

You grin back.

"Well, you could say it's exploitive, and takes advantage of . . ."

"You could say anything. The only way to be absolutely politically correct is never to have been born to begin with," she says with mock sententiousness. "The Greeks said that. They considered it their highest wisdom. It's what I always ask vegans: what if you found out that plants *can feel*? They look at me fit to kill. Have I alienated you?" she winds up with a sigh, and looking away.

"Not at all," you return. You feel like laughing—is this girl for real? She's so . . . what? . . . "What would 'friends of Bill' do?"

"Clinton!" she turns on you with pretend fury, her eyes laughing. "You don't defend that impossible Big Mac–eating philanderer with the doormat for a wife, do you!"

"Bill Clinton is the best president this country has had since . . . since . . ."

"Jimmy Carter?" she blurts innocently at him.

You want to say yes but are afraid of inciting a storm of abuse. You chance it.

"You said it."

Her face breaks into sunshine.

"I love I love I love Jimmy Carter. I would marry Jimmy Carter if Rosalyn would just get out of the way."

You laugh very hard at the idea of this seventeen-year-old lesbian marrying the septuagenarian ex-president.

Adorable . . . *that* is the word for this girl. . . .

"He's the greatest ex- . . . ." Miranda is starting to lecture when a cow bell sounds obstreperously, signaling the spectators to return to the viewing stands.

"Sitting with us?" she asks abruptly, almost as an aside.

"Ted must see the bulls," she continues as they join the crowd rising to the stands. "It'll be all we can do to keep him out of the arena. He was practically a bull rider from infancy, if you can believe him!"

"Who's Ted?"

"My dad."

"You put your own hand out far enough, that last rider."

"I could feel the wind off the horse's heels. I think that's what upset Elizabeth really. She said I could have gotten kicked in the head," she laughs as they rise into the air of the arena. "There are worse ways to go," she says blithely, gazing serenely across the expanse of trampled clay and gravel. She returns her hat, which has been hanging down her back, to the top of her head with a tap.

You take Elizabeth's seat, and soon the rest of the two families line up beside Miranda. She introduces them to you, and they nod, smiling and vague.

The announcer mumbles something viva voce, the crowd, still settling back in their seats, applauds, and three rodeo clowns barrel-roll and cartwheel out into the arena.

You can barely hear the garbled announcement for the first bull rider but catch something that sounds like "seventeen years old" (your own age, which focuses your attention) and "very first try" and "let's give him a really big hand."

As the crowd complies, you watch someone in a bright white hat—the same young cowboy you saw before, perched on the gate—standing on the fence of one of the pens nearby and arguing vehemently. The pen appears empty; the young man seems unhappy and points angrily at the next pen, where a grayish white back is visible, then jumps down and stalks to the pen, his hat bobbing above the fence.

"Did he say the rider's seventeen?" you ask Miranda, jumpy at your side.

"The golden age!" she shoots back cheerfully.

"Sounds young for bull riding," you say, looking back at the guy you've been following: you jam your finger hard down toward the white back of a bull, just visible.

"Ted used to ride his farm bull when he was eleven, didn't you, Ted?" Miranda says, shouting down the row.

"What did ya say?" A middle-aged man with a small, prematurely balding crown, sitting at the far end, turns with a questioning smile.

She repeats the claim, with a prim look of triumph.

You peek over at the youthful rider: he steps across the bull's back, straddling the bull while talking with a man at the fence. The man scratches his head and shrugs.

"The truth comes out at last!" You hear a middle-aged woman's voice say: a slightly younger, portly woman sitting next to Ted presents a look of pretended shock. "'He wasn't a full-grown bull'! *Now* he tells us! And now you'll tell us your prize Brahma 'wasn't a full-grown bull' either! I'll tell you where we can find some 'full-grown bull.'"

They're all laughing when there's the crack of the opening gate, and you see a huge white bull leap out with the young rider on its heaving back.

It bucks into the arena—enormous, a wall of white gray, muscles rippling down the flanks, a dead, determined look in its eye, implacable, not nervous or panicky like the horses; ruthless, bigger and more inhuman, it jumps without grace, vaulting at the sky to shake off its intolerable burden.

The crowd has become quiet, watching the young man, almost frail-looking, bounce like a toy on the bull's back, flailing about, barely in control of himself, hopelessly out of control of the bull, which treats him with irritation and contempt, as though trying to whip a mosquito off its back. The crowd goes completely silent.

The bull, perhaps sensing the uncertainty of its rider, leaps forward and stops in its tracks, and the young man tosses like a puppet over its head and lands on his back under the bull's face, and the bull, exasperated, throws itself onto the boy despite attempts by the clowns, who stayed in the arena after their act—dancing near the bull in bedraggled clown outfits, white face, and big red noses; smeared with dirt—to distract its attention and pull it away from the fallen rider. But the bull will have none of it and savagely tramples the source of its humiliation, heaving above the body curled up in the dirt, aiming its horns down at him, dragging the points through the dirt, and the crowd gasps as one and rises. The bull jumps on the boy again—turns and leaps again, under the frantic shouts of the clowns—and then again, and again, then leaps away, heavily kicking its back legs triumphantly in the air.

It has lasted less than eight seconds. The buzzer never went off, at least you don't remember hearing it. One of the assistants runs past the bull's head and hits it with a stick, and the bull charges him, leaving the boy's body flat in the dirt. A small medical team runs out as the bull is distracted, panting and blank, its eyes impenetrable as it pauses near the bleachers where you and the others sit: balls of stone and metal shining, blind with suspicion and wrath, idly distracted, ignoring its victim, already forgetting it.

The boy is raised on a gurney and moved quickly out of the arena, and the crowd, many still standing, stare vacantly at the bull. It stands silent—suddenly it sneezes—then gradually is goaded backwards, its head nodding threateningly, toward the exit by the assistants and a lone clown. Then the bull abruptly raises its head and stops, then turns its back with contempt, and trots heavily out.

A murmur as of wind or sea rises from the still-standing crowd. You look at Miranda, who looks in shock at the dirt rectangle beneath them. The two families are silent.

You suddenly realize you're holding Miranda's hand. You don't remember taking it—maybe when they all stood up— maybe she took yours.

She stares hard at the loud speakers arrayed on a pole in front of the judges' stand.

A long minute passes.

The arena is silent: no sound comes from the spectators, none from the participants as they stand waiting at the edge of the arena. There are snorts from a waiting bull or horse. A dog barks, a high nattering sound, somewhere behind you, maybe in the parking lot. The Tetons stand, impassive, wreathed in clouds, in the far distance behind the stands.

Then you hear a distant siren.

On the way back to the hotel, they talk, in subdued voices, about the boy's death, the last-minute switch of bulls, the decision to call off the rest of the rodeo. You sit squeezed in the back seat next to Miranda, who is pressed against Elizabeth.

The two girls, usually so talkative, say nothing: you can't

94

see Elizabeth, but you caught her sour look when Miranda invited you to drive back with them. Elizabeth, sitting in the car after her quarrel with Miranda, turned a blunt face twisted in physical repugnance as you advanced toward the car. You had cringed and bent a little in reflexive apology. But Elizabeth turned away with a sniff.

"It's only for ten minutes, Elizabeth," Miranda whispered, exasperated.

"Give me some air," Elizabeth replied and angrily pulled down her window. As they drove off, she narrowed her attention to an intense study of the mountain ash and cottonwoods lining the road, at one moment pointing out the window and saying, at full voice, "Look! A *weasel*."

During the ride Miranda withdraws into herself and stares through the windshield, where she has a clear view of the mountains bright in the midafternoon light.

"No," she perks up, in response to something said in the front seat, "he was not wrong to try. They were not wrong to let him ride," she says in a tremulous voice combining confusion, exasperation, and a pugnacious certainty. "It was terrible terrible terrible, but it was his most glorious moment. Glorious! He was *so young*, but he may never have had a more glorious moment in his life, never again. He died but he died at the highest moment of his life so far. I know nobody can know how he might have lived, he might have had even more glorious moments, but he didn't, and he might not have had any, it might just have been a long dull slide into the suburbs and an office job, though he would probably have had a job in a gas station or on a wildcat derrick, and a dull wife and too many kids, think about those young girl gymnasts whose careers peak at the Olympics when they are, what, fourteen, he died, and if he had to die, it may as well be in glory, if I die I hope I'm so lucky!"

"Whoa!" her father says, laughing dryly. "Was that just a condemnation of everything I've done with my life, or what . . .?"

"It sounds like he deliberately chose a bull that would kill him," snarls Elizabeth from the side, speaking at the same time Miranda's father does. "It was suicide. An exhibitionist and a suicide, that's what *he* was."

"An idealist and a bull rider, *that*'s what he was!"

"Same thing!"

"A *hero*!"

"A stupid fool who got what he deserved from a smart bull!"

"Settle down, back there," Miranda's mother intones from the front. "We're not going to settle this today."

Miranda and Elizabeth withdraw furiously back into themselves, deliberately looking away from each other despite being squashed against each other in the back seat.

Miranda gives you a quiet smile as you part at the hotel entrance. Her expression has a new serious, steady look. The theatricality has vanished, replaced by a subdued gravity.

"You were right, I think," you chance, "about . . ."

"Oh!" Miranda brushes it aside. "I was just babbling. I don't know anything!" Her eyes seem suddenly to take it in, sadly—the absolute depths of her ignorance. "But I *am* glad you drove with us—in spite of the company . . ."

"So am . . ."

"And I'm sorry about Elizabeth, she was very rude. She can be very immature . . ."

"You're not responsible for her."

"Sometimes I think I am." She glances away, her color rising a little. "How long are you staying?" she asks.

"We're flying out tomorrow morning. Late. For Columbus."

"We're going tomorrow too. In the afternoon. Back to Denver."

"You live there?"

"Yes, and you in Columbus?"

"Just outside. We have to take the hub at Denver."

Miranda pauses, seems about to offer to shake your hand, then hesitates.

"Maybe we'll see you at breakfast."

"Sure!" Your reply is swifter and louder than you had planned on, and you halt in embarrassment.

"With your friend."

"Yeah."

"Maybe we can sick him on Elizabeth!"

The two of you titter as you look at each other.

"Till tomorrow then," she says, with her little wave, and they part.

Calm down, you tell yourself while waiting for the elevator. *Calm down. Calm down. Don't get excited. All I am doing is this: I am going to have a breakfast date with a lesbian, I am going to have a breakfast date with a lesbian lesbian lesbian*, you think while entering the elevator. *Wait till I tell Steve we're having a double breakfast date with a pair of lesbians!* you think while riding up the elevator, and you get an attack of the giggles.

Steve is probably on his way, on the shuttle, to Jackson. He'll find everyone gone. . . . You imagine the empty rodeo arena, the custodians collecting the trash in the viewing stands, the ticket agent explaining to him, in a subdued voice, the reason . . .

He left so fast he forgot to close the door.

You stop.

A rhythmic huffing and sound of sliding cloth, like sheets, a regular creaking, as of springs, softly fill the hall. As you approach their room door, it grows louder. You peer in through the crack in the door.

The room is dark, the curtains drawn, you can see almost nothing but hear clearly the strange, regular sounds. Then there is a sound like a sigh.

The maid and her boyfriend—they think everyone's away at the rodeo, so-oo . . .

You quietly open the door, carefully sneak inside, one step, then another, past the bathroom and the closet, into the dark bedroom, grinning to yourself.

Wait till I tell Steve about this . . . he missed all *the excitement!*

An orange backpack lies at the foot of the nearby bed. In the other, near the curtains, kneels a humping naked figure sighing as it straddles another naked figure lying on its back. A head of black hair with a streak of blond turns suddenly to you with a cool look above her small dangling breasts, her legs straddling a man's waist and thighs. Steve's face, harder to see in the shadow, also turns to look. They halt.

Maven twists around and stares at you, her black hair with its streak of blond streaming down her naked back.

On the bed next to Steve's—your own bed—Max and Charlotte are sitting, watching the two. They turn to look at you. Max's face breaks into a grin.

You look back in a kind of blank daze, then storm out of the room, slamming the door, then race down the hall to the emergency stairs—leap down the stairs, dry-heaving, barely able to breathe, the tears spilling from your eyes, then out the lobby to the parking lot. You trip on the curb and fall to your knee, scraping it and straining your ankle, but you're almost too upset to notice and limp through the streets, impatiently wiping the tears from your face—you keep seeing the white bull leaping with the boy clinging to its back, Maven humping Steve in the half-dark room, and the bull trampling the boy's body in the arena; you see all of these, pointlessly and obsessively— till evening falls and you find yourself in the dusk beneath the cable of the aerial tram to the first range of the Tetons.

"Grand *Tetons!*" you say out loud to the twilight and the darkness above you and the black shadows of the mountains. "Big *tits!*" You give a nasty laugh. "And Jackson Hole is *your cunt!*"

You stare at the mountains, weeping, confused, furious at your friend, at Maven, at yourself, at life, until the mountains go black against an indigo sky.

It must be the heat, wrapping the Hummers like a python. It can't be anything else. It mustn't be anything else.

Pebbles skitter and rattle against the van's underbelly. The reg shows flat for the most part due north, wadis and depressions appearing in shallow shademarks and the false cloud shadow you saw the day before.

You had been discussing the politics of North Africa, the war of the Islamists in Mali and Libya over the last decade. At one point, you asked each other where you had been on September 11, 2001, when Al-Qaeda attacked the World Trade Center and Pentagon and crashed into a Pennsylvania field.

The old man had been in Central America on a dig. Vivian had been a twelve-year-old growing up in corn country at the time and remembered seeing the burning towers on TV, watching in terrified wonder, alone, her mother having left her to go on errands; she had known there was something wrong here, this was not a movie, it was not an illusion. She had wept hysterically all night, thinking the terrorists (she was already in thrall to the word) would come after her. It had changed her, turned her from being a free-spirited, happy-go-lucky child into a nervous, worried, overly careful adolescent, and yet it had also left her fascinated by the desert people who had had such power to wreak havoc on "our conceited civilization," as she put it.

You had been a student in New York.

The two others turned to you when they heard that: what had it been like? It must have been awful . . .

The air seems to go dim, and you shake your tight, pounding head.

"Yes," you say tersely. You have no intention of telling them what happened afterward.

But you don't need to. Something catches your eye and you look back over your shoulder.

The landscape seems to displace, overshoot where it ought to be, then snap back.

"Hey," you say thickly, "dust."

In the southwestern sky, a vast wall of brown, like an enormous sail, a lurid pink at the top, looms silently, bearing down behind them: a dust storm covering half the horizon. You glance again, leaning over and down for a better look. The old man reluctantly follows your eye.

"Dust storm," you say, louder, and barking the klaxon with all your might, stick your head out the window, looking back and braking, and shout: "Dust storm! *Dust storm!*"

The Hummer behind you halts, and you can see Peter look at you puzzledly as you point wildly back past him, then Peter cranes his head to look too. At that moment, the top of the dust cloud meets the edge of the sun, and the light goes bright pink. There's a blast from Jack's horn.

"Circle! Circle! Circle!"

They stop and, lumbering, pull the three Hummers into a distorted triangle, anchored on your van, the other vans aligning accordingly, *I can't see them, of course they are, there's the back of Peter's Hummer, Jack's must be nearby, I have to seal the windows, doors, got to use towels, rags, off with the shirt, there, whatever,* you direct the old man in the front and Vivian and Husayn and Umar in the back, but your head is spinning, your motions are ridiculously slow, petty and absurd, you aren't even sure what you're doing or should do, everyone seems to be moving through a lava of glass even though the air outside is growing gray as dusk, you can see nothing but what hangs just behind your eyes like fog. *What's wrong with me? I can't think.* The Hummer is suffocating, the heat is unbearable, you're overwhelmed with heat inside you and heat outside, you feel something wet suddenly smother your face and cry out, a woman's voice says, "You have to cover your face with this to keep the dust out, wait, you've got a fever, your face is burning up," and you feel like saying something silly like "Of course my face is burning up, I'm locked in a Hummer in the middle of a dust storm in the middle of a fucking desert," but you look up and sees the dust storm sweep in—an arm of brown air that

100

sweeps across the windshield, a hissing and spiraling of dust along the backlights in front, the outside mirror is shaped into a funnel of dust and wind, and sand along the white salt around the tires of the Hummers, licking around the fenders and corners of the vehicles. *Vehicles! God damned traps . . . .*

We're trapped, I'm trapped, the wind shakes the Hummers, dust seeps inside, you are trying to stuff a handkerchief, you don't know whose, into a crack in the front door, or are you just dreaming it, then you feel vomit surging up from your stomach, filling your mouth with acid, and abruptly the desert goes silent and dark.

As you step into the parking lot, the lot lights switch on. At the edge of the lot you see a figure, standing alone in a cone of light against the last glow of the sun and looking in the direction of the mountains, their eastern faces black, the western flanks quickly fading.

You walk toward where she stands; when you're a dozen feet away, she turns toward you with a soft look.

"What brings you to these parts, podner?" she says with sad gaiety, then notices something in you in the artificially lit twilight—the expression on your face? your slightly unbalanced stance? your limp?—and her face becomes grave.

You stand beside her, unable to speak, embarrassed and nervous . . .

She looks at you levelly, but you can't look straight back into those strange, beautiful eyes, disturbing and inviting and warning and strangely compelling—your eyes dart away to the brush in front of you, a clump of mountain ash down the embankment, an oddly shaped stone. . . .

You feel as though you may be the guilty party in a crime you first thought had been committed against *you*—if crime indeed it was. Some of the humiliating ideas that have been charging through you like electric jolts include the idea that you have no actual right to feel betrayed, despite the emotions that overwhelm you, and a self-contempt and self-blame for letting yourself get into a position where you could be betrayed.

"What's wrong?" Miranda asks you firmly. She suddenly seems ten years older, even her face has aged.

You sag into a squat on the parking lot barrier, and she crouches beside you.

She looks down, spreads her cowgirl skirt flat over her knees, biting her lower lip, then looks at you. She hugs her knees up closer to her chest, and waits.

Each of the mountains looks sharp as a claw, reminding you of your innocent ecstasy a week ago—a memory that now makes you feel like an idiot, deserving of the most severe and shaming punishment; an illusion torn from you now like a layer of skin.

How can you *tell* her what's wrong? You are not even sure yourself.

"Tell me," Miranda says.

You smile helplessly—there is a curiously maternal tone in her voice—and stare down at the patch of gravel and weeds, grass and clumps of paintbrush and a nameless blue mountain flower, randomly distributed near your feet, and you shyly, brokenly, divulge the story—it feels almost like pulling out your own teeth, one at a time, though teeth not of enamel but of shame—the shame of young love in the long curse of adolescence—if not always directly and in detail, indirectly and by implication. You are surprised at how little time it takes to tell. And what a relief it is to tell someone who is listening, seriously and patiently, something that just a little while before you would have sworn you would, you *could*, never say to anyone. The twilight sky is still vanishingly radiant in the west, still darkening at the end of it, though you had half expected midnight would not see the end of your story.

". . . and I came back here. I don't know where to go. I can't go back there. I don't know where I'll sleep. Maybe in the lobby. Or out here."

"It'll be too cold out here," Miranda says.

"It'll be too cold out here," you repeat, suddenly feeling like a child, then furious because you feel like a child. You glower at the dirt.

"I'm so sorry, Ariel," Miranda suddenly says, watching you, in a gentle, serious voice. For the first time she has used your name.

The sound of your name in her mouth is sweet, but you still haven't quite forgiven her for making you feel like a child.

Suddenly you feel her arm cross your back, and she pulls you lightly toward her. Then she kisses you on the cheek.

You stare into her pale blue irises.

"We both thought you two were lesbians." Your voice is like a child's.

Miranda crows a little laugh toward the dark crown of the sky slowly being pointed with stars.

"I am! And I'm a rodeo dyke to boot!" and she sticks out her foot in its small, stitched western boot, with its tassel. You both look down at her boot, already a shadow in the dusk.

"Doesn't that make you feel safe?" she says looking back at you gaily and mildly.

You fold your arm around her waist, almost without thinking about it, it seems just the natural thing to do, and lean against her.

"We are such stuff as dreams are made on," she says in a little sing-song voice, quoting her favorite play, "and our little life . . ."

Suddenly the immediate past is far away, as far as the mountains disappearing into the night, and the future—tomorrow, the summer ahead, the coming years—seems not worth a passing thought; unreal. The only things that exist are the first hand-throw of stars in the night—Venus, Mercury, the distant polestar—and the darkening peaks to the north, rising higher and higher in the sky, and the warm body of this girl against you and her patient breathing and the feeling that surrounds her—of a kind of gleeful sweetness and bright, goofy, great-hearted kindness—of beauty and love—like an aura.

You turn the page and let your eyes fall across the badly scrawled words, smudged and corrected, erased, recorrected. You imagine yourself, as a young man, hardly more than a boy, speaking them, looking into your eyes, as if on a screen; a kind of video diary. Then you read the words aloud, testing them in your mouth, listening to them.

The shadow of a plane moves across the screen
and buries itself in flame in the southern tower

[   ]

The fist of a cloud crumbles above the island falling
toward into the streets submerging the city

[   ]

Across the air draws a curtain of oil and fire

[   ]

Intolerable white light washes the gray streets
in the crushed mouth of the horizon a white ember

[   ]

In television silence in the falling night crowds stand
above a wilderness flickering

[   ]

Behind the noise silence behind the words silence behind
the wrath of the assassins silence behind the anguish of the
grieving silence behind the terror of the survivors silence
behind the guilt of the survivors silence behind the silence

at the foot of the ruins silence behind the buildings looming
in the night silence behind the heat of the late summer streets
silence behind the neon-lighted bars silence behind the roar
of the final trains silence behind the slow claw of the back-
hoe picking at a slab of twisted cement with the sensitive-
ness of an insect in the hush of an obsessively repeating col-
lapse silence behind the obscenities of the unbelieving fac-
ed with the proof of what they cannot believe silence be-
hind the smiles on the photos of the dead . . .

Faces rustling on lamp poles in the evening

Having been separated embattled
battling one another for many years
the fingers of the hand close softly bruised and wounded
around air around perfect air

You, carefully, as if handling a relic from a distant past, turn
the page.

The Lost Oasis

The fierce cheep of a moula-moula bird soars away, and the early dew scent of a markouba plant fills your nostrils with its sharp smell.

Your eyes start open. Your body is a mass of cramps, your head is jammed into a corner of metal and vinyl, a trace of sun reflects through a half-open window at your feet. You feel weak, how long have you been out . . .

The memory of a strange, wild thrill. . . like a scene from many years ago . . . suddenly dissipates.

You pluck at your chest, at the unfamiliar material.

Then you remember, vaguely—what? vomiting?—then passing out.

You pull yourself half-way up against the seat's backrest and peer through the windshield.

Vivian stands across from you, her haunted, haggard face staring moodily at the ground, her hair pulled back in a frizzy pony tail; as though remembering something she has long been trying to forget. You shake your head vigorously; suddenly she's gone.

You look upward. Early morning light fans out across a range of familiar-looking mountains. They seem to be back where they camped—the day before, longer? The Hummer they'd left for Brian stands a few yards away.

You squeeze your eyes. Your dry, thirsty mouth feels like shoe leather. You kick off the blanket and pull yourself from the car.

Umar is the first to see you: the boy comes up to you with his soft brown eyes.

"You sick?" he asks.

"No." You're surprised to hear Umar's English. Then you reconsider: "Maybe. A little. Thirsty . . ." You mime rubbing your eyes and drinking.

He runs off, shouting for water in Arabic.

Soon you're half-surrounded by the rest as Umar comes up, bearing a leather winebag of lukewarm water. You wipe your eyes with the water before chugging.

Peter's face looms nearby, with the results of several days without washing, his hair squiggling in all directions, his cheeks grizzled, his grin a shadow of its old bravado. "How ya feelin', mate?"

"Better," you say. "Till I saw you."

"Shall we take pity and," says Peter, "not tell him the bad news?"

They all laugh.

"How long was I out?"

"Twenty-four hours, almost," says Vivian.

"Give or take a day," quips Smuts.

Smuts glances at Vivian with disappointed eyes.

Sorry not to oblige you, old man.

"Never eat a chicken in this heat unless you've killed it yourself. That includes canned."

They give another, strained laugh. The three young assistants stand in the back, officious and nervous, imperturbably fresh, a little awed.

Nothing shocks the young like the vulnerability of their elders. Correction: the stupidity.

The water has helped, but you still feel weak.

They walk you to the camp fire and watch you eat breakfast.

Umar and Hussayn stare at you across the fire, with looks of curiosity, even a little triumph.

The nazreens are mortal after all. Only God is great.

There's little talk while you eat: a description of the storm, the trek back to where they'd left the vehicle of Brian, the sighting of a hawk, a cloud of bats that crossed the moon for an hour.

"That was no hour."

"It felt like one."

"It wasn't bats, it was a lunar eclipse." *A storm cloud. A flock of migrating cranes.*

Bickering. What other adjustments have there been in the delicate battle of wills?

There's no mention of Brian.

The air is beginning to warm.

After finishing (your stomach is still unsteady, but your light-headedness has disappeared), you give them a comprehensive look. They could abandon the reconnoitering equipment, pile into two vans and return to Ouadane in a couple of days on siphoned gas, but the old man vehemently opposes. The old man has become determined to go south; it's as though your fever was a sort of omen and Brian's disappearance a challenge. The old man is uncharacteristically adamant.

Smuts resists.

"You can't move for another day anyway," Smuts says to you. "You aren't ready, you can hardly walk straight."

"So rub it in," you say, with a smile, "why don't you."

"Well, you can't. And so that means three days of living on our supplies. And what if this place, this, this . . ."

"Ceruza," says the old man.

Smuts looks queerly at the old man, then at you. "Ceruza?" He snorts, then continues impatiently. "Anyway, what if it's more than two days off? We know the map, as it is, is *wrong* so there's no point trusting it at all. This place may be a hundred miles farther south, or nowhere near. Does it even exist? We won't have enough supplies to get back if we're wrong."

111

"There's a road just south of here," the old man retorts with a smile and a crazy, cunning look. "From Oued to Edeyen. I used it the last time I was in North Africa. It crossed the Trans-Saharan, camel caravans used it for centuries. Once we're on it, we can get to a way station and get enough supplies to find . . . our city." He stops short and gives another cunning look. "This way was shorter." He glares petulantly at the puzzled looks from the rest (why hadn't he mentioned this before?). "Would you really have preferred an overland journey of 2,000 miles from Morocco? I didn't think so. And we'd still have to chance it south to the Hoggar."

A weak, stubborn old man craving control? Or just deter-mined not to give up his baby without a fight? Regression? Senility? Courage? Denial?

Vivian gazes at her old prof with a pained look, her pecu-liar, frightened smile slipping in and out of focus.

Or just the "curse of Zerzura"?

"What do the drivers think? They know these parts better than the rest of us." Smuts turns to you.

You shake off the indifference of your fatigue. Peter, Cees, Jack all have strangely neutral looks, though Cees—with a per-sonality so neutral you often forget him when you're off the road—seems anxious, twitchy.

"Who has the map?" you ask.

Jack spreads it over the hood.

The marks are teasingly opaque. Between where they are and the patch marked "Ceruza" could be ten miles or a hundred. Or they could be standing on top of it. The marks suddenly blur and swim before your eyes.

You shake your head clear; you really aren't well.

"Does anything show up on your satellite maps?" you look up at the old man.

"They stop too far south," the other says curtly.

They stare back at the map in silence. Its lines and shad-ings, contours and speckles, so misleadingly clear and definite, tease them, like a treasure map leading to an empty grave.

You say, finally, "If we hope to get to the city and back before it gets too hot . . ." You pause, from a sudden wave of light-headedness, and jerk yourself up. ". . . we'll have to go south." Again you pause, winded. "As soon as we can move."

"Maybe we should take a vote?" says Vivian.

"We're not a democracy," the old man responds grimly.

Smuts returns, with a little acid: "We never were."

"Who votes for going south?" you ask, ignoring them.

"Six and six," you say, after a quick show of hands. Awkwardly, you find himself and Smuts on the same side—to go back—and Vivian among those voting to continue south. With some hesitation, you ask, "Can anyone guess how Brian might have voted?"

They shrug uneasily.

The temperature is starting to climb. You're beginning to feel weak again.

"I have to lie down."

You nap for a few hours on the Hummer's backseat, dreaming the same dream you'd had before coming to, now you recognize what it was: the mountains you visited as a teenager—the Tetons, at the western edge of Wyoming—though something important is missing. Then you see Smuts looking down at you from under a handkerchief tied around his forehead. He's staring through the back door window near your feet. You shake off your half-dream and struggle upright.

"Maybe we should have another vote." Smuts frowns. "After people have had a think."

You grunt.

"It's because . . ." Smuts looks bleakly at him. "It would seem . . ."

He stares at you, then turns and walks hurriedly away.

At first your own mind is blank, then you think, *It would seem futile and pointless and cowardly and moronic to give up now, after we've lost Brian.*

You slump suddenly back in your seat. It's the first time you have realized it, or allowed yourself to think it.

We've lost Brian.

You feel your lower belly go slack and the blood drain from your head.

6:58 a.m.

". . . Miranda . . . ?"

Her face hovers above you, laughing, a cowgirl hat peeking out behind her shoulders. But there's someone else's leg over your own. And a heavy cloth shifts, twists, binding, across your chest. Then a hand withdraws from your waist, and the young woman's eyes shift away. They have a little fold over them and pale ice-blue irises, like the eyes of an Alaskan husky. Her face—full-cheeked, child-like, both sly and goofy—also turns, and a ruddy swag of her hair sweeps into view.

The name you always think of for her—her secret name.

Then, abruptly, she vanishes.

Slants of dim light cross the ceiling in the stark and silent room. They cross the wall near the closet. They cross a window sill.

A dream? . . . a dream . . .

Why then why then why then this feeling of overwhelming loss?

The leg lifts from your own as swift as a kick, and the sheet sweeps away.

"The name is Pamela. *Cyril*."

You grab an edge of the sheet and pull it back over you, and you curl back into the warmth of the bed. You hear the trickle of Pam's feet as she walks across the floor, and feel her irritated silence.

We're not going to wake up fighting again, please . . .

You bury your face in the pillow and grope for a memory of the dream.

She flickers—Sally Miranda!—giggles, shifts, turns; giggles, shifts, turns, once, twice, three times, four times. . . .

She seems to be in some kind of desert, her face set against a range of black crags and rolling, Hollywood Sahara dunes (you saw something on the subway that looked like them . . . or was that some other dream?) —her spooky blue eyes, cream-white skin, orangey red hair, her sharp, funny smile.

She's chattering away, he has no idea about what.

The sun glares like a shout.

It suddenly feels suffocatingly hot.

Then something seems to hide the light and a rag covers your mouth.

You can't breathe, you panic, hear a voice muffled through the cloth, a woman's voice but not Miranda's—or is it? Then you see her face above you, giggling wildly. And suddenly she turns, as if summoned by someone you can't hear.

The sound of the shower stops, and you wake up again. The air in the room is stale and muggy. The traffic is an impatient rattling hum through the window you can't open in the scruffy Brooklyn apartment you and Pamela moved into last winter; it was painted shut long ago. . . .

You haven't thought of Miranda in days. You've tried not to think of her in days. Haven't even seen her in weeks. It feels like months. Years? . . . There's not much to do for Miranda now, except think of her.

Miranda. Sally Miranda. Salina Miranda Wild.
Sally in Our Alley.

You stay in bed one last minute, watching the thought of her fade into the light before you pull into the uncertain New York day ahead of you.

115

Lower Manhattan glitters through the kitchen window, coolish morning air drifting in in little, creosote-flavored breaths.

Against the September sky, the towers stand like the two sides of a gateway without a top. You can't see the opening from here, but you can guess. *Strait is the gate and narrow the way.*

You're always hated those buildings. Slick, impersonal, looking down on those mere skyscrapers at their feet. Flaunting. In your face. Like New Yorkers at their worst. Now every day you have to look at them.

But today there are more urgent concerns.

"It's not my fault she's so sick," you say in response to a snippy remark from Pam.

The fight you anticipated has begun.

"Maybe it is, for all I know."

You screw your lip over your coffee mug.

"Both her parents are *Irish*, her skin is as pale as—" You wave at the Half-and-Half. "—*that*. She grew up in *Hawaii*, there's an ozone hole the size of a *continent* every year, and she's out playing in it every day. What were they thinking!"

"Just don't mention her name in my bed."

"I didn't do it on purpose!" You give Pam a disgusted look. *As if you considered our bed so god-damn sacred.* You shrug cockily. "Maybe she was sending me a message."

"How very California."

"Than which there is nothing more . . ."

"Do you have her number?"

"No." You shrug again, look at her challengingly, then reconsider. "I could email her boss."

"Well then, be a Good Samaritan. 'Hi Miranda, I woke up this morning with your name on my lips (smiley). I hate cancer (groanie). Let me know if you're still alive. Please (exclamation point exclamation point). If you are, don't worry—asterisk *my girlfriend* asterisk will kill you. Love, Cyril.'"

You can't help smiling as you swirl your cup.

"You're mean."

"Lean and mean, but what a sex machine." She leers at you over her coffee. "Nobody named Sally or Miranda or whatever her name is, with carrot-red hair and a smile like Kirsten Dunst's, dies of cancer at 24. Except in bad novels and worse movies."

She splashes coffee on a script lying on the table as she cocks an eye at you, then plucks your napkin and wipes it.

"Maybe." You give her a quick squint. "Rehearsals today?"

"Coach-ing." Detaching each syllable. She sticks out her tongue and touches her upper lip. "Did I keep you awake?"

You stare back vacantly.

"I was doing my character's big speech. Her *only* speech. I wake up to the world after having slept for a generation. Little old Pinteresque Rip van Winkle me. Well, if I didn't manage to keep you awake, what'll I do to the director?" You give a smirk she pretends not to notice. "But Ilan can actually sit through an Andy Warhol film, so all may not be lost." She looks at you brightly, ignoring your curdled stare.

"Must go, Cyril. Sally and Cyril: sounds like really bad Dr. Seuss! We're still meeting at Barney's, I take it?"

You shrug assent. "No kiss?"

She puts her fingers to her lips to blow you one, then stops.

"When you've earned it. *May*be."

She smiles scornfully and flows out the door.

Have a nice day to you too.

Duden speaks with a certain glum satisfaction after the new vote. "All right then. Fine."

He tries the old avuncular smile, soft and sly with Yankee reasonableness, but it comes out both testy and triumphant, like a cockcrow. You think for a moment: *the old man really is crazy.*

Duden continues with a suspicious glance at you.

117

"This means we head out tomorrow morning. Am I right?" He turns to you. "You sure you're up to it?"

"I'll be fine after a good night's sleep in my own tent."

"Good." Duden nods with an attempt at firmness that seems merely anxious. "Good. Good."

As long as I don't die before we get to your precious city.

And Duden abruptly walks off to his tent.

You check the oil gauges with Peter, who grins at the folly of your clients but keeps his comments to his body language, then goes to the pup-tent set up near your paint-stripped Hummer. Vivian and Cecilia's tent is nearby, and Vivian is shaking out her sleeping bag near the entrance, a precaution against scorpions: Cecilia's feet, in athletic shoes, stick out of the entrance, toes dug into the sand.

Vivian presses her finger to her lips.

"Lucky young," you whisper. "Even scared out of their wits, they sleep like the dead. That's one thing I regret about my youth."

Vivian looks at you from the shadows. "Regret?"

"I thought I was miserable. I had no idea how happy I was."

They gaze absently at Cecilia's sleeping feet.

"It's a curse. We never know," she says softly, "till we've lost it. I sometimes think that will be the last thought I ever have. I thought I was so miserable, but I was happy! I was alive."

"Do you think," she asks after a moment, starting too loud then quickly softening her voice back to a whisper, "it'll be all right?" not looking up.

"We'll . . ." You think before completing your sentence. ". . . We'll be all right."

Her look is both grateful and skeptical.

"She would never forgive us," you try to joke, with a strained smile. "Good night."

"She'd do more than forgive us," Vivian says. "She would thank us. Good night."

118

The rocky maze seems to get denser as they move south. With each turn, the rock is folded, frozen, into granite twisters or petrified fire or familiar grotesques: here a lizard, there a frog, there a blind owl, a plummeting falcon. Above all there are human faces, leering or clownish or angry, and human forms: a girl in a burqa, a laughing woman, an old man with a missing chin; a woman out of de Kooning, a child molded by Picasso, a man's face smeared and torn via Ensor or Bacon, a Warhol lampoon. The gallery of bizarre shapes towers all around them, at once personal and aloof; they seem to call to you, beckon you, warn you off, mocking and baleful and weirdly beautiful.

By 11 o'clock, when you start looking for a place to rest through the heat of the day, you've driven almost fifty miles, though it may be only ten or fifteen due south of where you started.

As you circle a building-sized dome of volcanic intrusion, you come upon the first vegetation seen in days: a row of arid acacias, leafless, apparently half-dead.

You stop and get out to check them—you split a parched-looking twig and expose a tiny ooze of sap.

The vehicles carefully negotiate the gully past the acacias—they are barely larger than bushes—as you look for signs of water.

Then, just as the day's heat is starting to peak, you notices in the distance, above a wall of slaty scarp, what looks like the top of an enormous, dried-out bush.

"Eu-reka!" someone cries out from the van behind you.

As you cautiously swing around a slab of rock, an immense, massive, ancient cypress, gray and solitary, gnarled by the wind, looms above you, weather-beaten and alone in a shallow wadi between walls of rock. You catch your breath at the sight of it.

Sand the color of rust rolls away into the distance beyond a corridor of whirlwind tors behind the great tree. The tree

119

bristles with broken boughs and branches and thick masses of thick, tiny leaves. At its foot a dry gully snakes away.

You stop. Duden and Vivian, beside you, gawk at it in silence.

"I can hardly believe it," the old man sighs out. "How anything this big, this old, could have lasted the centuries it needed to grow to that size in this place . . ."

Umar and Husayn look out alongside them, but seem confused: what is there to see? Why are they stopping? There's nothing there, just an old, ugly, dead tree.

"Does it mean there's water close by?" Smuts asks, from the Hummer drawn up beside him.

You look at him and finally say, "Maybe a hundred feet down."

They nevertheless check the area for water, though unsuccessfully, then ease the Hummers under the cypress. They break for a quick lunch, then each of them curls up for a nap under the broad tree's generous shade. You keep the window open a crack to listen for the breeze that moves, hot and unhurried, through the crowd of small leaves.

The tree's shadow slowly crosses the hood with the movement of the sun.

To be able not just to live but flourish in this place . . ., you think dreamily as you doze, staring up through the patchwork of sunlight and shade.

After the siesta, they leave the cypress and its shade, somewhat reluctantly, and wind their way, through the rock tors, south. In the distance you glimpse sand and mountains and mounds of softly carved tassili, like frogs sleeping in mud.

You keep your eye on the top of the enormous tree—for as long as you can in the rearview mirror; you feel curiously attached to it, its ancient boughs alive, like great snakes, its branches bristling, motionless, defiant in the hostile air.

Then, after an hour, it's gone.

The cell phone sounds. Vaulting from the kitchen, you bump against the door jamb, stumble into the common room, search for the phone under the sofa cushions, find it, and stand staring at it, stupidly. How do you turn it on, again?

You press a button. The phone keeps ringing.

Goddam technology . . .

The ringing halts on the third try, and a familiar voice crisps half-audibly at you.

"Dude, I can't hear you, wait . . . wait I said I can't . . . ."

You stand listening to ambient static, truncated syllables, and a flickering aural strobe as the phone on the other end slips in and out of range. You imagine your buddy Dan, also with cell pressed to ear, somewhere in motion—on subway, skateboard, scooter. You lean over and switch on the PC, half listen to Brian Eno's take-off music for Windows with its organ-like resolution, with the impatient, vaguely detached excitement you always feel when powering up your desktop. You *so* need an Apple . . .

When the screen comes up, you go to the browser, wait for the dial tone on the land line, and click for the computer to dial up your service provider. In the upper corner spins Netscape's little earth.

It feels novel, sophisticated, "powerful," connecting to the World Wide Web on the Internet. It's inane, it's addictive.

It shows your account name: "Good morning, Ariel Hunter!"

Man, it feels cool. Still.

"You're at Spring Street? Good, now I can hear you. . . . No shit, *here*? Oh, dial-in . . . I don't know, I'll check it out, I've got some questions I want to ask that guy. Not that I expect a straight answer—after all, wouldn't doing that upset his entire philosophical pro-. . . ? Come on! Aren't simple declarative sentences phallogocentric intrusions enforcing the . . . ? I'm *not* kidding! What's the ultimate postmodernism if it ain't . . . Down with the Enlightenment! Down with Descartes!

Did anybody ever tell the guy he's the perfect philosopher for the age of Reagan-Bush? That should get his goat. Let's go back to Torquemada, forward to the ayatollahs, all you rationalist scum! If you can't persuade 'em, kill the bastards . . . Osama bin Derrida! . . . I can't hear you either. So, lunch at MacDougal? . . . I said 'Lunch at MacDougal'! . . . Right, ciao."

You type "google" into Netscape's search box. After a moment, a white page pops onto the screen with, at top center, the nonsense word suggesting absurdity, a dead Russian existential humorist, and a very large number, in big, multicolored, oddly formal type, and, underneath the word, a small search box, like a horizontal peephole in a guard box or a duck blind or a tank. The page is a clean, white oasis of calm in the data-frantic pages of cyberspace. You type in "derrida online interview" and then, after hesitating, click on the button that reads "I'm Feeling Lucky."

You owe me, lady.

A fraction of a second passes and a page of type appears, with the logo of the University of California at Irvine and information about an interview and Q&A with the celebrated—*notorious? infamous?*—French theorist, tomorrow at noon Pacific time. You bookmark the page, then go to America Online to check your email.

The connection is slow this morning. Everyone's dialing in at the same time. So you go back to your coffee in the kitchen, and stare at the cubist al-fresco glare of late summer Manhattan. The air through the window is almost chilly, though you barely register it. Your mind, as soon as it touches technology, launches into a virtual space of its own. You see, feel, notice everything as if through a wall of frosted glass, find yourself looking at the world with a detached tenseness, as at a screen, watching for its next move—*waiting* for it to move—not moving your eyes to follow the world, but, in some strange sense, expecting it to follow you. Oddly, as a result, the world has become even more slippery. Elusive. Ungraspable.

Noli me tangere.

Can't touch it. Can't smell it. Can't taste it. A completely visual and aural world. Just beyond my grasp.

It's addictive. You can't keep away from it. *What was it Oscar Wilde said about cigarettes, that they were the perfect pleasure because they were unsatisfying? He should see the Internet.*

Ungraspable because the world is now becoming an extension of yourself.

Right.

Is that bitch sleeping with him.

What you think is a statement, not a question.

A shadow moves across the south tower. You go abruptly back to the PC.

As usual, "You Have Mail"—and your mail box, as usual, is full of the already detested and detestable thing called "spam." Some of it is well-intended jokes from friends, classmates, workmates at Oglala. Most of it is useless nonsense or obnoxious insults to your intelligence from web entrepreneurs and *ueber*-hip geek idiot-savants. There is one email from Dan, from last night. There is one from his supervisor at Oglala, Ken Brown, that looks ominous. He wants a special meeting with you as soon as you get in, at 1:30. There have been talks of more layoffs. And there's an email from Schwartz, your academic advisor, confirming your meeting this morning. You'll have to make tracks. You notice the time at the bottom corner of the screen: you have been online for almost half an hour. It's now 8:45. *Time vanishes when you're online. It's positively creepy.*

You suddenly close your eyes and listen.

You hear Pam's last word to you as she leaves.

Bitch.

The computer fan hums. There's no other sound—you can't even hear the traffic outside, sirens, choking water pipes, neighbors' morning TVs or radios, the usual New York sounds. All you can hear is the fan humming in the CPU at your feet.

Your first day at Oglala, over a year ago. You're walking fast along the line of warehouse windows overlooking the back entrances of the local store strip, and make a quick turn around a corner when you see a tall redhead leaning in a shadow next to the free coke machine. She's looking straight at you as if she's been waiting for you, with that knowing smile.

"Howdie, podner?" says Sally Wild, almost repeating the last words she said to you years ago in a Wyoming parking lot. "What brings you to these parts?"

You halt, stunned, catch your breath, choke out a happy, astonished laugh.

You breathe deeply and open your eyes. One of life's little miracles, finding Miranda working in New York, at the same company, in the same department, how many years since you first met her, "fell" for her, badly, no matter what you knew about her, and then thought you'd never see her again.

You look at the clock: 8:47.

You finish your coffee, dress, jam your satchel with books, notebook, and cellphone, and leave, hammering blockily down the stairs.

On either side, long, low mountain ridges seem to follow them; to the left, a long mesa-like tableland, much further off, dominates the eastern horizon.

A line of buttes, geyser-like surges of basalt with whacked-off tops, march into the distance like an orderly herd, repeated exactly at left and right—mirror images of each other, like a symmetrical stage set, as neat as bowling pins.

After a time, Vivian perks up from the back where she sits with Umar and Husayn.

"They look like they're melting." She puts her head through the seat gap and gestures ahead, pointing.

The farthest ones do indeed seem to be disappearing from

the bottom up, hovering on invisible cushions as they vanish into thin air.

Duden trains his glasses on them.

"I can't see their bottoms," he says quizzically. "I can't see anything."

The invisibility slowly rises, like a mist of blue and yellow, and erases the buttes ahead of them as the caravan travels south. First the farthest ones, then those closer slowly dissolve as the sun descends. Less than an hour later they are, all of them, gone, dissolved into the yellow horizon haze and a pale sky blue.

Only two of the buttes are left, or seem to be, one on either side of the valley. One, farther off, is thick and tall; the other is closer, short and skinny.

Duden and Vivian look perplexed, staring suspiciously, not only at the last visible buttes, but at the mountains and mesas.

"Mirages," you say.

The old man smiles.

"Like being in a barbershop," you continue. "Reflections following reflections following reflections. Like I said, you can't always trust what you see out here."

"Are *they* mirages too?" Vivian asks, gesturing toward the two remaining buttes.

You shrug.

"They look so . . . real."

"Another mirage?" Duden suddenly says, gesturing ahead.

You look through the glasses yourself.

To the southeast, at the end of one of the ridges, you see, squiggling in and out of view, mounted on a bare escarpment, an oblong of rock with squared-off peaks.

Vivian takes the glasses,.

"What if it vanishes too—from the bottom up?" she asks.

You turn the van toward the rock spur where the square of rock stands, or at least seems to, in gray-green silhouette.

The Brooklyn streets are a human-sized rat's maze.

A thirty-foot-long square Hummer looking like a tank passes by. You snort a laugh: you've seen stretch limos galore, but never one of these monstrosities. You gape as it passes.

It's almost 80 in the sun. The humidity sticks your collar to your neck.

A plywood fence is covered with posters. One of them shows the pop singer Mariah Carey lying upside down, in a tilt. Her body looks like a playground slide; her feet pointing toward the sky, a nutty smile on her face.

There's a sidewalk sale of books that were in stores earlier in the year: *Underworld*, a couple of Doug Coupland novels, *The Road Ahead,* with Bill Gates on the cover. He also is smiling.

A furtive panhandler approaches you.

He's bearded, his gray hair wild, a still-raw cut over one eye; cocooned in layers of clothing, his whole wardrobe probably: a torn nylon shell over a filthy red sweatshirt, who knows what bulging inside the shell around his torso; stained pants, unlaced Reeboks from the '90s.

His body gives off an unbearable stench.

They're walking back from lunch at Cha'am Thai when they pass a middle-aged Latino with black glasses and a white cane, standing stiffly, in a dark three-piece suit; in his other hand, a mug with "I ♥ NY" on one side. She comes to a halt and gives you one of her peculiar, soberly ironic looks.

"Shall I or shanty?"

Before you have time to say "You haven't lived in New York very long," she's fishes a dollar bill out of the tiny bag she sports, and, looking the man in the face, deposits it in the mug.

"Tha-anks you, lady."

There's something hurt and frightened in his face, the look of a beaten dog.

"Por nada, señor," Miranda responds gravely.

126

After walking on a few feet, she gives you a mocking side-glance.

"If I don't, who will?"

You protest. "He was a fake! How'd he know you're a woman!"

"He's a fake, you're a fake, I'm a fake, we're all a fake!"

"You've been reading too much postmodernism. Anyway, he'll just use it on drugs and booze."

"Oooh! Drugs! And booze! And sex! And gam-bul-ing! Drugs! Booze! Sex! And gam-bul-ing!" she mocks, skipping in rhythm to the words. "And so what, Mr. Virtuous? You've never made any serious mistakes in your wonderful life? . . . Drugs! Booze! Sex! And catch me if you can!"

And she bolts toward the building entrance down the block. You give chase, and trail in the wake of her irresistible laughter, but can't catch her.

You take out a couple of quarters and deposit them into the callused, molasses-brown palm.

The panhandler says something you can't quite make out; it sounds like "God bless you . . ."

Most of the people around you are lightly dressed, rushed, focused, ignoring each other as much as they can. Some toss away cigarettes as they descend the stairs, others finish coffee or a danish. Some are plugged into CD players, their ears held by headphones wrapping around the backs of their heads. A number carry newspapers—the *Times, Wall Street Journal, Daily News*. One nattily dressed older man presses the *Post* against his chest like a banner, with a tartly proprietary air.

You jog along with the crowd, feeling numbly anonymous, absorbed into the small mass of almost indistinguishable identities. The subtle drug of being paradoxically seen and hidden. Watching.

"Technically, it's called a ksur," the mustache says, in his best lecture manner. "A fortress, built by Arabs to defend against the natives. And invaders like us."

They stand at the foot of a high stone wall beneath a pair of broken-down towers, looking at Smuts politely, like tourists facing a docent.

"Could be centuries old. Maybe a millennium. History, in stone."

You peer at the assistants, registering their impression: the guys are playing it cool; Cecilia looks more frankly impressed.

"See how the tower walls flare down from the top? Like narrow truncated pyramids. And the little clipped cornices? Classic. Probably built to protect caravan traffic from the Tuareg."

"Exactly," Duden interrupts. "The Oued-Edeyen road is close by." He smiles slyly. "Even if we've somehow missed Ceruza."

"Maybe," you say. "Caravan trails shift all the time."

"But mountains do not." Duden gestures disdainfully toward the landscape surrounding them.

"You'd be surprised," you say.

As they speak, Smuts climbs to the half-ruined entrance, a collapsed gate and a wrecked iron-reinforced door revealing a dark interior.

"Well, look at this!"

Smuts picks up a battered, blackened helmet lying in a pile of detritus nearby.

"French!" he declares, waving it at them. "They haven't used these since the second world war. Abandoned during Rommel's campaign, no doubt."

"No doubt," you echo.

"Last outpost of Beau Geste," says Jack.

"Beau Geste?" asks Cecilia.

"Ever see the Gary Cooper movie?"

The group pulls a blank.

"Ancient history," Smuts deadpans. "So. An Arab fortress overcome by Tuareg at some point and then manned by the French."

"Who owns it now?" someone asks.

"The bloody government," says Peter.

"Finders keepers," quips the Okie.

He then reaches up and pulls at a slat in the gate. It sheers off, dropping at his feet.

A bird, an unidentifiable raptor, flaps from a guard tower and soars off toward the north, eyeing them a moment as it flies.

The rest of the gate sags inward, and a great shadowy interior opens before them: stuffy, baked with the day's heat, lightless except for the dusky glimmer coming in through the opening and loopholes high up in the walls; the interior is dusty and stinks of hot alkali.

They stand without speaking, waiting for their eyes to adjust to the darkness. Then they hear a flutter and rustling, beginning close and just overhead, then rippling ahead of them and down what sound like narrow corridors along each side of the gateway. There's a chorus of high-pitched squeals and the air suddenly crowds with black.

"Bats! . . . Get out!"

Cecilia lets out a shriek, and they all escape as a cloud of bats crowds them, soaring up and swirling and squealing around the fortress walls in a viscous mass virtuoso display of coordination, a few peeling off and winging alone around the towers, the mass of them swirling and swirling and swirling, and then, after their brief disorientation in the late afternoon sunlight, all of them, as if on command, shooting once again down through the gate as they retreat in a long, ragged stream to their shadowy lodging, leaving the travelers staring after them in silence.

After a few moments of awed silence, you speak, bringing them back to dull, dangerous reality.

"I need to check something before it gets dark."

The four adults pass down a trail around the fortress's eastern flank; cross a line of log-like rocks lined up near the base of the wall, smoothing the surfaces with your palm. They're almost cool to the touch . . .

"Petrified trees," says Duden.

You suddenly remember a fossil you once found, many years before, at the top of one of the Rockies in the states. You had tossed it out a bus window in a fit of pique. Where was it now? Might be picked up by another fossil hound in a hundred million years, if there were fossil hounds then.

At the back of the fortress you're greeted by a sweeping view of the valley below. The sun, an egg-shaped oval, is slipping behind the horizon, and long deep shadows cross the land, brilliant toward the west, almost black to the east.

You sweep the binoculars over the horizon

Luck owes us, you think. Your inner devil immediately responds: *Luck owes us nothing.* To which you respond, in turn: *Luck owes us.*

You sweep the same arc again, then give Duden the glasses.

"Look just ahead," you say. "Between the butte and the outcrop east of it. It's dim, but tell me what you see."

Duden trains the glasses and looks.

"Can't see . . ."

"Steady them on this," pointing to a boulder, which Duden kneels down on.

"All I see is red sand and . . . Wait, something that looks like big ferns, above some sort of . . ."

"Ferns?" asks Smuts, taking the glasses from Duden. "My eye! Palms."

Smuts passes the binoculars to Vivian, who looks for a long moment, seeming to catch sight of them immediately, but saying nothing.

"Well?"

"I can't tell, it's too dark," she says.

"Neither can I," you say, guessing her suspicion. "But you

130

don't see mirages at dusk. My vote is for palms. And that means water."

"Ceruza?" From Duden, in the rapidly falling darkness.

Smuts gives Duden a hard look again, as he had before at the mention of the name; then he glances at you, as though half-expecting some comment.

"Maybe. Though if it is, it's even less than we thought," you say, looking through the glasses. A spark seems to ignite among the distant trees—a fire? a sign of people? a refraction from the setting sun? a reflection off water, or just volcanic glass? You drop the glasses, and the spark vanishes. You look through them again, but the light has gone.

"Less of a city?" asks Smuts.

" . . . than a sand bucket!" you grin.

You return and tell the news to the kids, who stayed with the vans. Soon after, the little caravan is back on the valley floor, where they search for a place to set up camp near the base of the fortress's escarpment.

The mood among them is almost cheerful. They keep teasing the girl about her shriek.

Later that night a cloud of bats—perhaps the ones from the abandoned fortress—crosses the full moon, playing across its face back and forth for almost an hour.

"Eclipse, my lips! I told you the bats covered it for an hour," cracks the victor in the previous quarrel.

Just like Peter; he loves to crow.

I can almost hear the whistling of their wings.

Waiting for the train, you feel the excitement that always catches you up whenever you're in a crowd, a sense that you are on the verge of an insight into the chaos, straining after it: it's almost *there, that,* under your nose, at the end of your tongue, just beyond your grasp . . .

Then it slips away like a fish in the darkness.

You gaze around you.

131

You feel teased with an embarrassed self-consciousness, goaded by an aimless longing—to *know*, to grasp and hold firmly in your mind—even though everything you are being taught, from all sides, from the florid vapidities of the media to the metaphysical sneers of your professors, from the know-nothingism of your well-healed relatives to the patronizing burbling of Buddhist converts, is the hopelessness of understanding anything beyond the hopelessness of the struggle to know, that knowledge either is power, or is not even that; is a blind impulse toward what it can never grasp, a grasp that exceeds anyone's possible reach—you are not to know even what you are waiting for, even if it *can* be waited for, if there *is* anything to wait for. You are not allowed, it seems, even to know what it might have been.

Yet you continue to expect something; even when it's not something from the world but from you.

Still, the maddening question—expecting *what*?—sticks like a nail in the bottom of a shoe you can't take off. Would you even know it if you saw it; *could* you know it, could anybody?

You have never discussed these thoughts of yours with Pam: you can hear the sneer she'd raise, shielded in the wounded fury of her feminism: "Only a guy would worry about such metaphysical bullshit."

The possibility that she might be right, that it might be "merely" a "gender-specific" concern, only adds to the confusion.

It doesn't alleviate it: even if it were true, your hunger, this demand for an answer to your *need to know*, won't just shrug it off and go away. It will only bury deeper in, And stick. Like a fish hook.

Sometimes it seems to you that everyone, including those around you, here and now on the subway platform—that everyone is enclosed in a kind of translucent bubble no one can see clearly through. Inside each bubble a projector plays a continuous looping tape based on—what? Memory and dream, say.

On top of this continuous screening, some light manages to get through the bubble, like light leaking through a translucent screen in a movie theater—light from inside the bubble when you're outside it, looking in (imagine seeing a weak tungsten filament inside a frosty gray light bulb); and light from outside the bubble when you're inside it, looking out (imagine the glass door of a steam room, the shadowy figures of people beyond the door moving through a dense, hot mist). But little light gets through, in either direction. Just enough to show you shadows, to let you know something is there beyond the perpetual screening of your fantasies, but never enough to let you know truly, clearly, without question or doubt, not what it *seems* (that epistemological cop-out so many people like to hide behind, you often think; anything can *seem* like anything at all), but *what it is.* Just enough to frustrate you and bewilder you. . . .

The air in the subway station is stale, sticky, even warmer than on the street.

A line of sweat trickles down the back of your neck.

Breathing is difficult, almost oppressive, as though your lungs resist taking in the sickly warmth, the foul air.

Glances, when traded by accident, bounce off like a ricochet.

A teenage girl, her hair up in a tight bun (a ballet student?), stands tightly erect at the platform edge, in lowcut denims with a naked midriff and a vest-like sweatshirt marked "Guess?" on the back.

She stares coolly across the tracks with a preternatural—or illusory—self-possession.

You watch her furtively. *If she turned toward me, I would run to the ends of the earth. She will not turn toward me, I'm invisible, safe.*

A poster across from her advertises a new movie based on a comic book: *Ghost World.* A photo of a nerdy girl in glasses and her blond sidekick stare skeptically at the viewer. Above their heads are the words "Accentuate the negative."

The ballerina leans over to peer down the tracks, under her arm a notebook and a paperback pressed firmly to her side.

You feel a familiar compulsion to read the title of books you see people reading.

You can see a Penguin logo, the border of shiny aubergine, and a few words of the title: *The Sickness Unto . . .*

. . . *Death,* you, mentally, conclude.

Why would a dancer would be reading Kierkegaard's tortuous disquisition on despair?

What genuine despair could she possibly know?

Unless she's just one more intellectual poseur.

Another existentialist fake.

Though what if that whole elaborate appearance of aloof and elegant calm were the pose, and the half-hidden cover of the book a chink in the armor providing a look into her . . . soul (there is no soul, but what else to call it)?

But wasn't that part of the Great Dane's point?

A hip-hopper, a honey-pale black boy in over-sized cutoffs and a football T and reversed baseball cap, appears from behind a column, moving to his own rhythm on the player he carries.

He almost aggressively ignores the girl.

You feel an immediate sympathy for him.

He's given up. He knows he'll never interest her or anybody like her. Or he thinks he knows. Why try, why not offend, with clothing, body language, pose. Hey, it keeps him in control of the situation. He's nowhere? Tell the bitch to care.

A train, charging into the station, moans to a halt as if in pain.

You crush in with the crowd of standees and lose sight of the girl.

The doors slam and the train groans on.

The hip-hopper is still dancing in place as the platform slides past the glass. He flips the train a bird.

Maybe just on principle. Maybe a little vendetta against the ice queen who never noticed his existence when he was dancing his morning away just for her.

A stream of thick warm air slips across your face from a half-open window.

Lamps flash by in dingy yellow smears.

The train rocks rhythmically.

A couple of young Hispanic guys in fashion T-shirts and spider shades trade a cell, hands over the phone.

One of them catches you looking at them and stares at you hard.

Three women sit on the other side of the car. A Filipina with a frayed shoulder bag, the top of a bottle of Mr. Clean sticking out. A little, plump Chinese in a cap with raised ear flaps, glancing wonderingly up and down the aisle. An elegantly dressed Iranian woman with an intimidatingly perfect profile, staring at nothing.

A short, thin Sikh with a large apricot turban and manicured beard with curling moustaches gets in at the next stop and takes the seat the Filipina vacates when she leaves, brushing modestly through the packed crowd.

The door closes violently behind her as she leaves.

A Hasidic Jew, an older man, with long beard, fetlocks, and an old-fashioned hat, stands quietly nearby, with a tensely inward gaze.

The Sikh sits down, very erect, next to the Chinese lady, who glances at him between her ear flaps with mild wonder, then quickly looks away.

He ignores her, stares ahead, glancing at you with a slightly wounded expression.

Above the man's turban a photograph shows a rocky island in a tempestuous sea white and black with wind-blown waves, a lighthouse beaconing weakly in the distance.

A sickly white beam stands in profile, a truncated triangle of dirty light, against crowns and towers of purple-black cloud.

"Pilot Safe Into Harbor With Vesuvius Term Life," reads the tag line.

"*When you've earned it*," you remember Pam saying. "*Maybe.*"

"Where do you fit in all of this? Where do you fit in all of this? Where do you fit in all of this?" the train's wheels repeat noisily.

You keep seeing Pam walking out the door.

At the next stop, three people get off and a mob jams in.

Your vision is reduced to a small tunnel more or less directly in front of your face.

You lift your eyes above the silver gray shoulder.

An ad rises above your head, past the silver gray shoulder, with "YOU Ready fuh US? *WE* Ready fuh *YOU*!" in heavy block letters.

A crowd of youngsters in rap outfits are photographed frozen in a frantic leap across the type, grasping futilely for something just out of reach above their heads, above the top of the ad, train, tunnel, streets, somewhere far up in the New York sky.

The silver gray suit with the shoulder presses against you, leaning on your foot. It seems to lean in toward you even more heavily as the subway hurtles through the hot, stale darkness. You can barely breathe. The suit is bright, shiny, impeccable—an Italian cut, the lapels strongly flared; the tie is a soft mauve, the shirt a cream white. You can't see the face. Then the train reaches Cortlandt Street, a few blocks from the towers you dislike, and the suit gives your foot a parting crunch and slips out a nearby door.

You feel a surge of resentment similar to the one you saw in the hip-hopper on the platform.

"Capitalist whore," you say under your breath as the suit leaves.

But the suit hears and turns to glare at you as the doors slide shut. For the first time you register the man's face: thick, heavy-browed, sandy blond, with black eyes.

The idea presents itself with sudden clarity: *I have got to get out of this place.*

You twist around. . . .

A word in large serif letters crosses a cinematically wide poster above the door opposite. The upper parts of the letters have been deliberately cut off by the top of the ad.

A L S A R A B.

Visible through the sheared-off letters of the word, as through bars on a window, an ocean of sand rolls away, empty, velvety, like the dips and swells on an ocean—or like a nest of enormous snakes asleep under a vast, rumpled sheet—almost a living thing—under a brilliant sun, its rays extending in four directions, a cross made of daggers of light. In a corner is a picture of an old-fashioned cut-glass perfume bottle. A phrase near the bottle reads, "Succumb to the mirage."

Mounds and valleys of desert sand roll on and on, an immense billowy maze, toward a distant horizon. *There.*

There.

A L S A . . .

You're having your usual friendly quarrel about politics.

"So then, according to your theory, Mr. Marx Man, I'm just a capitalist stooge"

"No, I . . ."

"So, which one am I: Larry, Moe or Curly?"

"Excuse me?"

"Larry, Moe or Curly? If I'm going to be a stooge, I'd like to know which one. Moe is too obnoxious. Larry is kind of cute, but that hair! I think I'd rather be Curly. He talks so pretty. You, of course, are all Moe." She sticks her tongue out at you. "Without any Jo at all!"

And she walks off down 52nd Street, toward her date with Sharon, the girlfriend she'd found in a New York drag-king club. You stare after her, a dumb grin on your face. Suddenly she turns back.

"You should see the look on your face, Ariel, my Ariel!"

Her smile flashes at you gleefully, and she turns and vanishes. Three days later she is taken to the hospital.

They're up early in a cool dawn. The feeling among them is relieved, almost cheerful.

The sun, for the first time since they left Ouadane, is a welcome presence as it rests briefly on an eastern mesa before launching into the sky like a fiery balloon.

As they move toward the western butte, Duden trains the binoculars past it, south. But between them and the oasis stands a huge column of basalt, a truncated, headless form soaring above them in dead mineral nobility.

Like the neck of a guillotined aristocrat, you think.

After briefly conferring at its base, they decide to push on through the midday heat and try making the oasis by nightfall.

"If I *can* find it, of course!" Duden jokes with excessive energy. He's overemphatic, as though this time he has got to get it right.

They laugh. Not find it! Now *there*'s a joke. Duden beams at the success of his joke. You notice his hand is shaking.

The ground heat is even more intense than the sky's as Duden and you climb up the next elevation after parking in a sand pocket. You feel compressed between two soft, smothering vices. After a few moments Duden is gasping.

"All right?"

"God Almighty it's hot. I'm fine, I'm fine!" Duden waves you on feverishly. "Let's go!"

Heat waves swim off the dune ridge ahead.

They look back at the rocky spur where the ksur stands like an abandoned fort on a barbarian frontier.

"If I recall right," you say, squinting hard, "the palms should be about *there*." You point. A barrel dune lies a mile or so away, barring the view.

As the two of you stand silent, you again hear what sounds like running water, just behind you. You say nothing but turn, looking down at the sand.

There's nothing there but your shadow, compressed behind your legs.

"What is it?" Duden asks sharply.

"Nothing, I just . . ." But you don't finish your sentence. "We should get back."

138

"Right. I'm about ready for my daily heart attack!" Duden tries to laugh but can't; he just smiles helplessly.

Jack's head pokes out into the heat as they climb down to the vehicles, and Vivian's face shows in the square of front-door window.

"One more dune to scout," you call out. "We're pretty close."

"Really?" Vivian says doubtfully.

"Close to *something*," you say.

Duden, catching her skepticism, speaks over your words. "O ye of little faith!" he shouts.

As you settle behind the wheel, you try to catch Vivian's eye in the rearview mirror, but she's staring into the distance.

"How are our camel drivers doing?" you ask, referring to Umar and Husayn sitting next to her in the back. They have been extremely quiet, even for them, over the past hour.

"Sleeping the sleep of the just," she replies. She raises a piercing look at you in the mirror.

10:37 a.m.

With a worried half-smile, Dr. Schwartz looks over the paper. His silvery eyebrows jump up and down, over and over. *Like Howdy Doody's*, you think.

I turned in the theme for my thesis a week ago. Hasn't he read it before now?

Your heart sinks.

"You know," Schwartz says, clearing his throat carefully but still smiling, "you know, Arik, this . . . this really won't do."

You look at Schwartz dejectedly. You were half-expecting this. After a moment of Schwartz's irritating smile, you can feel yourself expand, like an internal balloon suddenly inflating, and you go into imitation-professor mode.

"I must say that that surprises me ...."

"No, no. It shouldn't. Really. It's too ... well, provocative? This isn't creative writing class, you know, where provocation

139

can be a plus. I know you took creative writing as an undergrad
. . ."

The reminder is annoying, though it's nice to know your advisor has been paying attention.

"Yeah, but I wanted something with more, I don't know . . . Too many navel-gazers in that class . . ."

"There are worse things to gaze at than navels!" Schwartz chuckles. "Well, be that is it may, the committee will never accept this. It's one thing to be *political*, that's expected if anything, but . . ." Schwartz twists his mouth and looks over the sheet of paper before him, "but Marx is just no longer an option. If this were a degree in obsolete theories, that would be one thing. It's like proposing to dissect a dodo! It's dead. It's gone. I thought we had acknowledged that."

"We talked about it, but . . . I never *acknowledged* it."

Schwartz looks puzzled.

"I never acknowledged . . ." Black blind fury lunges from the back of your mind. "I didn't, I *don't* ac*cept* . . . ."

"Well, maybe *you* don't, but they *won't* . . ."

"Marxism" —*Voice sounds strangled, control it, I have to get this.* Then the words come bumping awkwardly out. —"as a, as a, as a *heuristic*—" *Am I using that word right? He'll slam me if I'm not.* "—is alive and well, even Bourdieu says so—" Schwartz frowns, "—even if he doesn't specifically . . . Marx was the first to categorize capitalism as a coherent system, though one that is inherently self-destructive, and, well, he describes in detail, that—" *Shit, I mangled that.* Schwartz opens his mouth to object. "*And* he just didn't live long enough to see it play out on such a huge scale, I mean, globalization is a gigantic laboratory for Marx's ideas, I'm not trying to justify his predictions, anyway he didn't make any at least in his lucid moments." Schwartz looks profoundly skeptical at that. "But he did name and describe the beast that's eating us alive *now*, he'd find nothing that's happening today all that surprising." Schwartz grins. *I'm getting in deep, oh what the hell.* "He'd

140

even feel *vindicated*—a voracious corporate class, run-away debt, a squeezed middle class, pauperized workers, international economic balkanization, NAFTA destroying Mexican agriculture and sucking U.S. jobs across the border, just like Ross Perot predicted, growing homelessness, economic bubbles, accelerated business cycles—it's all there, most of it's been there for over a century . . . "

Schwartz sits there, waiting for more. At your pause, he suddenly stoops forward.

"As Ross Perot, that great Marxist, said! Yes, you do think you're still in creative writing class. But none of that's really the point." He shakes his head dismissively, smiling at the student's enthusiasm, that touching willingness to defend a hopeless position. *The jerk!* "The point here is preparing an acceptable thesis. Without that you can't get a degree, and without that you can't continue in the field. You may want to get a doctorate someday. Hold off on Marx until you have tenure somewhere, then you will be free to do whatever you like." *Catching himself like the cautious man he is.* "Within much broader limits, that is."

"Sorry, Dr. Schwartz." *Why do I feel like I'm choking on the words?* "That just doesn't make sense to me, I've heard the arguments and I don't . . . I'm sorry." Schwartz shrugs grandly and gazes back at you. "The reason I came here is not just to get a degree for its own sake, it's to study, study society, the world I live in" *(God, bring in the corn!)* "to *find out* something about it and say what I *find out* as clearly and as loudly as I can." *Fuck!* "That's my understanding of it, anyway."

"I admire that. I really do. It's very . . . *idealistic* of you . . ." *Dickhead!*

". . . but the requirements for the degree include your submitting a thesis that is acceptable to the committee, and this simply won't fly. Would you seriously propose a paper in alchemy for a chemistry degree? I don't know about Jungian psychology! Its entire conceptual apparatus is—well, it's been judged as outmoded throughout the profession for a very long time, and certainly will be in this department, blasted as it is by everything from the Austrian School to game theory. At best, it's eccentric; at worst, hallucinatory, oneiric. You understand what I mean by 'oneiric'? After all, someone who throws around words like 'heuristic' should." Looking at you doubtfully.

You nod even though you have no idea precisely what "oneiric" means. You feel yourself blush.

" 'Wishful thinking,' in this case. The committee will not accept your thesis. I can guarantee you that based on my own experience. Don't throw away a year of research on certain failure." Schwartz suddenly looks at you with gentle eyes. "You're a good student, Arik—better than good, you have a better head on you than most, you actually make connections between what you study and, well, what you know. You have a talent for this, you can go somewhere with it. And you have a good heart. Don't sneer—it's as important as having a good head."

The bastard actually does mean well . . . damn him! . . .

"Let me tell you something. Twenty-five years ago I was in a very similar spot as you're in. This was in the seventies, when things were a lot looser than they are now. I wanted to do a thesis on Marcuse—the one-dimensional society, the limits of tolerance, repressive desublimation, that sort of thing." He smirks and shrugs, with resignation, as though at his younger self. "And I was stubborn about it, I insisted, even though there were objections, I had warnings. It was passé! There's nothing like a reactionary to tell you the avant-garde is out of date. It would hurt my chances for a Ph.D., it would never get me a job. Academic freedom is for the tenured. It's a bit like freedom of the press—you need to own a press!" He smiles his kind, if maddening, smile. "Anyway, there were thousands of Ph.D.'s driving cabs, why make it even harder for myself. So—what did I do?" He leans forward across the desk, almost meeting your nose. "I did it!" And he pulls back, with a triumphant smile. "I immersed myself for almost two years in Marcuse,

142

the Frankfurt School, the polemics of the sixties. And I did a good job of it, if I say so myself. I was proud of it. If it had been 1968, a publisher might have snapped it up. But it wasn't 1968 anymore. A year and a half passed, and I submitted it. In 1974. And the committee sat on it—deliberately sat on it for eight months. They wouldn't move on it." He waves his hands with a panicky look. "And I was desperate—I actually had a job offer! But it depended on my having the degree, and the committee wouldn't move." He slumps back in mock despair. "Eventually I found out what the problem was: the committee only acted on consensus, and one person objected to my thesis." Schwartz raises his finger. "*One person.* The other members held out, trying to persuade the objector. Well. He wouldn't budge." He stares at you triumphantly. "*And he was a liberal!*

"In the end, they rejected it and I had to start all over. Of course, I didn't get the job, and it took me another year to get the degree. That was another year of living on student loans, by the way. I was nearly sinking under debt when I finally got out."

"You make it sound like a prison sentence."

"It was, in its way."

"What was your thesis on? The new one."

"It doesn't matter now. It wasn't on Marcuse."

And did you ever return to Marcuse? Not that I've noticed on your biblio. If you start safe, you stay safe. Once they break you, they crush you. As soon as you're gelded, you can do anything you want. You can have any mare in the stable you want, or you can handle, now, sir.

Schwartz sighs, looks away, then back at him. The smile is gone.

"What used to be one objector is now everyone on the committee. I'm telling you: *this*"—slapping the thesis description lightly—"will never pass. We live in different times."

"All the more reason to bring back the Great Subverter himself . . . "

"No, no! That's 'grand narrative,' totalitarian, that's dead white male country. That's patriarchy. That's history. There's nothing to *change* because there's nothing to *understand*, except what we say there is."

And that depends on who's in charge. . . . Exactly who is in charge?

You stare at Schwartz, a wiry man with friendly eyes, thin but sturdy shoulders, a hesitant, well-meaning manner; watchful, skeptical, your own eyes are locked on him with unnerving intensity. A sweet man at bottom, you know at the back of your mind, though given to devastating frankness. His look locks on you, tight.

Is he preaching the pomo word, the post-Nietzschean apotheosis of apocalypse and liberation through nihilism, or is he ridiculing it? Of course, under the postmodern dispensation it was possible—it was mandatory—to do both.

You feel half sick: part of you rejects in disgust what Schwartz says, part ruefully accepts his common sense, part wants to please him and at the same time is terrified of not being accepted by the one world you have cared about for years: the university—the place where ideas were taken seriously, the one defense against the nihilism of the marketplace, of American capitalism. A place where when one was encouraged, commanded, to search for knowledge, meaning, truth; to understand the human condition, the world, and mold it, re-mold it, if possible, into something closer to the mind's, and to the heart's, demands.

You have become sickeningly aware of what motivates academics as much as it does everyone else—not the disinterested search for truth, beauty, the good, but *the same thing*, in a word, "careerism"—ambition, greed, power, the fear of being left out, of being despised by one's peers, colleagues, neighbors, friends, and torpedoed by one's masters, even when they are dupes or liars. The religion of self-interest.

The university seems to you little more now than a

reservation for intellectuals, where they are kept politically impotent, an asylum, a low-security prison, where intellectuals can be kept out of harm's way and the guards are made of degrees and student loans and tenure. A soft prison. A tin Theresienstadt with velvet gloves.

The sickness in you goes deep. Like any love sickness.

In the hallway, waiting at the elevator after leaving Schwartz, without having reached a conclusion, you think, bitterly yet lucidly: *You are in charge only because I let you be in charge.*

Again you have a rush of desire to escape.

Get me out of here . . .

"So. What are you going to do with your wonderful life?"

Miranda's private motto. That enchantment of a smile flashes by and vanishes.

And so, Miranda: what are you *going to do with your wonderful life?*

You can almost hear her reply: *Defeat* cancer, show them *how it's done* at law school, and become the *first bisexual comedienne* on the Supreme Court!

The thought flushes you with happiness.

You smile to yourself as you get into the empty elevator, which plunges directly to the ground.

"*There!*" Duden shouts, wildly waving his skinny arm.

His mouth pinches and slackens convulsively.

They're standing atop the dune they saw twenty minutes ago.

"I see them as plain as . . ." Duden stops then laughs that new cracked laugh of his. ". . . as plain as the hair on my head!"

The few hairs left on it waft as he wags his pate.

Duden thrusts the glasses into your hands. Then you see them: close enough to count the fronds, though as still as statues in the midday heat—a screen of palm tops like a row of aspidistras on an old-fashioned suburban patio, their heads hanging over the railing, or in a garden shop. The fronds curl up and out, like ferns. The very look of them is cooling . . .

The top of the dune cuts them off, but behind them, clearly there are, there must be of course, the rest of the trees, and a patch of green. A well. Food. Shade. Maybe a settlement, a bedouin camp. Above all, water.

You almost feel like singing.

Desperate too, old boy? you say to yourself.

Duden giggles and grins from burnt ear to ear; you've never seen the old boy look so frisky.

You slap each other's shoulders, and after checking the exact orientation on a compass and sketching a quick map, go back as fast as you can manage (you're weaker than you realized) to the waiting vans.

Duden cries out, "We've found it!" in a voice a little cracked from thirst (they've had only two small water rations since breakfast) and pumps the air with his bony fist.

You notice a tear running along Duden's cheek.

He was frightened. Now he's overjoyed.

So am I. . . . So am I.

11:49 a.m.

As so often after an argument, your hands feel itchy. Displaced aggression. A difficult day: two fights already. *And I lost both.*

You would like, right now, to be working on your vehicle: Jenny, the ancient Jeep Pam wants you "to lose"—it's drafty, uncomfortable, and only useful, as she puts it, for fighting World War II—but you love it, partly because it's so inconvenient and has such an ugly mug. You won't have time to tinker with it until the weekend.

So you drum on the table in the café on MacDougal, waiting for Dan.

146

"Hey."

Your scruffy school buddy from undergrad days, with the angry bald head and buzzed eyes lopes into the café in a bulky gray hoody with "Nirvana Next" in blood-red splash type on the back. He totes a net backpack with the cover of a copy of *The Idiot's Guide to Derrida* showing through the back. He catches sight of you and slides into the seat across from you with an intense look.

"Gonna eat?"

Dan screws up his face at the novelty of the idea.

"Why not," he shrugs. They head for the counter.

In a few moments a couple of plastic-wrapped sandwiches and two cans of coke stand in front of them at the table. They tear in.

"Schwartz is fighting my thesis."

"He's—" Dan starts to respond, stops, then swallows the bite of turkey sandwich in his mouth. "—an asshole."

"I wish he was, it'd make it a lot easier. He's basically a decent guy. He means well. He isn't a bitter loser out to crush his students out of jealousy and resentment because we're young and have a future. He may even be right about my thesis. And I hate that! But that's not the point."

"I never liked the guy, he's meshuggah. How old was he in World War Two?"

"But he's Jewish!"

"In his dreams!" Dan, who is, looks appalled. "That's what he *wants* you to think. He's friggin' Bavarian—or 'Boyern,' as the linguistically correct would have it. Did you ever see him with the chair? Talk about ass-licking."

"You like *your* advisor?"

"We get along like a house. He doesn't know shit, but he doesn't get in my way. Of course, I'm not trying to sell him Marx!"

They eat in silence. A young woman with a dog comes into the café.

"Have you decided on your thesis?"

Dan snorts between chugs of coke.

"Something about the undecidability of referentiality in deconstructive strategies. Turn Derrida on his head."

"And he *bought* that?"

"He loves it. I wanted to do something on Foucault, but he shot it down. He said it was too late."

You give him a look.

"'Forget Foucault,'" he says, quoting the title of a book by another provocative Frenchman.

"Then he suggested something on Derrida. But that was my backup plan anyway."

"At least it isn't Baudrillard!"

"You should go after some post-Marxist. Like Jameson. Or Terry Eagleton. Or, hey—Leo Strauss! Hell, his acolytes just took over the White House."

"Post *shit*. But that's not the point."

They eat away in silence, avoiding each other's eyes. You want Dan to follow up with a question—"Well, what *is* the point?"—but that would just tempt Dan's passive-aggressive side.

You put down your sandwich and look Dan in the eye.

"I'm thinking of bailing. Of leaving."

"From what." Dan looks sleepy, clueless.

"Everything. School. The city. The country. I'm sick of it."

Dan's face screws up in scorn.

"Fuck me! No way are you going to *bail*." He looks disgusted that you would even expect him to believe such a thing. "What would you *do*? Where would you *go*? That's bullshit."

"No. No. No," the firmness you wished for in Schwartz's office but find only now stiffens your voice. "*This* is bullshit. My life is bullshit. I am surrounded by bullshit, and I want out of it. Nothing . . ." —You pause, groping. —"Nothing here is *real* anymore for me. Nothing I do seems to have any weight to it, any heft or pull or . . . It's all wheel-spinning. There's no . . ." —*There*, something you can almost grasp, just beyond your fingers. —". . . There's no *reality* to it, I feel nothing but a kind of . . . I don't know . . . it's chaotic, it's senseless, but it's also frozen. If *that* makes any sense!" Dan nods in grim agreement. "There's no order or direction or purpose, it falls apart just as I'm reaching . . . I can't describe it but it feels wrong, not *real*. Even when it's real, it feels fake . . ."

"Well, according to Derrida . . ."

"Fuck Derrida. That's the bullshit people actually believe, or pretend to. Or not even *pretend* to, they just repeat and nod, like a crazy parrot!"

"I've seen them, on a PBS special: they nod and nod and nod, compulsively. 'Der-ri-da, Der-ri-da! What, *me* make sense? Cuckoo!' "

You giggle and shift in your chair. "Everybody in this country has become a fucking bullshit artist!" you say, laughing in despair. "Have you noticed that?"

"Well . . . duh!"

"I fucking expect it from politicians and lawyers and celebrities and CEOs—everybody 'on the make,' who *runs* this place. It's in their interest to keep the rest of us *morons*. But universities . . ."

Dan nods gravely.

"That's serious."

"Fuck all." You snort. "That's the *one* place in this fucked up society I expect to be based on . . . *truth, honesty, goodness, beauty*—go ahead, laugh, I know it sounds so fucking naive, *but I don't think it is:* that is the *point* of it. And now it seems to be committing, what? A kind of suicide. Universities were institutions based on something like the disinterested pursuit of truth, and they could be held accountable. They may have been beholden to their regents or board of directors or whatever, but at least in principle they held themselves, they could be held by others, to essentially disinterested standards. But they seem to have given up, they suck up to power or money or the hottest trend, because they've abandoned any other standard.

149

They aren't even called to account for it. The Internet seemed to offer some hope, but it's being taken over by business, the way everything is in this country, and that means destroying everything for the sake of adding digits to somebody's asset portfolio. Fuck, the globe's warming, the ozone hole's growing, people are getting skin cancer, species are dying, workers are fucked over right and left, and that means the rest of us are not far behind, and we just party and burn oil. The corporations are taking over everything through globalization, even people's clothing, even people's skin, they want to tattoo people with product brands for fuck sake, and they don't give a flying fuck about tomorrow. They are not even allowed to, by law—they've got to put their shareholders' interests above everything, even basic common decency. But even *that*'s not it." You frown at the crushed plastic, crumbs, spots of coke on the wooden table.

"It's quite an indictment if it isn't," Dan smiles at you, seeming to enjoy the rant.

"It's as if I never touch bedrock under my feet." You stare into space—*maybe that's it, what I'm trying to grasp, that thing, that* . . . "I feel like I'm on a slippery floor covered with ball bearings. I can't keep my balance from moment to moment, I'm always shooting off in a different direction, or not moving at all. Either paralyzed or shooting off all over the place. I can't tell if what I'm doing is worth the effort. I'm not sure that what I'm doing, even what I *intend* to do, has any value. I'm sick of everything."

"You need better drugs."

Dan looks away, sucks at his coke, looks back. The air rests a bit.

"You been thinking about this a long time?"

"Over the last year. . . ."

"What about the job?"

"An *ontologist* at Oglala!" You bark a free laugh across the café. The young woman with the dog leaves, glancing at you. "Oh. They don't even know what 'ontology' *means*, they just think the word sounds cool." You pause, watching the woman walk away down the street. "The whole company is based on a bizarre, inflated fantasy about itself, a business model that never existed. They claim they want to take on Yahoo! They have no money, no income, their stock price is collapsing by the hour. I have to see my supervisor this afternoon, probably about more layoffs. They've already *reorganized* twice since January. Get that! Euphemisms. Everyone fucking lies or hides information to protect their holy legal ass or the bottom line. What *is* this country? What has it become? And look who we've let become president! If *that* doesn't condemn us, what could?"

Your cellphone sounds in your book bag. You pull it out, flip it open, see Pam's phone number on the display, flip it shut, and shove it angrily back into the bag.

"*We* aren't getting along either. We fight every day. We haven't had sex in three months. She says she's too tense, rehearsing. What is she rehearsing for—*life*? Unless she's off getting it from her director." His voice, irritated but lucid, has suddenly risen in harshness and volume, then breaks off.

Dan looks at his friend piercingly. "I'm sorry, man." His face displays genuine pain. The reflexive compassion a man feels for another man's panic and anguish at the suspicion of sexual betrayal. "I'm really sorry about that."

"Sorry . . ." A sudden pullback, shame over having revealed too much. "I'm just venting."

There's a pause between them, Dan watching you and pulling back a little himself. When Dan continues, he retreats into his detachment: it's safer for both of them.

"Fuck-school rage. It happens in the middle of every degree program. It's okay. Sometimes you gotta let it out."

"I'm just so fucking frustrated about everything I don't know what to do. Everywhere I turn, there's a fucking wall." You look at Dan, at once vulnerable and shielded. "Know what I mean?"

"Shit, yes."

Dan leans forward lightly on his elbows.

"Think twice before you leave everything. If you really are thinking about it."

"I swear to God I've thought about it a thousand times. But if I do, it'll be complete. I'll disappear. There's a town outside Burlington . . ."

"Not Jersey!" With an appalled look. "You really *will* disappear."

They guffaw.

"Vermont. We were up there this summer. I wanted to visit the city that had voted a socialist for mayor. Bernie Sanders— my main man! Like, a generation ago. Man, I just wanted to stay there and sit tight for a year."

"Remember 'Twin Peaks.' Those country places are weird. You're a city rat now, dude. You'd never survive a New England winter."

"We have bad ones in Ohio. Or I could try Boston."

"Bostonians will freeze you faster than a Canada January. Be warned. I lived there a summer once. Nearly lost my balls to the frostbite."

"Well then, maybe not."

They pause, drinking the last of their cokes, looking out the windows at the steady trickle of pedestrians.

"Catch a smoke?"

They stand outside on the hot street smoking American Spirits, not talking.

"Going to Todd's tonight?"

"Maybe. I'm doing the sound at The Billy Club, so I won't be there till after midnight anyway. How about you?"

"Yeah, we'll be there. That is, if we don't fight first. What's the band?"

"Three girl bands: Rabbit Ears, My Dwarf Please, and somebody else." He crushes the butt under his heel.

People pass: a girl with purple hair and big fairground glasses, her arms crawling with tattoos; a middle-aged gay in a black Polo shirt tending a bichon; a tiny old lady arguing furiously with the air in front of her.

152

Dan looks you in the eye with a serious air. "Well. Gotta go. Take care of yourself."

"See ya."

Dan waves off and lopes down MacDougal, his bald head gleaming in the afternoon light, the backpack jogging on his shoulder, a cartoon of Derrida ogling through the mesh.

The heat is suddenly oppressive, clammy, and the soot, oil, and garbage late-summer stench of New York is more penetrating than usual. Ineffectual fluffs of cloud lie at random across a dull whitish sky.

Breathing is once again somehow oppressive, as though something is lying on your chest and pushing.

You head broodingly toward the subway for Queens.

"'Ceruza'?" Smuts laughs into the wind, a fleck of saliva on his jaw—"'Ceruza'!"—then he swivels angrily back at them.—"*Zerzura*! Shangri-la, Camelot! The kingdom of Mu of the Sahara! Your 'Ceruza' is a, is a, is a what—a mistransliteration of a myth, a fantasy—the legendary 'Lost Oasis'! It never *existed*." He glowers despairingly at the others, who stare blankly back. "A hundred years ago the great dune scientist and wizard of sand, one R. A. Bagnold, and the romantic 'knight of the desert,' a Hungarian Nazi aviator named (and I kid you not!) Count László Ede Almásy de Zsadány et Törökszentmiklós—better known to you, maybe, as Ralph Fiennes, the frigging 'English Patient' of ancient cinematic history—spent ten years looking for Zerzura and never found a trace, though they were always told you could just see it over the next rise, not a day's camel trek away. It's Ali Baba's cave, the Lorelei of the desert. The Oasis of Little Birds and bird-brained romantics! There was never any such place as *Zerzura*. And I don't care how you spell it on your *map*. We've been chasing a fucking will-o'-wisp. Your friend Amri has been laughing at us. How could we have been such idiots . . . !"

Exhausted, filthy, parched, they stand at the rim of a kind of crater in the sand heaped in a crescent around them. Duden grins like the skull of an idiot.

153

In a huge crater of sand at their feet is a spiral of old fences, built long ago and long ago abandoned, a shield against the invading desert; gradually overcome until the sand has filled most of the crater. Half-buried, the palms rise, pulsing gently in the wind.

You think: *An oasis drowning in sand.*

Duden's eyes stare wildly, his cheeks scarlet with embarrassment. Vivian's face seems drained of blood under her burnished skin. You try not to look at them.

The rest seem to combine incredulity with the vindication of a secret cynicism. The youngsters show their feelings transparently: the redhead sneers in knowing disgust at the wolf, who looks hollow-eyed with a sense of betrayal.

Cecilia stares at Smuts in a kind of self-conscious shock. As if her innocence might save her.

"There's a story about Zerzura," Smuts says, always the professor even in the midst of a disaster. "When you go to the splendid city of Zerzura, which lies upon the desert as white as a dove, you will find on the gate to the city the carving of a bird. Take the key from its beak and open the door to the city. Enter and you will find a great treasure, and a palace in which a king and his queen lie sleeping. Do not approach or wake them, so the legend goes. But don't forget to take the treasure. . . . And took it, somebody sure did!"

You motion toward a cluster of green moving in the wind on the grove's far side.

"The green over there might mean water," you say. "Peter?"

You hardly feel like moving, but you and Peter, always your sidekick of choice despite the slight resentment you can detect in Jack's eyes (not in Cees', which rarely seem to express anything), clamber into the nearest Hummer. The rest look at them blankly. Smuts glares petulantly; he wouldn't mind if they failed, just to prove his point. The group sinks raggedly to the sand, their shadows, first long and narrow, then shrinking down to squat-like silhouettes with nobs for heads.

The grove is smaller than it seemed—narrow and winding, like a snake of grayish green—but the green patch is considerably bigger. The sand there, away from the wind, is shallower, and the palms rise a good deal higher above the sand than did the half-sunken trees to windward.

Way over their heads, fruit hugs some of the trunks. *And that means . . .*

". . . there's water down there!" you say excitedly, gesturing to a depression between the palm trunks. "Our oasis is teeming with riches. The royal couple yet doth sleep!"

When they return, you are surprised the news doesn't cheer the group more. They stare at you as if you'd just said the trees were dead. As though they're too wearied out, or too often disappointed, or both, to be cheered by a mere prospect of survival for a day or two.

They eat a quick cold meal in silence among the palms, washed down with a half-cup of water, and go to sleep almost immediately, as the sun disappears under the horizon; some of them are too exhausted to set up tents and sleep, curled up in the van seats.

One thing: the petty tensions of the group—the professional rivalries, the sexual competition for Vivian's attention, the tiny bits of backbiting, sarcasm, flippancy—seem to have disappeared.

You take a long last look at the sky as it darkens: the palm fronds blank out half the stars even before the moon, just beginning to wane from its full, mad face (you think of Duden's crazy smile), has a chance to rise and erase the rest.

You're bitten by three mosquitoes at almost the same time: one on your neck and two on your right arm. You slap fiercely, then slip under the mosquito netting inside your tent and fall almost immediately asleep.

1:28 p.m.

Her chair is empty. The desk is a little stage for a dozen

plastic figurines, sitting, standing, lying in funny poses at the side of the cube-like monitor and an ergonomic keyboard split like a pair of blessing hands. The mousepad is bright cream yellow (her favorite color after orange), and a photo of herself with a group of friends sits inside a thick, pink frame beside a row of sharpened pencils and a clock with a Betty Boop face. A pair of fluffy rabbit slippers lie near the bottom of her chair.

The corner of the office where she usually sits with her work team is quiet, the light kept low to ward off glare from the computer screens. It seems even darker without her presence. It's been like this for weeks, since her last hospitalization.

A get-well card is taped to the top of the monitor screen between a tiny Barbie-like figure and a raffish Humphrey Bogart. It's been there a week. On top of the monitor is something new: a small pink rose.

Even quieter here than usual. None of her team members is in.

You remember the last time you passed by: she suddenly spun around in her chair and gave you a big loopy smile, spinning in a complete circle back to her computer again with a "Well! That was a nice break!"

I could almost feel the silliness of my grin as I walked back to my desk.

The silly grin has come back. I can feel it.

You have to pass her desk on your way to the conference room to see the big boss.

Suddenly you notice something pinched into the antiglare screen: a folded piece of soft paper, like a napkin, faded, its corner curled like a much-thumbed book page. You remember something but don't have time to check it.

The company has named the conference rooms after the planets: this one is called Uranus, by someone with a curious sense of humor. It is very small and hidden in a back corner, between the supply closet and desktop services. It has the air of a small interrogation cell.

156

You sit down nervously near the speaker phone and contemplate the silence concealing the sullen distrust that has gripped the company since its stock price went into free fall late last year. The only thing you can hear is the hum of a ventilator fan.

You always feel nervous whenever you walk into the company office, and don't feel calm again till you leave four hours later.

A woman you don't know passes by with a sheaf of papers and glances in with startled eyes.

Her eyes are wet as though she'd been crying.

The last mass layoff had been painful, but not as devastating as the first, in January. That one had felt like a massacre, with people openly weeping in the huge, pitilessly open office spaces. The second sweep found people hard-faced and grim. Now everyone works with the adrenaline of rolling anxiety.

To lay off, to divorce, to vacate the premises. When things are inconvenient, go. Loyalty is for the loser. Do unto others before they do unto you. It's as American as apple pie. It's the other side of the American Dream. It's the price of the risk society, the ownership society, where nobody owns anything unless they're a shareholder; it's a "hidden cost" of the land of opportunity. Though it's in extremely bad taste to mention it.

A layoff is like a very cold divorce: sorry, but I have to cut off your means of support. This might mean that some of you may end up homeless. But that's not my problem. I do not love you. I do not even like you. You are no longer useful to me. You are a drag on my balance sheet. Security will accompany you to the exit. Do not be seen within a hundred-foot radius of the building or we will call the police. Have a nice day.

Live scared and make someone else rich. Might be you some day. The law of the jungle is the only law we honor. Your freedom is my slavery. It's good. It's right. It's fate. It's unbeatable. There is no alternative. Adam Smith is the Father, Charles Darwin's the Son, Ronald Reagan's the Holy Ghost. Margaret

Thatcher's the fucking Virgin. For ever and ever and ever. Amen.

An exaggeration? Maybe.

My freedom is your anxiety.

With his false smile—perhaps not false at all, it merely says, "I'm on top," but it always seems false, unless charm is a principal key to his success—Ken Brown sweeps into the tiny room, compressing it even further.

"Ariel Hunter! How are you today?"

Ken Brown, a fleshy man who gives the impression he was once athletic and still thinks he is, deepens his impossible smile. He plunks down a small pile of papers and what looks like your HR file. He smiles even more broadly, if that is possible, as though reassured by your muted reply.

"Well, I'm glad someone is doing well around here." He suddenly gives you a serious, almost solemn, look. He seems uncharacteristically uncertain for a moment how to proceed. His mouth suddenly twists weirdly. Whatever he was about to say, he has decided not to. He stares hard at the papers in front of him.

"Have you tried to get into your computer yet?" His thin eyebrows cock with an odd neutrality.

Tried?

"No, I just got in and came right here after dropping my stuff off at my desk."

Ken Brown considers for a moment, frowning at the papers. Then he snorts, gives a deep, plangent sigh as he turns to you a face suddenly pale and soft, even sad. He pinches his eyes with the requisite look of sincerity he probably learned from management training. "Arik, this is one of the hardest parts of my job." He suddenly looks down and wipes the side of his mouth with his thumb, then looks back up again. *A spontaneous gesture: he might actually be feeling uncomfortable.* "We're going to have to let you go."

Up until now feeling more coolly detached by the moment, you suddenly feel the blood drain from your face, for a moment almost dizzy. You had known this might be coming, but you never actually believed it, even when people were falling around you like bowling pins. Tears fill your eyes. You rebel at them, the shame of them. As long as they don't spill . . .

"Oh?" you say, trying to control your voice.

"Yes." Ken Brown yields to his "I'm on top" smile again, though his eyes continue to pinch with compassion. He looks reassured. "As you know, we've had to make a number of difficult decisions to reorganize over the last year, and as part of that, we have had to reorganize your department, consolidating ontology."

His face freezes, watching your reaction. You almost laugh, out of nerves, at Ken Brown's stupid use of a word he clearly does not understand. *And yet this idiot has the power . . . !*

"Was there anything wrong with my work?" you ask after a moment.

You can hear the croak of weakness in your voice, a sense of pleading you immediately despise. Your last performance review, in late winter, had been excellent.

"No, there's never been any complaint about the quality of your work." Ken Brown's smile deepens. The pinch goes away. It's plain sailing from here. "This is strictly organizational." He almost grins. "The position is being eliminated." The pinch suddenly comes back. His lips drop compassionately. "As you know, in such cases we try to find other positions for the people affected. Unfortunately, we are not able to offer you another position at this time." With a consciously sincere look.

"What about the future." Spoken in a thin, dry tone. At least the tears have held in his eyes, like the water at the brim of an overly full glass.

"That's another matter." Businesslike, a half-smile. "We can't guarantee anything, of course, but it is likely that people who were let go in good standing will be given consideration for any new position." He pauses, then says rapidly, almost worriedly "If they *apply* for it, of course."

159

That must be for pleasing the lawyers.

Brown looks relieved, as if he's gotten through the worst. *I have behaved reasonably, I haven't broken down, shouting and screaming and threatening to sue. I have been "mature," like a good sheep holding my neck up helpfully so the executioner can get his ax in with one quick blow. I loathe you, and I despise myself.*

"We're giving you two weeks notice, but you can go home right now if you like, there's no reason to continue working."

He opens his arms with a generous sweep.

"Right." Your voice is shaky.

Brown pushes some papers toward you after thumbing the top one or two. The words come trippingly off his tongue with barely a pause. He's been through this many times.

"Here's information on unemployment insurance and health insurance, COBRA, I think they call it. HR will set up an appointment with you for an exit interview and for your final check which will include any unused vacation and to collect the forms after you've signed up if you elect to sign up that is."

He beams like Santa Claus. *I am giving you money, a vacation, insurance, the world.*

"I probably will." Your voice is clearer now, discussing technical details.

"Good! Well!" Ken Brown stands, rising to his full six-foot-one-and-a-half-inches. *Height gives power,* flashes across your mind. "If you have any questions, just call or email Amanda at HR. They're the ones with the best information anyway."

In other words, don't bother me.

You get up too, standing awkwardly at the side of the table.

Outside Uranus, a security guard looms just beyond the door. A thirtyish Hispanic with a suspicious look.

"Enrique will help pick up your things." Brown nods cordially, as if the security guard were a special benefit and not a protection against vandalism. "Good luck in all your future endeavors."

He thrusts his hand forward, with a genuinely sincere smile.

You take it firmly, and Ken Brown shakes your hand, smiling hard into your eyes.

You can't help smiling back, then walk away with Enrique in tow.

A twinge as you pass her desk again.

You see the folded paper and stop, pluck it from the anti-glare screen and open it.

"Ariel to Miranda: Take
This slave that will kiss thy lips for the sake
Of him who is the slave of thee"

is written across the wrinkled, frequently unfolded napkin from a Wyoming hotel breakfast buffet in your handwriting, in faded ink, of seven years ago, when you first met her, long before you met her again, by one of the loveliest of all accidents, working in the same office. . . .

You stop and stare at your old scribble, amazed. *So she did find it and she did read it, and she kept it, and she knew, and she never said anything. . . .*

"What you doing? That you property?" Enrique asks gruffly.

"Uh . . . it's okay," you say. "It's a note I once gave the person who sits here."

You lay the napkin carefully on her desk and walk away, your mind bewildered and confused, and filled with a painful feeling of strange, wild joy, yet also of having missed something—or almost missed something, it was a terrifyingly close thing—something immeasurably important, something overwhelmingly good.

You are in a cold room in a stormy Atlantic night in a sleep from which you—a king near the queen you have never seen but who sleeps the same sleep, not an arm's length from you and yet infinitely far away—cannot waken, in a dream from which you cannot emerge. "Sleeping the sleep" then a pause "of the dead," says a woman's voice. The voice is familiar but you can't place it. You're on the verge of remembering when you wake up to a teasingly fresh morning of shadow and brightness and cool air, however evanescent.

Oh God not here. Not now. Let me sleep . . .

You try to go back to your sleep and the dream; gone for good, like all dreams. Back to the sea and the kingdom and the sleeping king and the mysterious sleeping queen, whose eyes have a little fold and the ice-blue of a husky's eyes. . . . Then you hear a strangled cry and panicky shouts.

Your eyes open to the white netting above your face.

It sounded like Cees.

You stagger out into the grove, disoriented at first, unable to place the palms exactly in the dimness, and not even sure where the vans are.

The shouts go on and on, somewhere behind you.

You turn and grope toward a Hummer parked against a wedge of palms. Then you stop: the chubby Dutch boy is struggling frantically up a sand bank, crazily kicking his bare foot, on the end of his heel a snake attached and flipping back and forth, writhing and dancing. His shouts fill the grove. His pants are half off, stretched tight at his knees. It was grotesque. He must have been about to take a dump . . .

"Hold on," you shout, pull open the Hummer's back, rummage but can only find a crossbar. You just manage to grab the base of the boy's jerking, kicking foot and press, and while Cees's other leg kicks at you in panic, trying to fight and flee at the same time, you hammer at the snake with the awkward bar. The crossbar strikes Cees' leg as often as it strikes the snake, a viper. "Sorry!" you shout over Cees' snarls of pain whenever the bar hits wrong. "Sorry!"

It takes almost a dozen strokes before you strike the viper's head, and half a dozen more before the head loosens its grip and the long body, separated from the head, skitters down the sand bank and rolls, a twisting mass of blood and sand and scales writhing in automatic reflex after death, under the van.

The head rolls away, its fangs locked open.

162

Cees keeps shouting, and his foot streams with blood where the fangs penetrated his heel and ankle.

"Roll over, roll over," you shout, taking out your Swiss army knife. "Hold him down!"

By now Smuts, Duden, and the rest have come up, and Smuts and Chad and Sean, leaning against the sand bank, hold Cees, face down, the young golden-haired manboy still in hysterics.

You lean hard on Cees's foot and cut deep gashes into the four holes made by the snake's fangs, and Cees shouts in pain again, twists on his flank and kicks savagely, the other foot landing in your belly, winding you.

"Stop kicking . . . !" you shout.

As the blood flows freely from the enlarged wounds, you take Cees's heel in your mouth and start sucking the blood and spitting it out.

You yell out, "Where's the goddamn bite kit?" and "Stop *kicking!*"

Cees starts to sob. Then suddenly he stops and goes limp.

"He's fainted," yells Chad.

"Keep his head down." You go back to sucking and spitting: how much is enough is hard to tell, and Cees mustn't bleed too much, weakened as he is from little food and water over the last few days.

At one point you stop and hold Cees's foot, still bleeding, between your hands, tightly squeezing to stop the bleeding. Peter has brought up a first-aid kit, and between them, they wind a tourniquet around Cees's thigh, then Peter wraps the foot in an Ace bandage while someone gives you water to wash out your mouth.

Cees is bundled, still unconscious, to your tent, and Vivian volunteers to watch over him.

Duden stays behind.

"There's no bite kit," he says hollowly. "Somebody must have left it at Ouadane."

He walks unsteadily away.

"I think you smashed his ankle with the crossbar," Peter says.

"Right." You spit out the last taste of blood and wipe the bar clean. "It was that or let the snake kill him." After thrusting the bar back under the rug, you wipe your eyes, then look hard into Peter's blistered face, with the crack in his swollen lower lip.

"Poor little Dutchboy," he says. "I never knew he was such a kid."

Vivian and Cecilia watch over Cees—"It's not perfectly PC to nurse—and it's even less PC to let him die," Vivian says coolly to you. "Which he might do if left to the ministrations of the male."

"Look who's being sexist now."

"'Realistic' is more the term."

"Same thing."

She shrugs.

They make no attempt to bring the unconscious boy to.

The need for water is now acute. You drive several of your group to the grove's young palms. Husayn and Umar shimmy up the trunks and Jack catches the fruit they drop. In the meantime Chad and Sean start digging at the drift's low point; Smuts and you help by spreading the dug-up sand away from the pit so the sand doesn't slide back in.

It's slow work. After an hour of digging, the pit shows no sign of water. So they move to another spot and start digging again. That is also dry.

Sean and Chad look worn, too exhausted to be afraid, but already complaining of cramps. They break open some of the palm fruit Husayn and Umar have retrieved and toast each other, with a weak laugh.

After the short break, they dig again, with you and Smuts now in the pit, Sean and Chad at the buckets.

After ten minutes Smuts hits a thick cable of palm root. Just beneath is a thin bed of gray, moist sand.

You grin at Smuts: for the first time, you feel genuinely happy to look at the man's face.

"Are we thirsty yet?" you say and look up at Sean and Chad busy at the lip of the pit the older men are almost head-up in, standing in it.

"Yes?" says Chad, panting.

You grin even more broadly.

"Is that a *question*?" You bend back down with Smuts in the pit, digging at double speed, following the root to a shallow pool that slowly fills the pit bottom with a sludge of wet sand.

An hour later, you've built out the pit enough so you can dip buckets into a pool of dirty water, and you soon fill the water tanks and the Hummer's radiator.

"We can fill the other radiators tomorrow," you say, just before all of you wash up in the shallow muddy well.

"Water is glorious!" Sean, usually so silent, suddenly shouts, his face running with water, to the sky.

The rest give a laugh of relief, with a kind of gleeful, boyish joy.

You and the others return to the camp with lighter hearts than you've had in days.

Once back, Smuts carries a bag of water directly to where Cees is lying in your tent. You follow close behind.

Cecilia looks up at you, her chopped-off hair smeared against her temples, tears streaming down her sun-blistered cheeks. Vivian kneels at Cees's golden blond head, gently smoothing his brow. The pudgy, slightly under-sized body is crooked and still. Vivian doesn't look up at first.

"Nice try," she says gently. She looks at you with great tenderness, her hand coming to rest over the young Dutchman's eyes.

6:37 p.m.

"It was the most humiliating thing I've ever . . ."

To Pam later, at Barney's Bar, on Canal Street.

Pam frowns at him, withdrawn, cool. *So you didn't make the cut,* her silent face seems to say. She looks with detachment into her glass.

Your mind still rings with Ken Brown's words, which have the iciness of a death sentence spoken by a smiley button: forthright, common-sense, perky, brutal.

"Maybe there's some legal recourse," says Pam, almost indifferently. "Have you thought of that?"

"It's 'at-will employment.' They had us all sign an agreement last year. As though they saw the layoffs coming and their lawyers got on their case."

She considers.

"That might be a basis for a class-action suit."

You shrug harshly.

"They tried it already. The first batch out the door. The lawyers said forget about it—take the severance and go."

Pam perks up.

"Are you getting severance then?"

"He didn't say. I have to call HR."

You take a long swallow of beer.

"I was getting sick of that place anyway."

"I know. You certainly talked about it enough."

You look at her sharply.

"You seem to think I shouldn't have."

"It's your job, it's your life. Talk about what you like. Or what you *hate*. It's the same thing."

You glare at her. She stares back with her most queenly look, then looks smoothly away while sipping her cocktail—a red thing in a martini glass.

Your mind goes blank, briefly.

"You won't have to listen to me talk about it anymore now."

"What a relief."

Don't be a bitch.

"Pam. Would showing a little sympathy cost you your goddamn cool?"

She looks crisply down at her drink, twists her lips, then raises her cold eyes to your own.

You look away.

This is turning into a fucking shipwreck...

You flash on the memory of something you saw recently, a photograph of an island in the middle of a storm, a lighthouse weakly beaconing across the sea.

She stares at you as though from a distant planet. But without curiosity.

You suddenly imagine her and Ilan wrestling half naked on a sofa.

"I *am* sympathetic. This is your first layoff. It hurts your ego."

"Of course, it hurts my *ego*. Why *shouldn't* it!"

She waits for you to continue. When you don't, she goes on. With self-conscious patience.

"You should think positive. You'll get unemployment for six months. They often extend it to nine. In the meantime you can concentrate on school and have all of Manhattan as your playground. You should be happy. I wish somebody would lay *me* off."

She looks as if she's about to continue, but thinks better of it and pulls her mouth back in a deep, angry smirk.

You stare down at the beat-up bar top.

Pam. Schwartz. Brown. Miranda. You remember the napkin...

The bar is beginning to fill with after-work types from uptown and after-school types from NYU. The background music has changed, from blues to something electronica with a beguilingly strange, familiar voice.

Pam has turned away, swaying her head to the music. Then you recognize the voice, though not the song, breathy and crazily lyrical...

You make out a few words, repeated over and over: "the hidden place" or "a hidden place." By that cracked, angelic

167

voice you always liked. And you imagine volcanic rock rising in folds of granite, shards of onyx, rocks of whisky-black glass, ascending in a great cold sea. Swept clear of humanity, of all life. No lighthouse beaconing on the ancient coast.

Rock, ice, snow, a black sea, a sky of solid gray. A hidden place.

And over it the odd, sweet singer's voice, softly crooning, almost whispering.

Vesper time. Vespers time. No—it was called something else.

Pam is staring away with her look of general disapproval, a look she has long been master of.

"Do you hear it?" you whisper.

Pam looks at you as if you were a stranger.

"Hear what."

You stare back at her blankly, then go back to your beer.

"How did your rehearsal go. I mean your 'coach-ing.'"

Without skipping a beat, Pam says, in time to the song she has been listening to all along:

"It was in—a wonderful place."

And she looks at you as if to say, And if you don't know what *that* means, you're a bigger idiot than I took you for.

Fuck you. Fuck you. Fuck you.

You play with the edge of the glass's bottom on the counter for a moment, then suddenly pick up the glass and smash it against the bar. Pam flinches, freezing. You walk out to Canal Street. She doesn't follow.

They bury Cees near the heart of the palm grove. It is a brief ceremony. You had written up a short description of Cees's life, with notes from Jack, who seemed to know him better than you or Peter did. You had known him only a few months: Cees had been a newbie from Europe, one of the many cast up by economics, ill-starred romances, frustrated hopes, the melodramas of the young; you'd expected him to get his fill of the desert

168

quickly enough and pack it up back to cooler and wetter climes. Even though Cees had told him early on that Holland "had no future—the rising ocean's going in twenty years to eat it up," he said in his quaint English. He had also said, in his grimly absolutist, youthful way, "If Earth is going to turn into a desert in my lifetime, I might as well get used to living in it now."

He would have lived longer in Amsterdam.

What else had the boy told you? You had wracked your brains and come up with almost nothing.

Peter and Jack lower Cees's unexpectedly heavy and awkwardly slack body, rolled up and zippered into his sleeping bag, into the sand, with the few possessions he had brought along—his clothing, boots, a clutch of indecipherable books in Dutch with soft-porn covers, his razor, toothbrush, soap dish (empty) (Vivian had insisted you include these, even as you had been in the act of throwing them into the trash pit), his coffee mug and utensils, had been zippered into the bag—and they stand in the evening in a circle around the grave.

You speak from a paper hastily scribbled over during the afternoon during talks with Peter, who had hardly ever spoken to the fellow, and Jack.

Jack had stared into space for what felt like five minutes but couldn't have been more than two before he said:

"He hated windmills."

"He what?" you said with a start.

"That's the only thing I'm absolutely sure of. He mentioned it more than once. He just hated them. The wooden ones. He said all the ones left in the Netherlands were fake, put up for tourists. And he hated that. He said the whole country was being turned into a fake for tourists—'bloodsuckers,' he called them. There must have been more to it than that, but that's what he said. 'All my life,' I remember him saying, 'all my life the Netherlands and Europe, it's just turning into a gigantic tourist trap. All past and no future. Total fake.' He hated all that."

You had stared, a bit nonplussed, at your almost blank sheet of paper. You could hardly open your funeral oration with a statement that the deceased hated windmills and thought tourists were bloodsuckers.

Later, you can barely remember what you did say about Cees, though it must have been acceptable, no one seemed to take exception at the time. If they had been listening, which was doubtful. It had been a sequence of vaguenesses and clichés, the hoariest one being, "The earth takes back its own." But what else could be said that had any relevance, any truth, even humanity; that wasn't rancid with untruth? No one had known the boy—now that he was dead, he was "the boy," they would never have called him that when he was alive, it would have been at worst "young man"; but that was the truest word for him, a boy; at the furthest reach a man-boy. No one had known him well: he was just one of the crew, taken relatively for granted as long as he performed, noticed only when he was needed, or managed to disappear *when* he was needed. Had you even liked him or disliked him? You can't say. You try to see his face, as it was when he was alive, but now, after the funeral, all you can see is the face dead, at Vivian's knees, with her hand on his forehead.

So young . . .

Your eyes open.

There's nothing I can say about it except there is nothing I can say about it. I just keep repeating it. I must keep repeating it. I feel that I must. Death is loss, pure and simple, terribly pure and repulsively simple. It's a little nothing torn from, from everything. Where there was a body with memories, fears, angers, hopes, purposes, but who knows what they were, he was still learning them himself—there is now only skin, bones, organs, meat, a few undependable memories in other people's heads, a few personal belongings that will be scattered, sold, burn, rot. A corner is wiped clean and awaits a new occupant, or no occupant at all; not waits, is available again. A biological niche is opened up. For another temporary occupant. Until . . .

170

But however temporary, briefly—oh briefly—alive.

You forgot to offer a prayer. You knew you had forgotten something. That was important. If anybody needed a prayer, you did, all of you. And you had forgotten.

You focus through the darkness on the ceiling of your tent through the mosquito netting.

Suddenly you see his face, alive: the expression is his usual one, of a kind of blank good will, awaiting orders; well-meaning, but closed in on itself: bright blond, dark blue eyed, with child-fatty cheeks and a lumpy shapeless nose. Ugly in the Dutch way.

You feel a little guilty for not feeling more grief than you do. In fact you feel no grief at all. Just a kind of dull numbness.

"Sorry, Cees," you say aloud to the top of the netting, which peaks just above your head. You begin to mumble the Lord's Prayer under your breath, the only prayer you know.

You had looked over at Vivian at the end of the ceremony: she was standing with her head bent over the grave, her face open with a deeper and more complex grief than any you, surely, had felt, and you had been struck once again by the thought of how she reminded you of someone you had once known.

It hits you, now, in the darkness.

The girl you had known twice so briefly, who perished during that week when life's savagery opened to him, and to many others, its hellish maw. And you feel an overwhelming sorrow.

9:52 p.m.

The crowd at Todd's is still thin when you arrive. The DJ, Bad Tomás, in dreads and a floppy cap despite the heat, is scratching and looping samples from a couple of disks from the late '90s, his face already shut down in concentration between thick headphones. A few knots of people in trip-hop tags enliven the corners. The central dance floor is still empty; the kegs have just been opened.

171

You stand with a can of Red Bull, brooding off to the side.

After a while the room begins to fill. Corey brings the pot, and you stand on the fire escape smoking in the cool night air.

The lights of Bleecker Street shine in the distance.

Shaking your mind to forget, for a few hours, the day's damage, you shift from spot to spot, trading small talk with people you don't know. Mostly students, undergrads and grad grinds like yourself, a few ex-dotcommers gone back to school after the crash. Some Ogladytes you keep your distance from. The air is subdued, not like the late wigged-out '90s, when everyone expected to be a millionaire before reaching 30. The laptop projections, slipping, sliding, shape-shifting along the walls are tweaked to be a tad less exuberant, have a lightly nasty edge, of bitterness. *The self-pity of Gen X. First generation of billionaire slackers. So what are we, the ones following? Gen Y? Gen Why? Gen You? Gen Who? Gen Web? Gen Rim? As in, rim of the volcano, dancing on. Gen Lost. Another one.*

Sooo last century.

But then we won't even have our own decade.

The Zeros?

You go inside.

Pam shows up, with Ilan.

Bitch.

You keep a wall of crowd between you and them.

Little Miriam, with her blond half-head buzz cut, walks by, passing out tabs of "natural ecstasy."

"Par-*tay*!" she shrieks in falsetto, her eyes goggling.

You take one, slip it into your back pocket.

Dan's bringing the coke. *That* will put this party on the road.

You take a couple of cold Jaegermeister shots and follow them with a Rolling Rock.

The DJ's pounding is unrelenting. The crowd on the dance floor rocks together with it, each dancing alone yet connected to everyone else through the DJ's beat.

Fuck 'em all. I'm gonna dance.

You join the dance in free form, defiant, alone, dancing with everyone to the DJ's thumping bass, scratch electronica, smearing vocals.

Hey, it's like a Jackson Pollock but with sound.

"*You*, man, are a *genius!*" someone beside you shouts to the DJ as you contort and writhe with the rest on the dance floor. Then you realize it was yourself.

Toward midnight you wander back to the fire escape. "Wander" is the right word: in the state you're in, Todd's has turned into a vast dark jungle of writhing tribalists, a jungle swallowing you in, you're beyond pain, sucked into the groove, you go with the flow wherever it go, it takes you fifteen minutes to negotiate the walk to the toilet, and another fifteen minutes to find the way to the fire escape again. Which is packed with smokers of tobacco and weed.

You find yourself in a corner against cool iron and look down the street, toward shining Bleecker. Beyond, to the west, the twin towers stand, ugly and serenely arrogant, columns of money and power, monoliths lined with light. The antenna on the north tower blinks rhythmically in a sharp point against the deep gray Manhattan sky.

You look straight up. New York's sky is never quite black. *The city that never sleeps is a city that never knows the night.* You consider this a particularly profound insight, and are repeating it to yourself a few times when you notice Amos Bernstein standing at the far end of the fire escape, crying.

You know Amos from Oglala. He works in Miranda's team. A specialist in sports, of all things. A quiet, diligent type. Gay.

The sight of him weeping so openly is embarrassing. Maybe you should at least acknowledge he's there?

You don't know him that well . . .

You look away, then back.

Amos has seen him, pulls himself together, tries a smile. Despairing.

"Hey."

"Hey."

Amos stares at you for a long moment, his face bright with tears, as if waiting for something. Then looks away, hastily wiping his face.

Doesn't want to deal. Why should he with a practical stranger.

I don't want him to think . . . what, exactly?

When you look back Amos has disappeared inside.

You look at your watch. 12:27. Dan should be here soon.

You go back in, suddenly feeling impatient.

Another beer. Another hour of dancing, this time partly with Tina, who has always shown a liking for you, though she doesn't do much for you, frankly. Eventually you dance off into a corner, by yourself.

You've managed to avoid Pam and Ilan, miraculously. *Unless they've left and are fucking back in his studio.*

Fuck. Fuck. Fuck.

There's no more Jaegermeister so you chug another Red Bull, then go out with a second toke from Corey.

1:48. *Where the hell is Dan.*

You flip open your cellphone and call Dan's number; the call goes immediately to his voice mail. Then you call for your own messages.

"Hello, Ariel?" It's a woman's voice that at first you don't recognize. You cup your ear closer to the phone to keep the music from drowning it out. "This is Lisa, Sally Wild's team lead. I have some very bad . . . "

You can't hear it. You press your hand against your other ear.

" . . . to tell it to you personally since you were such a good . . . . "

Again you can't hear. You re-key the number, cover your ears with your shirt collar, and push yourself as far into the balcony corner as you can.

" . . . passed away early this morning from complications caused by the . . ."

You are staring blankly up at the towers, the tall antenna blinking somnolently in the dark early hour.

Your face knots into a savage grimace. Then the blood drains from your face.

No . . . no . . .

Your re-key and listen again to the message. There is a lull in the pounding DJ mix.

You shake the phone, staring at it, confused, suddenly enraged.

. . . No! . . . No! . . .

You grab the other side of your head and bend down farther, pressing the phone against your ear, though no longer listening as the message repeats, then abruptly ends with a click. More messages are read back to you, one of them from Dan, but you register none of them.

. . . early this morning?. . . when I was waking up? . . .

You remember the gleeful look on Miranda's face in the dream you had just before waking. And her abrupt turning away, as though someone was calling her.

Inside your head a silence expands.

No! You can't, you aren't allowed to . . . not . . . you, not . . .

You're drunk, you're high. *You can't . . .*

You remember Amos weeping on the fire escape.

You have to go. You can't stay here, you have to get out.

You walk straight across Todd's floor.

It seems to take forever.

The DJ's pounding thumps have returned in full, cool relentlessness; you feel like your legs are made of sand, fighting your way through the music. You walk straight through the crowd, bumping through people, repeating mechanically, "Sorry sorry sorry sorry . . ." You get to the door. You walk through the door. Then you walk, concentrating heavily, down the steps to the street.

"Hey, Hunter! You lost or something?"

You look at Dan.

"You're white as a sheet. You on bad drugs?"

You stare back at him.

You grab Dan and pull him with him.

"Come on. Come on. Come on."

"The Oued-Edeyen road—and it *was* a road, with macadam—sometimes, that is!—and even signs," Duden says from his perch against a van's tire; he's fresh after sleep, a wash-up in the sand well, and a bellyful of the oasis water, "wasn't far south of here. If I'd known Amri's map was so fallible, I might have chanced it. Not that I'm blaming you," he turns to you.

You frown and shrug from your squat.

Vivian folds her arms tightly across her chest where she kneels in the sand.

"We can't stay *here*," she says.

The rest hover nearby, looking at each other, considering their situation or pretending to.

They have water and food supplies, and gas from the abandoned van. They even have a little time. Very little.

"Maybe we can," Smuts suggests. "Maybe we should. Settle in and wait for visitors . . ."

"I don't think so." You raise your head with what you hope is a sagacious look, not the vacant-eyed blankness you feel. "There are no firepits, there's no trash, no clearing, nothing's been disturbed. No sign anyone else has been here since the last sand storm. Not even camel shit." You peer up briefly at the sun, peering in light bursts through the fronds. An unusually frothy sky full of clouds surrounds the sun and hangs over them, mockingly gray-bellied, promising unlikely rain. "We can always come back here, of course."

"Exactly," Smuts says, with a little snarl. "You can tell Amri when we get back that his map wasn't entirely wrong. Just off by a hundred miles and a couple of centuries."

176

"I'll be sure to let him know," you say, "when we get back."

"Well. Unless anyone else has a better idea?" Duden waves his depressed chin authoritatively from right to left.

He has, at least briefly, vanquished his shame.

Their movements are ponderous, mechanical, as they pull themselves from the ground and pack to leave.

Less than an hour later, the caravan moves out . The prevailing wind kicks up as they rise from the half-buried oasis.

Soon afterward, as they cross the shoulder of a dune, Vivian points east. "Look."

In the distance a cloud piles up an anvil head into the high air; from it a gray column falls, perpendicular, to the ground.They can see lightning charge once or twice between cloud and earth, bright cracks in the air. It's too far away to hear the thunder. "Rain in the desert," she says.

"Yes," says Duden. "Nature's irony."

"If you want to see a real dose of nature's irony," you say, "catch a rain storm in the middle of summer: the rain coming down in buckets and evaporating before it reaches the ground, obscenely beautiful, absolutely useless."

Within a mile, the sand dissipates into a plain of uneven paving-stone-like rocks.

And before you, a lake appears, shimmering with intense silvery brilliance, boulders strewn across it, reflected upside down.

After the distant downpour, it's hard to convince yourself it's all an illusion. It looks so completely convincing: a vast lake inviting you in for a swim. Its near edge vanishes just as you approach it.

Everybody's too quiet.

"When the disciples saw Jesus walking on water," you say, "could it have been a mirage? Like this one."

Duden says nothing.

"The disciples were in a boat at the time," says Vivian. "So the mirage must have been pretty convincing."

A pause.

177

"But if you want to give them the benefit of the doubt," she adds.

"How do you mean?"

"That they genuinely did think he was walking on water."

"And not as if he did."

She pauses.

"Is that your theory?"

"I avoid theories," you say.

"Oh? How about faith?"

"Even more. I'm suspicious of anything that's been made by people."

Duden glances at you with an enigmatic look in his eye.

They are quiet for a time.

Vivian speaks up again.

"Do you think this part of the Sahara was man-made?"

"Hold on," you say, as they lurch across a depression in the rocks. When they've steadied again, you answer.

"They called it Rome's bread basket. Some basket! Some bread! The desert west of here was farmland, pastures, covered with roads, towns. They over-grazed it, over-farmed it, over-irrigated it, then one day the desert marched all the way to the sea. That's one story, anyway. But I thought you knew all about that."

Vivian pauses, then says, dryly, "That was after my time. The more important question is will it ever come back."

"It's had a long enough time, if it wanted to." You glance around at the parched landscape. "But it doesn't look good."

"A debunked theory," Duden brusquely perks up. "Under the Tanzerouft, south of here—'absolute desert,' they call it, a desert within the desert, a gravel hardpack the size of Arizona—there's a layer of dormant soil, rich enough to feed Italy for a century, thousands of years old and just waiting to break out. All it needs," he cracks a grin, "is water."

"Exactly," says Smuts.

"And guess what?" Duden turns bodily toward you, with

178

a desolate grin. "A thousand feet below *that* there's an entire formation saturated with said miraculous liquid. A little salty, and not exactly the best thing to drink with your scotch, but good enough for prehistoric spores. This desert is like a layer cake that has all the elements of life in it, in sealed compartments, walled off from each other by heat, bad choices, and geology. There's nature's irony for you! It beats man's clever stupidity by a long chalk. Of course,"— He goes back to staring ahead through the windshield.—"it doesn't help that half the Tanzerouft is radioactive from atomic testing by the French last century. So maybe the irony of man beats it after all."

You walk, hard and fast, preternaturally aware of your surroundings and inwardly silent and vacant, dimly aware of your friend walking at your side in the half-darkness of the East Village.

You have been waiting for this phone call for weeks. Perhaps since she first told you months ago about the tumor.

You have been playing a game with yourself. You have allowed yourself to be deceived. You have allowed yourself to be blind. You have blinded yourself.

"Arik, wait up! Can we sit down a second?"

How long have they been walking?

The two of you sit on the white marble stoop of a brownstone, near a street lamp and a tree winking dustily through the light. A breath of wind cuts through the leaves. No traffic, no pedestrians.

A taxi pulls into the street and passes them, taking home a late bar patron, probably.

"Cig?"

"Yeah."

They light up. Natural American Spirit. That used to make you smirk. Natural poison.

The sound of a plane rolls across them from the night sky. A late flight from Asia maybe. A long, drawn-out, slightly light-toned peal of thunder: a dry, throaty tenor sound peeling off to a low, mellow rolling bass before dying away to silence. In the pauses between sighs, sounds of shifting limb or clothing between the two friends, the high whine of air molecules against the ear drum. So quiet, here. Strange for Manhattan. Not even a far-away siren.

You look up and see a billboard brightly lit on the top of a building several blocks away. You remember seeing an ad poster like it somewhere: it shows a large cut-glass bottle of cologne or perfume, with a desert of yellow sand rolling into the far distance beneath a brilliant sun—shot with a star filter so that rays of light extend from it like a cross made of brilliant daggers—and with letters, cut off at the top, that seem to read A L S A R A B printed across the enormous photo.

You curl up on the stoop.

Dan isn't always so good a listener, sometimes he'll zone out after the first few words or change the topic while you're in mid-sentence, his own life is so full of epiphanies and collisions, but tonight, or this morning, he's quiet, silent, perhaps it's just exhaustion and he forgot to take his coke, was saving it for the party, whatever; he's attentive and waits for you to speak.

In the middle of the second cigarette on the stoop, you tell him. Tell him about how you had been waiting for this news without knowing it. And you mention this morning waking up with her name on your lips, the dream she was in.

You tell Dan what you hadn't told Pam. About your meeting in the Far West and meeting again, by chance, working at the same company in Manhattan.

You tell him how you'd told Pam nothing about knowing Miranda before. You and Miranda kept the friendship inside the office. Miranda had a new girlfriend she always introduced as her fiancé (she always wrote it with one "e," as if the other "she" was the husband, and Miranda the queen bee), with a giggle and a whoop as if she herself could hardly believe it.

Then, less than a month after you met her again, toward the end of last year, she told you over lunch one day, with a shrugging insouciance that masked what must have been a state of panic: a mole on her back, which she'd never even seen, had been discovered one day during a routine exam, and when biopsied, found to be malignant.

At the beginning she was very brave, turning it into a running joke: her humor, always a little goofy, often sharp, turned devastating. People at work often passed along her emails. Whenever someone sitting solemn and silent at their computer broke out into a squeal of laughter, likely as not it was over an email from Miranda.

She was a favorite, and fully aware of it, and nobody had resented it, or could, now. As she became increasingly frightened, she became even funnier.

Months followed of a chemo regimen that sapped, then erased her energy. She moved slowly around the office, her face gray, puffy from steroids. Her eyes—ice blue, with an unexpected epicanthal fold over them, which gave her the look, as she once called it, of an "Irish Apache"—looked terrified above the latest joke on her lips.

Periodically she went into the hospital. Usually she would be back in a week or two.

The last time she went in was a month ago.

By then you were working part-time as you prepared for the new school term. You hadn't let yourself make the clear and obvious deduction.

"That's not surprising. Since you hadn't let yourself in on the big secret yet."

Dan's words have come out of the blue. Or the shadowy darkness of Alphabetland surrounding you.

You look directly at your friend.

"What do you mean."

"That you're in love . . ."

You look vaguely startled.

"Everyone's in love with her."

Dan gazes at you. Looks down, twists his face, looks back. his mouth pinched with concern, but in his eyes an irresistible grin. He wants to laugh.

"That's the sign. When you think everyone's in love with her—well, you're *gone*. No wonder Pam's pissed at you. She must have known for a long time."

"We never . . ."

"Sure. You didn't have to." Dan looks up at the night. "Don't ask me how they know these things, they just do. Now, if you had just been sleeping with her. . ."

"I *never* slept with her."

"Exactly." Dan looks at him. "It was more serious than that."

They sit together on the stoop for a time, staring in opposite directions.

"I have to go home," you say, standing abruptly. The word "home" has a slightly acid taste.

Dan peers up at you.

"You'll be all right?"

"Yeah. Yeah."

"You're sure?" Dan is looking at you closely, standing next to you, almost breathing in your face. Strange: you don't remember seeing Dan stand up. You must be more tired than you realize.

"Yeah. I'll be all right." Your words are detached and too quick. You find it hard to look your friend in the eye.

He reaches over and hugs you, slapping you once on the back. Then he looks at you, keenly, one more time, then turns, flips his hood over his bald head, and heads back, toward Bleecker.

Once, about thirty feet off, he turns, points at you, and shouts, "Go home!" He turns and walks a few more feet, turns and shouts, "And don't leave without telling me!"

"Shut the fuck up down there!" a voice yells from above.

You look up toward where the voice came from, see nothing, then look down as Dan's gray hoody with "Nirvana Next" on the back disappears into the darkness.

You are suddenly alone on the silent street. You look back up at the billboard, with its vast landscape of sand seen through bars of Roman lettering under a stark artificial light. Near the bottom are the words "Succumb to the mirage."

You can't stay where you are, and feel a numb compulsion to move, so you head east toward the river, your head bent toward the ground, your mind a buzz of exhaustion, grief, anger, and hyper-caffeinated energy.

Talking has helped. There may be something to the talking cure. Then, as you walk, you feel a sucking emptiness pulling at the back of your mind, a vacant, obsessive howl of *No! no! no!* and a tide of fury, your mind opening like a lament, and you nearly stumble to your knees, tears streaming down your face.

In a few minutes you are at a park along the East River, and you cross it in a darkness dotted with overly bright lamps. You glower at the vegetation, benches, trash barrels, half expecting a mugger, drug addict, hooker with a trick, at least a homeless to appear in the shadows. But there's no one else there.

You reach the cement wall above the river and lean against it, staring through your tears across the river at Brooklyn, its lights and darknesses and silences in the gray New York night.

You feel a thudding, empty fury smote with lashes of grief. But fury at *what*, at *whom*?

You lift your face higher, until you are looking almost straight up at the deep charcoal sky with its handful of stars. The moon has long gone.

"Damn you, damn you, damn you," you say, or think you say, or just think. "Damn you, damn you, God! . . . You *fucker!*"

You must have shouted the last words, you can feel the back of your throat tight and abraded after the final word's harsh, drawn-out snarl.

You remember the note you wrote so many years before

and that you found sitting on her desk. "Ariel to Miranda: Take
..." Again your eyes stream with tears. And you say aloud: "...
this slave that will kiss thy lips for the sake . . . of him who is
the slave of *thee*."

You thrust your hands over your face, but then pull up, wiping the tears from your face with your sleeve.

"No. I won't let you . . ." you say aloud in a gurgling voice.
"I will not let you . . . Not let you . . . Not let you . . . Not let . . ."

You almost break, then seize up again, pulling yourself
together. Then you stare blankly, vacantly across the river, at
where you think the water meets the opposite bank. You sniffle
from the phlegm in your nose and again wipe your face. After a
few minutes, your feelings seem to go numb. You lift your stare
to the cone of a distant street light over a section of street; a car
passes through the cone, and you wait for the next car, counting
the seconds, one at a time, in a slow whisper to yourself:

"... 7, 8, 9, 10 . . . 256, 257, 258 . . ."

At one point you lose count—were you at 561 or 651 when,
finally, something passes through the unwavering cone of light.
It looked like a truck—was it? —you're not sure, lulled as you
have become into a kind of trance by the silence of the night
and your methodical counting.

Time to go home.

The Red Bulls have worn off, and you're too tired for either
anger or grief. You head out of the park, staggering like a drunk.

"What brought you *here*?"

The two of you squat on a boulder with a long shadow pointing away from the setting sun. Vivian is watching you with a
deeply serious look. Beneath and around the two of you is a tangle of wadis the caravan has parked in and among—somewhat
dangerously but unavoidably, at least for tonight. Tufts of drinn
grass and one or two gnarled figures of acacia, a hardly more
vibrant medlar, draggle at the edges of the dried-out channels.

You both crouch down under the rock, out of the wind.

The sky shows a regatta of clouds dabbed like a baroque ceiling in an immense cathedral.

"A need to escape," you say. "I needed to find something that wasn't where I was."

"What were you looking for?"

"I don't know. I thought I'd know when I found it. . . . Maybe I was just running away."

"From what?"

You frown, look out across the desolate landscape.

"Family. 'Friends.' My workmates and schoolmates and roommates and country mates. Home. The silliness, the stupidity, the irresponsiblity of money. The war without shame. My life. My weaknesses, my stubbornness, my self-indulgence. Myself."

"Did you succeed?" she asks.

You snort and grin.

"We're everywhere. *I*'m everywhere—everywhere I go, that is?"

In the shadows of the evening, she looks even more like Miranda. The planes of her face, the bone structure, even the epicanthal fold over her eyes. But thinner, bonier, ruddier. The softness gone. The giddy, untested confidence. Only the hair is wrong: not a smooth orangey red, it's a rich auburn. And there is no goofy, carefree joy, only a kind of bleak sadness, a curious, probing wariness.

"Well," you say after considering some more. "Partly, I guess. The part I could escape, I did. The part I couldn't escape, I didn't."

"You'll go back?" She pauses. "It *has* changed. Though not always for the better."

"I may. I'll have to, I suppose. I have this recurring dream. I'm on an island off the coast somewhere. I live there alone. Walk the beach, fish, watch the sea, follow the birds. Trying not to leave my print behind. That's all. Weathering storms. Watching the ocean. Trying not to inflict any damage, any more

185

damage than I have to. In one dream I'm walking down the beach, and I suddenly make the mistake of stopping and turning around. The line of my footprints runs down the sand to where I'm standing. And I don't know whether to laugh or cry!" You pause, glance at her: her eyes glow in the last sunlight. "Whatever I do, I leave a mark. All I can do is hope it doesn't cause too much damage." You look away. "I'm only taken here on sufferance. Tolerated. Useful for the time being. It was as far from home as I could imagine."

"You talk as if the whole country's home. Did you ever think . . ."

"There was something about it that just made me furious, something I couldn't take. Maybe it was me! I was being super-seded, maybe that's it. Or maybe I was trying to remove my own bad seed. If I ever had any leanings toward Catholicism, the world I lived in would have been enough to prove, to me at any rate, the existence of original sin. But I don't. And that makes it worse. The world's now our fault. There's nobody else to blame for it. Not God, or nature, or our enemies."

"You're more of a patriot than you realize."

"I was a patriot once. I was a child of the Reagan era. I swallowed his line whole. It was inspiring, perfectly attuned to a six-year-old mind. Freedom is such a seductive word."

"Like love."

He continues without hearing her. "I think of America as having this double soul. One of them is a twelve-year-old girl, with a heart of gold and dreams of happiness and love forever. The other is a cross between a snake-oil salesman and a revival preacher. And a sadistic thug. And they feed off each other's perpetual disillusion and eternal spring of hope. The country of life, liberty and the pursuit of happiness had become a country of lies, egotism and self-deception. The entire place was in love with its fantasy of itself. Who can hate a naive twelve-year-old who has such marvelous dreams? But my God what it perpe-trates while stumbling toward wisdom. Or is it just the skill to lay traps for the next gullible generation? I moved away to clean my mind."

"I think America doesn't have a double soul, it has a million souls. It has souls that haven't been born yet. It has the whole future for its soul."

The sun disappears beneath the horizon.

"What future?"

She says nothing.

"The sin isn't original with us," you continue. "We're in the crap too deep—we're too much part of the evil we're sinking in. Adam was made from the mud, and the mud clings to us till we finally melt back into it."

Vivian shrugs irritably in the quickly falling darkness.

"That all sounds too neat. And convenient!"

You give her a sharp look.

"'Convenient'?"

"Yes. A convenient form of pessimism. It gets everyone off the hook. Especially *you*. You're not the first man I've heard talk this way, and it took me a while to figure out why."

You give a look of mock surprise. You can barely see the details of her face in the quickly falling darkness.

"You mean this isn't the first time you've heard this. You mean I'm being—gasp! —a plagiarist?"

She laughs.

"Sorry, darling, there's nothing original about it. Men like to keep in touch with their inner Eeyore. Tell me: does it give you guys a feeling of strength to look at the bleakest possible side of things? 'I'm so tough, I won't be fooled by anything, I can take total despair.'"

You smile into her disappearing face.

"Touché."

"Who said, 'Pessimism of the intellect, optimism of the will'?"

Touché again.

"An Italian. A hero for me till I lost most of my hopes. A Marxist and communist. Guy named Gramsci."

187

"Hm. Never heard of him."

"Of course not! You grew up in America," you snarl gaily at her.

"Well. From Reaganite to communist—that's quite a leap. And by the way, I grew up partly in Sasketchewan, which hasn't been annexed yet."

"I've always had a soft spot for Marx, but I was never a communist. Though it's only to be expected, before I settled down into crypto-Catholic nihilism."

You can feel her frown cheerfully next to you, rather than see it.

"And how does *that* go, podner?"

You flinch at that before going on.

"One day, a group of very smart apes woke up with the power to master the earth. So they did. Unfortunately, one thing they forgot was what to do with their shit, so one day they woke up drowning in it. We're hardly masters of the universe, we can't even master ourselves. If any creature needed a god to save it, we're it. A god—a sentient, intelligent being immensely more powerful and wiser than we can ever hope to be. But we can't find this being. Anywhere. And we have been looking for a long time. It may not even exist. In fact, it probably doesn't exist. It's like starving for a food that never was. Strange! How could that be? But there it is! Without it, we die. It's like water. We need it to exist. Yet we seem to have been born in a desert."

Vivian has almost entirely vanished beside him on the rock.

"Not to insult your ego, but don't despair. What you describe has been suffered by anyone before the relief for their suffering was discovered, or invented. Maybe that's our job: to create the gods that will save us."

And what if we corrupt them, you think without speaking, with our touch.

"We're getting awfully deep. Must be the moonlight. Maybe it's time to turn in." You pull yourself back up into the night breeze curling around the back of the rock you both have been leaning against. "Thanks for the bullshit session," you say, the wind flapping your collar. "Haven't had so much fun talking trash since I left school."

She looks at you.

"Anytime," she says softly, with a smile you can barely see.

You are shaken awake by a crashing of what sounds like a train roaring past or a plane taking off not a dozen yards away. You blink open your eyes in the dark, half thinking it's another nightmare. Then muffled yells force you up and you scramble half naked out of the tent.

The sound is already receding, like the rush out of a tide, a distant ocean-like sigh. The yelling has stopped.

A shape stands near your tent, staring over the edge of a wadi. You go up to it; it's Sean, standing in his underwear, shivering in the stiff night wind.

He gapes at you in the moonlight with a terrified look.

"They're gone," he says. And he looks back down.

You can see clearly below them a shining bed of wadi, wet with mud and strewn with newly deposited gravel and small scattered boulders. Near the center lies a Hummer knocked over on its side and washed with gravel and mud. The tents where Duden and Jack and Chad had been sleeping are gone. The sound of the flash flood has fallen, leaving the sounds of water draining out of puddles, down gullies, and the desert wind.

"What was that?" You hear Vivian's voice behind him.

You turn and reflexively clasp her in your arms.

An hour passes during which you futilely scout the wadi in the moonlight for signs of life or remains, even of the tents. But you find nothing but a gunny sack, caught against a rock, filled with salt tablets, and then someone's hat, probably Duden's, wet and stuck in the mud, then picked up by a breeze and rolling down the wadi too fast to retrieve it.

You all return to your tents and the vans, making sure

they're secured on elevations to protect them from further flood bursts.

Peter crouches outside his tent. Smuts holds his head in his hands in an attitude almost of contrition or prayer. Cecilia and Sean, who have until now avoided closeness beyond the usual professional banter, sit for a while wrapped silently in each other's arms.

"You should get some sleep," you say, approaching them from behind.

They glance up with vacant eyes and immediately gaze back down at the wet, empty wadi.

"I hate this place," Cecilia says with a flat calmness you have never heard from her. As though the child in her has suddenly died.

Umar and Husayn are the only ones who seem able to sleep: Umar, after gazing over the wadi in the moonlight with a mournful look, had knelt down and bowed three times to the east, bending his head till it met the ground, and is now curled up, sleeping, on his prayer rug. Husayn had returned as quickly as possible to his radio, still receiving a flicker of rai through the static, and gluing the radio to his ear.

The moon, its edge eaten by shadow, lights the plain with a bony glow.

Vivian stares at you outside your tent in the moonlight, and you go up and clasp her once more in your arms, though whether it is for her or for yourself, you don't really know. Then you pull her gently first into the tent and then into the sleeping bag.

"What's happening? What's going on? What's happening?" she sobs, repeating the words obsessively.

You stare into the darkness, your mind spinning about nothing.

Every so often, in little nightmarish stabs, you imagine sharply, mingling with your memories of the sounds, the water crashing down the wadi in the night and sweeping over the three men: the "irony of nature," as Duden had put it, these

190

unpredictable walls of water from distant rains suddenly flooding the desert. And you shake your head impatiently in the dark, fighting the temptation to go out and keep looking for them, absurd and hopeless as you know it to be, between vacant obsessions and nightmares, until a gray dawn shadows the tent flap and you fall finally, with Vivian, asleep.

7:13 a.m.

The sun is rising as you ascend the subway stairs. You'd gotten one last surge of energy and are able to hold yourself and behave almost naturally (you think) as you negotiate the subway, turnstiles, stairs, though you have to work against the flow of early commuters headed for Manhattan, including the man in the silver gray suit who stepped on your foot the day before, and now the Brooklyn streets of early morning.

You pass the same homeless man with the gash over his eye, begging at the top of the stairs, pass the fence covered with posters of the young singer tilted upside down with her nutty smile. You pass down the street to the first intersection, cross at the light, then go left, walk a block, maintaining yourself rather well, you think, then go right, for a block, then left again, a few doors down to your small apartment building. You walk up the stairs to the fourth floor, and stagger a bit as you walk in the door.

You pass the window and look briefly out at Lower Manhattan, the towers sparkling in the sun of a beautifully cloudless September morning.

Strait is the gate and narrow the way.

A reflection from the sun flashes off one of the top stories.

You throw off your clothes.

You feel something in your back pocket, reach in and take it out. It's Tina's tab of natural ecstasy. You stare at it stupidly for a moment, then carefully put it on the chipped child's bureau— the one Pamela and you scavenged from the street last spring, "all-natural stress, Martha Stewart would love it," as Pam put it—next to Pam's black hair-squeegee.

191

But Pam isn't home.

You are too tired to care.

You must sleep.

You pull down the blinds and get into bed. The alarm clock says 7:48 in red digital lights.

You'll have to get up in six hours for Derrida.

"Forget Foucault" and screw Derrida!

You laugh grimly to yourself and sink into sleep as your head sinks into the pillow.

Your dream fills with the nagging face of Schwartz. No matter what you do, you can't shake that gentle, relentless smile. The slightly irritating voice keeps repeating: "You can't do Mars, you can't do Mars," obsessively, maddeningly. You're trying to shout, "Yes I can, yes I can," but nothing comes out of your mouth. You try running away instead, through a maze of corridors in an endless building, with Schwartz in pursuit: "No you can't!" Run on and on, the air getting hotter; it's sweaty, suffocating. Then suddenly you levitate, flying, in a jeep, high above a land you don't recognize, the views superb, a magnificent sky open before you. Netscape's little earth spins in the rearview mirror as you sail into the clouds. Then you hear a voice that sounds like your mother's telling you to come down for dinner. You drop precipitately, plunging toward the globe which is suddenly frozen in its rotation at a spot just off the coast of Africa, the jeep disappears and you land gracefully, a little regretfully. And find yourself in front of a window looking out over an unknown city.

An enormous fist falls toward the city. You hear a sound like a deep booming crash and wake.

The room is calm and dark except for morning light showing around the edges of the blinds. Shouting comes from the street.

"Holy shit! Holy shit!"

You almost laugh and immediately fall back to sleep.

A pile of dog-doo appears briefly on a golden baroque

altar table, which dissolves into a drift of sand blanketing a lighthouse, and a breeze stirs the hair over someone's mouth, someone you don't recognize but who answers to the name of "Wanda."

You're walking hurriedly down a beach, looking for something, but it is an odd beach, there's no sign of the sea though you can smell decaying clams and half-rotten seaweed. You walk under a sky full of umbrellas, past driftwood, toward a wrecked ship in the distance, half-sunk under a sand dune, which looks like a collapsed circus tent blown across it. After a while, you stop and look around you, breathing deep the smell of the ocean. "Succumb," someone near you says.

You feel impatient.

Yes, right, but there's something else about it that . . .

The ocean smell has vanished, the beach has vanished . . .

What is it, what's happening, something's happening . . . Get up get up. Get up.

A hip-hopper dances on the edge of a wharf, a young ballet dancer stands on point with her nose raised snootily toward the sky, a man with a huge apricot on his head and a wiry mustache stares fiercely at you from a passing train, a man in silver armor stands on your foot till you shout. The man turns and stares at you with black holes for eyes. A computer mouse crawls out of his nose.

Then Ken Brown gazes down at you benignantly from the top of a huge skyscraper. Why, it's King Kong! And he lowers his great hairy face as close as your nose, grins a huge grin, and says, "We have to let you go. We have to let you go. We have to let you go. We have to let you go. So sorry we have to let you go!"

Then you see her. She is sitting silently on a rock, her orange-red hair pulled back in a French twist, and looking away from you, a dark red rose perched above her ear. She quietly turns toward you her startling eyes, and when she sees you, she seems surprised: her face breaks out in gleeful happiness, like a child, like the sun. She sings out to you with a kind of crazy joy, "Azrael to Zirpanda shake 'tis mave of juicy for the take off Wanda Wanda Wanda whee!"

A meteor shoots across the sky toward the earth, and you hear a second crash and hear loud cries and shouts. They sound next door, across the bedroom wall.

A woman's face opens up and shrieks. "Oh my *God*! Oh my *God*! Oh my *God*!" Behind her a small, ragged group stands, looking over your head and behind you. Silent. Frozen in a kind of amazement.

The face dissolves.

You try to turn and look but you can't.

You picked up the moleskine notebook at a stationery in Portland shortly before you made your decision that autumn. The pages are faded along the edges but still surprisingly white, and the ink has not faded. Your penmanship, never very legible, was at least still sharply drawn if tangled and inconsistent; it did not have the humiliating shaking of your late age. You haven't read it through in decades. Now it seems imperative to do so—it may contain something you need to remember, something important, perhaps vital, that you have forgotten.

Oct. 17, 2003 : Dennis, the freckle-faced nerd sitting next to me, just told me (he's tracking the flight on his computer) we've just entered Turkish air space—woo-hoo! And it really hit me: I'm in a Muslim country. I'm going to someplace stranger than I've ever seen, than I ever hoped (or feared) to see in this lifetime. Or the next. Punk, pierced, snarky, new-wave, geek-snuffling, Cap'n Crunch-eating digirati are nothing to where I am going, man. Man, I am going to Iraq. . . . A place where they'll kill you because your great-great-great-great-grandfather consorted with the diluted spawn of the assassins of Ali.

Or something like that.

Dennis has been there on a short tour already, and he's been giving me the lowdown, the stuff the folks at BlackRock forgot to tell us. One thing: they have long memories. And they'll *never* forget us.

I'm wondering, for the two-hundred-sixty-seventh time, what in the bleeding *hell* am I doing here? (Dennis knows: it's real simple, man. First, it's the money. Second—it's the money. Third, it's all those sexy girls in the veils that you never get to see! Correction: it's the money.)

It's not the money.

Maybe I have a gene for sadomasochistic Dantesque inferno-gazing. Or maybe I am just one more late-adolescent male hysteric who couldn't find his masculinity under a goat. Then for the two-hundred-and-sixty-eighth time, I trotted out my reasons: Grad school was a waste. Pamela and I broke up the month after Miranda died. I wanted to do something, anything, after September 11 to get back at those . . . fuckers.

The army was no option for a recovering Marxist (Note: Dennis is a Bushwhacker; better not tell him he's sharing air with an unreconstructed pinko.) I watched the Afghanistan war, Kabul, Helmand, the idiocy of Tora Bora—thinking how they let bin Laden escape still makes me sick. Trusty Jenny the Jeep took me cross-country—Illinois, Minnesota, South Dakota, Montana, Oregon. So I worked at a bookstore while Bush planned his assault on Saddam. Oedipal angst meets Butthead dumb fuck romantic ex-drunk. Then Powell lied to the UN, and I knew it was all over. Prepare for shock and awe, towelheads! Rummy and Tommy Frank had their way with Mesopotamia, and I figured there is no way I'm staying in Portland when Ali Baba has just taken Baghdad. But how to get there? The Green Tortoise was a dead turtle long ago. Then BlackRock, when

196

they heard about me and Jenny, made me an offer I couldn't refuse. . . . uh-oh, here comes my last beer till I get back to New York. Cheers, Dennis! Suck it up, baby!

The next page is blank.

Nov. 12: I have been here a month.

I was first attached to a food concession unit in an area in Baghdad called the green zone.
I'm running food between it and someplace in the south called Najaf.

No one will ever believe this. They'll think I'm hallucinating or an embed for Al-Jazeera. But what do the Americans serve, for breakfast, lunch *and* dinner, in a Muslim country where you can get your head chopped off for just thinking about eating pig? You got it: bacon, ham, sausages, tenderloin, ham hocks, chitterlin's, pepperoni, pork chops, pork cheeks, pork bellies. *All* pork, *all* the time.

Anyway, BlackRock looks like it's running half the military.

There are soldiers everywhere.

There are bombings every day.

They gave me a Hummer that used to belong to my boss—it looks like it's been through three wars already.
I can't describe the chaos. It's a kind of hell

One of the first things I saw after I landed was the burnt-out hulk of the National Library of Iraq, where three thousand years of the country's history were annihilated within hours of the Americans' arrival in the city.

What are we doing here?

I saw a truck get blown up not a block ahead of me on my third day at the concession. ~~I think I saw a guy's head~~

The next page is blank.

Dec. 9: A bomb in a dead dog by the side of a road near one of the presidential palaces blew up. It killed Dennis, the guy with the freckles I flew over with. It blew him to pieces. ~~I don't~~

Dec. 20: I keep remembering the morning of 9/11, telling myself this is the reason we are here, *I* am here, ~~but I have seen such things~~

~~Jan. 2, 2004: I don't think I can write about this~~

On the following page you read these words, written in large letters in an unsteady hand (it is your handwriting, though you don't remember writing this; in fact you don't remember writing any of this):

The Terrorist's Waltz

The White City

It is still night when a stiff shake of the tent pulls you from sleep.

There is another shake of the wind, just sprung up, making the tent flap languidly like a loose tarpaulin. It's very cold; you shiver. There is a strange taste in your mouth you haven't had in many years, since the long year in Iraq . . .

You try to shift in the sleeping bag. But you can't—there's someone beside you. You jerk over on your shoulder.

She presses against your back.

Vivian.

Then you remember the sound of the crashing water through the darkness the night before.

My God . . .

You slump on your back and stare up into the darkness of the small tent, listening to the tent lough heavily in the early predawn wind.

All of you sit in a rough circle to the leeward of your van in the early morning, near the edge of the wadi where the three men were washed away the previous night. You look from face to face—burnt from the sun, wild-haired, haggard, in clothing stiff with sand and dried sweat. You dumbly eat a ration of breakfast, drink a ration of water, look across the still-wet gully. A long ribbon of sand blows from the vehicle's grill.

"If we," you begin, then stop. Vivian looks into your face, her own streaked with dried tears. "If we all use one vehicle between us, we may have a chance to make Tamanrasset."

They look at you dully.

"Where's that," Smuts says.

"South of here. I was there a few years ago. On a run from Timbuktu to Djanet. A few hundred miles."

"A few hundred miles!"

"Did you hear what I said?" you reply testily. "Using one vehicle will save us gas."

"I can vouch for his veracity," Peter perks up. "I was with you, remember."

You recall Peter bouncing beside you, riding shotgun, in the battered truck as you gritted across the unending hamada.

"The road Duden . . ." You pause, then go on, coolly. "The road that Duden talked about might be close. He said it crossed the Trans-Sahara Highway. *That* hasn't been used in years. Still, if we find what's left of it, and follow it, we might reach Tamanrasset in a few days."

"Lot of ifs," says Smuts.

The girl and the redhead stare wide-eyed at the older adults, the redhead's face showing a blend of fear and contempt, the girl's half-teary, blinking with a kind of awed self-pity. Husayn and Umar are inscrutable: they watch like small animals waiting for their chance to escape the trap they sense closing over them.

"We should search the wadi first," Vivian says.

After clearing breakfast, the six of them search the wadi more thoroughly than they were able to the night before. The flood waters have vanished into the sand. There's no trace of the men or their equipment except for the overturned Hummer half-buried in the silt that swept down with the flood. It looks like it's been there for years, catching a hillock of dirt blowing over it for many seasons.

After a desultory search, they go back, siphon off the gas from Peter's vehicle into yours and a few empty canisters from the overturned vehicle, and after pushing with their last supplies into the last van, cautiously move south.

Vivian, sitting against you, stares straight ahead, not looking at the cross she had placed near the overturned vehicle as they pass it. The cross flies a scarf the girl had tied over one arm, at the base is a book Peter left ("I borrowed and never returned it, bastard that I am"). You can hear a squeaking from the back and catch in the rear-view mirror the girl's ear and the edge of her hand over her face, shaking.

"Crying only increases dehydration," Vivian had said to you as she turned away from the cross she'd made from a couple of sticks and a pair of socks and pushed into the sand. You had looked at the cross and gotten as far as "Our father who art in heaven . . ." then turned and walked off, a bitter taste in your mouth and sand gritting your teeth. You had to spit several times to get it out of your mouth.

A few miles south, they come across the remains of a roadbed covered with a sheet of sand, going straight east and west, a phantom highway.

"But is it enough to drive on?" you ask no one in particular. You squint east toward a lunar grove of tors and inselbergs and west, past the S-curve, to a single tall dune with a faded, shaggy range of mountains behind it. "Which direction. Oued"—turning to the west— "or Edeyen?"—to the east.

"It looks," Vivian says, staring at the tent-like form of the dune in the distance, an opaque prism in the process of melting, a torqued cube of butter, a woman's lazy breast, "like a sphinx."

You go west, toward the dune. The phantom road, rough from rocks and gullies, never as smooth as the sand surface seemed to imply, goes before them, sometimes bending for unknown reasons before returning to its western march, through groves of wind-worn tassili and by the rims of wadis. For miles ahead, the great sphinx-like dune grows to meet you, sometimes directly ahead, sometimes off to the side, its peak dominating the western horizon until finally it hides the distant peaks.

You think you're fooling us, but you aren't. You draw us on the way the Yetti Eglab draws the sand.

At one point the road makes a sudden turn, and the sphinx-like dune stands starkly before them.

At its foot lies a road: an abandoned breadth of tarmac crossing the wisp of highway they're on; the tarmac disappears north beneath the dune's stately paws. The dune will continue to stalk its way south, you think, now that nobody bothers to bulldoze it away; covering more and more of the road as it retreats before the prevailing wind.

Southward, the road runs straight as a die to the horizon.

"The gods are showing us mercy."

"At last."

"Or preparing better jokes."

A road untouched in years. Wars in the Maghreb, collapsing economies, drying-up oil, or no longer "economic" to produce. The return of the Sahara to sand and sun.

The two roads meet in a perfect cross.

"Ladies and gentlemen: the Trans-Saharan Highway," you announce. "Or what's left of it. Man's bid to conquer the desert."

"Now she's getting hers back," says Peter.

"You've had your fun," Smuts quips mirthlessly. "It's time to put away your toys now and go back to sleep."

The arms of the great sickle dune seem to reach toward them. A scurl of sand twirls away along the top ridge—a sand devil.

"The efreets are dancing for us," you say. "They're overjoyed we've made it this far."

"All the longer to torture us," says Smuts.

They turn onto the cracked surface of the highway and proceed, for the first time in a week, on a flat road, south.

"Why, I do believe we've returned to civil-i-zation," the Aussie drawls.

"To luxury," says Vivian. She suddenly drops her face into her hands. You're afraid at first that she'll start crying, but she doesn't, she just sits there, swinging slightly with the vehicle.

"I think we're lost."

The two young boys are surrounded by a tall verdant mesh of woodland, towering trees, entangled underbrush, weeds exuberantly flowering, bright with young green. The boys are tired, hungry, thirsty. There's no sign of a trail, no sign of people—no fields, fences, roads, signs. The sun is far down the western half of the sky. The woods are growing darker.

The afternoon had sped away far more quickly than the morning, as if the sun finds it easier to fall than rise. The early morning feels so long ago—you can barely remember it.

"I guess so," you reply.

Your bedroom, pierced with early light.

What a dream *that* was!

You had been guiding an expedition, exploring a jungle, a desert, a cave. There was danger and excitement and fear and thrill, it was a blur of surprises and strange people who loved and admired you, and others who hated and wanted to defeat you, because you were the leader, you were the hero, it all depended on you, you had to save them from danger, but you came through—or you would in the end, because the adventure wasn't over yet, you woke at the moment of greatest danger, they were afraid they might die, but they wouldn't die, you would save them all, and you remembered a voice asking excitedly, "What are you going to do now?" so clearly you can still hear the words in the room—maybe you said them yourself? your mom says you sometimes talk in your sleep—and suddenly the entire dream collapses in memory like a house of cards, and all you have left is a memory of romance and excitement and tremendous light, and those words, and then they too collapse in the flood of the light of the day waking with you, and the dream disintegrates into a few vivid images, sounds, an indecipherable word, a rush of air, and then not even that—as if it had never been.

Yet something is left: a sense of anticipation, sharp as a knife and fresh as morning, as though something wonderful is coming: a surprise the day has in store for you, Ariel Hunter—an unspoken promise, just over the horizon. It's a sense you often have. It's just keener this morning after your dream: a sense that something extraordinary is about to happen . . .

You jump from bed, throw on your jeans, T-shirt, running shoes, check the weather (patchy high white clouds, torn, smeared cumulus—you've been teaching yourself the names of the clouds: cumulus, nimbus, stratus, cumulo-nimbus, cumulo-nimbus-stratus, cirrus . . .), with its warm sun, in the cool, early morning air, just shedding its dawn yellow against the brightness of the late spring day.

Softly, you walk downstairs, through the walnut-furnished dining room and the marble-topped kitchen, open the freshly painted back door, close it gently behind you, and scamper around the corner past the wild rose bushes to the apple tree, blossoming and fragrant, white and pink (the apples will come in the fall, you can almost taste them, almost smell the tart, rotting ones in the grass in November), and, applying your rubber soles to the dewy, slippery bark and the first crook in the trunk, climb up to the first bough, then to the second—then pull yourself up to the little network of branches that holds the nest as the mother robin screeches in alarm and flies above your head.

Hugging the trunk, you push up through the branches with their pink-white blossoms and panoply of new leaves and raise your eyes above the nest.

A squealing of tiny voices greets you. Three scrawny, fluffy necks topped with open beaks above still-unopened eyes shoot up, alarmed and demanding.

The mother shrieks and flaps around your head.

The chicks hatched several days ago. The stupid mother hasn't figured you out yet: *I'm not going to steal your babies.*

You know enough not to touch them, though you're sorely tempted to stroke their heads, gently. You imagine doing so, then shake yourself—you sometimes have the uncanny feeling that merely by imagining something vividly, you are in danger of actually doing it.

A bumble bee lands on a flower near your hand, and the buzzing stops as the bee digs into the petals.

A bee once stung you several years before. It was the most painful thing you ever felt.

You freeze and stare at the enormous, yellow and black hairy insect, its transparent wings tucked up behind it, absurdly small for the bee's size, at the multiple, inhuman eyes that seem at the same time to be all-seeing and blind.

A shaft of sunlight streams through a hole in the apple blossoms, dazzling you.

"Ariel!" your mother calls from the back door. "Breakfast!"

The bee launches into the air.

You reach your foot down to the next bough, can't find it, kick in panic, reach down again, holding on by your fingers to the branch under the nest; then you suddenly lose your grip and fall.

They drive straight south down what's left of the highway as it dips in and out of little sickle dunes that look like hands trying to hide the road—they drive cautiously over these dunes and, each time, a little farther on, find the trail again where it emerges from the dune like a hiding child.

Soon they pass a ruined sign sticking out of the sand: a circle of metal hanging from a gibbet-like post.

"Used to be one of these every fifty miles along here," you say. "Abandoned gas stations."

No one responds. A desolate silence forms over the vehicle as it progresses south.

It isn't long before you feel Vivian's head rocking in sleep against your shoulder. The rest of the van is soon folded in silence as everyone but you sleeps in the heat's shell.

Once again, a lake seems to shimmer in front of them.

The engine's roar feels like cotton in your ears, the familiar clanks like a soothing chant, a murmur of repeated phrases from an old, cranky friend, lulling you almost to sleep.

You pinch your leg to keep awake.

"TamTam, Tamanrasset. TamTam, Tamanrasset," the vehicle's clanks seem to be saying, over and over. *How many years ago. Four, five?* The minaret of the sole mosque, the pie-like formations of courtyards and covered alleyways surrounding it, like a little Ghardaïa, the people in their mixed clothing, half traditional, half dirty T-shirts and old baseball caps, the lake with its palms, the marvel of water birds nesting at its edges. The muezzin's call to prayers—a man, standing at the edge of the minaret (you could see him), not a recording through loudspeakers, like almost everywhere in the Maghreb. Regular as church bells. Like visiting a scene from centuries ago: a town embedded in its past, its little eternity. The camels, the dogs.

They gaped at our trucks with envy. Even then, it was out of reach for all but the big traders. They wanted either to get out or bring as much of the modern world as they could to them. The disks for long-unusable satellite television—the mirage of a generation ago, like the Internet—still displayed, dirty, broken, aiming everywhere but the sky, on the rooftops.

High above the town lay the snows of Mount Tahat, leaning like a hand along its north face, never seen by the sun.

Snow. Just seeing it would cool you about twenty degrees.

You flash on last night.

I can hardly remember the Okie. . . . let alone the Dutchboy . . . and the old man . . . was he bald or not? . . . and someone named Chad: a complete blank . . .

You pinch your leg again and stare hard at the south, looking for the toothlike line of uplift announcing the Tassili

208

N'Ajjers in the distance. You can feel someone (Smuts probably, but you feel too weary to look), glare at you with Vivian sleeping on your shoulder, then slowly look away.

"What's that scratch on your forehead?"

"Nothing."

"And you're limping—what's the matter?"

"Nothing."

"You've got flower petals in your hair, were you climbing the apple tree again?"

"No."

Your mother, a small red-haired woman with delicate features and a steely voice, brushes your head with her knuckles.

"Your father told you not to climb that tree. You'll damage the bark, do you want to kill the tree?"

"No."

"Then stop climbing it. You'll poke your eye out on a branch. And you'll break your neck if you fall—do you want to break your neck?"

"No."

"All you can say is no! Yes, you did climb that tree. You're scratched all over. Next time you'll break your neck!" She gives you a glare. "What am I going to do with you?" She points to the kitchen table. "Eat your breakfast."

You sit down to your cereal and moodily dig in.

You know that the life of a tree is in its bark—if its bark is damaged a tree can die. But you hadn't seen any sign your shoes made any impression on the bark, so you suspected his mother is "exaggerating" again (as your father often accuses her of doing).

"Have you made your bed?" your mother stops you as, breakfast done, you take a flying leap at the back door.

"No!"

"An honest answer at last."

She gives you a level look as you tramp out of the kitchen.

At the top of the stairs you pass your father leaving the bathroom: he is a big man, with thinning hair, an appraising eye, a dry sense of humor. He passes without looking at you.

"Morning, Arik."

Then disappears into the master bedroom and closes the door with a click.

It was a friendly enough greeting—not cold or dismissive—if preoccupied, as his father often is. He called you "Arik," not "Ariel": which means he isn't feeling angry or disappointed with you. You exhale; you hadn't realized you had been holding your breath.

After making your bed, you lounge across it, and that strange, sharp sense of anticipation returns.

"There's something in the air."

A phrase your father used. You like it; it makes you pay attention to the smells, coming from outside, of trees and flowers, weeds and hay, the juniper bushes blooming just now, and nearby cornfields, and wet earth and Mannahawkin Creek at the edge of the family property—or indoor smells of cooking and baking, floor wax and dust polish, soap and shampoo and shaving lotion and after-shave and baby powder from the bathroom, your mother's perfume and your father's cologne when your parents are going out for the evening.

You breathe in and concentrate, except now you ignore the smells coming in from outside, of grass and juniper and mud, and try instead to imagine what might be coming ahead—today? tomorrow? years from now?

"Tomorrow, and tomorrow, and tomorrow, and tomorrow . . ." you say in a sing-song whisper to yourself.

You imaginve a chain of sunrises and sunsets glowing and billowing like great multicolored sails above the Grand Tetons, your favorite mountains, which you saw one day in a children's encyclopedia Grand-nan gave you last Christmas; in brilliantly colored sunlight, flashing among anarchic flotillas of cloud, leading you from today into the tomorrows of the future . . .

a dozen, then dozens, a hundred, then hundreds, into years, decades—and what must a decade be like, you aren't even ten years old yet, but people can live for many decades—five, six, seven, eight, nine (like Grand-nan), even ten—ten decades, who can imagine *that?*

You can feel the future spread out in front of you like an ocean, though you have never seen an ocean, never anything bigger than Lake Erie, though you have seen it on television and in movies.

You imagine yourself standing on the bow of a ship as it disembarks from shore. The ocean goes on and on under a sky filled with great cumulus clouds like a great armada of ships or warplanes or birds accompanying you as you launch out onto the sea, into the future.

You imagine what you will be when you grow up, what you will do and how you will do it.

First of all, twenty years from now, you will be famous. Like one of those famous people written about in the books in your parents' collection. Whatever else you do, you will at least be that: admired, "from sea to shining sea," as they sing in "America the Beautiful" (you like the words "the sea," they make you day-dream; you like even more the words "the ocean," they suggest immense space and a vastly long time, they even sound something like falling waves—something like what you feel when you look up at the night sky in the middle of summer—a warm darkness around you, with a deep-down, dazzling brightness), but you'll be humble and modest, quiet and gentle (you hate proud, pompous people, like the ones you sometimes see on the news).

You will be strong and kind, because strength is shown in kindness, not anger—only the weak get angry and need to show off their power, the strong are afraid of hurting others, their strength makes them shy—they are always thinking, "I could so easily hurt you, I must pull back, I must hide my power, it would scare you, I like you too much to see you hurt even in thought, I'll hide my power, that way we can be friends."

An impulse strikes you, and you lurch up from your bed and tramp downstairs.

"I made my bed!" you sing out as you race out the back door. "I'll be down by the creek."

"Don't go too far," his mother exhorts. "Don't get your shoes muddy. And be back for lunch!"

But you have already run too far to hear, and feel no need to acknowledge any more than with your catch-all response—"Okay!"—as you fly across the yard.

The Hummer suddenly stumbles and rocks on its springs.

"Sorry," you say. "They really gotta fix these potholes."

"If one is mentioning potholes purely of themselves, *that* was a ball breaker," Smuts quips.

To their left the earth falls away to a canyon three hundred feet below them. You roll the vehicle to a halt a dozen feet from the edge.

"No kidding," you say.

On the other side, a landscape opens, flat as a plate, extending to a horizon drawn tight as a string. Mushroom rocks, glazed and black, dot the surface; between the cliff you're on top of and the plain, the canyon descends into abrupt shadow; it's just beginning to be touched by the mid-day sun. A few medlar and jojoba trees, stumpy and gray, cluster at the bottom.

Vivian cranes over your shoulder and peers into the defile. "Their roots can just about reach the water, if they stretch far enough. Like kids in the kitchen stretching for a forbidden cookie jar—except it's *down*. An ocean of water buried under the desert. There's nature's . . ." She stops.

Something twitches among the medlars. Foraging, stepping delicately. It looks up. Its face is white and brown and black, a dramatic mask, with upright, twisted horns. It stares at them. Then, probably deciding the metallic box is too outlandish to be dangerous, returns to its probing for food among the rocks.

"Tanezrouft," Vivian says, echoing Duden's lesson and

looking out across the vast flat waste. " 'Land of terror.' Desert within the desert. Absolute desert."

"Sean, Cecilia," you suddenly say in a loud voice. You need to get Vivian off this subject. "You still breathing back there?"

Their sleepy voices—they must have had no sleep last night, must sleep now no matter what—roll forward in an incomprehensible mumble.

The shadows in the ravine below them, even as they shrink toward the walls, are tantalizing as a siren: there's no way to reach them, of course, and the landscape beyond and the way before them show no other shade. The heat begins to press down again.

"We can rest here, or we can continue south and try to make it to N'Ajjers before nightfall," you say.

"What's that?" Smuts asks glumly.

"High country. It'll take us out of the worst of the heat, till we get to TamTam."

"It will do *what?*" Smuts pounces. "Take us out of this *heat?*"

"You've got my vote, mate," Peter puts in.

Vivian nods, a little reluctantly; perhaps reluctant to abandon her old professor's country now that she's seen it. Then she shakes herself.

"All right! Anywhere out of this world."

A few minutes later you're back on the highway.

———

You turn the page of the old moleskine book. The words there are barely legible, deleted, erased, stuck back in again. You can hardly read it. But you can't *not* read it.

Tal Afar

Ignite
o shards of Nineveh
compiled into a manual
for soldiers and surds,
an indefensible liberation
out of a cunning, dark-eyed hope
no one can wholly shrive
or condemn —

the mound of cities
rises in a sandstorm
delivering
vengeance
to the avengers

*

A cuneiform of tablets
counting tares, trade's traces
for the king's taxes
and chartered warriors' wages,
baked four millennia
in the dust crossing two rivers,
can now add
the silica of child-men,
pixels bravely strobing,
wedging Sargon's spidered successor
engrossed between tank treads
and the ooze of the Cambrian

burning them

*

214

Thunder from Mosul
thunder from Najaf
thunder from Basra

a finger scores a rip down a mapfold

*

Legitimation crisis
Failed snark of longitude
A crick in a boundary
between a fabled cigar and a scotch
A mass grave is lit
by a gas flare
Oil turns to powder
in the air

*

At the head of the victims as they marched
marched a killer drinking their blood

At the head of the ignorant armies
marched a fool spilling their blood
When they met, the smoke billowed
across the scorched gray land
the fool kissing the killer
the killer fucking the fool

The gates of Paradise opened
in the palace's pit

*

The place is not tall
and is not far

it lights the night streets
between two vast seas
with sewage, empty pill bottles, blood
and fear's sweat

Bracelets of eyes
adorn its cities,
ditches filled with faces
open their mouths

*

In the middle of the battle
a hot fog rises.
Who will lose — who will win?
The loser will spit on the end.

————

Mannahawkin Creek rushes close to the top of the banks it had flooded only the day before.

The bank under the weeping willow is still waterlogged, and you step carefully. The willow branches drag in the water, and the shadowy morning air fills with the many voices of the stream.

A splash near the bank. A frog? You jump to a rock near the bank, peer into the water for the green form, feel the warmth from the sun as the sunlight creeps down the willow's trunk.

A dragonfly weaves back and forth an inch from your face, then buzzes off.

You listen intently. If you listen hard, you can hear what sounds like voices: you can hear words, can even make out the sound of your own name.

"Ariel. Ariel. Ariel. . . .," the gurgling water seems to say as it runs over the stones.

You listen for other words—"Easter lily" . . . "dungeon drum" . . . "if it weren't, if it were"—then just to the murmuring

216

of the water, then back to the voices, back and forth; the illusion is entertaining, the idea of the water blithely chattering away.

It isn't so, of course. But it's fun to pretend, especially when the sound is so close to that of a human voice.

Long ago you used to play a little game when playing alone near the creek, though not so much anymore—it was okay when you were five or six, though not now that you're nine. You pretended you were a giant walking across the world, and that everywhere you walked in this part of the backyard, near the creek, in the shadow of the willow, whole worlds existed to which you brought sunlight when they needed it, shadow when they craved it, wind when they suffered from the heat, warmth when they froze under ice and snow, all without your even knowing it, just by following your own sweet will as you played or loafed about the yard.

At the same time, you could destroy civilizations, continents, worlds of tiny animals and plants and people, with an equally inadvertent step or a sweep of your arm.

You daydreamed about tiny planets swimming through the air; made of grains of dust like the ones you saw riding sunbeams in the house, especially after your mother cleaned: worlds that you swept through as you ran about, sending them hurtling through the universe, breathing on them and cooling them in the hot summer days, or breathing them in with every breath, destroying them in universal catastrophes like great planetary hurricanes—lord of the winds, master of tempests.

And you imagined messengers being sent out from these tiny worlds, some to thank you for your unexpected gifts, some to beg you to spare them from destruction, and you would patiently listen to their thanks and their pleas, and then boom out, in a voice that must be, to them, terrifyingly loud and deep, your thanks or your apologies, and send them a kindly wave of your wind-stirring hand and tip-toe quietly away, holding your breath; and later you would breathe very gingerly.

You became thoughtful about the burden of responsibility

217

this dream, if real, would imply: providing benefits you never intended, even the very existence of life on these tiny planets, and equally without intending it, threatening them with the greatest suffering, even wholesale destruction.

But you couldn't always help yourself: no matter where you went or what you did, there was another civilization, another world threatened by your footfalls, or even by an absence of the right gesture, wave of an arm, sigh or breath in the right place at the right time—there was nowhere you could go without affecting whole worlds for the better or, usually it seemed, for the worse. What were you to do? You had a right to live as you could, didn't you?

It occurred to you that, just as you might be almost a god to the little worlds around you, giving and taking away life and death, you might yourself be only a tiny member of a little world to some even bigger giant who just thought he was taking a walk through his house or in his backyard, all the time bringing happiness or catastrophe to myriads of creatures, with even bigger giants above them, and bigger giants above them, in an infinite series above, and an infinite series below.

Then you stopped thinking about it; it was too dizzying. You stopped playing the little game, because if you started taking it seriously, you might become paralyzed with a sense of responsibility, unable to take a step in any direction, take a breath, move, live—as if, as long as you didn't think yourself a giant saving and destroying pygmy worlds, you wouldn't have to pay the price of being yourself a pygmy living on a world thriving or shipwrecked, triumphant or annihilated, living or dead, at the whim of greater giants stalking the universe above you.

You poke your finger into a fan of water falling over a little rock. The top of the rock wavers under the thin layer of water. Your finger breaks the liquid fan in two, making each side curve out slightly from your finger, like the eddies made by the detritus in the creek. You poke your finger in and out several times, watching the fan open and close like a little curtain in

218

front of the face of the stone: a little stage or theater.

The rush of the water surrounds you, tumbling, surging, streaming across and away, toward Darby Creek and the distant rivers—and on to the Great Lakes, the St. Lawrence, the Gulf—on, finally, to the Atlantic—almost with a mind of its own, like a living thing, a multitude of living things.

You hear the choke and chuff of a tractor starting up behind you. Mr. Palmer, your neighbor, perched on his beat-up farm machine, is edging his tractor backward. Little clouds of black smoke puff from the smoke stack. The enormous back wheels, more than twice your height, roll tentatively back. Squawking chickens and geese flutter out of the way. A waft of exhaust smoke, acrid and sweet, blows over the creek.

The farmer, a beefy middle-aged man with heavy eyes and a fist-like jaw, swings the tractor around and, driving up the driveway to Carter's Road, after a quick check for traffic, chugs and chuffs into the road and away. The rushing of creek water after the tractor's assertive groaning sounds almost quiet.

Tractors. Car engines. Lawnmowers. Carpenters. Clocks. Church bells. Sirens. Rock 'n' roll. And sounds of wind, water, bird song, buzzing of flies, of bees, thunder.

Human sounds, natural sounds. Human smells, natural smells. Human lights, natural lights.

You think of the smell of flowers and the smell of cooking, the smell of cut grass and the gasoline smell of a lawnmower. You think of sunlight and moonlight and starlight and lightning, and light bulbs and candles and the light from the television . . .

Sunlight breaks from a cloud above the house, and a shaft of light strikes the creek a few feet ahead. The mud and rotting leaves at the shallow bottom of the creek bed suddenly shine, a flat, decaying, shapeless matt, ugly but oddly reassuring under the loose, running, cold, bright water.

In nature something soft and powerful and slow and constantly moving, you think, hesitantly . . . *in people something assertive and insistent and fast and small and . . .*

219

You hear a high-pitched knocking: it bursts out like a hard rapping on a door for a few seconds, in a quick decrescendo down to a halt, followed by a brief pause and then another insistent knocking.

A woodpecker drilling a hole into a tree.

Well, that idea was wrong! Unless woodpeckers are like people! But then what is it . . .

You continue your hesitant, groping meditation—there seems to be some difference, a break, between human beings, on the one side, and, on the other side *everything else*—you can almost put your finger on it, but you are never able to put into words without immediately being given, like a slap, a refutation.

You've been luckier than you had any right to expect.

The highway comes and goes, disappearing under dunes like a wire under a rug, re-emerging a quarter, half a mile, once almost two miles, south of where it vanished, as if playing a game of hide-and-seek with a not very bright child.

Now it winds up an escarpment one thousand, two thousand, three thousand, feet to the hamada of N'Ajjers eroded into combs of granite and volcanic extrusion spiking along the crest like an imperial crown made of stone.

You carefully drive up the switchback road, roaring away on a choky-sounding low gear, over the remains of landslides, skirting cliffs falling starkly from the road shoulder, until you finally cross the edge of the tableland and you and the rest of your remainng band, getting out briefly into the cool air—breathing in sudden relief and sheepishly smiling in the new, delicious ease—gaze across the hot plain you spent the day crossing.

It stretches north toward a soft line of barely visible hills; splotched with ancient lakebeds white with salt and fields of dark gray lava, and dotted with black outcroppings like bands of nomads sitting randomly on the desert floor, their shadows stretching in the evening.

Then you turn to the hamada, the rock shadows strafing

220

the cliff walls above like scratches in the late afternoon sun, its punishing heat weakening as it falls toward the horizon.

"The promised land," says Smuts wearily.

"Land of milk and honey," you say.

"Land out of the heat." From the plainer Peter.

Their voices chatter deliriously.

"Our motel for the night. With air conditioning!"

"How about a steak dinner?"

"And a keg of beer."

"And ice cream . . ."

And they laugh at their own extravagance.

A large predatory bird flies across the view, descending from above, soaring down the escarpment.

"A hawk," the mustache asserts.

"It's an eagle," the redhead cries out in an unsteady voice. He's been silent most of the day; his voice sounds cottony, phlegmy from disuse. "I know from its shape—look at its head, the tail. It's not a hawk," he repeats, stubbornly, looking back at the bird. "It's an eagle."

The mustache smirks but says nothing, and you look at Sean watching the eagle as it disappears beneath them.

You flash on an old memory of an eagle you once saw, soaring toward a setting sun, as you stood next to your old friend, Steve.

They cross a scattering of splintered, sand-blasted rock covering the highway they hope they're still on. Shortly afterward, they pass a narrow ravine at whose base is a dark glimmer and a shadowy clumping of gauzy forms.

A tiny pocket oasis at the bottom of a canyon. *Water,* you think.

They get out for a better look.

"The only way's down the rock side," you say. "Peter, if we still have that rope, we can take the bucket down."

"What if it's undrinkable?" Smuts objects. "We'll waste a morning."

"We can use it for the radiators. We'll find a use for it. You don't pass up water when the desert hands it to you like this."

A cliff stands black in the twilight not far from the ravine's edge, little teeth of mica-like rock shavings glinting among the scree.

The group of you set up camp nearby, eat a quick supper and are soon asleep after nightfall.

"So you're admitting you're wrong, are you? *I* could've told you that."

You grab a pebble, spin around, and shoot it at the feet of the short towhead grinning on the bank.

"And *you're* always right!" you jeer as your friend skips out of the way.

"Always! Especially when I'm talking to myself," the towhead grins back. He stands a few feet away, a slight figure wearing scruffy old jeans with holes in the back pockets, a faded flannel shirt, torn sneakers.

You jump back onto the bank and throw yourself at Frankie Palmer, feigning a punch to the belly.

"Let's wrestle!" He swivels in the mud and makes to seize you by the shoulders.

"It's too wet. Mom'll have my hide if I get all muddy."

"So, what's wrong with your forehead?"

"I scratched it." You shrug. "I fell out of the apple tree."

"You did *what*?" He giggles at you.

"I just saw your dad on his tractor."

"He's going to plow the Prices' field."

"Why doesn't he have his own field?"

"It *is* our field."

"But he rents it."

"So? If he rents, it's ours."

"But it isn't the same thing as owning it."

"So?! Do *you* own everything *you* have?"

You're about to say yes, because it's true; anyway, if you

222

have it, you own it, don't you? But the look on Frankie's face—defensive and defiant—makes you hesitate. You're tempted to say it anyway—after all, it's true, and your father never beats you more severely than when you tell a lie. You hesitate. Is being silent the same as lying?

You say something else instead.

"I just heard a woodpecker boring a nest."

Frankie peers into the trees, shading his eyes with his hand.

"I think we scared him off."

Another burst of knocking.

"There!"

It comes from up the wooded slope on the other side of the creek.

"Let's look for it," says Frankie.

You both run over to a ragged line of rocks crossing the creek. Frankie almost loses his balance between the last rock and the steep bank, which dives straight into the creek, and curses before scrambling to the other side.

The footing is treacherous as they climb. The slope is covered with brush, grass, snapdragons, morning glories, daisies growing from a layer of decaying leaves at the feet of sycamores and hickories, birches and maples, and a line of firs long the top ridge. For a moment the woods seem filled with birdsong—a quiet, brief, chaotic concert—under dappled sunlight. A wave of air crosses the cover, a sigh and sough above their heads.

"Shh," Frankie says. He points toward the top of a shaggy hickory twenty feet off. You can see nothing at first, then, at a burst of knocking, catch the silhouette of the woodpecker, with a red head and a long sleek tail, as it knocks into the tree like a hand sized jack hammer.

An oriole perches on a lower branch of the hickory between bursts, then sails away as if startled.

"He thinks he's being shot at," says Frankie.

The woodpecker halts. When they look for it again, they can't find it.

"He can't have flown away."

"Scaredy cat!"

"We're not trying to shoot you, you silly pecker!" Frankie turns to Arik. "Ever eat a woodpecker?"

"No," you reply with disgust.

"Tastes like chicken," Frankie replies airily.

"Liar."

They look back up at the hickory, but the woodpecker is gone and the woods are suddenly quiet.

"Let's check out the fox den," says Frankie, heading up the slope.

Beyond the ridge lies a field of alfalfa starting to sprout, light green, from rows of turned soil. Most of the trees lining the field are posted with signs:

NO GUNNING

or

TRESPASSING

with, underneath, instructions written in tiny letters: "The land beyond this sign is PRIVATE PROPERTY and trespassing on it is a MISDEMEANOR. All Violators Will Be Prosecuted to THE FULL EXTENT OF THE LAW, According to the Provisions of Ordinance B-639 of the County of Pickaway Real Property Code. BY ORDER OF THE SHERIFF OF PICKAWAY COUNTY, OHIO."

"An' if yr'n *close enough* to *read this sign*, bud, y'rn *violatin' it!*" Frankie says with a guffaw.

Keeping your eyes peeled for inhospitable landowners, the two of you follow the line of trees along the field.

You can hear a tractor chuffing in the distance—a newer model than Mr. Palmer's, with a smoother, higher pitched growl. It's probably Mr. McClatchy, invisible beyond a low ridge near the center of the field; he is the irascible owner of the field and neighboring woods. Your father often says Mr. McClatchy is a man too much in love with his rights, and his "No Trespassing" signs: "How unsociable can you get? It makes you feel like you're in a hypersecurity vault when you're just trying to take a walk across a field."

"What poet was it who said that 'Life is not a walk across a field'?" your mother had said.

"He didn't know McClatchy's."

Noli me tangere. It's a Latin phrase you learned from your mother's art history book; the title of a painting of Jesus risen from the grave and talking to Mary Magdalene kneeling in wonder at his resurrection. "Don't touch me. It's dangerous to be too near me. You might be hurt if you touch me. Stay away."

Like your fantasy of being a giant in command of countless worlds: "Don't get too close! I'm dangerous."

The two of you scamper around a field corner and along the edge of the woods until you reach a gnarled, old oak, then take a sharp turn into the woods. A tangle of new grasses, thistles, and Queen Anne's lace screens a trail leading deep among the trees.

Monuments of rock half melted away by wind and sand stand bolt-upright around you like—depending on where you look at them—Buckingham Palace guards, or great chess pieces set randomly on a board, or flames of rock frozen at a moment of futile aspiration. Flames of smokeless fire. Djinn.

The uncanny humanness of many of the forms: the appearance of faces, snarling, gaping, laughing, weeping, grotesque masks, misshapen bodies, cripples leaning against the wind, wounded, lying in uneasy sleep, sitting in monumental chairs, thrones, above which an abstract head, reduced to a pin, solemnly overlooks the waste.

"'My name is Ozymandias, king of kings: Look on my works . . .'"

"A Shelley reader!" Vivian interrupts from her seat next to you.

225

"Was I muttering again? This kind of country always brings out the failed poet in me."

"It's no wonder," she says.

She gestures toward a wind-carving that bears an eerie resemblance to a mother gazing at a child in her lap. Only the child has no head and only one arm, raised blindly. Almost immediately they change perspective, and the forms disappear back into misshapen stone. Like a cloud.

The highway can be followed only with difficulty once they're deep into the tableland, and they often have to halt and scout ahead, examining for traces of the road under quilt-like sand hummocks. But the cool buoys their mood, and the sombre nobility of the desolation around them, with its quirky mockery of humanity, has the effect of cheering them up.

They look so weirdly alive. So, what is wind, heat, light, a flash of lightning balling into a fist, if not alive, as if nature were a kind of seed in suspended animation waiting for the right conditions to burst alive—sentient, thinking, feeling, imaginative, curious, examining, creating ever more life in some universal drive toward intelligent being throughout space and time . . . and that would be, that must *be . . .*

"Ilaman, mate, that's what it must be," Peter says suddenly from the back, throwing his voice forward toward a distant brown nob of basalt that has just appeared in a gap in front of them.

A few moments later they cross the last crest of the tassili.

And before them spreads the mud-colored range of the Hoggar, the ancient remains of an enormous volcanic explosion that tore through the heart of the continent millions of years ago, spilling the oldest rock beds underneath into the heart of N'Ajjers. And, commanding them, like the hub at the center of a great spoked wheel, the mist whitening under the high sun, the great holy mountain, Mount Ilaman, wreathed in a mantle of cloud.

Even older than the plateau we're on is the Hoggar, says the legend. It casts a spell of a time before time, a creation that perished before life itself was even a possibility: a Leviathan of molten rock, a mind of no-mind, a thinking, calculating, dreaming chaos, an earth roaring as it was being born. The chaos of the real, not the genteel fractallage of academic papers. The catastrophic drive toward creation.

Before Being, they say, was the Hoggar . . .

The group of you move toward the mud-red majesty of this pre-human, pre-living, almost pre-existent world. A world that to *know*, it is said by the mystics, the fabulists, the poets, is to erase all knowledge.

It seems to dissolve behind a curtain of fog.

A few dozen yards from the oak tree appears a clearing dominated by a massive black trunk broken into chunks—the tree was split by lightning years ago, with a long gash along the trunk's upper part, and all its branches were split and scattered—the trunk's main body has been eaten to dust by termites. It's a majestic fallen pillar, with its mass of roots lofted into the air like the skeleton of a huge foot clotted with mud.

The air is tangy with the smell of grass and damp soil. Along one side of the trunk a mass of blossoming honeysuckle sweetens the air, a few bees working among the flowers.

You point to something lying on the ground, half hidden by the lowest blossoms.

"Somebody and his dad was here," you whisper: three spent shotgun shells, thick as a man's fingers. Frankie smirks as you pick one up, look over the weathered red cardboard, the dull brass cap, the charred mouth. You sniff it: it still smells, lightly, of gunpowder. Then you put it in your pocket.

You both tip-toe to the other side of the trunk, near a hollow cushioned with milkweed. Peering down the bark to a small opening in the ground, you see some reddish fur through the weeds—it twitches slightly and turns, and a couple of little snouts poke out, with mouths panting, and two small pairs of beady eyes that almost immediately disappear behind another twitch of the mother fox's tail.

"They're still there," Frankie whispers excitedly.

"Shh."

The tail switches again, but you don't see the fox pups again. The mother must be asleep after a night of hunting in Mr. McClatchy's fields.

McClatchy is always chasing the neighborhood boys off his fields, sometimes using his shot gun; just showing it, muzzle up, near his tractor seat, or ambling in your direction with it casually tucked under his arm is all he needs to do to make his point clear. So there's little sorrow when he loses the occasional hen to a neighborhood predator.

"The robin's chicks in the apple tree are still blind. I checked this morning," you say after you return to the other side of the tree.

"They're late, chicks' eyes sometimes never open. I once found an arrowhead near here."

"Hey, listen." You stop. You hear a kind of crowded buzzing coming from nearby.

"Bees."

"Look." You gesture toward a paper hive attached to the bough of another dead tree, a dozen feet from the ground. The hive is surrounded by a thin glittering haze.

Three of the insects—huge and shiny brown—appear with a buzz harsher and deeper than a bee's. One of them lands near Frankie's elbow and crawls deliberately over a blossom.

"Shit! Wasps! Let's get outta here," he says. The boys walk rapidly, then break into a run out of the clearing.

The highway has vanished into a warren of goat tracks and gullies squirreling through steeps of volcanic slag and cliff walls the color of rust or dried blood. Your movement slows painfully, the compass twitching between irrelevant points on the dial, idly leaning in random directions or turning on a dime as the sun seems to appear through unexpected chasms, above the wrong peaks or down dead-ends. Yet in this wilderness of petrified mud, you pass signs of monastic retreats, long abandoned; the Hoggar has been a magnet for the religious for millennia—animist, Christian, Muslim—empty hermitages once belonging to French holy orders, cairns of white-washed stones where holy men once stopped for rest, or temporary encampments in little valley shelters. On the flanks of a high hill you pass a small, square, once-white building topped with a decaying dome, a tall cairn a dozen yards from the entrance. A forbidding dark horseshoe-shaped gash marks the doorway. It's a saint's tomb.

You pass a shrine proclaiming its dedication to Si Aissa—Jesus, "the prophet."

Some of the cairns are overturned, some of the shrines destroyed, after the salafists's revolt that swept North Africa a decade before. But the ruined ones become less frequent as they drive deeper into the Hoggar.

The cairns seem even to multiply: multiplying saints, holy sites. At one point they pass a group of tassili like a cluster of black-robed men and women kneeling in a pocket of sand.

You note it, the sand making a backdrop against which they stand like silhouettes; you've gotten so used to the rocks' mockery of humanity you're hardly moved anymore to stick your tongue out mockingly, as you've been moved before, in reply. The sand has been polished off most of the mountains, leaving miles of denuded bedrock pocked with outcroppings, like a vast ossuary picked clean by dinosaurian vultures and maggots.

They pass beneath Tezouyeg, beneath Souninan—fat peaks of basalt, thrust in fasces of organlike flutes toward wispy cirrus—and volcanic extrusions grotesquely bulked like huge, swollen catcher's mitts—into the Atakor. Mount Adedou rises like a huge lonely tent. Then, after a bafflement of valley and compass dance and confusion of the sun, you turn out of a narrow gully into what looks like the exploded ruin of a palace built by drunken giants: platform, altar, stage.

Mineral towers, tall prism-like forms stand alone or lean together precariously in clusters across a flat plain of rock, and near the center of what falls more and more into the shape, as one looks at it, of an enormous open-air temple, a gigantic nub of basalt rises, stark and clear in the sunlight, a plug of volcanic rock in a weird shape of holiness, surrounded by the soldiers of its faith petrified into columns supporting an invisible roof, or the sky: at last, clear under a now cloudlesss blue, Mount Ilaman and the Mosque of Tarmergidan.

They stop. Valleys stretch out around them, lined with columns of rock, an immense plein-air mosque beneath a vast cerulean tent penetrated by the sun as by an eye: a view of such desolate grandeur in this place of immense and casual destruction that you all go silent, leaving the vehicles, and stand for a time without speaking. Umar and Husayn suddenly kneel and, after a moment contemplating the holy mountain, bow low before it, touching their heads to the earth.

"Just a Lego with bigger pieces," Smuts says.

No one bothers to respond.

After slowing to a walk in the thickening forest, you say, "I've never gone this far into McClatchy's woods."

"I did, last fall. With my dad hunting pheasant."

"So McClatchy lets your dad hunt his land?"

"They got a deal. Dad can as long as he gets a share."

"He shoot anything last year?"

"Nothing on McClatchy's land." Frankie gives you a look. "At least that's what my dad told him."

You guffaw. "Serves him right."

You stoop and pick up a small jawless skull.

"Baby rabbit, I bet," Frankie says. "Too short for a fox, wrong shape for a squirrel."

You smooth your finger along the top of the skull and look it straight in the eye sockets. They're empty and stare back eerily.

"Wait till you find one with a jaw."

"This'll do for now." You slip it into your pocket next to the spent shell, and you both walk on.

There's another tree fallen across the path, smaller than the previous one. On either side a rusty wire fence extends into the woods: on nearby trunks are tacked torn, weathered no-trespassing signs.

"He thinks he'll scare away the *skunks*?" Frankie asks, disgustedly.

You remember the smell of a dead skunk you and your parents passed through in the family car while driving across a stretch of rolling farm country last fall, as the trees were turning red and gold on a wooded rise, a bullet-like silo shining at the foot of the hill in the dusk. "Pee-ew!" your mother said. "What a smell!" But you thought the slightly beery stench of the dead skunk didn't really spoil the view. As long as it didn't last too long.

The two of you scramble over the trunk and peer curiously around this new part of the woods, as though crossing the boundary might miraculously transform the landscape.

"Dad and me never went this way," Frankie whispers.

The woods are the same woods—the same kinds of trees and brush—but there seems to be a keener smell, darker shadows, brighter sunlight in the dapples shifting over the forest floor.

"You know who owns this part of the woods?" you ask, also whispering.

"It's ours for now," Frankie whispers back, and leads the way into the undergrowth.

A small opening in the trees you can see dimly through a sunlit tangle of brush and trees, seems to beckon.

"Watch the poison ivy," Frankie says, using his adult voice.

A bird bursts up at their feet, whirring straight toward the patchy clouds above the trees, briefly startling the boys.

"Pheasant," you say.

"Your dad ever hunt?" Frankie asks in challenging voice after a moment.

"Sure he does," you reply, defensively. "Not much around here, though. He usually goes with his friends to Michigan for a week. He says there's more deer up there."

Frankie doesn't reply.

"I once saw a white-tail deer at the edge of the Prices' field," you say.

"They're supposed to be protected," Frankie responds in a huffy voice.

"Oh?"

"But I know Bobby Miller and his brother poach them."

"What do they do with them?"

"They eat them. They're *poor*," Frankie sneers.

Your mother once said something you didn't understand at the time: "Don't brag about your advantages to your friends." *What advantages?* you had thought. Now you get it, in a flash. You peer briefly into Frankie's closed, resentful face. *Frankie's family is poor, too.*

"I once saw Mr. Hurley on a rabbit hunt in the Prices' woods," Frankie continues after an awkward pause. "Last fall."

Mr. Hurley is your fourth-grade teacher. You scowl at the mention of his name: Frankie knows you hate him.

"I'm surprised a rabbit didn't shoot *him*!"

"Maybe your rabbit tried."

"He should have aimed higher."

The bushes crackle as you move through them.

"How was Mrs. Gates?" you ask. "I may get her for fifth grade."

"She's okay." Frankie shrugs. "I could have gotten worse—I could've gotten Brooker. You afraid you might get her?"

"In the worst world of all."

"And welcome to it," he says.

"Hurley isn't that bad," you say. "He just tries too hard to be your friend. How can you be somebody's friend when you can flunk him? Ouch!" You pull a thorny branch that had grabbed your shirt.

"Did he catch any rabbits?" you ask as you approach a clearing. A few butterflies flicker over a haze of tall weeds, grass, a pageant of ferns. You both crouch down on a rock in the shade.

"He shot a rabbit as I was watching. A little thing. It kept twitching in the grass as if it was still running and alive after it fell. He looked way too proud of himself for such a dip-shit little thing."

"He's got a mean smile. When he isn't trying too hard to be nice."

"Can't say that about McReady. She *never* smiles. But she seems to know what she's doing. She even makes Bobby White keep quiet."

"Didn't his father used to be an air traffic controller in Columbus?"

"Until Reagan fired him for going on strike. Served him right! That's what my dad says."

"But . . . now he's got a lousy job. That's why Bobby White is still wearing clothes that are too small for him. That's what Tommy said, anyway."

"What does Tommy know? He's a jerk."

"My mom says they should have had a national strike. Like the French."

"Like the French! Gimme a break. People will never do that. Anyway they're too wimpy. Except when they're behind a gun."

"What 'people'?"

"*Us.* That's who!"

You look gloomily at the tangle of weeds and grasses at your feet, some already beginning to turn a whitish yellow.

"How is McReady in arithmetic?" you suddenly ask: you know arithmetic is Frankie's worst subject. You feel a mean little joy as Frankie flushes from his neck to his bangs.

"I hate fucking arithmetic. There's no way she'll ever make me like that. *I hate fucking arithmetic!*" Frankie yells.

A rabbit suddenly shoots out from a bush and runs away through the woods."Fuck you too!" Frankie shouts after it.

————

You turn another page. The words here are clearer, easier to read. Maybe because they are angrier.

Sun rims the horizontal forests, blear
the sky attempts at seizure (he reports),
night venues galled in portcullis and lime
to testaments of earth in white cement.

A tattered triumph hangs on buttercups
as the wind sports a grit leaved with dust.
Above expands a crown of clouds, nearby
collects a polite curiosity of crows.

The barnyard rings with chestnuts cut to fuel,
the crank of a tractor whines, the morning draws
the fox out of his lair, repenting but
the stiff, bald limits of foxy appetite.

He works his snout between the links of chain,
the razor wire holdings cleared of straw
of petulant emollients and cocks
wooing spinster misses in each maw.

The mantled handyman returns with rust
up to his elbows, rancid peat and jeans.
The darkling thrush reminds of him who knows
the bitter essence of the scent of crows.

Immediate to sky, the blind king claws
the rude earth with his sceptre, strike and jerk:
I came unto this field, I laid them waste
that dared deny my privilege, my right.

You read the words a second time, this time aloud.

————

You watch the sun descend behind Mount Ilaman.

To set up camping, you had found an immense barrel-like rock vault facing the mountain in the twilight, and set up tents under its coping.

Vivian suddenly bends forward with her hands in an attitude of prayer, her eyes squeezed shut, her lips murmuring. After a moment you turn away, embarrassed. You once felt that holiness in the mountains, and you flash on a view of a valley descending beneath you as you rode up a mountainside in a cable car, and of mountain scenery spread before you behind the whirring propellers of a plane through which you peered. You wince at the memories of your childlike wonder.

As you and Peter are building a fire, Cecilia suddenly looks up, drawing in her breath and staring intently at the overhanging vault. You ignore her, concentrating on the fire, as she stands and walks up to the rock surface.

"It's carved," she says, in a deliberate, professional voice. "And painted."

The twitching light of the fire shows a frieze of carved rock: a row of abstractly shaped cattle, not much smaller than the living animals, with great sleek horns and heads reduced to blunt, oddly perky triangles, their bodies simplified but immediately recognizable, the whole carved in low relief along an unseen baseline a meter and a half above the ground.

She smoothes her fingers across the surface of the carvings.

"How old do you think they are, professor?" you ask her.

She looks back with a gaspy little smile that almost undermines her professional poise.

"Oh," she says, "Neolithic, for sure. Ten thousand years, maybe. They call it 'Pastoral' here, though."

"I know," you say with a smile at her unconscious patronage.

"Could be Paleolithic, of course," Smuts speaks up.

Has to stick his oar in. Can't just let the girl have her moment.

Cecilia doesn't object, though she looks skeptical.

"However old they are," Vivian says, admiring the art from the other side of the fire—and they are truly fine, for vigor, grace, a fine complexity of composition combined with the simplicity of the shapes, for a cunning respect for subjects and material: an instinct for the jugular, "they're older than this desert is. This place could never have supported those animals today."

When you see the rest of the inner wall of the vault illuminated by the fire, you hold your breath. It is covered, spectacularly, with paintings and carvings—carvings of large animals, bulls and cows and something like a hippo; paintings, above, in red, of hunters and their prey in a jumble of abstractions; the figures seeming to move in and out of the wavering and flickering of firelight.

A crowd of hunters swarms across the high barrel vault, aiming a flock of spears at the herds of prey, with one lone archer superbly arcing his weapon at a shaggy beast in the lower corner from his spot half a wall away. A flock of birds sweeps up in red along the far side, ignored, oddly, by the hunters. Unless the birds were never meant to be taken by the hunters, and the artist was just letting his inspiration run away with him, inspiration flying away with the birds of his imagination.

"Maybe they fled here," you say meditatively. "Maybe they were just painting and carving what they knew—memories of their life before they were driven into the desert."

Vivian looks out from the vault, where Ilaman stands invisible in the darkness. "They're offerings. To the mountain."

She turns back. "All this time in the sun and wind, and they haven't broken or eroded or even faded."

"The gods don't mind wrecking a civilization now and again," you say, giving a glance to the invisible mountain. But you can see nothing. "Though," you say, turning back to the glow of reflected firelight, "they always seem to save the art."

"Look over here," says Sean.

Cecilia steps up to a series of red hand prints on the wall, just above her shoulder. She leans over and places her hand over one of them; it's a close fit. She looks back, startled, as Sean suddenly aims a throw-away camera in her direction. It flashes.

As the group goes to sleep around the dying fire, bats zig-zag across the rising moon, gibbous again along its other edge, and they hear the growls of lynxes coming from somewhere nearby.

"We're going in circles again," Smuts snaps at one point.

You grin, bizarrely, back. You feel a happiness you're almost afraid to show. Yet how real can it possibly be?

Vivian is asleep on your shoulder.

They have lost count of the days. They lost their only calendar. They only know of sunrise and sunset, sleep in the darkness, the hours between brief rationed meals.

In the distance Mount Tahat raises its head, half white on its snowy north side. Yet it has a way of appearing at different points on the horizon after they dip in and out of the Hoggar's valleys, as if playing blind man's bluff with them, daring them to catch it.

TamTam is near Tahat's base, so the mountain dictates their direction. Which it cannot do if it keeps changing place on the horizon. But even the distance between them and the mountain seems to change, shift, as if the air contained different kinds of magnifying glass that cheated the sense of distance. Everything about the mountain seems illusory, teasing, baiting, pretense.

The cragginess of the Hoggar, and the resultant inability of the travelers to focus on a landmark for any but brief periods, increases their difficulties. They are at the landscape's mercy. The farther they go, the deeper into the labyrinth they seem to be. The highway has become a maze.

Your eyes brush the old broken GPS screen on the dashboard. The last GPS satellite went down over the Pacific years before. The next step back would be to camel caravans. *So much for the industrial age: good riddance! A fool's paradise. The world's most powerful psychotropic, creator of the most potent of all hallucinations—of metal and glass, concrete and plastic, electricity and oil; hallucinations you could weigh in your hand, throw at your enemies, wear, wear out, smear over your body, eat, drink, absorb, consume, they seemed so real; even when you couldn't touch them, could only watch them on screens, they promised to overwhelm every other possible reality . . .*

"What is 'reality,' after all?" you had found yourself replying to Vivian the night before as you talked before bed, after night had fallen, and you gazed out toward the dark form of Mount Ilaman (it had subdued even the mustache). "Reality is what doesn't let you get away with it. Reality is what is hitting us now."

"Now? Us? Hitting?" Vivian had asked, with an ironic look, watching you through the darkness. A bit of moonlight caught her eyes.

"Hitting. *Me*. Now," you had said.

You looked steadily at her, she at you.

They had almost kissed, at one point. But it seemed hopeless, ridiculous, irrelevant. Vaguely indecent.

You shook it off. Again.

Maybe when they found TamTam. Returned to *their* reality. This was all mirage. A nightmare, but a mirage.

"What if it's a mirage that won't let you get away with it? Then the mirage becomes reality." Who said that—Vivian?

You turn in your bag to her, lying in a separate bag less than a foot away.

Her dark profile makes her look even more like Miranda. She seems to be sleeping. *Is she, too, just an illusion then? Is memory an illusion? The wishful thinking of the lost?*

Bad philosophy. Go to sleep. Besser zu schlafen, as the crazy German poet said. When in doubt, go to sleep. Meine

238

Dichter. Mein Dichter. Und denker . . . you thinkers . . . you dreamers . . .

Suddenly she turns to him.

"Me," she whispers, as if answering a question. "You."

And he falls, spiraling into the darkness of her eyes.

Frankie almost stumbles into a small stream shaded with ferns. He pulls back sharply. You both peer into the rushing water, avoiding each other's look.

The glassy water moves, almost silent among a few stones. You can see a handful of leaves pressed against the bottom, the muddy bottom magnified by the water. You crouch down and stick in your finger: the end of your finger in the water seems to break, shift to the side, and expand the moment it crosses the surface: an optical illusion, as Mr. Hurley had explained in science earlier that year.

You withdraw your finger, then stick it back in. A minnow appears—or maybe it's a tadpole—and wiggles, a narrow inch of blackish brown with big eyes, near your finger. It must look bigger than it is, and that must help birds and animals that hunt it for food; but also it isn't exactly where it appears to be, so that must help the minnow. Or the tadpole.

Suddenly it's gone. You withdraw your finger and look up and down the spring as it runs in a crooked channel across the forest floor. It probably ends in Mannahawkin Creek.

"Think it's safe to drink?" you ask.

"Sure."

They bend down and slurp the fresh, cold water.

"Don't drink a minnow."

"Ugh!"

"Would you call this forest or woods?" you ask Frankie as they walk away.

"I'd call it woods," Frankie says without hesitation. "A forest is what they have out in California, with redwood trees, going for, like, hundreds of miles."

239

You imagine the immense trees, a thousand feet high, and forestland covering valleys and hills without a break for as far as your eye can see, filled with bears, wolves, cougars, wild sheep, elk, moose. Forest is wilderness—untouched by people, alien, pure.

This was "woods," small, broken up by farmers' fields, with nothing in it bigger than an occasional white-tail deer or more dangerous than a wild cat or water moccasin. It still had its mysteries. Little gods seemed to hide behind the trees—little crooked Indian tree spirits, whispery squaw phantoms of vines and grasses.

After staying late one night, you had walked from Gabriel and Topher's house through the woods back to your house—it wasn't that far, down a dirt drive that touched the edge of the Palmers' backyard, but it had felt like miles, as if you had been walking for an hour under the dim light of a half moon, a light more frightening than darkness, under a shell of sky pocked with a dark, cold radiance of stars millions of miles away in the cold wash of darkness of the universe in which the earth swam, lit temporarily by a small star called the sun and the reflected face of the moon—as you walked through the tangled blackness of the woods that seemed to hide demons and monsters and zombies appearing briefly behind trees in the moonlight, weighing whether or not you were worth catching, toying with, eating . . .

Something came toward you—a form in the darkness walking up the drive with a small light bobbing in front of it—just someone walking up the drive with a flashlight, you had told yourself. But as it came closer, you suddenly thought, *It's a witch*—you could see the blacker form of the hat thrown into huge, black shadow by the bobbing light against the scraggly shade of the underbrush and the witch's profile falling in and out of the light as she stared down, still unaware of you, watching the path ahead of her as she walked straight toward you.

You panicked and irrupted in a run down the drive past her,

imagining a crowd of demons behind you chasing you like a pack of hounds . . .

You ran till you reached the back door of your house, with its single bulb above the lintel, and leapt through the screen door to safety and slammed the screen door and the wood and glass back door behind you, breathing heavily as you looked through the window into the wall of black caused by the radiance of the porch light against the night. You felt caught between shame and the terror you had felt in the woods as your heart beat long and hard.

"You think Gabe and Topher are back yet?" you ask Frankie.

"I saw Topher on her bike last night."

They go single file between a pair of birches.

"They're lucky."

"About what."

"Not having to go to school."

"I don't know," Frankie scowls. "Imagine having to live with your teacher. Home would be like school. There'd be no escape."

You consider this. Gabe and Topher were being home-schooled by their mother. You love your mom of course, but the thought of having her as your teacher watching over you ever day, day in, day out, with nowhere to escape, no one to complain to, nowhere to hide, was not a nice thought.

"Gabe and Topher don't seem too hurt," you say.

"They're weird anyway. How would anybody know?"

They *are* weird, but in a way you like, even though you can never quite relax around them the way you can around Frankie. Your parents call their parents "old hippies" and "pseudo-gyp-sies" and pretend to look down on them; they even show a contempt they would never show the Palmers, as though it was, in some sense, okay to be rude to the Wheatleys, at least when discussing them—though his parents were always cordial, in a slightly brittle way, when they met. You sometimes feel a little envious of them. They seem exotic; in some ways freer, in the way they dress and their manners (both children call their parents by their first names—"Howard" and "Debra"—which you always find a little shocking), their home-schooling, their sudden going off on long trips around the country, even abroad; but in other ways, they seem less free, even constricted, inhibited, as in their speech, at times almost too careful, oblique, priggish—they never swear or say anything harsh about anyone, or even bluntly direct, except against the president, who seems in their eyes to be little better than a dolt, or the puppet of Satan, which confuses and alarms you, given your generally warm feelings for the country's avuncular leader (your own parents are studiously silent on this subject, except for an occasional sigh and shrug— "There he goes again," is your father's favorite comment when watching President Reagan; this makes your mother laugh ruefully, for some mysterious reason). It makes you wonder if you are missing something important.

The Wheatleys don't eat meat or wear leather, and they had looked solemn and sad when you showed up one winter day in your coonskin hat (made from real fur) that Grand-nan gave you the year before she died. ("Make you look like Danny Crockett," she had said in her thick accent as she placed it carefully on your head and admired you in it. "*Davy* Crockett, Nan," Mom had corrected her with a thin smile. But Grand-nan ignored the correction and ever after always asked about your "Danny Crockett hat.")

The Wheatleys can be a little prissy despite their gypsy-like ways, a little "holier than thou," your mom says. ("Like all atheists," your father sometimes adds with one of his ambiguous looks.) There's always something brittle in the air at their house, especially around the mother, who is thin and elegant, with her strange eyes and brilliant but ambiguous smile and her delicate, intense way of speaking. She always wears, draped loosely across her shoulders, a brightly colored scarf from her large collection. Mr. Wheatley is zealously pleasant, and prematurely bald.

242

You're not quite sure what to make of them, but they intrigue you. Especially Topher, the little girl a year and a half younger than you. Gabe is eleven and treats mere nine-year-olds with weary condescension. He tries to be nice (as his parents have no doubt dictated he must be), but it always comes off as tolerating slightly damaged goods. This sometimes drives Frankie to distraction, but it makes you curious: it reminds you of how your father treats people outside the family—even at times inside the family. It makes you try to do what you know is almost hopeless: impress Gabe, which Gabe allows only very grudgingly. When you succeed, usually by coming up with something even Gabe doesn't know, it is profoundly satisfying though always short-lived.

Topher is a bit of a mystery: small, with long hair the color of dark honey, full cheeks, and a strangely expressionless mouth. She always wears old-fashioned dresses that go down to her maryjanes and is usually silent in her talkative brother's presence, which is much of the time, since they generally go about together. She has her mother's strange, staring eyes, and a way of staring at people and things as if from a great distance. You feel a little, funny thrill, vaguely unsettling, whenever she looks at you, unlike any sensation the girls in school give you; *they* are generally annoying. But Topher's mysterious reticence and her composed look, so uncannily self-possessed as she always seems, stay with you in a way you just don't get.

When you think of the presences of the woods, the little nymphs and fairies in the shadows of the daylight, they often have her solemn eyes. As when you think of the tree spirits, they often have Gabe's superior glance.

"It was a brand-new bike," Frank says with disgust.

"What?" you perk up.

"Topher's bike. She broke the old one just a few weeks ago, before they left. So what do they do? Repair it? That's not good enough for them! Spoiled brats, my dad calls them."

You imagine Topher riding down the long drive you ran

down in a panic that night last year, on her shiny new bike with her long hair riding the wind.

"Yeah," you say half-heartedly.

Maybe spoiled. Maybe not. Maybe lucky. Maybe not.

"Damn! Look at that." Frankie halts.

A deserted house, half in ruins, rises among the trees. Most of its windows are broken, torn shingles hang from the walls, a brick chimney is scattered over the sagging roof. A smell of wet ashes fills the air.

On turning out of a small valley, you see them in the distance—half a dozen or so, on white camels. It's almost startling: the first people you've seen in almost two weeks. Like seeing a particularly exotic form of animal. At first you don't quite believe your eyes.

They don't notice you at first: at least a hundred yards away, they're slowly moving up a defile with their backs toward you.

"Blow your damn horn," Smuts suddenly shouts. "*They* know their way out of here."

When you hesitate, Smuts reaches over and presses with all his might on the klaxon.

The ugly sound, like the roar of a gigantic camel, fills the valley.

They stop and look back; the camels especially alert.

You suck in your breath: you could turn and drive off, fast, now—the camels won't be able to catch you on this terrain—but you are indeed, truly lost, you need help to get out of this place. You have little choice now but to trust the Bedu. It is now the Bedu's choice to trust you and help you, or ignore you and proceed on their way.

For several minutes they don't move as you drive the vehicle slowly, rocking, down a dry creek bed toward them. *Perhaps they're conferring,* you think. Then they slowly turn their camels on the narrow track and cumbrously climb down the track to the valley, toward where the Hummer is headed. At one point the six or seven of them stop and wait, staring at you, wrapped in long, white robes and topped with headdresses of a deep blue, atop the pale, patient animals, as the Hummer, suddenly seeming the acme of loud, intrusive vulgarity, lumbers toward them.

You pull the vehicle to a stop twenty feet away.

"Tuareg. Maybe from Adrar," you say.

"What does that mean?" Smuts asks.

"You don't want to know, mate," says Peter.

"You mean they're not safe?"

"Only," you say, "if they think we aren't."

You know this is not entirely candid but there's no point in alarming everyone.

"Stay here."

You and Frankie briefly contemplate the building. Black smoke-smudges smear the wall above a corner window. The rusted-out skeleton of a reaper lies in the front yard, overgrown with ferns, with corroded gas and oil canisters and sheets of corrugated iron lying about, a bed frame with rusted springs, a sofa frame, its upholstery long eaten away, a rusty saw, a set of corroded files.

"How old do you think it is?" you ask.

"*Real* old."

"Older than our parents?"

"Older than our *grandparents*."

You look around. "There's no sign of a road."

"The trees've all grown up since it burned. *That's* how old."

You imagine the land around them empty as a field, then the trees growing from saplings around the abandoned house, growing over decades until the trees returned, surrounding the house in a curtain of thick, jungly green, taking it back into the woods.

"Want to go inside?" asks Frankie.

"What if it's got a ghost?" you say with a weak grin.

245

"There aren't any ghosts!"

You shrug and waggle your head as Frankie trots up the steps to the porch. The second step cracks under him, and he sinks briefly to the ground, then leaps up onto the porch.

A damp, ashen, decaying smell, as of wet charred planks, spring mud and old mushrooms, enfolds you, stronger as it comes through the half-open door. Frankie pushes the door inward, then it sticks; he pushes it harder and it still won't give, then you help him, and the door moves inward with a harsh scrape.

The dark inside has a danker, mustier odor, and a cobweb covering the doorway shreds and sticks to you as you walk in.

"Ugh," Frankie says, waving the web from his face. A spider scurries into the ceiling shadows.

Inside is pitch black, with a vile smell; then the dusty light slowly reveals an old front parlor with sticks of furniture in the corners, a broken stairway to the second floor, a hallway leading to the back. Down from above comes a sound of rustling birds. The floor sags as you creep over it, rotten with termites and damp.

The walls at the top of the stairs are a carbonized black under a sprinkling of light from the caved-in roof.

At the end of the hall a doorway glows dimly.

You tip-toe down the hall, the light ahead vaguely brightening—or rather, seeming to grow less dim. A dirty counter, a deep, corroded sink, a scarred, filthy stove, a gaping icebox from another era and webbed with spider silk gradually appear beyond the doorway. The collapsed surface of a table next to the door. A pair of dirt-smeared windows above the counter. A rug rolled up at the bottom of the far wall, with a decayed shoe, torn sole upward, lying at one end.

You pause at the doorway.

Frankie gives you an arch look, as though to break the spell that had settled over the two of you, and takes a step into the room.

"I don't think anybody's home," he says cockily.

Something moves at the bottom of the wall and at the end of the rug a head turns to them bearing an old, bruised, bloated face with iron-gray hair, a broken nose and staring eyes.

"Shit!"

You run back down the hall. You see other faces, shapes of heads, arms, shoulders, in the parlor's shadows, emerging from the broken furniture, staring from the walls, though you know, you know, you know they're just cracks of light in the walls, spots of light from the roof, shafts of sunlight from the broken windows. The hallway, the parlor seem suddenly immensely long.

A rat shoots ahead of you out the door.

Then you see it, in a corner under a window: a dog curled up, emaciated from hunger or disease, mangy, its skin covered with scabies. It turns its unnaturally large, shiny eyes to you and whimpers and you stop momentarily, or think you do. Its tail weakly thumps the floor. Frankie dashes out the front door and you run after him.

Frankie's foot again falls through the same step as you both dash across the porch, and he hops out of it in a panic.

"Did you see the dog?" you say, as the two boys run across the front yard.

"Who has time for a damned dog!" Frankie shouts, and you both run as fast as you can into the woods until you can no longer see any sign of the house behind you when you glance back, terrified, over your shoulder.

You're starting to slow down when an animal you can't identify shoots out from the brush nearby, and frightened again, you set out again and run deeper, in panic, into the woods.

At last the both of you stop and look at each other, panting, at once frightened and embarrassed, suddenly ashamed.

"Must be some homeless guy."

"Yeah, just some homeless guy."

You stand there, looking at each other for a long moment, panting.

"Ugly old bastard!" says Frankie mad at having been so frightened. He suddenly kicks a tree stump. "If McClatchy finds him he'll shoot him."

You caught only a glance at the old, dirty face, battered, grizzled, the milky eyes blinking with a crazy at them—like a severed head turning to them from the roll of filthy rug by the wall. You remember the shoe, the torn bottom of the sole in the dim light.

"D'you think he'll chase after us?" Frankie asks.

"Why would he do that?"

"Kidnap. Ransom. He could use the money." Frankie tries to grin. "There were more of them in the house. I saw one of them sleeping under the couch in the front room."

You remember the forms you thought you saw in the shadows. No. They were just shadows and random light. . . . Only the dog was real. You remember its look of helpless pleading as you turned away and ran. You think of challenging Frankie, but what's the point? And you begin walking again, at a rapid pace, crashing deeper into the underbrush.

"Maybe we should go home," you say after walking in silence for a time. "I've had enough exploring."

You stop and look back again. No sign of anyone in pursuit. No sign of where you are or where you've been. You could be in the middle of a forest. A wilderness.

The sun is almost straight above your heads. It warms the air of the clearing. It must be past noon, lunch time—your mother will be angry at you for missing it.

"Which direction?" Frankie asks.

"Back where we came."

"We'll have to pass the house."

"Maybe we can go around it."

Frankie shrugs with a scowl.

And you both head back the way you came.

But after five, ten, fifteen minutes, you find no sign of the house, nothing you recognize: you had run in a blind panic, noticing nothing. Now you have no idea where you are.

"God damn," Frankie says.

The birdcalls have fallen since the morning, as has the breeze, and silence reigns in the noon. The air is warm. A few white butterflies flutter over a patch of weeds. A snail oozes its way along the ground. A gecko appears in a flash on a nearby stump, takes a brief pose, then flashes off.

A little beetle with a round, tomato-red back with two black dots suddenly appears, crawling along your thigh.

"Lady bug, lady bug, fly away home! Your house is on fire and your children will burn," you recite. The bug opens its red carapace and flies off.

"Too bad the sun's still so high up," you remark, looking up at the sky through the trees.

"Yeah."

"You bring your compass?"

"No."

You try to remember the rules of what to do when you're lost in the woods: stay where you are and call out loud if you've been separated from your group, or, if you're alone, start walking in a straight line—sooner or later you'll find a stream, a road, a field.

From there, you're half-way home. *We're hardly lost at all*, you think, looking coolly around you at the trees disappearing into the shadows.

Someday I want to be really lost. So lost I don't know where I am. Like in a movie . . .

You remember the dream you had the night before: the immense wilderness you were lost in . . .

"Watch that poison oak," Frankie says, pointing to a plant beside your foot.

You step away carefully from the weed's glossy, oak-shaped leaves and then go deeper into the woods.

————

249

On the next page the following words appear, written in block
letters, carefully shaped, as though your younger self had meant
to engrave them in stone.

Welcome to the chalked tangle,
welcome to the dead mine,
to the un-elmed street, the dead seat
of the unthroned. Where the bog darks.

You do not have a visa?
Go to the wall, or better yet, a cell. You do not
have a constitution in your pocket?
The buzzer emphatically screams. Go to hell.

Believe, oh infidel, in the apodictic
right of freedom's lie,
of the unconstrained pursuit of happiness
into the labyrinth of the dog's tail.

March, smile, wave. The scag unfurls
into the eagle's might. A president
descends into pitch black.
Everyone says please and thank you.

Off with the shoes. Spread those legs.
Aim high. We're all in the all-together
since slammed and burned. You didn't know?
Not the difference between gizmo and Gitmo?

And Elmo! He's our king! or is it
Spongebob of the Squarepants?
March, march, to Ur, to Kabul,
to Baghdad beneath a bloody rag.

And drawn and quartered the city
gives good head abruptly detached,
brands in bloody letters Liberty,
hung mouths, the muted kiss.

The peak shafts to the core.
Snow lards the sandstorm,
covering tanks and Blackhawks with a gravy
succulent and deeply strange. The big dog eats

off on his own. Crumbs fall like bombs
exploding at his feet. He doesn't care.
The mountain rises at his whipping tail.
Thunder blacks his teeth. He eats alone.

The final words seem to echo long in the darkening living room
where you sit, reading, the sound of the surf coming in through
the open window.

———————

One of them has green eyes—not the leader; a younger one
on a camel off to the side. An ax head and handle show along
his upper thigh. The eyes of the others are as brown as watered
coffee. The eyes are compelling if only because they're the
only features you can see besides the hands, gracefully holding
the camel reins. Their faces are swathed in veils of blue—for
two of them, white—that cover everything but the eyes beneath
crown-like turbans. The veils make them look mysterious,
intimidating. The robes hang like lazy wings along the camels' flanks. The camels stare, sleepy-eyed and indifferent, at the
blankness of the landscape.

The men watch in silence as you approach, stumbling
among the splintered rocks. You can feel the heaviness of your
exhaustion, the weariness from lack of food and water from
the strict rations over the past few days: you hope it isn't too

apparent—the show of weakness is irresistible to certain kinds of evil. Rifle butts stick out of the robes of most of the Tuareg. *Never felt so naked, never felt so the color of my skin. Like chain mail. Never irrelevant, especially now. They're appraising me, weighing me in some internal balance. Guessing the price I'll command in the market?*

You bend and fold your arm in greeting, displaying a palm pale and empty; motion toward yourself, back toward your companions, then ahead, with a shrug.

"Tamanrasset," you say, and wincingly hear yourself mumble the word. You repeat the name, louder and more clearly. "Tamanrasset. Tahat."

"TamTam," says the leader in response, using the city's nickname, with a flicker of recognition, and says something in Tuareg you don't understand. You curse your intellectual laziness for not learning it when you had the chance.

Their leader is not a particularly large man, from what you can see of him, but has presence; sits more bolt upright on his beast than the others and stares out from his sleek blue veil with more detachment, without the pointed suspicion of his followers. His veil shines in the sun like new silk of cobalt blue. His camel gear is just noticeably more luxurious, and a dagger handle gleams at his waist. He is the only one who does not carry a rifle. Perhaps he doesn't need to.

The Tuareg repeats what he just said, motioning toward your vehicle then up the trail the men on camelback had been taking. The others merely stare silently, the green-eyed Tuareg boring his eyes relentlessly into your gray ones.

Again you bow and fold your arm in acknowledgement, and walk back to the Hummer, careful this time not to stumble.

"They want us to follow them up the trail they were taking. It'll be a test for this buggy but we don't have much choice."

They watch the half dozen Tuareg once again climb the narrow, rocky trail on their camels.

"Do you think it's safe to do this?" asks Vivian.

252

"It's even less safe to do what we were doing."

Slowly you drive up the defile, clumsily rocking behind the switching tail of the last of the camels.

You remember, for some reason, the profile of an elk you saw in another range of mountains, in America, that distant country of fable and mystery, known by everyone and no one—your strange and alien home—many years before.

After half an hour of moving through a maze of ravines and wadis, you come to a canyon, at the end of it, in the distance, a flank of Mount Tahat bright in the afternoon sun. The Tuareg turn in the opposite direction, and you halt and hit the klaxon. Its mournful blast fills the canyon, echoing back from the mountainsides, like a huge camel's moaning. The Tuareg halt and gaze back at you, the camels' ears perk up. You wave outside your window and point toward Tahat sun-drenched in the distance. The Tuareg shout something incomprehensible and point ahead. You motion again toward Tahat, and they insistently point again, crying out more vehemently. One of the Tuareg rests his hand on the rifle butt sticking out of his robe.

"We better follow them," says Smuts. "They at least know their way around here."

"I wouldn't trust them with me mother!" Peter says, with a broad Irish accent, from the back.

The Tuareg seem to wait.

As if challenging us to try and run away.

The Tuareg keeps his hand resting on the rifle butt.

You turn the Hummer and slowly nose it toward the camels.

The one weapon you've kept is a small .22 rifle, in the back under the spare tire. For hunting small game, should they need it. *Not the best tool for shooting men.*

You catch up with the Tuareg, and as a group they move forward; the broad hairy flank of one of the camels almost brushing your elbow as you rest it out your window.

You can feel the veiled rider staring down at you.

At one point they turn out of the mountains and you overlook a wide plain. You notice Smuts staring at something on the distant sand.

"Good God," he says, and points out his window. "I don't believe my . . . Vivian. Look."

Vivian pulls from your shoulder and cranes toward the right. It's the first time Smuts has addressed her directly in days.

You look too, seeing nothing but a sweep of perfectly level plain covered with a sheet of sand.

"Do we have the binoculars back there?"

Peter rummages a moment in the back.

"Here, guv."

Smuts raises them to his eyes.

"By God. . . . You can see it plain as day." He hands them to Vivian.

She gives a little gasp, then gives the landscape a long, questioning look.

"Dido's toehold," she says slowly.

"Legion camp," Smuts responds peremptorily.

"Or farthest outpost of Pharaoh?"

Vivian sighs and drops the binoculars to her lap. She looks at you, then lifts them again. You can see in her eyes her hesitation to mention Duden's crazy hope—there's little point now. And who needs any more of Smuts's scathing retorts? "We'll never know now."

"Never say die . . ." Smuts says. And they both stare across the plain, passing the glasses back and forth one more time.

You give the landscape a quick glance from your seat behind the driver's wheel. "So, what is it, exactly?"

Vivian points through the dirty windshield.

"Follow my arm," she says softly. "You can just see it on the ground—city walls—a complicated grid inside the box. Streets. And those amorphous areas may have been groves, or maybe a waterhole. The light just catches it."

Glancing hard several times in momentary glimpses from

your driving, you can make out a rough diagram on the ground, like the figure seen in the satellite photograph: a broad, loose polygon-like box, spread across the valley floor, with inside it vague spots where the waterhole Vivian mentioned may once have been or groves of palms, and a warren of broken lines, like ancient streets, the foundations of buildings, houses, a central square, a market, a palace. *Remains of a labyrinth,* you think.

"It's worn down since the satellite photo caught it," Vivian says.

"There must have been more water back then," says Smuts, his voice dragging strangely.

Around them in the sweeping view there's no sign of water except the white print of snow on Mount Tahat's peak, with its quickly vanishing hope of Tamanrasset and escape.

"We don't still have the picture, do we?" Smuts asks.

"No," Vivian says after a moment, quietly. "He kept it with him . . ."

Smuts laughs dryly.

"I wonder if it had a bird carved on its gate, with a key in its beak."

Vivian stares at the plain.

"And sleeping royalty. And a treasure." He looks at Vivian, who stubbornly resists the appeal suddenly in his eyes. "To think we may have finally found it. El Dorado of the Sahara, Atlantis of the sands. Maybe it wasn't a lie after all. . . ."

Smuts looks back at it lingeringly as they pass, then it disappears behind a boulder back into obscurity, lost again, a phantom city.

"I guess we're lost. . . ." says Frankie.

The woods are darkening under the falling sun.

"I think so," you reply at last.

A bird chirps, monotonously, a few trees away. "Do you think hollering might help?"

"Can't hurt," says Frankie. "We got to be real far from

McClatchy's." Frankie stands up, draws in a long breath, and lets out a loud yell: "Hel-looo!"

They listen.

"Hel-looo!" he yells again. "Anybody theee-re?"

Silence except for the chirping of the bird.

"He-eeey!" You join in, at the top of your lungs.

"Hel-looo!"

"We're lo-ooost!"

"Anybody theee-re?"

"He-eeey!"

"Hel-looo!"

"We're lo-ooost!"

"Anybody theee-re?"

"He-eeey!"

"Hel-looo!"

"We're lo-ooost!"

"Anybody theee-re?"

You listen hard. The bird has stopped.

The silence after the yells is even deeper than before.

Frankie takes a pebble and throws it at the opposite trunk.

"I think we should change direction," he says.

"Where?" you ask, feeling even more tired and irritated after the futile yelling.

"I don't know. Going west hasn't helped. Maybe south."

You bite your lip. You're tired and hungry and above all, thirsty—you haven't had any water since the little spring.

"We should keep going straight."

Frankie snarls: "Well, *I* say we should go south. Following your plan has just gotten us loster. And we'll just get loster if we keep doing it. You want to stay here the whole night?"

You have a flash of panic: in your mind you see the man's face as it turned toward you in the kitchen, and the shadows you saw in the parlor as you ran through the deserted house suddenly seem frightening.

"No. Do you just want to go around in circles till we die out here?"

"*No!*" yells Frankie. "*No, no, no!*"

They stand, face to face, their faces twisted and red, their arms raised and hands clenched like claws.

Frankie suddenly turns and starts hammering the tree.

"Fuck, fuck, fuck, fuck, fuck, fuck!" he shouts. He stops and leans his head against the tree, whimpering. He stops almost immediately, wipes his face on his sleeve, then leans his blond head again against the bark.

You feel too scared to cry. You look away, again listening intently for any human sound.

Somewhere farther off the bird starts chirping again.

The two boys stand against the trees for a long time, not looking at each other or speaking.

At the final turn, past a black tor at whose base shimmers a bed of shattered coffee-black onyx that creaks as they cross it, they see, spreading ahead of them in the light dusk, a vast sea of dunes, a mass of sand swirled and licked into a kind of enormous rumpled sheet blown by centuries of wind. The lowering sun sweeps it with shadows thrown from whalebacks and star and giant sickle dunes, like great herds, and glowing in brilliant shades of tan and pink and red under the setting sun.

At the edge of the sand sea, where it meets the edge of the blasted volcanic region they have gradually been leaving, you can see, dotted with early supper fires, the tents of the Tuareg encampment.

"The Great Erg, they call it," you say, as all of you gaze over the vast sea of sand opening out before them, rising enormously behind the camp. "The Big Egg, among initiates."

"Bahr bela ma," says Smuts, bluntly.

Husayn repeats it, in the back, softly and in a purer accent: "Bahr belà mà."

"Sea without water," you say.

Seems like an ocean. No, not seems—is, oh very much, sir. Ocean that drank all the water in the sea.

Their guides lead them down the last miles from the low rise to the long tongue of sand where the camp lies.

You take a quick glance back, but there's no more sign of Tahat, and only nebulous lumps of blackness on the horizon where the Hoggar stands. You wouldn't be too surprised if they'd entirely vanished by the morning.

Their guides give cry as they enter the camp, with answering calls from veiled men and unveiled women and a gaggle of barefoot kids who greet them with happy screams and laughter. The tied-up camels greet their returning peers with roars, and dogs yip and scamper around the tents. A few goats look up, laboriously chewing. The slow, lumbering Hummer, with its camel guard, is greeted with gaping looks; as it rolls to a stop near a fire, a small gathering surrounds it, ragged, touching the glass windows and wind-eaten, colorless metal body, the grill with its sinister idiot grin, the dirt-packed tires.

"Seems like we're either guests," says Smuts, "or prisoners."

"Maybe we're both," says Vivian.

"Maybe they haven't decided yet," you say.

You watch the leader descend from his camel and motion the other Tuareg to approach the vehicle as he discourses, with sweeping gestures toward it and the distant Hoggar. The other men gather around him, watching him intently, ignoring the Hummer, listening, sometimes responding, sometimes nodding, sometimes shaking their heads.

"Ever feel like meat in a butcher shop?" you ask.

"Not since I stopped hanging out in bars," says Vivian.

Eventually the leader approaches them, with the other men in a loose group behind him, and examines his prize with a quietly theatrical show of authority, pointing out various details—the goggling headlights, bruised lip of the bumper, institutional toaster grille, side mirrors, running board, on which he places one foot, either to display purpose or to show conquest, as on a dead bull—and making brisk, no doubt witty comments: at one

258

point, his men break out in laughter as the leader pulls the door handle on your side and gives it a hard yank.

Probably comparing it unfavorably to one of his camels.

You had prudently unlocked the door, and it swings open with an unoiled squeak.

You stare into the eyes of the leader standing over you in the darkening air. The dagger handle gleams dully at his waist. Behind him the other men, their laughter suddenly stilled, watch through their veils the naked faces before them.

You raise your hand, again, from the steering wheel, holding it up, palm outward, in a pacific gesture, and slowly climb out of the vehicle. Vivian climbs after you. The other doors open and the rest emerge.

The Tuareg look them over once more with that appraising, uncomfortable look through the slits in their veils. The looks of the women are more frank and more curious. They stand in a group slightly away from the men and watch as the whites stand awkwardly outside their vehicle, suddenly vulnerable and fragile-looking in the dying evening and the firelight.

One of the Tuareg women, a small older woman with whitish hair and fatigued, sad eyes, says something to the group of you; it sounds like it might be a question, but all you can do is stare back at her. She repeats her question.

The leader barks something and the woman snaps back at him, but ceases. He walks up to you and, sweeping his hand across the encampment, he says, "TamTam."

You stomach sinks at the extravagance of the lie.

You shake your head slowly, then gesture back toward where they came.

"Tamanrasset," you say, gesturing toward the vanished lumps of distant mountains standing somewhere in the dark. "Tamanrasset. Tahat."

The leader gazes at you chillingly in the eye. Then he sweeps his arm around the darkening landscape that surrounds them.

"Sahara," he says.

He leads them toward a small, square tent of animal hides and raffia screens at the edge of the encampment.

A shot rings out, an echoless report. A camel roars in response and a dog barks excitedly.

They stop and the leader shouts toward the back of the group of Tuareg. Several voices shout back, sounding apologetic and fulsomely explanatory. The leader briefly scolds them, then returns to leading his guests—or prisoners—to their quarters.

A fire burns in front of the tent, which stands with one wall open toward the fire, and you all stand about awkwardly in the enclosure after entering it, looking at each other, stared at by the Tuareg; silent, nervous.

The leader looks you over as if you were camels being readied for market. He suddenly takes note of Umar and Husayn, half hidden behind their elders till now; looking wide-eyed and blank with terror. And he abruptly orders something to a Tuareg near him. The Tuareg walks over and seizes the two boys by their arms and drags them, wailing with fear, out of the tent.

"Wait a minute!" you cry out indignantly and stand up to the leader. You suddenly feel the muzzle of a rifle in the soft flesh under your chin and find yourself facing another pair of eyes gazing into your own between layers of heavy veil.

You can hear Umar and Husayn crying out as they are dragged down the camp, and suddenly their voices stop.

You back down under the pressure of the rifle and the staring eyes. You can feel your companions press back toward the walls of the tent. You are suddenly aware of a smell: a harsh, gagging odor coming from just outside the tent.

The leader issues some orders to the Tuareg around him, then abruptly leaves. Three men sit on the ground across from them, rifles cradled in their laps, and a woman starts cooking what looks like a meal for them in the fire outside.

"I'm very thirsty," Cecilia suddenly says. It's what everyone is thinking. They haven't had water since midday.

You turn to the guards and make a drinking motion. One of them gets up and comes back five minutes later with a skin bag of warm liquid and hands it to you. You sniff it: it has a strangely reminiscent smell, both herbal and musky, but you take a quick swig and pass it around. It's only later that you remember where you have smelled it before: in camel tie-ups at oases near Djanet. Camel urine, the Bedus' emergency water supply. And you immediately realize why.

You had heard the rumors that the slave trade was returning to the southern reaches of the Sahara. That and the razzia—the custom of raiding neighbors and caravans—thought to have perished long ago after the introduction of roads, oil fields, artificial oases. You have fallen into the hands of the past, a past not dead after all, just waiting, like spores in prehistoric soil thousands of years old, for a chance to emerge again into the light.

No point in wasting good water on slaves.

You don't tell your companions.

"How do you ask to use the latrine around here," Smuts asks.

Without waiting for an answer, he crawls toward the guards, pats at his crotch, then points toward the ground, making an arcing motion with his hand. One of the guards barks something at him and shakes his rifle, motions him back and points toward a back corner of the tent. The eyes of another guard glitter with hilarity.

The domineering guard is the green-eyed Tuareg, you note. He seems younger than he did before. *Has to prove himself. Cocky.*

"You'll have to do your business here, mate," Peter says, unnecessarily.

"So I see," Smuts replies, and crawls to the back corner and, facing into it, unceremoniously urinates. The rest are too listless to turn away.

"Good thing we've been on low rations," Peter says with an attempt at a laugh where he crouches toward the side.

You squat down near Vivian, who is kneeling on the ragged piece of carpet covering most of the ground. She looks up at you with a smile. "It's an adventure," she says, as if answering your unspoken question.

Sean and Cecilia sit together behind Vivian, leaning against each other. The light and shadows from the fire outside the tent play across the five figures in the tent: the exhausted faces, weary postures, puzzled, anxious, not quite hopeless, not quite believing stares. The guards watch them with curious looks, their eyes especially taken, it seems, with Cecilia, who tries to shield herself, almost unconsciously, behind her elders.

"So what are they going to do with us?" Smuts asks while eating from their supper of corn fritters spread with camel butter and smeared tomatoes.

"I suspect," Peter says, with brutal candor, "send us south to a slave market, where they're liable to get a good price, especially for the young ones. Good thing Duden missed this."

"Oh?"

"He'd have been 'culled' as too old to market, I imagine."

"Will they keep us all together?" Vivian asks you.

"Who knows," says Peter.

"Till we get to market, probably," you reply, "if Peter's pessimistic assessment is right. Then it's every commodity for itself. Capitalism in its pure form: it should be a beautiful thing to witness."

Smuts looks disgusted.

"You and your 'capitalism.' To be stuck in a slave pen with a blithering communist," he says with a glare. "Didn't you notice socialism has been dead for fifty years? I always knew there was something wrong with you. Americans who live too long outside America go rotten, they live in the past . . ."

"I know," you pounce, "the twentieth century!"

Smuts glowers.

"Whereas capitalism, with its stench of the nineteenth . . . !" Smuts continues bitterly.

262

"Look at us," says Vivian, with sudden gaiety, her face flushed. "Is this premodern, or what? At least we chose the right profession!" To Smuts. "We not only get to study the past, we get to live in it too!"

"It's not really the time for this debate."

You look at Smuts.

I've always despised the man. Now my survival may depend on him.

"Who'd athunk the future had camel caravans waiting for us?" asks Vivian. "What'll they do with the Hummer? They look as if they have no idea what to do with it."

From outside come the sounds of camels, dogs, the complaints of a goat. The fire flickers low, the light is weak in the tent.

All of you lie down and try to go to sleep, though it's hard because of the big flies that buzz around your heads and settle on your faces, drawn by the dried sweat. In the darkness you curl Vivian into your arms and feel her arms instinctively fold against your back. You say nothing to each other. You simply breathe together.

Eventually her breathing becomes regular with sleep, and you too drift off.

A high scream almost at your ear wakes you. You can barely see Cecilia at the mouth of the tent under a dull moonlight, she's struggling with someone, she screams again, then again. You see a shadowy form lift something and bring it down hard half a dozen times, as though hacking at something, and Cecilia's scream changes to a gurgle and choke and a bizarre huffing, an almost animal-like whimpering sound. You hear a furious argument between several Tuareg over the animal-like groans and huffing noises from Cecilia, and then several more men come up from outside with torches, in the midst of them the tribe's leader. And on the carpet floor of the tent, toward the opening, you can see the girl, gagging and shaking mechanically, in the wavering torchlight, lying in a widening pool of blood, something lying next to her right breast. The leader looks down and starts shouting furiously at the green-eyed Tuareg, who is standing with a blood-covered ax in his hand.

You look hard at Cecilia, who chokes and gurgles in the blood. And you see more clearly what it is lying near her flank. It's her right arm, lying the wrong way next to her, chopped off at the shoulder, the fingers half clasped and still moving, almost touching her bleeding shoulder.

The leader gives the green-eyed Tuareg a furious dressing-down, nattering in a shrill, high-pitched voice, and sends him off, then looks down at his ruined prize, spits in disgust, and marches, with the torches, back to his tent.

Cecilia is left lying on the floor of the tent. She has stopped shaking and there is a quickening stench of blood. The four stare dumbly at the mutilated body in the fading moonlight as the flies settle on it. Sean whimpers in the back.

The dawn breaks cold and gray through the opening of the tent, like a screen showing the two guards asleep and in the far distance, waves of star dunes touched by a long ray of sunlight. You are the first to wake; the others are curled up or lying against the walls of the tent, asleep. The girl's remains have been removed, leaving a wide black-red stain on the rug near the entrance and in the sand at the rug's edge. A trail showing where her body was dragged appears dimly in the sand outside.

You shiver lightly in the cold.

Not a nightmare. Not a dream . . .

A camel snorts and snuffles somewhere outside.

You seem to hold no memories. You look inside yourself, and you find no memories.

You look at the others sleeping on the floor of the tent, and for a moment can't recognize them. One of them sighs and shifts a little. Another mutters a few unintelligible words, then repeats the same jumble of meaningless syllables insistently, rapidly, then again, even more insistently. Then a few words come out crisp and clear: "If only you had done that." Then silence.

A strange, sleepy voice. A young man's . . .

If only you had done that? Or: if only you hadn't done that?

The figure nearest you breathes in deep, holds it for what feels like a minute, then slowly breathes it out.

A woman.

Miranda . . .

You shake yourself.

Not Miranda. Vivian . . .

A form dimly crosses the entrance a few yards out, and vanishes.

A jackal looking for food? A dog? Too silent. It looked like it was carrying something in its jaws.

You suddenly visualize the young girl's remains hastily buried in a shallow grave in the sand nearby.

Don't think about it.

Brave child on her first expedition into the dangerous world. An adventure. An adventure is not supposed to end a tragedy.

That fear in her face. Its innocence. If I am just terrified enough . . .

Could that be why fear isn't the thing you feel? More a sense of unreality—or rather, of hopeless stupidity, of things, men, the world, life.

That, gentlemen, was the lesson, patiently, sometimes impatiently—beaten into your thick skull, fool—taught.

Under each footfall lay, not an abyss, infinitely deep and leading to the eternal regions of hell, but a shallow pit with a few spiders, a poisonous lizard, a snake: a hole just deep enough to break your foot in, and find you can't get out of, and die bitten by a scorpion smaller than your hand . . . That is the terrifying abyss.

The ray of sunlight starts to move down the flanks of the dunes, brightening them into a slice of silver, and throws long shadows toward the west.

One of the guards scratches his cheek in his sleep.

A shadow near and slightly behind you stirs, rising slightly. You watch it through the corner of your eye.

The figure, still dim, large, male, crawls toward the entrance where the guards lie asleep over their rifles.

"Don't," you suddenly whisper at the form.

The figure ignores you, suddenly fills the entrance of the tent.

Don't be an idiot!

Did you say it or only think it?

But the figure has gone too far to turn back, and suddenly scampers lightly out the entrance, stepping lightly over the sleeping guards.

You can see dimly in the light outside the man's head—an angry, petulant, stubborn face surrounded by a cloud of ragged hair torn in all directions, a half-crazy wretch with a thick, now almost Nietzschean mustache.

The man hesitates at the entrance, looks back, suddenly turns, stoops and, it seems, tries to pry the rifle from the loose hands of a sleeping guard.

Both guards wake, almost simultaneously, almost as if they had been faking it, waiting for the white fool to make his move, and they grapple him to the ground with a grunt. You can hear the man gasping and squealing just beyond the wall of the tent, his boots jabbing at the ground. One of the guards starts hitting him with his rifle, held by its muzzle and striking the man with the stock, again and again: he can just see the stock, rising and falling rhythmically, at the peak of its arc, above the man's jab-bing and writhing boots, until the man goes still.

The whole thing has taken place in near silence, without a shot, and no one else in the tent has woken.

The man is pulled away—his boots disappear, and you can

hear him being dragged across the ground. The other guard reappears at the entrance almost immediately, staring into the darkness of the tent with a frightened glare, and poking the rifle muzzle toward what must be for him a wall of obscure threat. You stare at the scared Tuareg with the gun. Behind him the sun continues to lighten the peaks of the dunes, turning them first silver, then gold, as the shadows lengthen farther and farther west. The man's face, outlined by the entrance, grows darker against the brightening sky.

Any movement and he'll shoot us all, you think detachedly. Nearby the woman sighs in her sleep and swallows hard.

You stumble through the darkening trees. Through an occasional break in the leaf cover, you can see ahead a pile of cumulus to the south (you've taken Frankie's direction), sailing like a great galleon, reflecting pink along its western side fading to gray against a deepening azure away from the sun, while long streaks of smaller clouds to the east catch flecks of golden yellow and turn them into long avenues fading away to eastern darkness. The birds, quiet for most of the day, are starting to whistle again in the trees. You're too hungry, thirsty, tired to take any pleasure in birds or sunset, too scared at the prospect of the coming night. You stagger forward through the darkening underbrush, looking nervously to each side for wild cats, snakes . . .

The sky above the trees darkens to a hard cobalt blue with a few tiny holes of light. The brush darkens, whipping your faces without warning as the tow of you stumble and stagger ahead. The trees darken, standing around the two boys like black giants.

You can hear Frankie stumbling beside you. You are both panting with fear as you stumble slowly ahead through the blackness.

"There's a light!" Frankie suddenly says in a quivering voice.

267

Ahead of you something glows piercingly, like a small star fallen among the trees. You stagger toward it, trying to run but prevented by the treacherous underbrush.

It's a small house, embedded in the woods. It seems strangely familiar, though you have never seen it after dark or from this direction. A driveway disappears into the gloom along the side yard.

You both become very quiet as you approach the backdoor. Alone, you go up to it and knock gently against the screen.

After a moment, the wooden door opens.

"We're lost," you say. You can hear a quiver in your voice, even though now you are safe, and home is just down the road. "Can we come in?"

Topher looks quietly down at you and Frankie with her strange, imperturbable eyes.

"Where's Ralph?" Vivian asks.

She sits, pulled up in a half-lotus, next to you, having just woken up; still groggy with sleep, her hair scattered and torn.

"He tried . . .," you begin, your voice thick. "He tried to . . . tried to . . . get out . . ."

She gapes at you, her eyes blinking rapidly, as if taking in more than they can quite receive. You had never realized how blue they were, like the sky. Miranda's had been paler—they may have faded like this with age, chastened, darkened by what they saw.

The top and back of the tent flaps stiffly with a release of wind. The other two—Peter and Sean—gradually wake and blink dumbly around them. Peter's grin has vanished in an unrecognizable flatness of mouth and a blank look that could mean stoicism, abandoned hope, or just a stark, willed mindlessness. His beard, unshaven in days as for all the men, has gone almost completely white, overnight or sneaking up on them over days of not noticing it. You wonder how you yourself look. You are, all of you, shaggy, burnt, with clothes stained with sweat, like beggars or homeless, with chapped lips, calloused hands, blistered and swollen feet for those who had taken off their boots to sleep. Even young Sean looks like a middle-aged wreck and crouches silently, his head bent over low, refusing to look at anyone, his face stained with tears, shivering in the early morning cold.

"Did they kill him?" Vivian asks quietly.

"I don't know. Maybe not . . . He's too valuable . . . but who knows . . ."

She stares at you expressionlessly.

Someone stirs the fire alive again in front of the tent, and the same woman cooks them the same meal as the night before. She hands each of you a corn fritter, looking each of you in the eye as she hands out the small meals with a strange softness and sadness.

The four of you accept the food, nod to the woman, and stare at the tasteless corn fritters with the smears of camel butter and crushed tomatoes in your hands, eating compulsively, without appetite despite your hunger. One of the guards brings back the skin bag of warm liquid for all of you to drink: he proudly plants it on the carpet between the four captives, and it strikes you, with bitter humor, that offering their captives camel urine is considered an honor, like giving the best garbage to a prize pig or the best feed to prize hens, plumping them up for market.

The guard looks at you fussing distractedly with your food, and speaks sharply. He repeats it, with rising emphasis and a glitter of angry humor in his eyes. Repeats it again, still louder.

You all cower and stare up at him from where you crouch near the center of the tent.

"Eat, drink, and be merry," you think, translating what you think the guard said. "Eat, drink, and be merry! *Eat, drink, and be merry!*"

You eat, you drink, slowly, doggedly, and the guard seems satisfied, though your merriment might leave something to be desired.

Your attention latches onto irrelevancies—you see a freeze-frame on the television: a huge wave on the ocean you have never seen crashing spectacularly against a wall of cliffs, seen from above, in grainy black and white (an old film your mother was watching for her history of film class), you notice your mother's notebook open on the coffee table, with a title "Le Tempestaire—The Tempest Master," written across the top—she had told you the story, about the old man living on an island off the French coast who could control the weather using a magic crystal ball, and she had promised to let you watch the movie with her, but that was clearly not going to happen now, though you had been depending on seeing the mysterious-sounding, fairy-tale-like movie, and had wondered if the old man at some point, like the Sorcerer's Apprentice, ever lost control of the weather, and the tempest got out of hand—as you are dragged into the living room under a hail of recriminations.

You knew you had to face this, so you take it stoically. Topher's mother had called your and Frankie's parents. Frankie's father came in his Chevy and drove the two of you in frigid silence back to the neighboring houses. Neither Frankie nor you said anything to each other in the car or since both of you you were picked up.

"Do you have any idea how worried we were!" your mother storms at you. "We were about to call the police and put a search out for you when Mr. Wheatley called."

Your father's silent glare at you is more troubling than your mother's yelling: it's the prelude to a more refined and painful punishment, though it might not be meted out immediately—as though making you wait was part of it.

"Go into the kitchen and eat your dinner."

The first thing you do in the kitchen, though, is go to the sink, turn on the cold water, and, sticking the faucet into your mouth, despite all parental injunctions for as long as you can remember against doing so, chug in great mouthfuls until your thirsty body is saturated.

Your parents say nothing, though, as you suck away at the faucet. You feel your mother grab the back of your head as you pull yourself away from the sink, wiping water from your chin. You feel almost sick from bloat.

"Don't move," she says. "You've got a tick." And she yanks at something sticking hard to the back of your neck: it feels like she's pulling out several hairs at once, and you wince.

You turn with a jerk and she shows you what she has just removed: a fat, blood-swollen tick—big as a pea, a disgusting beige with tiny, wriggling black legs.

You blanch as she throws it into the sink and turns on the garbage disposal.

"Rain," Peter suddenly says, looking north.

You are standing outside, having been taken out of the tent a few minutes before by the guards. It's the first word Peter, who looks more and more like a desert prophet, a nabi, lost and half-mad, God-possessed in the wilderness, has spoken since the day before.

A cloud is rising toward the already blazing sun—the Tuareg encampment is on the hot plain, and the heat is rising around you once again like the walls of an oven—and a wash of light gray rain, like a long thin fall of hair, descends from the cloud's gray belly. The cloud is almost on top of you, and Peter ecstatically opens his mouth for a touch of the refreshing rain that is unexpectedly upon all of you.

But the rain passes overhead and the cloud sails across, thousands of feet in the air against the stark blue above, south, the long fall of rain crossing without touching you, the rain never reaching the ground.

Peter stands there, his mouth open wide toward the sky, his eyes pressed shut, and only when the cloud has crossed completely, and the sun has returned, blazing his face and penetrating his closed eyelids, does he open them again and shout like a crazy man, "Ghost rain! Ghost rain! Ghost rain!"

271

The erg rolls to the south and west, under the curtains of ineffectual rain. The dunes tower away, rolling swells of milky yellow and tan as long as the horizon and soft, they seem, as skin and flesh, as smooth as cream, almost beckoning, like a hand, with a soft, seductive challenge.

The Hummer, battered and paint-peeled, stands off to the side, leaning slightly, one of its tires punctured flat, its doors sagging open, surrounded by water and fuel canisters, tools, equipment, clothing, the belongings the vehicle had been carrying ransacked sometime during the night and littered over the ground. The Tuareg have taken what they needed and left the rest.

You sigh as you look at it with a kind of pained relief. Before coming to North Africa, you had always detested Hummers on principle. Yet you had a fondness for that one, its face and skin, its vain complexion, ruined by sandstorms. Only Jenny had ever made you sentimental before, but seeing this thing ransacked and crippled, its doors sagging like the wings of a dead bird, pains you; what they have done to it so utterly disrespectful.

A rifle muzzle stuck in your back makes you move ahead.

The four of you—Peter and Sean and Vivian and yourself (there's no sign of Smuts, so the worst must have happened)—are led to a short line of white camels standing at the edge of the camp. Loose goats look up at the group of you curiously, black and white flanks twitching, ears jutting up, snouts wiggling.

As you pass one of the tents, you hear a high-pitched burst of Arabic and look over to see Husayn and Umar, crouching at the side of a tent, looking at you—Umar's funny little face frightened, Husayn's dark long face more stoic—with a kind of sweet hopelessness. A woman barks at the boys irascibly in Tuareg, which they understand no better than you do, you can see from their uncomprehending faces. A Tuareg guarding them waves his rifle at the two Arab boys—*what have they been, made slaves for the camp?*—and they go mum, their eyes round and staring, watching them walk away, Umar, with his funny egg-shaped face, plaintive and fearful; tall, bony Husayn looking resigned and already withdrawing into a dark future.

The other Tuareg in the camp—especially the women—watch all of you with interest as you walk past.

The little old woman who had the brief spat with the Tuareg men the night before appears near the last tent. She is carrying a large, red doum fruit, as big as she is—it must be a luxury here. She marches firmly up to you and stops the march with a surprisingly loud shout. The Tuareg guards look at her blankly, but obey.

She walks close to you and peers up into your face: she's a full head shorter than you and stands ramrod stiff.

Probably a handsome woman once, with her proud bearing, delicate face, strong shoulders and thighs. But the sun, the harshness of the climate, the unceasing demands of desert life, and the burdens of labor forever given to, and accepted by, women had harshly aged her: she might be no more than forty but looks a toughened sixty, threads of white hair escaping from her red hood, her fatigued, sad eyes and mouth a squash of wrinkles, her face beginning to collapse into formlessness. Her eyes are strangely warm. Like those of their brutal guard the night before, they are green.

She babbles something you can't understand and gestures toward you and your captive companions, then solemnly hands you the pale red fruit.

Its color shines out in the dull tans and grays surrounding you.

You take it and hold the large, surprisingly light fruit as she turns and gives a sharp nag to the Tuareg guards. She looks back at you one more time, and to the others, checks the fruit, shakes her head, looks you once more in the eye, mutters something, and briskly returns to her tent.

The fruit in your hands looks very tempting: the heat has already risen and the little liquid they'd had for breakfast is beginning to wear off. But there's no time now for it.

When you reach the camels, the four of you are draped in the same kind of heavy robes the Tuareg wear—maybe to camouflage you from possible passersby, or protect you (*precious cargo!*) from the sun, or both. Then all of your feet and hands are tied, the doum fruit is taken from you (the Tuareg laughing among themselves— "the old woman will never know the difference," or something like it, passing between them) and put into a gunny sack on one of the camels, and you are lifted, one to a camel, onto the kneeling beasts.

You have seen no sign of the leader. Maybe he's gone on another raiding expedition.

Along the northeast, as you sit awkwardly on the high bank of the docile animal, you see a dull, distant range of mountains, one of them high and half-white in the season's snows: the shape, clear as a mirage, of the futile Mount Tahat, and broadly to the side and farther off, the tall, narrow dome of ineffectual holiness—*or disdainful divinity*—Ilaman, with its great natural mosque open to the sky.

The four sit on the camels, their robes unkempt, in disarray, their attitudes ungainly, awkward. They look like drunken Tuareg.

"I've never been on a slave caravan before," a voice with an Australian accent suddenly says from a lump of motley robes on a nearby camel.

The lone Tuareg guard snaps a few words up at him—probably a call for silence.

So that's Peter. Vivian must be there—she sits on her animal more softly than a man, as though she knows her beast already. And that must be Sean, weaving between bolt-upright honor and limp despair, obscurely convinced he might be able to do something if he just tried and were clever enough.

From your elevation, you can see the layout of the encampment: a row of square tents with open-air enclosures for each, like front yards, where the meals are cooked and chores performed, the youngest children play, the adults relax in the

274

evenings. The larger children probably have the run of the camp, whispering and scheming among themselves, laughing, shouting, running with the dogs (several mongrels sit or lie casually around the camp, one of them worries a tent post and nonchalantly raises a back leg to mark it).

Or maybe not: now the children of the camp sit in a group near the camels and stare up at the four of you, watching with an animal-like fascination, their eyes large in their small, soft faces, the boys making superior remarks, the girls looking with frank wonder. When you look down straight at them, they stare up at you even harder, blinking in the sun. You wonder, idly, why they don't shade their eyes with their hands, since, looking up at you from the ground, with the sun behind you, must be blinding for them.

After almost an hour, with the four of you standing in the sun, watched over by the children and a lone guard, other Tuareg pack supplies onto several camels, then climb onto the camels, which lift them without complaint into the air, and the caravan moves off toward a broad gassis in the high dunes to the south.

You flash on a dream you had recently—it seems now from another life: the landscape here like the one in your dream—a high, long dune, like a giant whaleback hundreds of feet high, in the distance, with a single figure at the top, looking back toward you and slowly waving—beckoning or warning. Instinctively, you peer along the saber-edge of the dunes ahead of them—a soft, long curve of golden tan against a cloudless turquoise blue—looking for a nick or a knob, a figure, along its perfectly sharp edge.

The caravan moves out in a line, the children running after them, the dogs barking, goats briefly interrupting their daydreams, one or two of the women stopping their chores to watch as they leave. The whites bounce uncomfortably on the switching haunches of the camels, only mildly padded by the hump. *There seems to be no resting on a camel's back.*

In a few minutes, the little caravan is beyond the boundary of the camp on a plain of loose rubble, and in a few more minutes the camp is starting to drift behind them like a raft of flotsam on the ocean, to fold back into the landscape and merge into the misty vagueness of the distant mountains.

You glance back into the expressionless eyes of the rearguard, stolidly lumbering behind on his white beast.

The sound of barking dogs fades into the silence of the light breeze following you as the caravan rises out of the camp's sheltering chott.

You move your eyes forward again, to Vivian's back, covered in robes, looking both vulnerable and resilient, pliant and pliable, a woman's soft durability.

You feel a sudden plunge at the pit of your stomach as you look at Vivian's back.

The erg advances toward them like torn sheets being pulled up a vast cot, the dunes the knees of gigantic adolescents sleeping far into the morning.

The sand overwhelms the rubble in a low, long swell like sheet surf at a sea edge, and the caravan rises toward the great star dunes.

Vivian stares off toward her right as she bobs on her camel, and you follow the direction of her gaze. At first you can see nothing, as before, when looking at the shadows of the ancient city, but as the camels move ahead, you see a long crescent of blackened sand move toward them and pass toward the right. Vivian watches it until it is level with them, then snaps her head forward again.

It's something you have seen in northern parts of the desert near abandoned oil fields, result of a spill. Here it is clearly coming from beneath the ground: a seep. Vivian might not be able to apprize her oil industry sponsors for some time to come. The sand surrounding the black crescent is whitish gray and gold: silica and iron polished for millions of years, the bones of the land crushed into powder and blown around like children's toys by the wind.

The caravan moves slowly into the white silence of the gap between two of the star dunes, making its own path, created by the laborious feet of the camels stepping through the sand, snaking behind them until the sand blows over it, smoothing it over and leaving no trace.

It's when they are half-way down the slope on the other side that you notice a stiffer wind coming from the north, behind them, fresh, that takes off the edge of the heat. You feel thankful for it; the lightly blowing sand is against their backs, and you cover your face with a fold of your robe.

The wind seems to be increasing.

You look to your side. The surface of the sand begins to leap in little spurts and whirls. They're like skinny sand devils blown in little spouts as if from water jets in the sand; growing taller as the wind quickens. Sheets of dust pass across them, in layers and folds, still bright in the sun, then growing shadowy, thickening, like screens. The surface of the sand rises like a thin fog or a blowing carpet under the strengthening wind, and you can see small splinters of gravel strike the feet and legs of Vivian's camel ahead of him. The camel kicks lightly in irritation.

The wind starts to gust from different directions, stopping, then gusting again. In one of the lulls, you hear the Tuareg at the front shouting, and they stop the camels and make them lie down in a tight circle. The captives are pulled off and everyone crouches at the center of the circle of sitting camels, the heads of the animals bent under the coming storm.

The sand lifts around them in gray sheets covered with leaping dust, a thickening wall of sand and wind. The wind and sand snarl with the sound of a huge shovel raking gravel across a pit in a great roaring, intermittently quiet between bursts of wind. The sand drives like a blaster, filling eyes, hair, mouth with stinging sand and grit.

The wind quivers like a contracting bow.

Between blasts of sand and darkness that covers the sun with a gray mist, you can see between your eyelids, between the whipped flanks of the camels prostrate along the ground, something moving past, great humped forms, and it strikes you: the dunes are moving. The idea fascinates and terrifies you: if the storm lasts long enough, you will all be covered with sand.

You look up to see the crests of the nearest and highest dunes, just barely visible through clouds of sand and dust, turning to smoke and melting away against the dim sky.

You put your arms around Vivian, who clasps you in return. The wind drives harder.

The sense of a malignant force—a punishing, stinging, mocking torturer of a million tiny, maddening bites, like mosquitoes made of grains of stone, and a darkness suddenly covering the sun, descends on them; they are on a sea, pitching and heaving in a parched ocean, scorched and flailed, buffeted by a singing and roaring that fills their ears and scratches their faces and digs at their mouths and drowns out all other sounds, the moaning of the camels lying with their necks stretched across the sand, it is as though they have been caught in a huge wave of sand, tossing them, rubbing them down with sandpaper, a fury made of dirt and air, a raging shrieking of devils, trying to destroy them, willfully, with malice and sadistic delight, with a vicious, savage hate directed at the world, at life, at them, intentional, cunning in its insane fury, spiteful and evil, demonic. In triumph over the outcast of the demon, the rasim of the efreet.

The air goes black.

They clutch one another—the four captives and their several captors—in a circle within the rough circle of camels lying down with their necks stretched out straight in front of them as the storm frets and rages.

You hear Peter trying to shout something to you and you look up, but can see nothing and hear no more from him, and you pull your head back into the circle.

Then you hear the sound, a deep, cracking boom that shakes the ground, cutting through the high screaming tenor of the storm, and you turn where you crouch clutching Vivian (her

278

arm around your neck in a fierce clasp—it is the last thing about her you will remember), to see a huge shadow falling across them and above.

So, was *that* the adventure you had felt coming when you woke this morning?

You're lying under the covers in the darkness, a sliver of moonlight shining through the window. You feel in a luxury of comfort, with a deep sense of relief, wrapped in a sheet and light blanket. You shift and twist happily. "Safe and sound," those were the words Mr. Wheatley had used, with a laugh, over the telephone. You feel safe and sound.

The rabbit skull you found in the woods lies on your desk: you can see its profile from where you lie in bed. It stares blindly across the room. Next to it is the spent shotgun shell.

The adventure is already far away—almost a romance, now you know how it ended. You were the hero, and you are now home, free from danger. Well, maybe not quite a "hero," this time. You hadn't exactly been welcomed home—more reprimanded home: nobody was singing praises for the boys finding their way *out* of the woods; they blamed them for getting lost in the first place. . . .

Imagine if you'd had to sleep in the woods all night (it suddenly seems less terrifying, now you're home), and the police had been sent out looking for you, and they hadn't found you till morning (they would have found you in the morning, of course, just waking up where you and Frankie had slept in the ferns—you can almost smell them—near the foot of a tree), your names would for sure have been published in *The Circleville Call*. Maybe even your photos too, under the headline: "Missing Local Boys Found." Or something like that. "Ariel Hunter, 9, and Frank Palmer, 9, were found this morning after getting lost and spending the night in the woods—no, in the forest belonging to farmer Ephraim McClatchy, near Lehana. They were discovered hungry, tired and thirsty but otherwise in good health and happy to be home again after their ordeal in the wilderness. . . ."

Your eyes blink open as you remember Frankie's taciturnity as the two of you were being driven back by Mr. Palmer. Frankie hadn't even said good-bye to you when you were dropped off at home, he just looked away with a sour, petulant expression, as though their getting lost had been your fault and he refused to take any responsibility for it. The last you saw of Frankie that day was the top of his towhead above the backseat as they drove off.

As your mind drifts toward sleep, you remember the old man's face in the abandoned house and the sick dog whimpering in the front room, looking up at you . . .

Frankie is still your friend, isn't he? You look gloomily into the darkness. You had turned south, as he had demanded, and you had escaped the woods and gotten home.

You would have to find out about Frankie tomorrow. You'd find out tomorrow. You'd go with Frankie up to see Gabe and Topher at their house tomorrow, and they'd have a laugh about getting lost in the woods, and then play in the old unused barn on the Wheatley's land. Things'll be okay. Tomorrow.

"Tomorrow, and tomorrow, and tomorrow," you whisper to yourself, curling up into a ball and closing your eyes in the darkness, repeating your old daydream of sunrise after sunrise opening before you, over days, and weeks, then months, then years, with the sense of anticipation you have whenever you dream about the future, as though you are looking down a long tunnel toward a distant brightness. And that sense subtly blends with another feeling—that you are falling into someone's open arms.

Tomorrow, and tomorrow, and tomorrow. And tomorrow, and tomorrow, and . . .

Al Sarab

A shout of light.

He lunges, grabs at something, tries to pull it over his head like a sheet—anything to hide from this shrieking light. But it crumbles in his hands. The edge of it burns like splinters of fire, but his legs lie, cool, underneath its weight. He thrusts and shoves to bury himself inside the coolness, but it resists him, melting away back into heat. So, giving up, he yanks himself out, sand falling from him like water.

For a minute he sits, groggy, his legs drawn up, his face in the shade of his bent head.

Where am I—

A flickering of dream-like images passes across his eyes, like the flickering of a fire stared at in camp, in a fireplace—they dissipate immediately into the silence and the ferocious heat wrapping his back like a shirt of fire.

He squints and peers around, then squats in the sand.

It's a little valley between two steep dunes, the sand rippling like water up a near slope. The sun flares near the center of a sky black as steel.

His teeth grind on sand. Disgustedly, he starts spitting before stopping and swallowing the rest.

Save fluid . . .

His eyes hurt in the light, and he turns back into the shade made by his body.

He remembers, among the camels with their necks stretched out on the ground, the others, captors and captives, curled up in the sandstorm—the memory distant as another world.

Buried? . . . escaped? . . .

The sand is smooth, undisturbed.

He pulls himself up to his knees, then rises stiffly and beats the sand from his pants (hadn't he been wearing a robe?), looks around him for a sign of the others. He wipes the hair from his eyes, feels his beard, considers: last shave—when? Last saw his face in a mirror—when?

The ripples of the sand under his feet look like a vast school of waves. He trudges toward the ridge, his feet breaking their delicate forms into craters. He listens to the sand falling from his shoes: sif, sif, edge of the dune sword, sif . . .

Above the ridge he sees a long sand hammock swoop away in a hollow or coomb, then ascend again toward a far-off overhang. Past that, a maze of star dunes makes patterns of shadow and light in custard-like dollops scattered with pocket valleys. But at least there's shade. So he heads toward them.

The sand sighs as it falls over his shoes; he hears that, and the dry sound of his breathing—nothing else. He stops suddenly and listens.

The sound of running water.

He slaps the side of his head a couple of times, yet still he hears it. *Not that again!* . . . Then he glances anxiously around the slope. But there's no sign of wadi or gully, of any break whatsoever—not a stumpy clutch of grass or a half-withered acacia he'd expect near even the stingiest spring. A breath of sand crosses his face, and he crunches up his face and turns his head away. He almost remembers something, but the memory disappears before he can grasp it.

But the sound of running water is gone; he can hear nothing

again but his own breathing, and the whine of air molecules against his ear drums.

. . . choose a direction . . . then go straight . . .

He stops and stares.

The towhead he remembers—or did he just dream about him?—appears in his mind's eye and looks at him mutely. They seem to gaze at each other for a moment, then the blond boy vanishes.

To his left something unwinds swiftly from the ground: an S-shape makes a row of parallels in the sand as it disappears over a dune. A horned viper.

He sees something ahead that looks like a fallen tree trunk, sticking from the sand. A goal: something at least to head toward in all this blankness.

The dunes behind him take the shape of a long odalisque-like body asleep on the horizon. His footprints in the sand cross to where he stands, like the prints of an ant across dropped sugar. Ahead of him the custard-like peaks seem to have softened in the sun but hardly seem any nearer. "You can never tell real distances in this place," he remembers someone saying. He's parched, he needs water. The trunk in the sand is no nearer.

He bows his head into his own shadow and slogs on.

Something catches the corner of his eye: a black speck on the horizon. It shakes and jostles as he watches, coming toward him in a great hurry.

In less than a minute he sees a camel with an empty saddle, running toward him in panic, surging and tossing across the sand, its head and neck loping above its pounding legs. Its hump rocks from side to side, a look of terror on its face.

Then it's almost upon him, not thirty feet off, and dashes by, the ground rumbling under its weight, its lungs wheezing from panic or exhaustion, a thread of saliva hanging from its half-open mouth.

A moment more and it thunders away, soon a throbbing speck of shadow shrinking on the horizon. Then it's gone.

He walks up to the line of camel prints in the sand. A light wind moving across a slope is already effacing them.

With a sarcastic grin he faces the trunk.

Right.

Smashed-in jaw, half-a-grin of teeth, sunk-in nose, heat-sealed eyes over embalmed sockets gape at him. Leathery skin preserved in the heat. Most of the clothing rotted away, a patch still covering the exposed shoulder—probably a native, Berber or Tuareg. The withered hands seem to pluck at the sand, the knees curled up against the chest.

He stares dully at the corpse.

A thin lock of hair waves in the air.

After a long moment: Water.

Turns and slogs on.

A few minutes later he remembers something and turns back, following his tracks. But the corpse has disappeared. He shakes his head: he distinctly remembers seeing it, it can't have been covered up so fast, there's almost no wind . . . But there's no sign of it. No sign in the sand that he ever stopped: the line of his tracks wavers from side to side, unbroken over the ground.

. . . need water, hallucinating, maybe there's a gassi behind those . . . there's water a thousand feet below, that's what the old man . . . enough for a whole . . .

Grins.

. . . though not exactly the nicest thing to drink with your . . .

He keeps remembering the corpse in the sand and glances back several times. But all he sees is his own path across the sand.

Soon he stands at the bottom of the closest of the majestic, high-peaked dunes, and starts climbing.

On all sides spreads an ocean of dunes, huge whalebacks in the distance with deep gassis in the creases between; at another compass point, a mob of big sickle dunes entangled at cross purposes, like baggy tents collapsed across sleeping circus animals—the whole landscape looks like a sea caught between storms, swells petrified as they surged across the waters—an ocean caught in a freeze frame or a sea moving in infinitely slow motion.

Above it, like an enormous, metallic dome, the sky seems nailed to the sun.

Clouds, oceans, mountains, sand, water, dunes.

He's seen this before, many years ago; remembers it, through the disorientation caused by his thirst.

. . . chaos within order . . . order within chaos . . .

Illusion, inside hallucination, inside illusion.

Al sarab.

Mirage.

What does it remind him of, who . . .

He shakes his head and gazes around the horizon.

Choose a direction and stick to it . . .

Wohin der weg? Kein weg. . . .

He shakes his head again.

Where did that old shred come from? . . . haven't thought of that since second-year German . . .

Ins unbetretene.

Where's the path, Mephisto? There's no path, my lord Fist . . . into the unknown . . . or some such poetic bullshit . . .

But first: water.

The sun still hangs high, offering no help regarding either compass points or direction.

Ins unbetretene, my lord Hunter . . .

A clump of drinn sticks up like a cowlick a quarter mile away: it might mean there's a water hole on the other side, or it might not. But it's the only sign of a hope of water for as far as he can see, so he walks down toward it in as straight a line as the dunes let him.

287

Kein weg . . . make your own veg in the vilderness, my boy . . . keep going straight . . . straight on . . . on the straight and narrow . . . or is that "strait and narrow"? . . . through straitening circumstances . . . up a queer street . . . up a creek without a paddle . . . up shit's creek . . . wouldn't mind any creek as long as it had water in it . . . Mannahawkin Creek . . . its little worlds . . . annihilating some . . . saving others . . . like a giant, master of the tempests . . . into the labyrinth . . . in broad daylight . . . lost without a compass . . . helpless giant . . . alone . . . you always wanted to be alone . . . well, what are you complaining about, haven't you gotten what you wanted? . . . nobody else as far as the eye can see . . . just you and the sun and a landscape so dead it's practically alive . . . proof if you ever needed it there's nothing more living than . . .

He flashes on the corpse he saw in the sand.

. . . probably never more alive since you smashed your nose . . . maybe that's what you were grinning about . . . now I'm dead I live forever . . .

Peter . . .

He remembers Peter's perpetual grin, that's what that corpse's toothy look reminded him of, turning toward him under worried eyes the last time he saw it—when was that? Weeks ago. Where is Peter now. Where are all of them . . . hauled across the sand on mangy camel backs . . . lying stuffed in a tent at a camp . . . buried under a sand fall.

Vivian . . .

He hears a low, distant boom and stops. It's followed by another boom, deeper, quieter, just over his left shoulder, and he turns to hear better. It goes on, a deep bass, pulsing gently. A quake. But no ground shake. Sand avalanche? But then why the pulsing throb as it slowly dies away. Like a gigantic boom-car.

The sound fades away, and he finds himself staring at his shadow in the sand: the only living thing he can see, aside from the half-dead patch of grass on the sif ahead of him.

Vivian . . .

288

Sally . . . Sally Miranda . . .
He returns to the path he is making in the sand.

An oil pipeline emerges from the landscape ahead like the body of a huge dead python, then disappears under a dune that had migrated over it. He feels a sudden flush of optimism. There must be a pumping station somewhere, he just has to follow the pipe till he finds it. And he climbs the dune at double time.

He's half-right: the pipeline re-emerges, then disappears into the side of the next dune. Just over the ridge is a wellhead, its arm moving regularly up and down like the head of a large bird. He lunges toward it down the slope .

The wellhead stands behind the ridge; nodding like a crazy bird obsessively dipping its beak into a water holder. It gives out a strange squealing, bleating noise.

He pulls up into a brisk wind.

The wellhead nods irregularly, pushed by the wind and pulled by a starved goat tied up to it and running back and forth, bleating.

The goat stares silently at him, with its strange horizontal irises. He stares back into its starved, scared eyes. Then he hacks off the worn rope, and the goat runs, hobbling pathetically, into the dunes.

With a curse, he moves on.

The tuft of drinn is smaller than it looked: a splay of scorched stems, pulled back like a shock of punk hair in the wind. On the other side of the drinn the sand runs down to a deep gassi along a low whaleback that goes on for miles. But this isn't what surprises him. It's what covers the bottom of the gassi for a mile in either direction.

A plain of wrecked vehicles and equipment, torn-up, burnt, damaged, rusted out: trucks, jeeps, earth movers, tractors, steam rollers, cranes, ambulances, Humvees, personnel carriers, tanks, rocket launchers, howitzers. *An army graveyard. A dump.*

He shakes his head, the astonishment clearing his head in a moment, and looks again. *How did this get here . . . who was idiot enough to invade this place . . .*

And he winces at a wall of memories he never managed to demolish.

. . . a scream far off, at the end of the sky of your mind . . . If not there, why not here? . . .

The dump spreads before his eyes like a mass of enormous husks, and, eerily fascinated, he investigates them.

The fourth wreck he checks—a crane with a broken lift snapped in two and listing in its own shadow—holds a canister which, using a hammer he finds nearby, he bangs till he forces a hole, lukewarm liquid spurting into his eye. He smears it off and licks it from his finger, then lifts the can and chug-a-lugs till his stomach aches with bloat. As he used to do when a child, sucking at the kitchen faucet. The vile liquid, warm as blood, tastes to him like nectar, and he flashes briefly on the idea how dangerous it is to drink it like that, only to dismiss the thought in the ecstasy of filling his belly. Then he drops the can, gasping—he drank so long he forgot to breathe—but feeling more refreshed than he can remember.

He gapes across the plain of wreckage.

Giant insects, burst by an enormous thumb and gutted by rot. The frozen legs of gigantic half-crushed spiders. Skeletons of downed lions, cougars caught in spasms of wrath, falcons locked at the end of their gyres, hawks frozen at the moment of plummeting, crazed, broken, reckless stallions, dragons seized in the eruption of their fire. Tar-pit dinosaurs petrified at the flash point of combat. The day after a battle between all of the world's mythical beasts. That's what it looks like.

A crippled Bradley stands near a drunken rocket launcher, its cannon aimed at his head, its turret half-off the tank's body, the treads broken where some roadside bomb blasted them. A personnel carrier lies ripped open into one long piece like a cereal box torn apart by some kid looking for a toy inside. Car hoods, doors, top frames littered on the ground like amputations, a tractor leaning crazily on the rims of long-rotted tires (the chuff and choke of Mr. Palmer's tractor), a lift raises its rusted arms as if in supplication, and here and there lie piles of engine parts, mufflers, transmissions, exhaust pipes, engine blocks, steering wheels, door handles, nameless devices in obscene couplings, tools, wrenches, hammers and screwdrivers, piles of bolts, washers, nuts, chains, everything rusted from desert dew and the odd rain over the years since the war that left this elephant graveyard.

He explores, peering into the wrecks, half-buried in the sand, most of them beyond hope of repair, kept at one time to cannibalize for parts and now rotting in the desert, many of them picked and pulled apart as if by a vulture with a taste for metal or a curious and cruel child.

Near the farther edge of the dump he comes across a half-blasted Humvee, its doors blown off but the windshield, hood, tires miraculously intact. He looks it over with a feeling of professional satisfaction, then climbs into the driver's seat and sits back comfortably. The rearview mirror is covered with dirt and he smears it clean with his cuff. Then he peers at the reflection of his face.

A stiff mass of wild grit-filled hair, grizzled unshaven cheeks, exhausted blood-shot eyes and burnt skin and blistered lips look back at him. A mad man. A homeless mad man. A piece of human wreckage. A lost soul. Scum of the earth.

If I had seen you anywhere else, that's what I would have thought.

He snorts.

Featherless biped. Forked radish. Unaccommodated man . . . Any other gems, o Western Civ? No doubt, there's lots more where that came from. All coming back to me when I can least use them . . .

A breath of hot air blows in through the side window.

His eyes fall on something dangling beneath the dashboard.

What the hell is that doing there. God damn fool left his key in the ignition . . . What if somebody wanted to steal it!

He plays with the key, then turns it.

His luck is holding: he sucks in a breath and holds it as the engine, long unused, kicks over. Then chokes and stalls.

God damn. God damn! All this buggy needs is . . .

He glances around the piles of wreckage, most of them attached to an internal combustion engine of some kind.

He takes one of the empty canisters strewn over the dump, a hammer, and a rubber gas hose from a nearby fork lift, and goes methodically from vehicle to vehicle, hammering off the corroded gas caps and sticking the hose in like the nose of an anteater, until he's found what he needs: residues of gasoline that have somehow survived the years and heat. He siphons until the canister is full.

The engine kicks over and, after stalling a few times, runs with a regular choking complaint and unsteady rumbling.

Holding his breath, he carefully turns the wheel. It's stiff and it fights him, *hasn't been oiled in forty years, what do you expect . . .* Then suddenly it takes a grip, and the machine lurches from the sand. And the crippled Humvee slowly drives, like a wobbly Lazarus, into the rough corridor down the middle of the dump.

Miracles do happen. Who's to say they don't? Not I, not I . . .

After picking up the water can, he drives the Humvee—or the Humvee carries him—to the far end of the gassi, past the last edge of the dump. He marks a point on the horizon, aims the Humvee's nose toward it, and drives. His satisfaction has a grim side to it: the victory, real as it is, is only temporary, it might last no farther than the next horizon. He listens closely to the creaks and squeals coming from the long-unused engine, the complaining chassis.

292

He drives, carefully, but almost cheerfully, over the sand.

Far beneath him spreads the great sand sea: bright dune and valley rolling away like a vast tangled sheet, in a tangled wilderness of shadows. He looks back where he came, expecting to see the dump, the plain of wreckage at the bottom of the gassi in the distance, but sees nothing in the gassi but the beginning of a shadow from the whaleback flanking it, an enormous culvert of sand, empty and white.

He shakes his head: he knows he saw it, he knows it was there, the Humvee he's driving is here to prove it. But then, where is the dump, where are the wrecks? . . .

Efreets, you're getting soft. If you wanted to make me really freak out, make the Humvee vanish! Where did it come from, well? Well?

I refute you—thus.

And he kicks the Humvee's tire.

In the far distance ahead a flat whiteness extends to the horizon.

He gets back in and drives down the slope.

When the Humvee stalls out, he's within sight of the salt flat spreading west from the slopes at the erg's edge.

A tiny village of low hovels with strangely shaped roofs stands in the distance at the edge of the flat.

He's heard of salt-cutters mining the flats for one of the desert's few luxuries—criminals, convicts, quasi-slaves, imprisoned for years by the landscape. This may be a village of them.

He abandons the vehicle and walks warily down toward the village. He may be stuck here for months before the next caravan arrives, as in centuries past before the automobile's brief victory.

The sound of a rifle shot makes him fall to the ground.

When he looks up, through the heat waves rising from the

sand, he can make out the shaky forms of three males, in filthy rags, heading toward him.

He rolls over on his back as they come up and stand over him, babbling in a Berber language he hasn't heard before. He opens his eyes and motions his hand toward his mouth. The sun blinds him where it stands motionless above their heads. The men stink of filth and sweat and rotten eggs.

They pass more words between them.

What should we do with him . . . we can't keep him . . . we can't feed him . . . we can't leave him out here . . . why not, the vultures will take care of him . . . let's bring him in . . . let him rot here, the nazreen . . . he'll die here . . . he'll die anyway, God willing, no man lives forever . . .

He imagines what they're saying since he understands nothing.

Suddenly he feels hands grasp him under his arms and lift him to a stand, and he mutters weakly "sala'am aleikum, sala'am aleikum," pointlessly, he immediately realizes, they probably understand as little Arabic as they do English, as they walk him roughly toward the hovel. They respond with contemptuous silence.

As they near the hovel, he sees why the roofs seemed so strangely shaped from a distance: each hovel is roofed with the body of a dead camel, buzzing with horseflies and rotting in the sun, lying across big slabs of salt upended to make the walls.

Inside the tiny, windowless hovel they drop him on the floor and stand above him, staring at him. The black air is thick with a stink of rotten eggs . . .

There's no way he can stay here. He needs to get food, water, rest; get out . . .

But exhaustion catches up with him, and he faints.

He has no idea how long he'd been out: from the light he can just see through the narrow doorway, it may have been a few minutes or an entire day. The men have left and the heat in the hovel is just bearable, though the stink is as strong as before. Horseflies buzz around his face. He stares up at the stiff, half-rotted flank of dead camel above his head. He bats one of the horseflies away, pulls himself up, and listens.

Someone is approaching the doorway, he can hear footsteps, then sees a fall of dark cloth against the light as the person stops and looks back. He tenses, wondering what the men have decided to do with him. Then the figure turns and enters the hovel.

It's an ancient crone, her face wrinkled up like a long-preserved date. She looks down at him for a moment. Her eyes are ugly and stern. Then she draws to his lips a gourd from which comes a sound of gentle slushing.

The woman is bringing me water.

Is it a curse or a blessing to be kept alive in a place where there is nothing but illusion and pain, the only comforts are lies, and the only certainty is I'll never know the truth about anything . . .

He almost drops the gourd when she hands it to him, but she grabs it and draws it back sternly to his mouth, and he slurps it greedily down, even though the water is foul, brackish, and stinking even more strongly than the air.

She looks outside furtively as he drinks. Then she turns to him as he finishes, takes the gourd and puts into his hand a cluster of dried dates, which he crams into his mouth ravenously, chewing and spitting out the pits. She stands watching him, the horseflies buzzing around her, then collects the pits from the floor and leaves as silently as she came, the cloth of her robe disappearing from the narrow doorway.

Less than an hour later, he is stepping cautiously through the collection of hovels, soon following the edge of the salt flat back to the desert.

The salt of the flat burns white and blinding for miles around him.

295

At one point he looks back toward the village to see how far he has come, but he can see nothing but the edge of the erg lapping at the edge of the flat whiteness stretching to the horizon. He walks on, limping on his left foot, which has gone bad.

He stops and looks up, blinking, half-blind.

Across the flat a few miles away—having snuck up on him as he staggered ahead in a half-daze for, he doesn't know how long, hours—stand long rows of white buildings. There are modern low-rises, a few higher, half a dozen sets of minarets and mosque domes, and what looks like city walls, bright white in the sunlight, straggling along a broad hilltop like a long tableland. He can just barely make out large signs painted like murals across several walls facing his way, some probably political, some commercial—he can make out the familiar red and flourish of a Coca-Cola sign. And a glittering and flickering of traffic moves back and forth along the bases of the walls—cars, trucks, busses.

A town. A great white goddamn city! . . .

He stands and stares, almost giddy with amazement.

Timbuktu? We were never that close, it was always a thousand miles west of us . . . I can't have gone that far, even on the slave caravan . . . I must have flown! Did the old lady stick a flying carpet in my pocket too? . . . Good old grandma! . . . TamTam maybe? . . . But TamTam's not so modern, anyway it's at the base of the Hoggar, so what is this . . .

Who cares—it's civilization! Home, food . . . water . . .

He limps onto the salt flat and heads toward the city.

He stops abruptly and listens.

Beyond the sough of traffic coming to him on a light breeze, he can hear the muezzins calling the faithful to prayer. He almost feels like praying himself.

Praise to Allah! . . .

If he weren't afraid he might not have the strength to get up again, he'd kneel and bow his forehead to the ground.

296

He continues limping ahead.

The white city seems to come no closer but glitters, tantalizingly clear, in the distance; it must be several miles away, and he makes slow progress. He sees a flock of birds suddenly irrupt above the roofs—small birds in a swirling flock, like starlings swooping over the city.

What is the word for those little birds—zarzar? So could it be Zerzura? Has he found the lost oasis, the white city of little birds? Has Amri's map been vindicated at last and led him to the fabulous city?

He sees something leaving by the nearest city gate, it looks like a horse and rider: it moves directly down the hill directly toward him, as though someone had seen him and was coming to get him.

He waves, first tentatively, then frantically, as the horseman steadily advances. He can almost hear the pounding of the hooves.

It moves onto the salt flat and grows in the distance—a small vertical black line against the horizontal white plain.

He waves again.

A breeze strokes his cheek—a hot breeze that carries a cloud of sand with it that briefly covers the flat and the sight of the horse and the broad stretch of the white city on the low hill on the horizon for a few moments, drawing a veil across his vision. And when the wind falls and the sand settles in little swirling dust devils across the salt flat, the horse and rider have vanished, and the city has vanished, even the hill where it stood has vanished, and all that meets his gaze is a level, blinding whiteness and all that meets his ear is the soft hiss of sand blowing lightly across the plain.

Duden's hat, picked up by the wind at his back, goes rolling down a gully. It lands briefly on its brim, then the wind catches it again and it flips over and rolls away.

Pam walks away from him down a badly lit alley with the words, "Now you know how I feel," spoken closely, almost whispered, against his ear.

His mother turns to him with a smile and flips open a book with large print and illustrations, called "Le Tempestaire," which she begins reading in a low voice.

Peter turns to him with a grin and opens his mouth as if about to make a clever remark.

Steve suddenly jumps off the top of the Tetons, shouting "See? I can fly!" And falls straight down the flank of the mountain.

Two large planes ram into the old towers of the World Trade Center in silence, one after the other. There are screams in the distance.

In a panic he tries to wake up but can't.

The sound of a child weeping outside in the rain.

Frankie picks up a stick, shakes it in the air, then starts hitting the ground over and over with it, with all his might. His golden blond hair turns into Maven's, and she suddenly shoves the stick into her mouth.

His grad school advisor Schwartz shakes his head at him, with sad eyes. "I'm very sorry," he says, "but it will never do."
"What?" he demands insistently, *"What?"*
Schwartz just keeps shaking his head. He smiles sadly.

Great herds of animals are moving down a valley toward lower land. A snowflake lands on his forehead, and he sticks out his tongue to catch the flakes beginning to fall through the winter air, but they blow away before reaching him. The snowfall grows heavier, thick as a veil of white, and he tries to run through it, but he can't move, it's as though his legs have turned to stone. He looks down and finds himself half-buried in a snow drift, and he suddenly feels deliriously happy.

Miranda smiles and talks where she sits across from him, making little faces and little jokes he can't quite make out. He glows inside, watching her. But he can't hear a word she says—he strains, but all that meets his ear is the sound of the dripping of a faucet. He raises his head toward Miranda as she babbles cheerfully on, and touches a surface of glass, strangely warm, even hot in places, that stands like a wall between them. He presses his hand against the glass. Miranda suddenly raises her own hand and presses it on the glass across from his, and she grins at him: their hands are almost the same size. Her pale blue eyes disappear behind a dark red rose. Someone is whistling "Sally in Our Alley." Miranda turns into Cecilia, who suddenly screams.

He wakes. Or does he—is he still dreaming?
A giant star stands in the middle of a dome of turquoise blue. Rays of light thrust out from it in four, in eight, in innumerable directions, like daggers. There are no clouds, it's blindingly bright yet sharply clear. It must be the sky, must be the sun, but it doesn't feel like sky or sun. It feels like . . . what? One of the knives of light seems to be aimed at him. He tries to walk away, his feet slogging through sand in a desert that suddenly seems strangely unreal, like a painting of a desert, or a desert seen in a photograph, cold and unchanging and still and without depth, but the blade of light follows him—it must be a trick of the light, a trick of the desert, one more of the desert's lies—and still it follows him, or seems to follow, it won't let him go, jabbing at him like a finger, pointing at him like a knife. And he

starts to run, and the blade of light seems to follow him, it seems to be meant for him alone. But it's just a trick of refraction, a hallucination, a mirage, it must be, like all the rest.

Suddenly he feels crushed with thirst and heat, an overwhelming craving for water and shade. He starts running, his legs suddenly feel light, and he runs off the flat up the slope of a sickle dune, its sif graceful, sharp as a saber blade, high against the blue. The sand at his feet ripples like the sand of a beach, trembling in the waves of heat rising from it, touched with wind and surf.

He looks back, almost by reflex, and his eye catches the brilliant star at the center of the sky, and the dagger-like blade of light suddenly reaches down to him. And the light goes black.

He staggers, blind, groping, frightened, up the rise, falling, gripping at the sand, pulling himself up, climbing again, feeling his way up the slope as the air presses against him like a white-hot boot. He climbs, staggers, falls, pulls himself up, climbs, staggers, falls, over and over, for what feels like hours but it can't be hours, he'll be dead in hours, in the heat of the sun he can't see. And he imagines a spider and a scorpion in a death duel in the white sand beneath the light he can't see.

Suddenly he gropes at what feels like a ridge, crumbling under his hands as he grabs at it, that slopes down dramatically on the other side, it's the great dune's sif, its saber edge, and he staggers across it, stumbling, then regains his balance and stands, straddling it, he must be at the very top of the dune. His sun-blindness dims in a froth of formless colors, roiling and clashing before, inside, his eyes, forming and re-forming and disintegrating, like the shapes that crowd the eye as you fall asleep, and as he stands on the crest of the dune, they grow translucent, in chains and broken segments, letting in a thick light, they become floaters, moscae and serpents that disturb his vision, riding it like bacteria in a petri dish, letting through brief patches of light, until they finally break up, become islets of broken cells like clusters of jelly fish on the sea of his eye, disperse, and then vanish, and the immense landscape appears before him like a vast quilt of a thousand subtle colors, pastels of yellow and red, silken and silvery, across an enormous bed, rolling away on all sides to the horizon.

He slowly turns, scanning the horizon and the sea of sand, a tiny being, a little spore, a splinter from a broken mirror, in an immensity of earth and sky. Alone under the eye of . . . what? God. The world, the universe. Himself. Nothing. It. Bad enough name for the Great Whatever but maybe no worse than others he has heard it called—Allah, and Christ, and Yahweh, Brahma, and Krishna, Osiris, and Baal, Ormuzd, Ishtar. The One. The Absolute. Tao. El.

He looks behind him. In the distance, at the far end of a plain of sand pocked with black outcroppings in strangely familiar shapes, he can see a tiny figure, alone, moving slowly toward him. The one living thing he can see. He hesitates, but if he can see him, possibly he can be seen by him. So he lifts his arm high above his head and salutes the distant figure, raising and lowering his arm, again and again. Then he slowly waves. He can't tell whether the figure sees him or not—maybe he stops, maybe he doesn't. He waves again. The figure halts . . .

He hears a sound of running water behind him and turns abruptly around.

The little old crone with the gourd is looking up at him with her ugly stern eyes. She raises the gourd with its stinking water up to his lips. She can barely reach them now that he's standing.

He reaches out without thinking—how did she get here? why is she doing this?—and the gourd turns in his hands into a red doum fruit. He stares at it stupidly for a moment, then raises the fruit to his mouth and sinks his teeth into it. The red moist meat of the fruit bursts like ambrosia against his parched mouth.

The woman's hands seem strangely young, hanging still open in the air below his face. He looks up suddenly into a pair of ice-blue eyes.

The last pages are dirty with erasures and deletions, revi-
sions, edits, changes of mind. You can just make out the ragged,
uncertain lines:

To begin, gentlemen:

    a line of dead kelp, like mermaids' hair
    on a thigh of sandbar

        on a breast of cloud one hand
        in the loins of the valley the other

        in the navel of the valley the mouth
        eyes nailed in an attitude
        of voluptuary prayer

    a grunt, a plea, granted

on a boulevard leading from desert to sea
        desert that began no larger than a handkerchief
to a sea as old as a blind god's eyes

on the coast three cities stand
less than two meters above sea-level

a spring tide laps
a cocktail cabinet

an enormous flatness
lies west toward the mountains

glaciers crack like bread

ghosts lounge in the halogen

you can count them:
lilacs and vampire bats
gladiolus, a peach, a parsnip
leaping troves of salmon
striations of dead raccoons

a bear kneeling in a creek

a grunt, a plea, denied
a sand crab trying to dig into my palm

"oh
they ate dreams of man-flesh and glory

like Cyclops in the Ithacan's jeering
howling in fables toward no one
swathed in clouds of light"

thus: five or six petals? or must we await the fossils
to freeze the mud
of the laurel

as they sleep, groping against the shed
their eyes happy, forgotten
between blood and a lotus
the sea belches comfortably
at the foot of the ancient garden

*

they shift, restless

what we knew was true, that is what is so terrible

the distant reefs roar with an unbearable singing

Kitt's Rock

The sound of thunder wakes you, your teeth coming together on a sodden corner of a pillowcase you've been chewing on in you sleep.

The house is thrashed by the wind, the rain pummels the window. You spit out the end of the pillow and pull yourself away from it in the darkness.

Such awful dreams, like memories from far back, long forgotten—no: they were harder, more coherent, more lucid, than memories—vivid, obsessive. Taunting. You shift over on your side, sighing hard and trying to shake them from your mind. Then you hear it again, through rain and wind. Something weeping.

You stare through the blackness hanging like a curtain between you and the bedroom wall.

Horrible . . . nightmares more real than . . .

You hear it again, then wipe your face with the blanket and hold your breath. The rain drums harder against the window.

Miserable creature . . . poor and lost and alone . . .

You stare into the darkness.

Suddenly you pull yourself out of bed into the ice-cold room, pull trousers and shirt over your long johns, then a sweater, and your heavy shoes, your teeth chattering, brush your hands together to get the blood circulating, then clump gingerly toward where you think the door is in the darkness, groping with your hands and barking your shin against a chair, then through the door and down the corridor, your hand following the wall, to the head of the stairs, then slowly down the stairs, forcing your eyes open wide, trying to catch what little light there is, though there's no light inside the house and none from the long-deserted neighborhood and none from the night outside, no moon or stars can cut through these clouds. The lightning has gone over the sea to the south like a drunken sailor trying to find his ship.

At the bottom of the stairs you turn into the kitchen, pitching forward like a zombie in overdrive, your arms waving in front of you, till you ram into a table, and groping over the tabletop, find the hurricane lamp standing where you left it the night before, then fumble with a box of matches and strike a match. The yellow glow shows a ghostly image of the kitchen, and you light the lamp.

The face on the calendar emerges dimly: the young woman's face, the reddish hair, the questioning look, the rose perched above her ear.

You gape at it a moment. Then rummage in a drawer, remove a flashlight and test it. Its weak light glows on and off.

You take lamp and flashlight from the kitchen, through the living room: as you pass the fireplace, the lamp illumines the hearth thick with ashes from the fire the night before. The letter lies half-closed on the rug, between sofa and hearth. You glance at the letter absently, then pass into the front vestibule and lay flashlight and lamp on the hall table.

You stop and, still rocky from sleep, briefly gape at the closet door, then open it and pull on macintosh, sou'wester, gloves, boots, and slip the flashlight into your pocket. A strong gust shakes the house as you pause at the front door. The windows suck in and out as though caught in a vacuum. You try to pull open the door, but it sticks, and you have to kick it half a dozen times till it opens a crack, and you press your ear against the crack and listen. Then you drag the door open, and wind gusts into the vestibule.

The door closes with a slam, and the house is empty, dark beyond the small glow of the lamp against the vestibule wall and silent except for the sound of the wind and rain and, when the wind dies briefly, of whimpering, of something lost and frightened in the rain.

Within half an hour the flame flickers out. The house rattles one more time as the storm passes beyond the island.

The windows are growing pale when the door shoves slowly open. Ariel Hunter, his face streaming with water, staggers back inside carrying a dog of nameless breed, frightened, wet, and shivering.

A hand is offered to you. A clock begins
its unspectacular routine,
like a donkey circling a water pump. The hand
writes, and then erases what it means.

The moan of the ferry rises from the bay waters below. You
look up and close the book before preparing to go down to the
wharf to pick up the week's supplies.

In memory of Aura Mayo

Voyage to a
Phantom City

Joan Gelfand, poet and author of *The Long Blue Room, Here and Abroad, Seeking Center: A Collection of Poems,* and *The Dreamer's Guide to Cities and Streams*:
If ever there was a time when readers are looking for explanations to life's mysteries, sordid events and shocks, it is now. Christopher Bernard, close observer of the Zeitgeist, answers with *Voyage to a Phantom City*. With a poet's eye and an archeologist's patience, Bernard brings his protagonist, Ariel, to the verge of death, only to be saved by a single act of kindness. Is his life a bad dream? An adventure of "Indiana Jones" proportions, or is he a modern day Ulysses slaying every demon in his attempt to come home to his self?

Peter Bush, award-winning translator of *The Gray Notebook* and *Life Embitters,* by Josep Pla; *La Celestina,* by Fernando de Rojas; and the fiction and nonfiction of Juan Goytisolo:
… an enormous achievement … The descriptions of the desert—its shimmering dangers and dangerous politics—are phenomenal. … the language and poetry is ever tight and sinuous—a spare beauty in all its baroque splendor.

Emily Leider, author of *Dark Lover: The Life and Death of Rudolph Valentino, Becoming Mae West,* and *Myrna Loy: The Only Good Girl in Hollywood*:
In tumbling, imaginatively rich language, Christopher Bernard upends convention as he braids disjunctive narrative strands, each with its own distinctive geography. From the stormy New England coast to the pitiless Sahara, from menaced lower Manhattan to Ohio farm country, from the Grand Tetons to exploding Iraq, each locale carries a story of loss, extremity and mystery. The narrator, desert tour guide Ariel Hunter, binds them together. This startlingly original quest novel conjures a line from Yeats: "man is in love and loves what vanishes."

Ernest Hilbert, poet, editor, librettist, author of *All of You on the Good Earth* and *Sixty Sonnets* and editor of E-Verse Radio:
Christopher Bernard's wide-ranging and ingenious picaresque novel *Voyage to a Phantom City* pays homage to both the fanciful meta-fictions of Jorge Luis Borges and the exotic bohemian travelogues of Lawrence Durrell, William S. Burroughs, and Paul Bowles, where "with each turn, the rock is folded, frozen, into granite twisters or petrified fire or familiar grotesques . . . above all there are human faces, leering or clownish or angry, and human forms: a girl in a burqa, a laughing woman, an old man with a missing chin." But first we find ourselves in an America that has abandoned hope, become fearful, as it slips into irreversible decline, where "the grand houses, handsome and abandoned, stand off to the side along the cliffs; staring out over the restless sea, their computerized safety features ludicrous and useless despite the aging solar panels and the elegant wind turbines. Dead television dishes point toward the sky like wistful faces."

The elusive Phantom City of the title—an ancient ruin rumored to be somewhere in Africa—may be construed symbolically as John Edward's promise of America as a "City on a Hill," a New Jerusalem and beacon to the world. It can just as easily be understood as the inevitable ruins left by once-powerful civilizations, sometimes so obscure archaeologists spend lifetimes trying to locate and understand them. Bernard seizes upon the ways in which we decipher, memorize, remember, and ultimately learn to feel the world around us through war and peace, through love and loss. His deftly drawn characters grapple with tragedy, yet they are always renewed by hope, their dialog lightly salted with gentle humor. All the while, "the hand / writes, and then erases what it means."

Voyage to a Phantom City is a beguiling and poignant book, haunted by history, capturing the long decline of America in the life and struggles of a single man, hinting that we've seen it all before, that we've been here, and that we'll be here again, no matter how much we hope to break free, a timeless human position Bernard conjures so well, as when "suddenly the immediate past is far away, as far as the mountains disappearing into the night, and the future— tomorrow, the summer ahead, the coming years—seems not worth a passing thought; unreal."

Jack Foley, author of *EYES; Visions and Affiliations: A California Literary Time Line, Poets and Poetry; The Dancer and the Dance;* **and** *O Powerful Western Star*:

"Le néant," "das Nichts," "l'abîme," "il nulla," the "nothing at the heart of being"—the words echo throughout the late 19th and early 20th centuries as the power of the negative asserts itself. Not plenitude and fullness—the richness of God's creation—but *un*plenitude, absence, loss: Eliot's "Unreal city."

It takes some courage to present such a vision in a popular form such as the novel—a form in which the "happy ending" still predominates. (Cf. the omnipresent theme of "coming of age": how I got to be the wonderful ego I am today. This book is a kind of *un*-coming of age novel.) *Voyage to a Phantom City* is a brilliant, unrelenting, exquisitely-written "voyage" into a consciousness which experiences nothingness at every turn: "The hand / writes, and then erases what it means." It situates itself as a "voyage" into both the personal past and the past of humanity as we are constantly engaged in situations which seem initially clear but which whirl-a-gig into uncertainty, enigma—and which are rarely if ever resolved. It is a world in which "your hunger, your demand for an answer to your *need to know*" comes smash against a situation in which "the only certainty is I'll never know the truth about anything," in which the very shapes you see, like the sands of the desert in which much of the action takes place, shift so quickly that nothing can be taken for granted—except for the likelihood that it will all come a-cropper: "The farther they go, the deeper into the labyrinth they seem to be." "Welcome," Bernard writes, "to the chalked tangle, / welcome to the dead mine, / to the un-elmed street, the dead seat / of the unthroned. Where the bog darks." Not where the dog barks: where the bog darks.

Voyage to a Phantom City is Christopher Bernard's (in Céline's phrase) *voyage au bout de la nuit*, his voyage to the end of the night. It is not for the faint of head and definitely not for the sentimentally inclined, yet I don't want to create the impression that it is "depressing," that it is a *downer*. A "downer" would be simply another mode of sentimentality—the flip side of the happy ending. Bernard's book is extraordinarily engaging, alive, bringing us into its world with passion and intellect moving all over the place. ("Fuck Derrida," says one character.) It is D.H. Lawrence's "one bright book

317

of life" tackling a theme that Lawrence never touched. Despite the many disasters its characters experience—*because of them*—it is ultimately a liberation from the false forms of optimism that surround us at every turn. Buy this toothpaste. Buy this car. Aren't these lovers sweet? Fuck all that, says Bernard: look at this darkness.

Curt Barnes, artist:

With Gilbert Sorrentino gone, Bernard is the most culturally knowledgeable writer I know of: his resources are huge, awareness of modernist and post-modernist forms, for all I know, total, his virtuosity awesome. Yet *Voyage*, paradoxically or not, is a real page-turner. His characteristic intensity propels you through it—that, the vividness of his descriptions, and the format itself.

The format consists of small episodes in the life of his protagonist, jumping back and forth in time from youth to mid-life to old age. Bernard takes advantage of the egalitarian realm of words to narrate, variously, external experiences, interior monologues, remembered experiences, and dreams, with a naturally transitional haze conforming to our dawning awareness of which is being encountered on each occasion (a kind of grace not possible with film, for example, with its jump cuts). These vignettes are short, usually no longer than a few pages, and concentrate on significant moments even as they propel us through the novel. All the while there is the suspense: where are we going? what is this leading to? how is this adding up? That, too, propels us forward, to the next vignette, and the next. And this format allows for real authorial economy: all meat and no extender.

It becomes apparent that the protagonist is an American born in Ohio during the Ford or Carter administration and lives beyond the present day, into the 2020's, where some of the action takes place. He's seen as a Marxist graduate student, a downsized employee of a large firm, a mercenary in Iraq and an expedition guide in the Sahara. This Ariel Hunter is no Everyman; he's also an amateur poet, and in fact, his unusual career path helps create a kind of epic, to inhabit a broad international canvas with political and social ramifications.

Bernard is a poet, with the care for language that that implies, and as with his novel, *A Spy in the Ruins*, you will be ravished with words, with intense and vivid description. (Many will rush past, given the momentum of this novel) There are fatalities and disasters in the

318

action, both near and far from Ariel, but the mood remains upbeat rather than tragic thanks to the sheer energy of language. A major theme, if it can be called that, is the human relation to nature—from midwestern woods to the southern Sahara to the coast of Maine—and as with Peter Handke (but in a different way), the most vivid and memorable passages are multisensory descriptions of landscape, or nature as moving, changing, raining and blowing, of being animate with life.

I don't know quite why, but I loved the novel being written in the second-person singular, maybe because it helped the momentum or made the descriptions that much more vivid. Jay McInerney used it throughout *Bright Lights, Big City* but it didn't have the same effect for some reason. A stronger association here is the narration of film noir of the fifties, establishing psychological intimacy (but not the paradoxically ironic distance).

Toward the end Bernard pulls out more Modernist and/or Post-modernist stops and we're presented with part of the narrative in play format, more of the protagonist's poetry and other literary flights, in a kind of virtuosic coda for this symphony, but I'm not sure if that will flummox any reader who's stayed with it till then. If you look at the customer reviews for such a pedestrian structure as Jennifer Eagan's *A Visit from the Goon Squad* on Amazon, or Penelope Fitzgerald's *The Blue Flower*, you'll find half the readers are baffled by switchbacks in time or narrator and disparage the novels for those reasons. So I'm not sure how *much* more "accessible" *Voyage* is than *A Spy in the Ruins*, but I do think it *is* more accessible, and would be my recommended place to begin an engagement with Bernard's oeuvre for most readers.

Anna Sears, poet and author of the novel *Exile*, and currently at work on a novel called *Espionage: A Love Story*:
A beautiful and haunting novel. Christopher Bernard has a poet's voice and the creative power to immerse a serious reader in human consciousness itself. In his magnum opus, *A Spy in the Ruins*, Bernard deliberately holds at bay most standard narrative devices, leaving his reader to swim freely in an ocean of evocative prose many have described as Joycean. In his latest novel, *Voyage to a Phantom City*, Bernard inhabits mysteries of memory, time, and identity. He transforms you, the reader, into you, the novel's character: an aged

recluse living by a northern sea; a voracious and erudite reader, poet, and intellectual; a youth encountering sexual adventures in the American West; a former mercenary in the Iraq war; and—most frequently—an experienced guide to the Sahara desert. Are you, as Bernard's character, perhaps, many men—or maybe the many a dreaming man can become? As a guide to the Sahara, you reluctantly participate in an expedition to find an ancient "lost" city—an expedition funded by an oil company. Bernard himself has spoken of *Voyage to a Phantom City* as a parable. As his reader, you—implicated by your author in the novel's multiple lives and viewpoints—are free to choose your own meaning.

David Grayson, former president of the Haiku Society of Northern California:

Voyage to a Phantom City traces the arc of a young man's journey, moving seamlessly from pre 9/11 Manhattan to the American West, the Sahara, and beyond. Christopher Bernard evokes a wonderful sense of place and of memory. In beautiful language, he articulates how we navigate friendships, our place in a shifting world, and longing and loss. *Voyage to a Phantom City* is a memorable read, and will stay with you long after you close the book.

D. Donovan, Senior Editor, *Midwest Book Review*:

Voyage to a Phantom City is a surreal, philosophical story that opens with a vivid description: *"You hear a creak, an animal-like squeal, and feel the breeze and hear the sound of surf against the rocks. The kitchen backdoor pauses and swings, in a little dance, awkward as a child; you must have forgotten to latch it. It finally makes up its mind and stops, stuck on the threshold like a half-open book, and you turn back to the broken hurricane lamp and the unopened letter lying near it."*

With such an evocative invitation it's hard to stop reading: captured from the first paragraph, readers are quickly immersed in a sensory explosion of images and description surrounding bad news brought to an isolated man. The 'you' referenced is an old man, his hair nearly all white, and the dreaded letter contains notice of the death of an old friend from years past. As readers gain understanding of the impact of this death and the strange experiences which follow, settings and perspectives change from the introductory 'Kitt's Rock'

320

chapter to the second chapter, 'In the Mountains,' which takes a flash of memory and moves the plot to an entirely new setting where 'Kitt's Rock' was just a dream ... or was it?

The protagonist here is one Mr. Hunter, a desert guide who leads professors and assistants into a barren world to check on a possible ancient city revealed by satellite photos. His work as a guide is not a joy, but his desert job offers much more than pay: it's a subliminal experience challenging perception, illusion, and memory; blending past, present and future with different worlds: *"Dozing: broken images of the professors blend with memories of your flat in Oran, the schoolyard of your middle school near Columbus, a road in New England, a silent bar in the East Village during the summer before the attacks on September 11, a rowdy Cairo dance club, a train stopped in the middle of a pasture in Spain, a foaming vanilla shake sliding toward his mouth, then the blocky face of your long-dead father...."*

Literary, allegorical and spiritual discoveries permeate the expedition and weave together literary and daily worlds alike, creating waves of surreal thought and interactions between very different protagonists. At the heart of *Voyage to a Phantom City* is a focus on these different directions and how these roads are chosen: *"Corn circles, witches' covens, corn wizards—corn was the basis of Mayan blood rituals. That's what got me into archaeology, when I discovered that. Midwestern corn no longer seemed like such an embarrassment. We had a secret, we were wild and weird, dancing bare-chested beneath the slowly fattening cobs. All summer long."* From drifters to anarchists, believers to students, each searcher seeks something different from the expedition ... more than archaeological discovery.

Being in the desert and encountering different people in singular ways leads to epic visions, dreams, and equally ambitious thoughts: *"And you drift off to sleep, with the thought of the night sky slowly turning, like a kaleidoscope. And your mind begins to turn with it, the night sky's stars turn and turn around you, in a great sweep between the poles and a long, flat horizon, as though you were on a sea or in a desert: a turning wheel of dark and light above your head, that turns faster and faster, the stars streaking in white arcs against the blackness, as long as comets, sweeping, swirling, faster, faster, until you feel yourself, as it were, shooting up in a fountain, a geyser, of stars, thrust into the sky, and you're flying, the earth shrinks below you to the size of a toy train table, of a doll house, of a map, as you soar into the night, the earth's shine surrounding the horizon like a corona, and you hear a voice saying, "This is you," and it says again, "This is you . . . this is you . . ."*

When survival and danger enter the picture, each explorer finds a different way of confronting mortality, *Voyage to a Phantom City*'s changing settings and reflections are evocative of the best of Proust's *Remembrance of Things Past*, in that the plot is enriched by a combination of reflection and tactile descriptions loaded with a sense of the moment. In such a surreal world the story line becomes quite simply an overlay for memories weaving past, present and future, and under Christopher Bernard's visionary hand each experience brings with it a burst of emotion and perception that goes far beyond the usual singular tale.

Without spoiling the plot's evolution, it should be said that all things return to Kitt's Rock: and in that moment readers gain true insight into the real goals and meaning of the phantom voyage they've just undertaken.

Heartfelt and brimming with experiential moments, this is a challenging novel recommended for readers with special interest in surreal and philosophical literary works.

322

Christopher Bernard writes fiction, poetry, essays, plays and criticism. He is co-editor of *Caveat Lector* and a regular contributor to *Synchronized Chaos*. His poetry can be found online at The Bog of St. Philinte. He lives in San Francisco.

CPSIA information can be obtained at www.ICGtesting.com
Printed in the USA
LVOW08s1105310316

481591LV00001B/20/P